Inspectors of Irish Fisheries

Report of the inspectors of Irish fisheries on the allegation that the custom of fishing for herring off the south west coast of Ireland before the 1st of June each year is detrimental to the mackerel and hake fisheries

Inspectors of Irish Fisheries

Report of the inspectors of Irish fisheries on the allegation that the custom of fishing for herring off the south west coast of Ireland before the 1st of June each year is detrimental to the mackerel and hake fisheries

ISBN/EAN: 9783742810311

Manufactured in Europe, USA, Canada, Australia, Japa

Cover: Foto ©Andreas Hilbeck / pixelio.de

Manufactured and distributed by brebook publishing software (www.brebook.com)

Inspectors of Irish Fisheries

Report of the inspectors of Irish fisheries on the allegation that the custom of fishing for herring off the south west coast of Ireland before the 1st of June each year is detrimental to the mackerel and hake fisheries

Office of Irish Fisheries,
Dublin Castle,
20th April, 1893.

Sir,

I am directed by the Inspectors of Irish Fisheries to submit, herewith, their report on the allegation that the custom of fishing for herrings off the South-west Coast of Ireland before 1st June in each year is detrimental to the mackerel fisheries.

With reference to their recommendation that a Close Season should be established for herrings, they think it desirable that it should only be taken to apply to herrings captured by boats manifestly fitted out and fishing for herrings, and should not apply to herrings captured accidentally in mackerel nets by boats fitted out, and manifestly fishing for, mackerel; but as they are doubtful whether such a saving clause could be inserted in the enactment, they have not introduced it into their report. They, however, consider it to be of such importance, that it should be given effect to if possible.

I am to add that the evidence taken at the Inquiries is being printed, and will be submitted for the information of His Excellency when completed.

I have the honour to be, Sir,

Your obedient servant,

(Signed)   M. P. DOWLING, *Secretary*.

The Chief or Under Secretary,
&c., &c., &c.,
Dublin Castle.

REPORT

OF THE

INSPECTORS OF IRISH FISHERIES

ON THE ALLEGATION THAT THE

CUSTOM OF FISHING FOR HERRINGS OFF THE SOUTH-WEST COAST OF IRELAND,

BEFORE THE 1st OF JUNE IN EACH YEAR, IS DETRIMENTAL TO THE MACKEREL AND HAKE FISHERIES.

TO HIS EXCELLENCY ROBERT OFFLEY ASHBURTON, BARON HOUGHTON,
&c., &c., &c.
LORD LIEUTENANT GENERAL AND GENERAL GOVERNOR OF IRELAND.

MAY IT PLEASE YOUR EXCELLENCY,

Acting in accordance with instructions received on the 20th October, 1892, to hold an exhaustive inquiry into the alleged destruction of immature mackerel off the South West Coast of Ireland by boats engaged in the herring fishery, we held a series of inquiries, commencing at Kinsale, on 20th December, 1892, and ending at Yarmouth, on the 17th March, 1893. Between these dates, we visited Cockenzie, Anstruther, Montrose, Buckie, Burghead, and Campbeltown, in Scotland, Peel in the Isle of Man, and Lowestoft on the East Coast of England. At all these places, witnesses who had personal experience of herring or mackerel fishing off the South West Coast of Ireland, came forward and gave evidence.

The fishermen from the East Coast of Scotland come to Kinsale for the herring fishing. Campbeltown men have engaged in both herring and mackerel fishing. Over 500 boats from the Isle of Man, Lowestoft, Yarmouth, Penzance, and all the East and South Coast of Ireland, from Belfast to Cape Clear, take part in the mackerel fishery. This fishery commences, as a rule, about the 1st of April, and lasts till near the end of June, and is of immense importance to the locality where it is carried on, as well as to the fishermen who come from other parts of the Kingdom.

Herrings appear off the same coast in April. As first they are in poor condition, but gradually improve until about the middle of May, and they seem to leave the coast about the end of June. The Scotch boats which fish for herrings arrive usually about the end of April, and commence fishing as soon as possible, but according to a mutual agreement between them, the buyers, and the mackerel fishermen, they have not for the last few years put their nets into the water, until the 11th of May.

The mackerel fishermen have, however, expressed themselves much dissatisfied at the herring fishing commencing even then, and allege : —

I. That an immense number of small, unmarketable mackerel are killed in the herring nets, thus injuring the more important mackerel fishery (which, we regret to find, shows perceptible symptoms of decline).

II. That the herring boats shoot their nets within a few miles from land, and force the mackerel boats farther out to sea than otherwise would be necessary, as herring and mackerel boats cannot fish in close proximity.

III. That quantities of mackerel too large to be caught in the herring nets are killed by them and sink to the bottom.

IV. That large numbers of small, unmarketable hake are captured ; and that the hake fishery, which is a very important industry to the Kinsale fishermen, is thus injured.

During the course of our inquiries, it was conceded by the herring fishermen that they did kill some small mackerel, but that they were saleable, and not killed in the great quantities stated. Some fishermen who formerly fished for herrings, but now fish exclusively for mackerel, stated that the quantities of small mackerel and hake killed in the herring nets were sometimes very great.

With regard to the possibility of the herring and mackerel fishing being carried on in the same water, the Scotch fishermen quoted the case of Lowestoft, where they alleged that the two fisheries are carried on, side by side, in perfect harmony.

The Lowestoft men, however, told a different tale, and stated that immense quantities of small mackerel are killed in the herring nets, and that only for the fact that the herrings lie far to seaward of the mackerel —thus enabling the herring and mackerel fleets on that coast to keep apart—they would seriously interfere with each other.

The evidence given by some English fish buyers, who frequent the South of Ireland during the Spring fishing season, was all on the side of the herring fishery. The more fish captured, the better their business would be, and as their view touches the question of the food supply for the public, it must be given its full weight to.

Having carefully considered all the evidence, the great importance of the Irish mackerel fishery, the comparative shortness of the herring fishing at that season, and the fact that the fishermen interested in the mackerel fishery are about four times as many as those who follow the herring fishing, we have come to the conclusion that for the protection of the mackerel fishery, both as regards its future prospects and the facilities for carrying it on, and for the protection of the other sea fisheries of the South of Ireland, a close season for herrings should be established off the coast of the County of Cork from Poor Head to Mizen Head, from the 1st of April to the 16th of May, in each year; and that during the time thus fixed, it should be illegal to land on any quay, bulk, or vessel within territorial limits of the United Kingdom, or on any portion of the coast of the United Kingdom, or to sell, expose for sale, give, transfer, or purchase, receive, carry, or have in custody or possession, herrings captured within the limits aforesaid. As we do not consider that we are possessed of the necessary powers to make such a Close Season Order, we have the honour to submit that it is for the consideration of Your Excellency to direct by what legal means an enactment may be made giving effect to our recommendation.

<table>
<tr><td>ALAN HORNBY,</td><td rowspan="3">}</td><td>Inspectors</td></tr>
<tr><td>WM. SPOTSWOOD GREEN,</td><td>of</td></tr>
<tr><td>CECIL R. ROCHE,</td><td>Irish Fisheries.</td></tr>
</table>

Dated at the Fisheries Office,
        Dublin Castle, the 20th day of April, 1803.

APPENDICES.

BOATS ATTENDING THE SOUTH COAST MACKEREL FISHERY IN 1892.

52 English Boats, .	29 from Lowestoft. 10 from Penzance. 9 from Newhaven. 3 from Yarmouth. 1 from South Shields.
229 Manx,	148 from Peel. 80 from Castletown. 3 from Ramsey.
12 Scotch,	4 from Leith. 5 from Campbeltown. 2 from Aberdeen. 1 from Inverness.
274 Irish,	89 from Dublin. 25 from Belfast. 19 from Newry. 84 from Skibbereen. 46 from Cork. 7 from Tralee. 1 from Wexford. 3 from Limerick.
97 French, . . .	67 from Boulogne. 29 from Fécamp. 1 from St. Valery en Caux.

NOTES OF EVIDENCE TAKEN AT INQUIRIES.

KINSALE INQUIRY.

Court-House, Kinsale,
Tuesday, 20th December, 1892.

Her Majesty's Inspectors of Irish Fisheries,—ALAN HORNSBY, Esq. (in the chair), Rev. WILLIAM S. GREEN, and CECIL BOOTH, Esq., B.L., held an Inquiry this day, at the Court-House, Kinsale, pursuant to the following notice:

"FISHERIES—IRELAND.

"32 & 33 Vic., c. 92, and the Acts incorporated therewith.

"HERRING FISHERY, SOUTH COAST OF IRELAND.

"NOTICE.—It has been represented to the Inspectors of Irish Fisheries that the custom of fishing by nets for herrings, off the South Coast of Ireland, before the 1st of June in each year, is detrimental to the Mackerel fisheries, and they have also received applications to prohibit such herring fishery before the date named.

"The Inspectors hereby give notice that they desire to hold a full and exhaustive inquiry into the matter, and with this object will hold a public meeting at the Court-House, Kinsale, county Cork, Ireland, on Tuesday, the 20th day of December, 1892, at the hour of 12 o'clock, noon, of which all persons interested are requested to take notice.

"Further meetings will be held in Scotland, in connection with this inquiry, of which due notice will be given.

"By Order,
"M. P. DOWLING,
"Secretary.

"Dated at the Office of
"Irish Fisheries, Dublin Castle,
"this 1st day of December, 1892."

Mr. *John Murray*, one of the officers of the Scottish Fishery Board, attended the meeting, to render any information or assistance which the Inspectors might require during the inquiry.

Mr. HORNSBY opened the proceedings.—We have been requested by His Excellency the Lord Lieutenant, to hold an inquiry here, with the view of trying to come to some settlement of this rather vexed question of the mackerel and herring fishing off the south coast of Ireland. We are sitting here to-day to hear the evidence of any of the fishermen from Kinsale, or parts of the coasts adjacent to it. We also, by his Excellency's direction, purpose holding inquiries at various places in Scotland, with the kind approval of the Scottish Fishery Board; and at those places we will take the evidence of the Scotch fishermen who engage in the herring fishing off these coasts, and will hear what they have to say on the subject; and when we have completed our inquiries we will report to his Excellency what we think ought to be done. Is there anybody here representing the fishermen?

Mr. *James O'Neill.*—As the Chairman of the Town Commissioners of Kinsale, I attend here to represent the fishermen at this inquiry. I may mention that from information that was laid before me from time to time with respect to the capture of immature fish by the herring fishermen, I have been in communication with the Member of Parliament for our Division, and he has made strong representations to the Government on the subject.

Mr. HORNSBY.—You had better bring forward and examine the men who can give the best evidence, as representing the general feeling of the fishermen on the matter.

Mr. *O'Neill.*—Yes, sir. I will first call the Harbour Master, who will give you statistics as to the number of boats that are engaged in this herring fishing; and I will afterwards examine some of the Kinsale fishermen.

JAMES COLEMAN, sworn; examined by Mr. *O'Neill.*

1. You are the harbour-master of Kinsale?—I am.
2. You are acquainted with the number of boats that are engaged in the herring fishing here?—Yes, sir.
3. Kindly give the Commissioners the figures; have you the figures for a number of years?—I have, from the year 1884.
4. How many were there in 1884?—About 185 boats.
5. Were those Scotch boats?—Yes.
6. How many were there in 1885?—Somewhere about 350 boats; but a great many of them left after a time.
7. But there were that number of boats engaged in the herring fishing during the season of 1885?—Yes, sir.
8. How many in 1886?—106.
9. How many in 1887?—53.
10. How many in 1888?—40.
11. How many in 1889?—45.
12. How many in 1890?—10.
13. How many in 1891?—49.
14. How many in 1892?—50.
15. How long do those boats continue to fish herrings here?—From the beginning of May till July.
16. Mr. HORNSBY—What do you mean by "the beginning of May"? What time in May do they commence?—They generally come from the 1st to the 10th of May; they do not arrive all together.
17. Can you tell us what number of Irish boats fish for herrings here?—In 1884 there were from about 20 to 25.

Mr. *O'Neill.*—They have never exceeded about 20; they principally come from Ardglass and the northern parts of Ireland.

18. *Witness.*—Yes; now and then we have a few Dublin boats fishing, but only very few.

19. Mr. HORNSBY.—Don't you keep a record, as harbour master, of the number of Irish boats frequenting this coast, as well as of the number of Scotch boats?—I do, sir, but I have not got it here.

Mr. *O'Neill.*—Then be good enough to go and fetch it; and, in the mean time, I will proceed with the examination of other witnesses. (The witness went to fetch the record.)

TIMOTHY HAYES, sworn; examined by Mr. *O'Neill.*

20. You are master of a fishing boat?—I am, sir.

21. You earn your living by fishing?—Yes, sir.

22. Exclusively?—Yes, sir.

23. You are, of course, acquainted with the fact that a number of Scotch fishermen frequent this coast every year?—Yes, sir.

24. Fishing for herrings?—Yes, sir.

25. Amongst the herrings do they catch small mackerel and hake?—They do, sir.

26. Small, immature fish?—Yes, sir.

27. Have you seen those fish?—Yes, sir; I have seen lots of them in the harbour outside.

28. Taken by those herring boats?—Yes, sir.

29. If that capture of immature mackerel and hake is allowed to go on, will it, in your opinion, be injurious to the regular mackerel and hake fishing?—Of course it would, sir. It must be injurious.

30. Have you seen quantities of those immature fish thrown overboard from the boats?—No, sir; I have not been near the boats when they go out to sea.

31. Have you seen them sold at the pier?—No, sir; I have not been there at the time.

32. But you know that they capture quantities of them? Yes, sir, quantities of them. I have seen lots of small fish floating in the harbour, after being thrown away, of no use to any one.

33. You never saw them throwing them overboard?—No, sir.

34. Or selling them at the pier?—No, sir. But I have seen them floating in the harbour, and there were no other boats that could have caught them but the herring boats.

35. The mackerel men could not capture them?—No, sir, they could not be caught with the mackerel nets.

36. You fish mackerel yourself?—Yes, sir.

37. Did you ever capture any of those small immature fish?—No, sir; I could not take them with my net.

38. Is your mesh different from the mesh of the herring nets?—It is, sir, a larger mesh.

39. And those small fish would pass through your net?—Yes, sir.

40. So that the mackerel men could not capture them?—No, sir; they would go through our mesh.

Mr. *O'Neill.*—I think the evidence of the other fishermen will, in substance, be the same as that which Hayes has given you, except the fact that some of them may have seen those people taking the immature fish out of their nets, and throwing them overboard, so that it might not be known that they had captured them; and sometimes, when they come ashore here, they sell the fish at the pier.

41. The *Witness.*—I have not seen them throwing them overboard.

42. And you have not seen them sold at the quay?—No, sir, I have not been there, but I have seen large quantities of small hake drifting about the harbour.

43. Mr. GREEN.—You say this does injury to the hake fishing?—Yes, sir.

44. How?—By taking the small fry of the hake.

45. Have you had good hake fishing lately?—No, sir; the hake fishing is getting slack on our coast.

46. Was not 1891 a good hake year?—Not very, sir; there was only about a month's fishing that we could call anything of a good hake fishing to.

Mr. GREEN.—Could any one give us a return of the quantity of hake landed here for a number of years?

Mr. O'Neill.—I am afraid not, sir; I don't think there is any account kept of it; but I think it must be obvious that the taking of that immature hake must injuriously affect our fishing, after it has been prosecuted, for three or four years.

Mr. GREEN.—One of the allegations is that the hake fishing here has been injuriously affected by the herring fishing, and it would be well to have some statistics of the hake fishing to show that.

Mr. O'Neill.—I think it a reasonable presumption that if a quantity of immature fish are captured in the way that has been described, the result must be injurious to the fishing of the matured fish.

Mr. HORNBY.—That is your argument?

Mr. O'Neill.—Quite so, sir.

JOHN M'COLGAN, sworn; examined by Mr. O'Neill.

47. You are Collector of harbour dues at Kinsale?—I am, sir.

48. And a retired officer of customs?—Yes, sir.

49. You are acquainted with this Scotch herring fishing which has been prosecuted here, for the last five or six years?—Yes, sir, and before that.

50. Have you seen them bringing to the pier large quantities of immature mackerel?—Yes; very often.

51. Would you consider those immature fish valuable for food?—I think not; I would not like to eat them myself.

52. Have you seen them sold at the pier?—Yes, sir; I have seen them sold in baskets full.

53. For little or nothing?—Yes.

54. Could you convey to the Commissioners what price they receive for those fish, and what value they would be if mature? Well, the English buyers would not buy them, in the first place; it is only the people in the town buy them in baskets.

55. Can you tell us about what they sell for per hundred, as compared with the price of mature fish?—No, sir, I could not tell that.

56. Are they sold, to your knowledge, for little or nothing?—Yes. The English buyers, to my knowledge, object to buy those small fish, and our fishermen complain bitterly that the taking of those immature small fish is destroying the mackerel fishing. Year after year, and time after time, they have complained of it, but we have no control over them whatever. Our fishermen would have no objection that the fishing should commence on the 1st of June, and that as many Scotch boats should fish as like to come; but they declare that to allow them in May is injurious to the mackerel fishing.

57. Are you aware of the fact that many of these fishermen are not permitted to fish in the locality from which they come, up to a certain period of the year?—Yes, I saw a letter some time ago, which appeared in one of the Scotch newspapers, stating that they had an agreement amongst themselves not to commence fishing until the 19th of July, from the Frith of Forth to Wick; that is an agreement amongst themselves; there is no law to compel them to observe it.

58. Mr. ROGER.—You say you saw that in a letter that appeared in a Scotch newspaper?—Yes, sir.

Mr. HORNBY.—If there is any such agreement we can get evidence about it in Scotland.

Mr. O'Neill.—Yes, sir; it shows that those people recognise the fact that such early fishing is injurious to their own locality; but they came to our waters, and fish here, when they will not fish in their own.

59. *Witness.*—Our fishermen have no objection to let the Scotch fishermen come here and fish after the 1st of June, but they object to their fishing here before that.

60. Mr. GABEN.—Are there no small mackerel or hake in these waters after the 1st of June?—We have never seen them, only in the fishing season, when they catch them in the herring nets; we never see them at any other time.

61. Is it only in the month of May the small mackerel and hake are caught in the herring nets?—We never see them, only when the herring fishing is going on.

62. But the herring fishing goes on after the 1st of June?—Yes, sir.

63. Have you seen any small hake and mackerel taken in the herring nets after the 1st of June?—No, sir, I have not.

Mr. *O'Neill.*—We have no objection to their fishing after the 1st of June.

Mr. GABEN.—Then we may take it that no small mackerel or hake are caught after the 1st of June.

Mr. *O'Neill.*—That is a question the fishermen will answer, sir. We submit that the two fishings cannot be advantageously prosecuted at the same time, namely, mackerel and herring fishing. It is well known that you cannot get mature herrings before the 1st of June.

Mr. ROCHE.—We would like to get some evidence as to whether there are any immature fish after the 1st of June.

WILLIAM ALCOCK, sworn; examined by Mr. *O'Neill.*

64. You are a fisherman?—Yes, sir.

65. You earn your bread entirely by fishing?—I do, sir; I have no other way of living.

66. Are you master of a fishing boat?—Yes, sir, for seven years, and beyond it.

67. Have you been engaged in the mackerel fishing?—Yes, sir, for the last 50 years.

68. Do you remember when the Scotch fishermen first commenced to frequent this place?—I do.

69. Since that has there been a complaint by our people that they are catching small, immature mackerel?—Yes, sir, and hake, small hake.

70. Do you think that is injurious to our mackerel and hake fishing?—I think it is, sir.

71. You think that if the Scotch fishermen are allowed to continue the herring fishing in the month of May as they have been doing the result will be injurious to the mackerel fishing?—Yes, sir, if they are allowed to go on they will spoil the mackerel fishing.

72. Are those small mackerel that they catch of any value?—No, sir, not at that time, but if they were allowed to come to maturity they would.

73. What do they do with those small fish?—I am told they throw them overboard outside the headlands, where they won't be seen.

74. Have you seen them doing that?—No, sir; but I have seen them floating in the harbour.

75. And your impression is that they were thrown overboard by those people?—Yes, sir.

76. Mr. GABEN.—Do you think that, if the Scotch boats fished for herrings after the 1st of June, they would not catch any small mackerel

or hake ?—They would, sir, to be sure; and you know, as we are engaged in fishing at the same time that they are fishing for the herrings, and the two seasons going on together, one spoils the other.

77. By catching immature fish?—Yes, sir, and cutting down the price in the market.

78. Mr. Rogers.—Cutting down the price?—Yes, sir.

79. Mr. Green.—Are any herrings caught by the mackerel men? —Very few, sir; there are a few, but very few; because our mesh is three inches; theirs is only two inches.

80. How does this fishing cut down the price?—By the two fishings going on together.

81. Mr. O'Neill.—It floods the market?—It does, sir; the herrings coming in as well as mackerel, at the same time.

82. Mr. Horsley.—Surely the evidence you have given has tended to show that the mackerel at that time would be valueless?—Yes, sir.

83. Mr. O'Neill.—With regard to the question whether immature fish would be caught after the 1st of June, do you think they would catch as many immature fish after that as they do before the 1st of June?—I think they would.

84. Wouldn't the small fish that they catch in May be matured in June?—They would grow bigger, no doubt, and be too big, most of them, for their mesh, after that time.

Mr. O'Neill.—That is what I wish to point out; that there would not be the same objection, on the ground of small immature fish being taken, after the 1st of June.

85. Mr. Green.—Do you say the mackerel are increasing in size after the 1st of June?—I do, sir.

86. You are sure they are not decreasing in size?—No, sir.

87. And that the smaller schools are not coming in?—No, sir, I think not.

88. Your evidence is that when the mackerel come in first they are small, and that they grow bigger as the year goes on?—Yes, sir, they grow bigger; that is my opinion.

89. And there is not the same chance of catching a quantity of small fish after the 1st of June?—No, sir. Their net is terribly deep; they catch all that is before them.

John Coghlan, sworn; examined by Mr. O'Neill.

90. You are a fisherman?—Yes, sir.

91. Have you been engaged at that occupation all your life-time? —Yes, sir, for 35 years.

92. Do you earn your livelihood entirely by fishing?—Yes, sir.

93. Have you been engaged in the mackerel fishing ever since it was established in Kinsale?—Yes, sir.

94. And your father before you?—Yes, sir.

95. You are acquainted with the mackerel and herring fishing here for many years?—I am, sir.

96. Are you also aware of the fact that those herring men take large quantities of immature fish?—Yes, sir, small little cocks we call them; small mackerel.

97. And small hake?—Yes, sir, very small; about four or five inches long.

98. Are you aware that those Scotch fishermen fished off Arklow at one time?—I don't remember it, sir; I don't know.

99. Or off Howth?—I know they fished off Howth; I fished off Howth with them myself.

100. Are you aware of the fact that the Howth fishing has almost disappeared?—Yes, sir.

101. What do they blame for that?—They blame the fishing in the south channel, that won't let the fish come up to them in the north channel; it breaks the schools: that is what they say.

102. Do they blame the means used by the Scotch fishermen?—Yes, sir; they say the Scotch boats break the banks of fish before they come up the channel. That is their belief; I don't know whether it is true or not.

103. They attribute the fact of not having herrings in their place to the means used by the Scotch fishermen?—Yes, sir.

104. Now, with regard to taking the small immature fish, have you seen them yourself?—Yes, sir; I have seen them floating in the harbour.

105. Have you seen them taking those small fish out of their nets, and throwing them out?—Yes, sir, alongside the bulks; if you were on the spot you would see them yourself; they throw them over the side of the ship.

106. Mr. BOURKE.—Have you seen them do that?—I did not see them do it; but I have seen the small mackerel in the nets, and I have seen the fish floating outside.

107. Mr. O'Neill.—Is it your opinion that if this goes on is our waters the mackerel fishing will disappear?—Yes, sir; they are a great break down to us; of course we cannot say positively; it is only our opinion. We consider them a great injury to us.

108. You would have no objection, and the fishermen generally would have no objection, to allow them to commence the herring fishing on the 1st of June?—No, sir, we would not have any objection, if they kept off the coast from the 1st of April till the 1st of June; they may fish afterwards, if they like.

109. Is it your opinion that there is not the same danger of capturing small fish after the 1st of June?—Yes, sir; and the herring is in better order after the 1st of June.

110. Is it your opinion that they would not catch as many small mackerel after the 1st of June?—Yes, sir, it is my opinion they would not; the mackerel are larger in size after the 1st of June.

111. Then you think that their prosecuting the herring fishing after the 1st of June would not be so injurious to the mackerel?—Yes, sir.

Mr. HORNSBY.—Can you give us any evidence as to the quantity of immature mackerel taken by the Scotch nets?—The witnesses say they have seen them floating in the harbour, but they have not given us any idea of the quantity taken.

Mr. O'Neill.—It would be very difficult to give anything like an approximation of the quantity; because, since our people have got dissatisfied with their fishing, the Scotchmen throw the small fish overboard outside, so that it is impossible to get an approximation of the quantity they capture.

Mr. HORNSBY.—It would be very important for your side of the question that you should be in a position to prove that owing to the large quantities of immature mackerel captured in the herring nets serious injury is done. Of course you know as well as I do that the fact of a few mackerel being caught in their nets would not do any substantial damage.

Mr. O'Neill.—We will give you evidence that they are caught in great quantities; but to give an account of the quantity, we could not do that.

112. (To the *Witness*.)—Have you seen great quantities of those small immature fish taken by the Scotch nets?—Yes, sir; very large.

113. Confine yourself to some one boat; keep one herring fishing boat in your mind; have you seen thousands of small mackerel meshed by one boat?—I have seen several baskets of them.

114. From one boat?—Yes, sir.

115. Several baskets?—Yes, sir; several large baskets.

116. About what number of fish would that represent?—I suppose about 300 a basket.

117. In your opinion have you seen, taken by one boat, 5,000 small immature mackerel?—Well, no, sir; I heard there was 5,000 of them taken by one boat, but I have not seen it.

Mr. Hornsby.—Is there any one in court who has seen it?

Mr. O'Neill.—We will give you evidence of it, sir.

118. At all events, you have, to your own knowledge, seen a couple of thousand of those small fish taken by one herring boat?—I have, sir.

119. Mr. Green.—Do you say you have seen 2,000 small mackerel taken by one boat?—Yes, sir; I saw that about four years ago; I was walking about at that time with a sore hand, and I saw a good deal of it that year.

120. We have got returns of the number of boats fishing, and there were a large number of Scotch boats fishing herrings here in 1885, 1886, and 1887. Do you remember whether there was any decrease in the hake and mackerel fishing after that?—Yes, sir; our books will tell that; we got better seasons eight or nine years ago than for the last few years. There is a pass-book of our earnings. This has been a very bad year entirely.

Mr. R. A. Williams.—I am managing owner of this man's boat, and I am aware there is a wonderful falling off for some years back; I can let you have the figures in about fifteen minutes.

121. Mr. Green.—One of the witnesses said that the herrings injured the price of the mackerel? (*Witness*).—Yes, sir; one evening a great lot of mackerel came into the harbour, but owing to the quantity of small mackerel and herrings that had come in they could get no buyers for them; one of the boats had to throw the mackerel overboard; they had no way of sending them off, on account of the steamer being full of herrings and small mackerel. Furthermore, I was told, and I suppose there are men can prove it, that as much as 7,000 of mackerel were sold for £1.

122. Mr. O'Neill.—Small mackerel?—No, sir, large mackerel.

Mr. Green.—What year was that?—This year, sir.

Mr. O'Neill.—The herring boats fish closer to land and come in earlier with the fish, and the consequence is the buyers purchase up the herrings and small fish, to the prejudice of the mature mackerel.

Mr. Hornsby.—I see that in 1885 there was a meeting of fishbuyers, boat owners, and fishermen, and they suggested that the fishing should not commence before the 11th of May. I suppose you have altered your views since then?

Mr. O'Neill.—Yes, sir; the circumstances have altered, and further experience of the way in which the fishing has worked has obliged them to change the data.

123. Mr. Green.—What time do you think the herring fishing ought to commence?—The 1st of July, sir, is my opinion.

124. Do you say the mackerel get bigger from the time they come in first?—No, sir, I would not say that; but we catch only the larger mackerel; we catch as large mackerel in March as at any other time

of the year, but we do not catch the small ones. They pass through our mesh; we carry nets with from 3 to 3½ inch mesh, and the small mackerel pass through our nets.

125. Mr. ROCHE.—What is the number of Irish boats fishing here? (Mr. O'Neill).—Our local boats are about 40, but we have boats from Dublin, Arklow, and Cape Clear. The fishing extends now from Kinsale to the mouth of the Shannon, whereas some years ago it was confined to Kinsale.

126. Mr. GARER.—Have you herring nets for your boats? (Witness).—We have nets for fishing for bait in the winter time.

127. Do any of the boats take up herring, as well as mackerel fishing? —Yes, sir, a few of them did, but it did not pay. They used to go to the North Channel to fish, but it did not pay.

JOHN RIORDAN, sworn; examined by Mr. O'Neill.

128. You have been acquainted with the mackerel fishing for many years?—Yes, sir, both herring and mackerel fishing.

128. Mr. GARER.—As a buyer?—Yes, sir, and seller also; I am an auctioneer.

129. Mr. O'Neill.—Have you seen those small fish that have been described?—Yes, sir; I have seen quantities of small mackerel caught by the Scotch boats; up to 4,000 or 5,000 at times.

130. Would that be the catch of one boat?—Yes, sir; about 4,000 a boat; I saw last year 10,000 small mackerel caught by one boat.

131. Mr. ROCHE.—What size mackerel would they be?—Six or seven inches long.

132. Mr. O'Neill.—As against fifteen inches, that the mature fish would be?—Yes, sir; about a half hundred of mackerel, if mature, would fill a box, but it would take 5,000 of those small fish to fill the same sized box.

133. Mr. ROCHE.—You say you saw 10,000 of those small mackerel taken by one boat?—Yes, sir.

134. Mr. GARER.—What is the average catch of herrings by the Scotch boats?—As high as 70 meases; one boat had 100; the average might be about 40 or 50 meases for each boat.

135. Mr. HORNBY.—What became of those 10,000 small mackerel? —They were sold.

136. What price did they fetch?—From 1s. to 1s. 6d., and from that to 3s. a hundred.

137. What price would be got for mature fish?—About 25s. a hundred.

138. Are those immature mackerel consumed locally, or sent away? —They are sent away to all parts; some go to the English markets, and some are sent to France for bait.

139. Mr. GARER.—Do you buy herrings?—I do, sir, sometimes.

140. In the beginning of the season?—Yes, sir.

141. How much do you pay per mease?—They averaged this year 15s. a mease; they were bought as low as 7s.; the price ranged from 7s. to £1; the average was 14s. or 15s. a mease.

142. If a boat had 150 mease would she get 15s. a mease, when there is a big haul?—Well, it would depend on the mackerel fishing, and the quantity of fish in the market; sometimes they go as low as 7s.

143. How much a box was got for the small mackerel the Scotchmen caught?—Do you mean in the English markets?

144. Yes?—About 12s. 6d. a box.

145. What effect has the catching of the herrings on the price of

mackerel?—It lessens the price of the mackerel, of course; when a quantity of herrings comes in the price of mackerel drops.

146. Mr. Roche.—That is a substantial part of your complaint? (Mr. O'Neill).—Yes, sir; what we submit is that, even assuming that the herring fishing would not be injurious from the point of view of interfering with the immature fish, the flooding of the market is injurious to our interests here.

The Witness.—It is certainly injurious to our interests.

Mr. O'Neill.—And that is established by the fact that they don't fish in their own waters until the 1st of June.

The Witness.—There is no doubt they destroy quantities of small fish, hake and mackerel.

147. Mr. O'Neill.—Can you give any figures of the small hake that are caught?—I have seen boats with 500 small hake, and I have seen them floating in the water.

148. Have you seen them unmeshing the fish at sea?—Yes; also gurnet and whiting; they destroy quantities of small whiting; I have seen them throw them overboard at sea. Their reason is that the people would kick up a row if they saw them, and they throw them overboard outside, so that they won't be seen.

Mr. O'Neill.—I may explain, gentlemen, that the buyers go out to sea to purchase the fish, and hence Mr. Riordan sees the operations outside; so that his calling gives him opportunities of seeing it; the fishermen have not the same opportunity.

149. Mr. Green.—Do boats come here from Campbeltown for the mackerel fishing?—Yes, sir.

150. They don't fish for herrings?—They do not. They know very well that if they did they would destroy the fishing on themselves.

151. Do any of the Irish boats change their nets, and fish for herring while here?—Some of the Arklow boats come down here in June to fish for herrings.

152. In June?—Yes, sir, in May and June, but very few; it is mostly Scotch boats fish herrings here in the early part of the season.

153. Are the Arklow boats the only boats that fish for herrings, besides the Scotch boats?—Some Manx boats come too, but they don't fish till the mackerel season is over.

Mr. O'Neill.—Our complaint is entirely against the Scotch boats; neither the Manx or Irish boats, practically, fish for herrings until the close of the mackerel season.

154. Mr. Green.—Some of the Scotch boats don't fish for herrings till after the mackerel season?—Some of them do not.

155. On what date, in your opinion, should the herring fishing commence?—I think the 1st of July would be quite early enough.

156. Mr. Hornsby.—The 1st of July?—Yes, sir; those boats come here to fish in May, which is too early altogether; the fish then are useless.

157. Mr. Green.—There is a great difference between the 1st of May and the 1st of July?—Yes, sir.

158. Do you think the Scotch boats would come here at all if they were prohibited until the 1st of July?—They would, sir, I think; the reason they come here in the early part of the season is because their own season is not open; and I don't see why they should come here when they are not allowed to fish in their own place. They come here and fish till their own season opens.

Mr. O'Neill.—We shall be pleased to see them after the 1st of June, but not when they destroy our fishing.

159. Mr. Green.—It would be a disadvantage to Kinsale to prohibit

them altogether from coming here ; the place derives a benefit from their presence here ?—Yes, sir, if they came at the proper season.

Mr. *O'Neill.*—What we say is that if by fishing here in May they injure our mackerel fishing, then, no matter whether they come from Scotland, Ardglass, Dublin, or anywhere else, we would be better off without them.

160. The *Witness.*—Their mesh is so small that they take the small fish.

161. Mr. ROCHE.—What is the size of their mesh ? (Captain *Hall*).— An inch mesh is the regulation size for herrings, and an inch and one sixth for mackerel.

162. Mr. *O'Neill.*—Do you know of your own knowledge that they adhere to the size you mentioned ? (Captain *Hall*).—If they don't they can be prosecuted.

163. Are the nets inspected ?—Decidedly ; both herring and mackerel.

Mr. *O'Neill.*—I have other witnesses in court, gentlemen, but their evidence would be a repetition of what you have already heard, and I do not think it necessary to occupy your time further. If there are any points which you would like to have explained, if you mention them, I will endeavour to provide the information for you. We contend, in the first place, that even if there was no complaint with regard to the capture of immature fish, the fact of having the two fisheries going on at the same time is injurious to both, particularly to the mackerel fishing. The month of May is the season for mackerel ; they are matured, and the herrings are not. It has been explained how, from a financial point of view, the herring fishing is injurious to the mackerel fishing. But in addition to that, you have also to consider the evidence as to the great quantity of immature fish that are caught by those boats, which must necessarily injure the hake and mackerel fishing. These are the points I respectfully submit to you.

Mr. ROCHE.—You represent the town of Kinsale ?

Mr. *O'Neill.*—Yes, sir ; we are practically unanimous on this matter. Our fishing is entirely confined to mackerel and hake, which is injuriously affected by the Scotch herring fishing in May.

Mr. HORSBY.—I suppose the fishermen of Baltimore and other places on the coast are of the same opinion ?

Mr. *O'Neill.*—Yes, sir ; their views are practically the same as ours.

Mr. GREEN.—And Arklow ?

Mr. *O'Neill.*—No, sir ; I won't speak for them.

Mr. ROCHE.—Our inquiry extends to the south and west coast. His Excellency's Commission gives us jurisdiction to inquire into the fishing on the south-west coast.

Mr. *O'Neill.*—I don't know that there are any other districts that have reason to complain so strongly as Kinsale. I desire to remind you that our community are supported exclusively by fishing, whereas the people of Baltimore and along that coast have other callings ; they are farmers on a small scale, and labourers ; but our people are entirely dependent on what they can earn by fishing.

Mr. GREEN.—What are the two fishings most important for Kinsale ?

Mr. *O'Neill.*—Hake and mackerel.

Mr. ROCHE.—You don't fish herrings at all ?

Mr. *O'Neill.*—No, sir ; except some small Seine boats that catch them close to the shore, but that is prosecuted only in a very limited manner.

Mr. GREEN.—Your contention is that the Scotchman should not be allowed to come until the 1st of June?

Mr. O'NEILL.—Yes, sir, till the 1st of June; we have no objection to their fishing after that, if they wish to come.

Mr. ROCHE.—You say that practically the herring fishing is not prosecuted by the fishermen of Kinsale?

Mr. O'NEILL.—No, sir; practically not; and we attribute the non-existence of the herring fishing on this coast to the fact that it has been fished out by those fishermen.

Mr. HORNABY.—But there is one fact that you must not lose sight of. These Scotchmen are not by any means fools, and they would not come here to fish for herrings if there were no herrings to be caught.

Mr. O'NEILL.—As I explained already, sir, these men come here when they do not fish on their own coasts; they fish here for a while, and then leave us, and go back to their own waters. It is my firm conviction that herrings could be caught here after the 1st of June, and good herrings.

Mr. HORNABY.—When the Scotchmen are able to get herrings here, how is it that the Kinsale men don't try for them?

Mr. O'NEILL.—The only way I can explain it is from the want of a market. In years gone by our men had herring nets; there were buyers then, plenty of them; and they used to go to Howth, and attend the fishing along the coasts; but there would be no use now in our men fishing for herrings, as they would get no market; since the Howth fishing went down our men gave up the herring fishing, for they had no buyers for them.

Mr. HORNABY.—Your people never went as far as Kilkeel?

Mr. O'NEILL.—They used, in years gone by, but very few.

JAMES COLEMAN, Harbour Master, recalled.

164. Mr. O'Neill.—Have you now brought the returns of the number of Irish boats?—I have, sir.

165. How many were there in 1885?—In 1885 there were 11 Belfast boats here fishing.

166. Mr. GREEN.—What class of fish were they fishing for?—Herrings, sir; and there were also seven Pool boats. That was the number of boats here, exclusive of the Scotchmen.

167. Mr. ROCHE.—They were not included in the figures you gave us before?—No, sir; the figures I gave before were only the Scotch boats.

168. Mr. O'Neill.—How many were there in 1886?—Nine Belfast boats, and 15 Pool; that made 24, irrespective of the Scotch.

169. How many in 1887?—In 1887 we had two Arklow boats, and five Manxmen.

170. How many in 1888?—None in 1888, and none in 1889; and in 1890 none, except the Scotch.

171. No Irish?—No, sir; no Irish or Manx boats.

172. How many in 1891?—Five Dublin boats in 1891, and one in 1892; making a total of about 55 Irish and Manx boats in eight years.

173. Mr. GREEN.—How many boats follow the hake fishing?—The local men do, as a general rule; about 40 boats; I think we are falling under 40 now.

174. Do any of the Kinsale boats go to the Scotch fishing?—None of them, sir; there was one left here a couple of years ago; she has been to the Isle of Man, I know; whether she went to the Scotch

fishing or not I cannot say ; but that is all, to my recollection, for the
last eight years.

175. Mr. HORNSBY.—What time do the Manxmen come here?
—Generally in March.

176. When do they go away?—In June.

177. Do they fish herrings?—Not of late years, only the few I have
given you the numbers of; as a rule the Manxmen are all mackerel
boats. Since the Scotchmen came here they have driven the little
boats off the coast.

178. Mr. GREEN.—Do you know whether the Scotch boats that
come here go to Castletownsend and other places? I do not know,
sir; they are boats that use our harbour for fishing, and pay dues
here, but whether they go anywhere else I cannot be accountable.
(Mr. O'NEILL).—As a rule, those boats that came here to fish do not go
to any other place, such as Castletownsend or Baltimore; they come
here, and remain here for a while, and go back again.

179. Mr. HORNSBY.—We are anxious to find out if all the Kinsale
people, or the great majority of them, are unanimous about fixing the
1st of June as the date before which herring fishing should not take
place?—They are, &c.

180. Traders, shopkeepers, fishermen, and all?—Yes, sir ; we are
unanimous as to the date; the 1st of June would meet the wishes of
the people of Kinsale.

Mr. HORNSBY.—We are here to receive suggestions or remarks from
anybody who wishes to say anything on the subject of the inquiry.

Mr. O'NEILL.—I think the fact that there has been no objection
raised here is conclusive to show that we are all unanimous.

181. Mr. GREEN.—If the effect of fixing the 1st of June as the date
for the opening of the herring fishing was to banish the Scotch boats
altogether, do you think it would be a good thing? (Mr. O'NEILL.—I
attach great importance to the question you have asked me, sir; and I
want to be perfectly clear on it. If I understand your question, it is that
if the herring fishing is put off till the 1st of June, and if the effect of
that is that we would have no Scotchmen coming here, and no herring
fishing, whether that would be a good thing. My answer is this. It
is better that we should have no herring fishing, than neither have
hake, mackerel nor herring. The feeling of the people is that if this
herring fishing is continued here in the way it is carried on, that even-
tually we will have neither mackerel, hake, nor herrings, and that it is
better to lose one than the lot.

182. Mr. ROCHE.—I suppose we may take it that the town is practically unanimous on that? (Mr. O'NEILL).—Yes, sir ; all the commercial interests are represented at this meeting. I need not tell you
that our resources are derived from the sea, and if our fishing is
interfered with, you will obliterate the town altogether.

183. Mr. GREEN.—The 10th of May was the date fixed on the
former occasion? (Mr. O'NEILL).—I can explain that. At the period
the inquiry you refer to was held, the mackerel fishing was earlier
than in recent years; it is much later now. It has latterly begun
about the middle of April, at that time it began about Patrick's Day.

183. Captain BALL.—It is a tradition I have heard here that the
mackerel fishing commenced on Patrick's Day, but it did not commence this year till April. They always used to say the mackerel
fishing commenced on Patrick's Day.

184. Do you remember when they commenced the herring fishing
this year?—On the 18th of May; I think there was some arrangement not to commence till then.

185. I know they were here for some time before, and upon that day they all went out together?—Quite so.

186. Mr. HORNBY.—There is one point which has to be considered, that of the supply of food for the public. If you drive the Scotch boats away altogether, and if your people here won't fish herrings, the result will be that a large quantity of food will be lost to the public? (Mr. O'Neill).—But the fish they catch in the interval from April to the 1st of June we submit are not good food; and that is recognised by their own people, by reason of the fact that they won't fish in their own waters until the 1st of June. We say the public would be hotter off without it.

187. Mr. HORNBY.—You must allow that that there is a considerable difference between the Scotch and Irish climates; here the fish strike the coast earlier, so that a later period there would be necessary? (Mr. O'Neill).—No doubt, sir, there is something in that; but my further answer is this. Even assuming that they were good food, if you permit this fishing, I submit that it is injurious to the capture of other fish which are good food, so that for what you would lose in one respect by putting off the herring fishing, you will get an equivalent in the other. For what you lose in the herring you will get an equivalent in the mackerel.

188. I want to state these things to you, because those objections will certainly be made, and I wish to put them before you, that you may not be taken by surprise, and say that we did not think of them at the time? (Mr. O'Neill).—I am greatly obliged to you, sir; we are so conscious of having a good cause that we do not dread an inquiry of the minutest character.

189. Mr. HOGIE.—Of course, there is one view you might put, that this being an Irish fishery, it is only natural that Irish fishermen should be allowed to get them—the fish that come to this coast are sent by nature for the Irish people, and if the native population can take them they ought to be allowed to do so. (Mr. O'Neill).—Yes, sir; that is what we respectfully submit. There is a question I want to ask Mr. Riordan in reference to the quality of the herrings that are taken early in the year.

John RIORDAN recalled, and further examined.

190. Mr. O'Neill.—Are you aware of the fact that a quantity of herrings that were sent across in the early part of the season were condemned at the other side as unfit for food?—I am, sir.

191. Have you known that to be done, of your own knowledge?—Yes, sir; they were bad; the bellies dropped out of them.

192. Who condemned those herrings?—The food authorities on the other side. I had some myself that were condemned. I had some boxes of them, and when they were sent over, the bellies of the fish were all gone; they were a bad quality of herring altogether.

193. Mr. GAREN.—You said that 15s. a mease was the price they averaged?—Yes, sir; that was low, of course. Of course it is all speculation; the buyers have to run that chance. The sanitary authorities condemned them when they got over.

Mr. HORNBY asked Mr. Murray did he wish to put any questions to any of the witnesses?—Mr. Murray replied he did not.

MICHAEL NEWMAN, sworn; examined by Mr. O'Neill.

194. You are a fisherman?—I am, sir.
195. And all your family, I believe, are fishermen?—Yes, sir.

196. Do you remember the mackerel season of 1890 ?—I do, sir.

197. Were you standing on the pier in that year on one occasion ?—Yes, sir.

198. Did you see a large quantity of small immature mackerel that had been taken by a herring boat ?—Yes, sir; as high as 30,000.

199. By one boat ?—Yes, sir.

200. Mr. ROCHE.—30,000 ?—Yes, sir; from one of the boats.

201. Mr. O'Neill.—How many boats were discharging on that occasion ?—There were only five or six boats, as far as I could see.

202. What quantity of small fish would each boat average, to the best of your opinion ?—I dare say they would average about 16,000 to 17,000.

203. For the other five boats ? -Yes, sir; for all the boats that were there. I don't know how many were there.

204. And one had 30,000 ?—Yes, sir.

205. Mr. HORNBY.—How did you make the calculation ?—From the quantity of fish that was there.

206. Mr. O'Neill.—Did you see the small fish put into baskets or boxes?—No, sir.

207. Where were they ?—They were on board the boats at that time.

208. You did not see them put into boxes or baskets ?—No, sir.

209. Mr. HORNBY.—In what way did he estimate the quantity ?—He says there were 30,000 in one boat, and an average of 16,000 or 17,000 in the others. How did he measure them ? (Mr. O'Neill).—From the bulk, sir; of course it is only an estimate, but though there may be some inaccuracy in that, there is no doubt there was a large number.

210. Mr. GREEN.—Did you see those boats come in on any other night ?—No, sir; I was not there any other day.

211. You went there one day ?—Yes, sir; one day only.

R. A. WILLIAMS, sworn; examined by Mr. O'Neill.

212. You are owner of some of the Kinsale fishing vessels ?—I am.

213. How many ?—Five, and I manage four more, so that I represent nine.

214. Have you got the returns of the fish taken by those vessels ?—I have got the returns of four of them. In 1885 the "Damsel" made by haking £190; last year she made £65; this year is almost a blank; at the very outside it would be only £50 this year.

215. Mr. GREEN.—How much did she make in 1889 ?—£55; I am talking now of one boat in particular.

216. Mr. HORNBY.—Can you tell us how much she took in 1886 and 1887 ?—In 1887 this boat made £75.

217. £75?—Yes, sir; £75 in 1887.

218. How much in 1886 ?—I have not got the figures for 1886 here.

219. Can you give us the returns for any of the other boats?—Yes, sir; I have the returns for the "Susan"; that is the boat the skipper of which gave evidence here to-day. Here are the returns:

In 1884 she made £100 by hake fishing.				
,, 1885	,,	135	,,	,,
,, 1886	,,	115	,,	,,
,, 1887	,,	130	,,	,,
,, 1888	,,	10	,,	,,
,, 1889	,,	55	,,	,,
,, 1890	,,	55	,,	,,
,, 1891	,,	100	,,	,,
,, 1892	,,	50	,,	,,

She only made £50 this year by hake fishing. For the five years from 1884 to 1888 inclusive, you might say the average was £120 a year, whereas now it is down to £50. I may mention that the "Susan" is one of the best boats to take as a test, because she is entirely engaged in fishing, while some of the other boats pilot. The next boat is the "Wood Nymph." I will take two years: In 1885 she made £140 by hake, in 1891 she made only £50, and this year about £40.

221. Did she fish in the other years?—She did, but I have not got the items; I had not time to make them up. Of course it is for my own information I keep an account of these things. The next boat is the "Stella." In 1891 she made £65 by hake; I have not got the other items of her earnings; she is a pilot boat.

221. Are those all the figures you have got?—Yes, sir; I have noticed that this year the hake fishing is almost a blank; in fact we may say it is a blank.

222. Is the conclusion you arrive at that the falling off is due to the Scotchmen fishing?—My conclusion is that the herring fishing so early in the year is most injurious. I have seen myself a great deal of small hake caught in those nets, and small mackerel.

223. What is your best season for hake fishing? What time of the year?—From July to Christmas.

224. Then the Scotchmen are not fishing at the time you fish hake?—No; they go away.

225. Mr. ROCHE.—But you contend that they have done the injury before the hake fishing begins?—Yes, sir; the hake have not come to maturity at the time they are fishing; they are very small at that time.

226. Mr. GREEN.—What has been your experience with regard to the mackerel fishing: is it improving or otherwise?—No; it is falling off to a wonderful extent, whatever is the cause of it.

227. Mr. ROCHE.—What is the difference in the size of the hake they catch early in the year, and the matured hake that are caught later on?—The hake I have seen caught early in the year was something about the size of a mackerel; they could not catch large ones. In fact, they are scarcely the size of a mackerel. The proper length of a hake is about three feet.

228. Mr. HORSLEY.—Could you give us any statistics of the decline in the mackerel fishing during the last few years—I do not mean now, but could you send them to us, to show what the decrease has been?—I will, sir, certainly, with pleasure; where shall I send them to?

229. To the Fishery Office, at the Castle?—Yes, sir; I will send them. I am sorry I did not know that you wished for them; if I had known I would have had them ready now. In fact, probably, I could do it to-day.

230. You need not give them to us to-day; any time within the next week or two will do?—Very well, sir; I will send them to you.

Mr. O'Neill said there was another witness in Court, who could state how his mackerel fishing was obstructed by the herring men.

ADAM M'CARTHY, sworn; examined by Mr. O'Neill.

231. You are master of a fishing boat?—Yes, sir.

232. Have you been all your life engaged in fishing?—Yes, sir.

233. Describe how you are interfered with by the herring men?—I have two nets, sir; but during the past year I had to keep my mackerel nets in, and not me alone, but I suppose a number of other men had to do the same, owing to the herring fleet coming on us.

234. Why had you to keep your nets in?—If we shot our mackerel

nets when the herring fleet was there they would destroy our nets. One night seventeen of them went over our nets.

285. Mr. GREEN.—Don't you shoot your nets a long way outside of where the herring boats shoot?—We are forced to do it now, sir; we can't interfere with the herring fleet; if we did we would lose our train nets.

286. Mr. O'Neill.—Have you seen large quantities of immature fish taken by those herring boats?—Yes, sir, thousands.

287. Have you seen them unmeshing them out at sea, and throwing them overboard?—Yes, sir; coming in seven or eight miles I would see them all the time throwing them over.

238. Mr. GREEN.—What size mackerel?—About four or five inches long, sir.

239. Mr. O'Neill.—What are called cocks?—Yes, sir; and those are only the mackerel that are seen; but how many thousands and millions strike against the nets that no one ever sees; thousands of them strike against the nets and down they go, and no one knows about them.

240. Mr. ROGNE.—Would they not float afterwards?—No, sir; no one gets any satisfaction about those fish; they are killed. Moreover, before those Scotch herring men came here our best fishing ground used to be a dozen to fifteen miles along the coast, but now we dare not shoot a net there. Some years ago we had fourteen or fifteen miles to shoot our mackerel nets where we had nice fishing; but now we dare not look at it.

241. Mr. GREEN.—How far off the coast do the herring men shoot their nets?—They have been off as far as forty miles this year.

242. The Scotchman?—Yes, sir.

243. What month was that in?—That would be about the end of May.

244. Forty miles off the land?—Yes sir.

245. Were the whole fleet at that time of the year forty miles off the land?—No, sir; from that to five miles; some five, some fifteen, some forty. They would go farther only the mackerel fleet were outside them; they went as far as they could go.

Mr. HORNBY asked Mr. Murray whether there was any question that he wished to put to the witness.

Mr. Murray.—No, sir, not now; I think not.

246. Mr. GREEN.—With regard to those small mackerel that you say were immature, and thrown overboard, were they saleable—are any of them sold? Yes, sir; I did not see them, but I am informed the buyers bought them, and sent them across.

Mr. O'Neill.—We have had evidence that they were purchased at 1s. 6d. per hundred. (Witness).—I have not seen them sold; because they are brought in before we arrive and we have no chance of seeing them, except an odd time when we would be in earlier than usual, but that would be only one time out of fifty.

Mr. HORNBY asked Mr. O'Neill had he any other witnesses to examine.

Mr. O'Neill said he had not.

Mr. HORNBY.—Then does that conclude the evidence?

Mr. O'Neill.—Yes, sir; I think so.

Mr. HORNBY.—Very well. As I stated, when opening the proceedings, we will continue the inquiry in Scotland, and when any decision is arrived at, of course those interested here will be duly informed of it.

The Inquiry then concluded for the present.

COCKENZIE INQUIRY.

———

Public School, Cockenzie,
Saturday, 28th January, 1893.

Her Majesty's Inspectors of Irish Fisheries—ALAN HORNSBY, Esq.
(in the chair), WILLIAM H. GREEN, Esq., and CECIL ROCHE, Esq., B.L.;
held an inquiry this day at the Public School, Cockenzie, pursuant to a
notice which stated "that the custom of fishing for herrings off the
south coast of Ireland before the 1st of June in each year, is detrimental
to the mackerel fisheries off said coast, and, as fishermen from Scotland are interested in the question, the Inspectors of Irish Fisheries
hereby give notice that they will hold inquiries into the matter at the
following places in Scotland, etc."

Mr. John Murray, one of the officers of the Scottish Fishery Board,
attended the meeting to render any information or assistance which
the Inspectors might require during the inquiry.

Mr. HORNSBY said—In opening the proceedings here to-day I deem
it right on the part of myself and my colleagues to make a few
remarks concerning our position. At the request of the Lord Lieutenant of Ireland, representing Her Majesty the Queen, we have commenced an inquiry into the question of the necessity of fixing a date
before which herring fishing should not be carried on off the south-
west coast of Ireland. In holding inquiries in Scotland we wish it to
be most distinctly understood, as we are aware that in some quarters
misconceptions have occurred, that it was never our intention for
one moment to interfere with the jurisdiction of the Scottish Fishery
Board, or to usurp any functions within the limits of their jurisdiction.
We, as the heads of the Government Department having control and
jurisdiction over the sea and inland fisheries of Ireland, are sitting
here simply to convenience such of the Scottish fishermen as fish in
Irish waters off the south-west coast, by hearing whatever evidence
they have to tender to us on the subject from their point of view.
Recognising the fact that it would be impossible for most of them to
appear before us in Ireland, we have come to listen to their story at
their own doors. We have already held an inquiry at Kinsale as to
the views of the Irish fishermen in that locality. I take this opportunity of tendering our thanks to the Secretary of State for Scotland,
and to the Chairman and members of Fishery Board for Scotland,
the latter for having placed at our disposal one of their fishery officers,
who has at considerable trouble submitted to us the most suitable
localities for sitting on the various parts of the coast inhabited by
fishermen, a large number of whom fish in Irish waters, so as, if
possible, not to shut out any important evidence. We trust also he
will be able to submit to us the names of such witnesses as can give
us reliable, intelligent, and unbiassed evidence on a question which
we must consider in its bearings on the fisheries of the United
Kingdom and not as a purely local one. Does anybody represent
the fishermen here?

Colonel *Cadell.*—I represent the fishermen. I desire to make a statement. As Acting Chief Magistrate of the burgh of Cockenzie, in the absence of my brother, General Cadell, it has devolved on me to represent the interests of the fishermen of this place at this inquiry. My first duty is to express our great gratification at seeing you here, gentlemen. The Chairman has explained that they come here with no intention of interfering with, or usurping the authority of, the Scotch Fishery Board. Far from that—they have come here as a very great favour to us, out of their way altogether. They would have been quite within their rights had they only conducted this inquiry in Ireland as it concerned Ireland. But, knowing that you men could not go to Ireland to give your evidence, the Irish Government most thoughtfully and impartially directed the Inspectors of Irish Fisheries to prosecute their inquiries, commenced at Kinsale, at various places in Scotland also, in order that they might hear both sides of the case. I am sure this shows a desire on their part to have the matter fully before them before coming to any decision, and I hope the Commission will accept our grateful acknowledgments.

Mr. Hornsby.—They can come forward as witnesses.

Colonel *Cadell.*—There are two—Mr. Flynn and Mr. Porter.

Mr. Hornsby.—They can come forward as witnesses.

Colonel *Cadell.*—I beg formally to hand in a statement drawn up by the Chief Magistrate of this place representing our views upon this case. I believe you have already seen this statement, but I am not aware of its having been formally before you.

The oral evidence which will be produced will deal with most of the questions which came before you at the inquiry at Kinsale on the 20th ultimo. There are some points, however, connected with documentary evidence which cannot well be made clear by the witnesses, and I would therefore with due respect submit the following statement for your consideration.

I would beg leave to point out that the statistics furnished by the Harbour Master, Kinsale, regarding the number of Scotch boats engaged in the herring fishing at Kinsale during the past nine years do not correspond with those contained in the Annual Report of the Inspectors of Irish Fisheries. The figures furnished by the Harbour Master are therefore inaccurate, or the reports embodied in the Blue Books are unreliable, and it is for you, gentlemen, to decide which of these conclusions is the correct one.

The Harbour Master also stated before you at Kinsale that the herring fishing commenced at that place between the 1st and 10th May. Oral evidence will be produced on this point, and I would also beg you to refer to the annual reports from which it will be seen that during the twelve years from 1878 to 1889, both years inclusive, the fishing commenced eight times before May, and four times during that month. The dates of commencement are not given in the Reports of 1890 and 1891, and the Report for 1892 has not yet been published, but we know that by an arrangement previously made, the date of commencement was the 11th May.

Mr. W. Alcock informed you at Kinsale that the two fishings, namely herring and mackerel, flooded the market, and "cut down the price," and the Harbour Master gave, as a reason for the soreness on the part of the Kinsale fishermen, the reduction in the price of mackerel owing to many more fish being brought into the market. On this point I would venture to mention that Sir T. Brady, in a letter dated 30th March, 1892, to our Member of Parliament, which he said, might be printed publicly, stated that this objection was unreasonable. It is evidently so, as the community benefits by the price being lowered.

The Harbour Master of Kinsale stated that the herring caught by the Scotch fishermen were unfit for human food. If such were the case, how was it for example that the 44,323 mease caught at Kinsale in 1884, in which year the herring fishing lasted from the 13th April to the 21st June, yielded £39,566, and that the 11,233 mease caught in 1891, the last year for which statistics are available, yielded £6,608.

On the general question of the value as food of immature fish, I would beg you to refer to page 236 of the 10th Annual Report of the Scotch Fishery Board, in which the following statement occurs :—" In the great herring fishery of Scotland the quantity of immature herrings caught last year amounted to over 25 per cent. of total catch and of a value to the fishermen, as near as can be calculated, of between £200,000, and £230,000," and the report goes on to say, " unless on economic grounds, it is as unreasonable to prohibit the sale of such immature fish, as to prohibit the sale of the eggs of domestic fowls, of chickens, lamb, veal, &c.

As to the alleged immaturity of the mackerel caught by the Scotch fishermen, the evidence of the witnesses who will be produced to-day will prove to you that the comparatively few mackerel caught are excellent food.

I would also request the favour of a reference to page 8 of the printed statement which I have submitted to you, in which scientific authority is quoted that " mackerel spawn in May and June. In three months the young attain a size of only three inches. It migrates to deep water in November, when it has grown to six or seven inches long, re-appearing in the following June eight or nine inches long." The Scotch herring net of 32 mesh or less to the yard could not hold fry which must at that time be three inches long or less, any more than the mackerel net with larger meshes could do so, and if you credit the evidence which will be brought forward the mackerel caught by the Scotch fishermen at Kinsale are about a foot long and must therefore be two years old.

Witnesses stated before you at Kinsale that the herring fishing if carried on would spoil the mackerel fishing and that the two fishings could not go on simultaneously. This is disproved by statistics, and I would refer you, for example, to the Annual Report for 1884, in which year 99,339 boxes of mackerel caught at Kinsale realised £86,111, and 44,323 mease of herring £39,566. Evidence will be laid before you regarding mackerel and herring fishing being carried on simultaneously, without detriment to either, on the east coast of England.

There are no statistics of the quantity of mackerel caught by the Scotch fishermen, but it cannot be large, as will be proved by witnesses. Their statements are confirmed by the fact that the mackerel fishing ground is thirty or forty miles or more from the shore, and the herring fishing from seven to fifteen miles from the shore. The proportion of mackerel caught in the herring nets must be infinitesimally small compared to the total catch, and it is surely absurd to suppose that it can possibly affect the general mackerel harvest either in May or June, or from July to Christmas, which latter period is, according to Mr. A. N. Williams' statement made before you, the best season for mackerel.

It is not known to us what decrease in the catches of mackerel is shown in the statistics which Mr. Williams promised to send to you. There undoubtedly appears to have been a falling off at Kinsale, but it would appear from the official reports that no practical harm has been done to the mackerel fishing by the early herring fishing, notwithstanding the allegations of the Irish witnesses to the contrary. In those official reports it is stated that the mackerel fishing was better in 1886 than in 1885; that hake in that and the two following years were taken "in large quantities," that in 1887 the number of mackerel taken was greater than in 1886; that in 1888 the mackerel fishing was "good"; that in 1889 all kinds of fish were "plentiful"; that in 1890 the "mackerel spring fishing" was "very good" that in 1891 it was "very good with better prices but fewer fish," and that "as a whole the fishing was above the average." As already stated, the report of 1892 has not been published and cannot therefore be referred to.

Might not the decrease in the quantity of mackerel caught at Kinsale be attributed to other causes than the herring fishing by the Scotch fishermen?—For example to those mentioned at page 32 of the Annual Report for 1891 (in which it is expressly stated "the fish were in great numbers off the coast and in all the bays"). "The mackerel fisheries for the spring of 1891 do not show as good a result as those of the previous year. Various causes have been assigned for this, but the departure from the engagement system on the part of the fishermen, and their desire to congregate at points where there was likely to be competition between buyers, such as at Berehaven, Baltimore, and Kinsale, have no doubt much to say to the falling off. More boats were concentrated on certain grounds while others were neglected," also to the recently introduced autumn fishing and to the action of the steam trawlers between Milford and the Irish coast, which two alleged causes will be spoken of to-day by Mr. Hugh Flynn.

From the official reports and also from the evidence taken by you at Kinsale, it is clear that herring fishing at Kinsale by Irish boats has been practically abandoned. If the herring fishing on the south coast of Ireland is closed up to the 1st June, it would not be worth while for the Scotch fishermen to go there at all. The fixing of that date would practically mean the entire stoppage of herring fishing on that coast all the year round, and I would ask you, gentlemen, if it would not be preposterous to make that coast the only locality in Her Majesty's dominions closed against herring fishing during a season when they are in good condition, the real reason for the closure being not that the herring and mackerel fishing cannot be carried on simultaneously, without detriment to each other, but the jealousy on the part of the local boat-owners and fishermen against fishermen from other parts of the kingdom coming among them and "cutting down the prices" by the quantities of fish landed by them.

It is hardly necessary for me to point out that if it were true that, as asserted by one of the witnesses at Kinsale, the mackerel boats had been obliged by the action of the Scotch herring boats, to fish further out at sea than formerly, and that the former were afraid to put down their nets lest they should be damaged by the latter, facts of such importance would not have been passed over without mention in the reports of the Inspectors of Irish Fisheries or by Mr. O'Neill in the several statements made by him before you at Kinsale.

A copy of the official report of the inquiry only reached me the night before last, and unavoidable engagements obliged me to go into Edinburgh yesterday. It has, therefore, been out of my power to criticise the evidence of the several witnesses, and to analyse the several inconsistent and contradictory statements, and, in some instances, their incredible assertions.

Mr. HORNSBY.—That is a most important statement. Will you hand it in?

Colonel *Cadell.*—I will have much pleasure in doing so.

JOHN BROWN sworn; examined by Colonel *Cadell.*

1. Mr. HORNSBY.—Do you live here?—Yes.

2. Colonel *Cadell.*—Are you a fisherman, and own a boat?—Yes, sir.

3. And are you skipper or owner of a boat?—I have been owner of a boat for the last fourteen years.

4. Have you been in the habit of going to the herring spring fishing at Kinsale?—I have been in the habit of going to Kinsale for these last ten years.

5. About what date do you generally commence, and when do you leave off?—The date is always stated to be from the 1st of May, and we always stayed at Kinsale till the 8th or 10th of June. If we were beyond that we found it to be injurious for us at the Howth fishing.

6. Did you catch as good herring at the beginning as towards the end of that period?—Some seasons we realised better fishing when we started than in the middle of the time.

7. Are these herrings readily bought by the dealers and others?—Quite readily bought when we come ashore.

8. Do you get as good prices for them at the beginning as at the end of the season?—Sometimes we realised more for the first shots than what we did afterwards.

9. Can you tell me what you realised for the first shots—give me any instance of prices?—There was one year we had over twenty-six mease, and 26s. the mease for the first shot, and in the second shot twenty-seven mease and got 20s. for them.

10. Mr. HORNSBY.—What year was that to the best of your recollection?—That would be 1882, sir.

11. Colonel *Cadell.*—Did you get many mackerel in your nets?—That season I am referring to we had no mackerel at all. Those two shots I can recollect as well as I do the present moment.

12. But in ordinary seasons do you get many?—The fewer herrings we get we seemed to get fewer mackerel.

13. What is the size of the mackerel you generally caught in your nets?—From ten to twelve or thirteen inches.

14. Is it the case that in the years you get most herrings they get most mackerel?—Yes, we have always experienced that. The more mackerel the mackerel fishers get it seems to me there are more herrings on the coast, but further out from the shore.

15. What was the size of the mackerel you got?—From ten to twelve and thirteen inches.

16. And do you get mackerel fry?—I have never seen any fry ever since I went to Kinsale—what we term fry in Scotland.

17. Can your nets retain fry?—No.

18. What is the size of the meshes of the nets used by the Scotch fishermen?—I have been in the habit of buying my nets from thirty-one to thirty-two meshes to the yard.

19. Are the mackerel caught by you good for food?—We have realised good prices for them—from 15s. to as high as £1 to 2s.

20. And that proves that they are good food?—Yes.

21. By whom are they bought?—The most of the Irish buyers buy them.

22. Are they general dealers or Irish buyers?—The Irish buyers, who send them through Ireland.

23. Do many local people buy them too?—There are a great many local people moving about—fishwives and people, but we do not care about selling many to them. There is always a squabble with them before getting our money from them.

24. You therefore sell them to the dealers?—Yes.

25. Do you catch many hake?—Well, we have caught a few hake, but very few.

26. And during the last two years have you caught fewer than usual?—Yes, we have not seen any for these past two years—just an odd one now and then.

27. Can you give any idea what you catch during the season, of hake?—They have been so few that we have never taken anything like statistics to know how many we have taken. We have taken no notice of them.

28. And of mackerel, can you give any idea of the amount you have caught?—I believe the most mackerel ever I had taken at Kinsale for a season on the average would not exceed four to five mease in the week.

29. Are you in the habit of throwing many fish overboard?—We have no fish overboard that we can get money for in Ireland. What the Irish fishermen call gurnard—we call them gurneys—we heave overboard. We can find no money for them—unless the old people ask them from us as a fry; but if they are not alongside we put them over the boat-side.

30. How do you account for the Irish witnesses saying they saw mackerel floating in the harbour of Kinsale?—I would not that as being false. I never saw mackerel come to the surface after being dead. It always went to the bottom like a stone.

31. Mr. Green.—Do you believe as a fact that mackerel do not float?—They never can float.

Colonel Cadell.—That is the general belief on the part of our fishermen.

32. How do you account for the assertion by Irish witnesses that the herring have been condemned in England?—I can give no proof as regards that—only that they might not be salted down enough when they got to the English markets.

33. How far off shore do you fish for herring?—We never like to go beyond fifteen to twenty miles at the very farthest.

34. What is the usual range?—From seven to fifteen miles is about the range where we have caught most herrings.

35. And how far do the mackerel boats go?—It is very seldom we see them unless when the weather is very quiet we come in collision with each other. But when there is wind for us to go to sea it is very seldom we see the mackerel boats, unless coming in in the morning along with us. They go as far, by their own statement, as thirty-five to forty-five and fifty miles always south-west of us—right out of sight.

36. And while fishing do the mackerel and herring boats ever clash together?—We have never seen it, because we always try to keep out of their way. The mackerel nets drift so fast and come quick upon us, and we always try to avoid them if possible.

37. Have you ever heard complaints of the Scotch herring boats breaking the mackerel nets?—I have never heard of any, and for my own experience I have never broken a mackerel net ever since I went to Kinsale.

38. Did you get on harmoniously with the Irish fishermen when you first began to go to Kinsale?—We always got on harmoniously

with them and with the Irish people until these last two or three years. We do not know what was the cause of the ill-will towards us. We have done no more during the past few years than what we did previously.

39. When did they begin to show ill will to you?—The most that ever we as Scotch fishermen felt was the year before last, they stopped us altogether.

40. Had you had any disputes with them before?—I think I can recollect no more than some people going to the public house and falling out. I have heard a few young fellows complaining about being too late out at night, but I always found that had been their own fault.

41. Did you get on well with them until the Irishmen practically stopped the herring fishing,—was it then they began to quarrel with you?—We always got on pretty well with them. We never could say anything bad about the men, because we always kept out of their way until that year they stopped us.

42. Can you tell us when the herring season commences at different places?—We go first to Kinsale. We find most herrings at the grounds at Kinsale. If the buyers would buy the fish from us, and we commenced at 1st April, we would find more herrings then than we do at the latter end of May. And when we go further north, we find that the fishing just begins about a month or six weeks later than at Kinsale.

43. Where do you mean?—At Howth.

44. At Stornoway, when does it begin there?—The 15th of May.

45. And then round Scotland?—It begins at Wick on 1st July.

46. And then further south does it make any difference?—In former years when the merchants belonging to Fraserburgh and Peterhead would not take herring from us before 20th July by agreement, it did.

47. Mr. ROCHE.—By agreement?—Yes, by agreement. But, now, these things are done away with, and we start now at 1st July, not to our benefit, but to our disadvantage a great deal.

48. Mr. GREEN.—Where do you start on the 20th July?—At Fraserburgh and Peterhead.

49. Colonel Cadell—Might you start earlier if you liked?—Is there any close time by regular or mutual agreement on the east coast of Scotland?—No; we have the boats catching herrings on 1st April all the year through—even now right on till September.

50. Mr. ROCHE.—Do I understand you begin on the 1st July?—From the 1st July is what we fishermen term the Lammas fishing.

51. Colonel Cadell.—But you might fish before then, or all the year round, if you liked. There is neither legal prohibition nor private understanding to the contrary? No; the fish make us stop in September, because they go to the south.

52. Mr. GREEN.—Is it on 1st July you begin to fish for herrings at Fraserburgh and Peterhead?—We begin fishing at Peterhead, Fraserburgh, and Aberdeen on 1st July, and as the fish go south we follow them.

53. Mr. ROCHE.—Not before?—Oh yes; but we fishermen reckon 1st July for our Lammas fishing to begin.

54. And you do not fish before then?—Oh, yes. The reason why we do not begin then is that we are out of the way of it.

55. Colonel Cadell.—Does it pay you to begin sooner?—It does not pay us to begin so soon. There are fishermen in Scotland who fish before that. You will find them fishing for herring at Peterhead if you go there now.

56. Mr. HORSLEY.—Let us understand. Is there a general close time on the east coast before 1st July, or are you only talking of what you do?—I am only talking about Cockensie fishermen.

57. Colonel Cadell.—Can the fishermen possibly feel the fish striking their nets, and being killed and sinking to the bottom of the sea, and never rising again, even if thousands and millions did so?—No we can never do that, for we lie sleeping before daylight. We do not know what is coming against our nets.

58. You could not possibly tell what fish touch your nets?—Oh, no.

59. Were you on good terms with the townspeople at Kinsale?—Pretty good terms. They all rejoiced to see the Scotch fishermen come amongst them.

60. And did you think that the townspeople were for having a close time up till 1st June, or only the people connected with the fishing?—They were all very sorry when the fishermen stopped us that season we were stopped.

61. Can you, for the sake of peace and quiet, suggest any compromise by which you would catch fewer mackerel in your nets than you do now?—There is only one thing we as fishermen have been bringing under your notice, and that is to lengthen our buoy ropes, which would cause us both toil and expense. That might serve a little, but as far as we know, there is nothing else we can think of.

62. What is the present length of your buoy ropes?—Two fathoms.

63. And what would you propose to lengthen it to?—Two and a half or three fathoms.

64. Do mackerel swim high?—Always to the surface.

65. And you think if the buoy ropes were lengthened say to three fathoms, many mackerel caught now in your nets would swim over them?—We are in that belief.

66. Do not boats fish for herrings all the year round in various parts of Scotland?—All the year round we find them.

67. Mr. GLENN.—Have you seen mackerel drop out of your nets when hauling them in?—Oh, not very many.

68. These are the large mackerel that are not caught by the meshes—they fall out before you can get them on board. Is that so?—Yes.

69. These mackerel have been in the nets probably all night and are killed?—Yes.

70. And they are lost?—Some of them are. The way our nets are mounted just like a barb. When we see either herring or mackerel we try to get the head of the net, and try to pull slow. We always sing out to the men who are pulling what we term a pull of the net " pull slow " and we commonly get most of them. I do not say we get them all. What we do get are few in numbers. There are not many at the best.

71. You have suggested lengthening the buoy rope to give the mackerel a better chance of escaping the herring nets?—Yes.

72. But your buoy rope is two fathoms long. Generally speaking you do not have the net slung to the full length of the buoy rope?—You cannot. You must have room to fix the buoy rope to the net. If the herring swim up we always like to get them.

73. In the spring of the year is it a fact that you find the herrings nearer the surface than in the later fishing?—Oh, no.

74. The more wind the higher the fish, is it not?—It matters not where we go. That may be to a certain extent.

75. If the buoy ropes were lengthened to three fathoms instead of

two there would be no way in bad weather for the mackerel escaping?—
It is not always bad weather, and if it is fine weather a great many
of the mackerel would escape because our nets would be below them.

Mr. GREEN.—If you were fishing to the full length of the buoy-
rope.

76. Colonel *Cadell.*—If any such by-law were issued by the Irish
authorities that the buoy-rope should be three fathoms the Scotchmen
would attend it?—We would do anything to have peace. We do not
like to have disputes with our brother fisherman. It is not agreeable
for any man to be in terror of his brother fishermen.

77. Mr. GREEN.—Yes, but what I mean is—supposing you had a
buoy-rope three fathoms long, you would use as much as you felt
suitable according to where you found herring swimming; so that
having a buoy-rope three fathoms long would not be any guarantee
that you would fish with three fathoms?—Then you, as Commissioners,
have no faith in what I say. There is no use asking us to come and
swear and then taking us up like that.

Mr. GREEN.—We have no doubt that when you are fishing you
will do the best thing; we are most anxious to let you fish in the way
that would be most suitable.

78. Colonel *Cadell.*—You stated how many mackerel dropped off,
commonly caught by the gills; does the same thing happen with
herring?—Yes.

79. Mr. GREEN.—As a rule, do you clear your nets on your way in
from the fishing ground?—Yes, we cannot do it any other way.

80. The mackerel you bring in and send away ten, twelve, or
thirteen inches long, they are the mackerel you have culled from a
general take on your way in from the fishing ground and have thrown
overboard?—Do not you believe that a Scotchman would be so silly as
heave anything away he is going to get 'siller' for.

81. Would you get money from the buyers for the small mackerel
under ten inches?—We never get any.

82. You never get mackerel under ten inches?—No, any mackerel
we got we take more care of than of herrings. They are all put in
a different part of the boat. Mackerel are easier destroyed than herrings. We stop and take them out to the best of our ability, knowing
that they will not buy those that are split in the belly.

83. Do you mean to say you never made a shot of such small
mackerel that you had to heave the greater part of them overboard?
—Not me, for one.

84. Colonel *Cadell.*—Have you heard of any other Scotch fishermen
doing that?—Never.

85. Mr. GREEN.—Is it small or large boxes that you send the
mackerel away in?—Just according to the buyers.

86. How many would go to the half box?—I found that when we
sold them to the English people they put them into small boxes and
iced them down, and all they could put into them was just a hundred.

87. Have you over seen 400 in a half-box?—Not to my knowledge.

88. Have you seen 300 sent away in a half-box?—No, that is
perfect nonsense. The box would no more hold them than it would
hold us.

89. Colonel *Cadell.*—Do you throw many gurnard overboard?
—The gurnard are all thrown overboard; with fifty boats there might
be any quantity of whiting and gurnard. The tide takes them to Scilly.
We see a great many birds resorting there about; but for mackerel
or any other fish swimming we never saw a mackerel swimming, and
I have been between thirty-five and forty years going to sea. I

have caught mackerel in Scotland and England, and never saw one floating after it was dead.

90. Mr. GREEN.—You say herrings can be caught on the Scotch coast all the year round?—Yes.

91. Why is it worth your while to go to Kinsale instead of nearer home?—There are two or three good reasons for that. The merchants go to Stornoway in May, and the English buyers, a great many of them, go to Kinsale and round to Baltimore and Berehaven and round as far as the Shannon. The consequence is we can find no buyers for our herring at that time of the year on this coast.

92. Colonel Cadell.—And do you find the herring not of such good quality in the early season as at Kinsale?—Nature tells us that. When we go round to Kinsale the weather is a great deal warmer there than in Scotland when we arrive home, and makes the fish a great deal better than in Scotland.

93. Can you tell us the difference in the price you get for your herrings at Kinsale in May, and what you would get for them in Scotland?—We can realise good markets for them at Kinsale, and when we come to Scotland we get no sale at all for them. We have found that by experience.

94. Mr. GREEN.—Is there much difference in the quality of the Scotch herrings at that time from the Irish?—There is as much difference as between a potato when it is not ripe and one when it is ripe.

95. When is a potato ripe on the Scotch coast?—When they are taking them out of the ground.

96. When is the herring ripe?—We find the herring ripe in July and August. We find them most mature in August.

97. Colonel Cadell.—And do you find them as mature at Kinsale in May as you do in Scotland in August?—Yes, we do.

98. Mr. ROCHE.—I suppose the same thing applies to the immature mackerel at Kinsale?—We cannot talk about immature mackerel at Kinsale. We never had any.

99. Mr. GREEN.—The fishermen talk about them and find the same fault as you do with the herring?—When we get them we will be able to talk about them.

100. Mr. HORNSBY.—Can you tell us how many first class registered boats there are at Cockenzie?—About 35 or 40 boats.

101. Do you mean all the boats that go to the herring fishing; how many of these go to Ireland?—There are 50 boats in Cockenzie and Port Seton go to the herring fishing. I do not believe there has ever been over at Ireland out of that number at the largest fishing more than 10, 12, 15, and 25 boats.

102. You say 25 is about the largest number going to Ireland?—That is the largest number ever I have known having been there from Cockenzie.

103. What do the rest of the boats belonging to Cockenzie do at the season when the other boats are fishing herrings at Kinsale?—The greatest part of them are at Stornoway fishing for herrings.

104. Mr. GREEN.—Have you been at Castletown?—Yes, sir.

105. Have you had any trouble there?—No trouble.

106. Why did you not continue to fish from Castletown?—Because we had no buyers.

107. Mr. ROCHE.—You had no trouble anywhere except at Kinsale?—Speaking for myself, nowhere except at Kinsale.

108. Mr. GREEN.—Have you fished from Baltimore?—No.

109. There are plenty of buyers there?—I could not say. I have not been that way.

Hugh Flynn, Liverpool, sworn; examined by Colonel *Cadell*.

110. Are you a fish merchant on an extensive scale?—Yes, sir.
Mr. Hornsby.—Well known to fame.

111. Colonel *Cadell*—You have had great experience of Irish and other fisheries?—I have.

112. And do you export many fish?—I do, sir.

113. For how many years have you gone to Kinsale for the fishing?—Since 1870.

114. Do the herring nets or boats destroy the mackerel or hake fry?—It all depends on what people call mackerel and hake fry. I have never seen them destroy or kill anything but what was fit for human food.

115. What is the size of the mackerel they catch, say, in May?—Do you mean the mackerel the herring boats catch? From nine to twelve inches perhaps.

116. And do the herring boats at Kinsale catch more mackerel than is usual—than herring boats fishing for herring in any other part of Ireland or in the Isle of Man?—I would say no. I have been at Howth and got good herring fishing in the winter time. I have seen as many as 40, 50, and sometimes more masse of herrings in the herring boats. The same at Dunmore.

117. Did you say you had seen any fry among the mackerel caught at Kinsale?—I have seen no mackerel fry at Kinsale.

118. Were they sizable mackerel usually caught in the herring nets, and were they eatable, saleable, good food?—They were.

119. Do you and other merchants purchase many, and at what rates?—I and other merchants purchase them when we can compete with the Irish buyers—I mean the people sending them to Irish markets. Sometimes Dublin merchants would give more money for them than we could get in England.

120. And did you lose by purchasing these mackerel from the herring boats?—Oh, no.

121. And would you not have lost if they had not been good food?—To commence with I do not think we would have bought them if they had not been good food.

122. How many of those mackerel that you buy from the Scotch herring boats go to a box?—As we send them, we would put a hundred to a hundred and a half into a box.

123. How many large mackerel would go into a box?—Half a hundred.

124. Have you ever seen mackerel from Kinsale go to England and France for bait?—I do not know what they use them for. I do not think they would be used for bait. We intend them for the market to be sold. Those small mackerel are never sent to France. We have sent large mackerel to France.

125. Are those small mackerel in good demand?—Yes.

126. Are they as much liked as small mackerel?—So far as the prices go; you cannot expect mackerel boxes that will hold a hundred and a half to bring as much as only half a hundred.

127. But they fetch good prices?—Yes.

128. Have you had any mackerel condemned as unfit for food?—I have heard of none of them being condemned as unfit for food.

129. Do you think the mackerel caught by the herring boats affects the spring mackerel fishing at Kinsale?—To give my own opinion I would say no.

130. To what do you attribute the falling off in the mackerel fishing at Kinsale?—In the first place, I do not think that the mackerel these men catch in the herring nets are the same mackerel at all. They are the same as are caught all along the coast during the herring fishing time between Kinsale and the Isle of Man. As for the falling off in the fishing, I am not altogether sure there has been a falling off. Although we are not getting as many mackerel at Kinsale, we are still getting as many mackerel or near about it as we used to get all through. At one time we had 400 or 500 boats fishing for mackerel at Kinsale. Now they do not all fish at Kinsale; they fish as far as Galway.

131. Mr. BOCHE.—The general quantity of mackerel is equally large but the Kinsale mackerel fishing is falling off?—Yes.

132. You would not admit that the Scotch herring boats have had anything to do with the falling off?—No.

133. How do you account for it?—Simply because there are fifty, sixty, or 100 fishing from Kinsale instead of 300 or 400.

134. Mr. HORNSBY.—They are more scattered now?—The boats used to go out from Kinsale and go up as far as Berehaven and bring all those mackerel back to Kinsale. Now they go to Baltimore, Castletown and all the places; consequently the quantity coming to Kinsale is less than it used to be.

135. It is not a fact that any boats going out from Kinsale are not at all likely to make the same shots as ten or twelve years ago?—The only difference is that the mackerel they would catch ten or twelve years ago are caught before they can get there, because the boats used to go from Kinsale to Baltimore, but now the boats can go out from Baltimore. Consequently the Kinsale people cannot get there in time and the people west of Baltimore take them before they can get them.

136. Colonel CADELL.—Do the herring boats take hake fry?—No, I have said that before.

137. Were there any large or small hake seen at Kinsale last season?—Very few, indeed, either large or small. I noticed a falling off in the hake.

138. To what did you ascribe this?—I do not know to what I could ascribe it; only that I do know there is a large fleet of steam trawl fishing boats fishing between Milford and the Irish coast as far as Kinsale, and further west. These boats have been seen landing cargoes of fish at Milford and Liverpool daily, and principally hake.

139. Has the number of trawlers increased much during the last ten years?—Considerably. Ten years ago none of these trawlers were to be seen on that coast.

140. And have the trawlers had to go elsewhere?—They did go elsewhere. They went to Baltimore, but came back again after giving the ground a rest. They could not get the fish ashore then.

141. After giving the ground a rest?—Yes.

142. Were the herrings caught at Kinsale in May, good food?—They were.

143. And did you find the herrings caught in May as good as the herrings caught in June?—Sometimes they might be better in May than in June, but they are of as much and more value in May than in June.

144. Why?—Simply because herrings have got scarce at that time of the year. The curers put in a good stock of herrings at Yarmouth and Lybster, and when they come to May they begin to get scarce, and as the herrings on the Scotch coast are not what they should be for curing purposes, all the people in England want to get these herrings

for curing purposes—that is for bloaters and kippers, and there is a larger demand for the herring caught at Kinsale in May, than there would be in June.

145. Are these herrings in May worth more money?—In May they are worth more money per hundred than in Scotland at the same time.

146. Mr. GREEN.—Than even at Stornoway?—They make more money than they do at Stornoway, and I conclude they are worth more.

147. Have any of the herrings consigned by you to England been condemned as unfit for food?—I have never had any condemned.

148. Have you noticed much fish thrown overboard from the herring boats at Kinsale?—I have never seen any.

149. Mr. HORNABY.—You are not in a position to say?—I did not say they were thrown out. I say I do not know.

150. Have you any reason to believe that some are thrown overboard there or elsewhere?—I do not think there is. I do not think they have ever been thrown overboard.

151. Can mackerel and herring fishing go on simultaneously at the same place without detriment to either?—I would say so. I do not see anything to prevent them. I will give you my reason for saying so. The mackerel fishermen go out in boats to the fishing, and land the mackerel from the larger boats into small boats, and these boats go alongside the hulk to discharge. The herring boats in the first instance go alongside the pier head, and the herrings are sold by public auction, and as they are sold they go alongside the hulk, but a different hulk together from that at which the mackerel boats go alongside. The herring boats are worked by an altogether different and separate staff from that which works the mackerel boats—different places and different men.

152. So that from that do you think that the herring catches affect the price of mackerel?—I would not say it did. They are a different fish altogether, and used for different purposes. The herrings caught at Kinsale, are principally sent to the English markets, and are used for curing purposes. The mackerel are killed and sold fresh.

153. Has the price of mackerel fallen off?—In what time?

154. Is it lower now, at the present date, than it used to be some years ago?—Mackerel are worth more for the hundred now, than ten years ago. Last year and the year before last, mackerel sold for as much money as ever they did—more in fact.

155. Have the mackerel boats to fish further out at sea than formerly?—I do not know that. I cannot speak to that.

156. Mr. O'Neill at Kinsale said their complaint was against the Scotch boats, not against the Irish or Manx boats, because the latter did not fish for herring until after the close of the mackerel season. Is that the case?—When first the herring fishing started in my time, it was not Scotchmen who did it at all, but Irishmen. They fished in April and May, and a good many fished until it did not pay them, and they gave it up.

157. When do you consider the herring fishing at Kinsale is over? —It is over so far as the fish on the ground is concerned about the 1st of June. Some Scotchmen last year fished herrings from 10th May till 1st June and went away because it did not pay them to stop. Some four or five Manx boats who had been fishing for mackerel then put their herring nets out and went on fishing for herring. They got 10. 15, or 20 mease of herring each for one or two days, and remained for several days, but never got anything.

158. So that practically that fishing is over when 1st June comes?—Is over so far as the fish are not there.

159. When do the fish merchants leave Kinsale—the fish merchants who go to the mackerel fishing?—The mackerel fishing ends from the 15th to the 25th June, and they go away then.

160. And if they continued the herring fishing longer than that would the fish merchants remain for the sake of the herrings?—That is a question I could not answer. I could not tell what anyone would do. If there was a fishing for herrings that would pay me to stop I would stop. But I do not think the herrings are there for them to fish.

161. Mr. Garden.—Is it not the case that the Scotchmen leave Kinsale about the 1st of June in order to have time to get home and fit out for the Scotch fishings, and that the buyers leave Kinsale as soon as the herring fishing is over for the Scotch fishing?—The buyers leave Kinsale when they find that it does not pay them to stay there. My business for instance is principally in Ireland. I only go from Kinsale to Dunmore. I simply shift there because there is nothing for me to do at Kinsale. If the herring fishing continued I would be there with them.

162. Last year was a very good herring year at Dunmore?—It was; but it was very late before we got them. The fishing is over at Kinsale in June; well, then, there is July and August—two months. Last year I was at Dunmore and had plenty of time to enjoy myself. We had nothing till September and then we had to go on fishing in September and October.

163. But then why is it that station has been given up by all the buyers?—Simply because it does not pay them to go there.

164. You were speaking of the herring boats going to a different bulk from the mackerel boats. Is that because the herrings are sent away in salt and mackerel in ice?—That is one reason. Not only that but there is a different process of working them.

165. When the herrings are sent away from Kinsale they are sent in salt?—Yes.

166. And they are chiefly for curing purposes?—Yes; there are no herrings go from Kinsale sold fresh, with the exception of what may go to the Irish markets.

167. Is it not the case that when the herring fishing opens and the herrings go upon the English market, there is a sudden drop takes place in the price of the spring mackerel?—I do not think it. We get forty boats fishing herring there. If they average twenty mease a piece they would only have 800 mease of herrings. That would be a very small amount to go into any one place to interfere with the market. I do not think it has the slightest thing to do with it.

168. From your handling of these herrings is it the case that when they first come they are so soft that they won't bear the salt?—I have never seen herring at Kinsale that were not fit to stand salt and be sent any place.

169. What truth is there in the statement that they are so soft that the salt cuts the bellies and they reach the market in a bad condition?—I do not think there is any truth in it.

170. In your experience are there any herrings so soft as to be injured by the salting?—Certainly not.

171. Mr. Hussey.—Such a thing could not have occurred without coming to your knowledge?—I think not. I have myself bought the

c

most herrings I believe of anybody in Ireland or in Kinsale, and I have never had any such complaint at all. As to the herring boats interfering with the mackerel fishing, I will just say that in 1884 we had something like 130 or 140 Scotch boats and some three or four or five hundred mackerel boats, and they all worked together there. They did not go to any other port to deliver their mackerel, except a few who went to Baltimore. That was the last year either the Kinsale fishermen or the Scotch fishermen had there, and I could not consistently say that one fishing was doing the other any harm.

172. Mr. GREEN.—I think it is very important, you have had such a long experience of the mackerel fishing, to get your opinion definitely about what is very often stated on the south coast by the fishermen, that even at Baltimore or Castletown or Berehaven, at none of these places can they make the same shots as ten or fifteen years ago, or that the same number of mackerel is brought in by any boat. Is that your experience?—I say that the mackerel is got and the pull of the mackerel is broken before they get to these places. The best of the boats get the big shots and they go up as far as Galway.

173. Do you fish from Bantry? Why were those places given up for the last couple of years?—The reason I would attribute is because they have fished it out. The fish was not there, and the men were not paid as well. The boats that went to Bantry were engaged at a certain price. Those who engaged them did so with the intention that there should be a good fishing. But it turned out otherwise. Whatever fishing there was on the south coast, the boats got more money for their mackerel, and consequently had more money. It did not pay them.

174. Mr. HORNBY.—Have you any idea or any knowledge, or what is your conception of the cause of the friction on the part of the Irishmen that has sprung up within the last two years to Scotchmen fishing in the waters?—I could not tell. The only thing I can think of is that they thought these people were earning money, and they were not.

175. I imagine they were earning money?—Well, so they were. They were doing very well.

176. Colonel CADELL.—Why could not the Irishmen earn money in the same way?—The Irishmen fish for mackerel. Their boats are adapted for the mackerel fishing, and were not ready for the herring fishing.

177. Mr. GREEN.—You have engaged mackerel fishing boats. Have you engaged boats for herring?—Yes, I have engaged boats at Castletown and they fished there. Those that were not engaged to buyers had the best of it. Those who made engagements were engaged at a price that paid them well, but those selling in open market got more money for them, consequently they were better off.

178. Mr. HORNBY.—Have you ever had any reason assigned why the Irish fishermen gave up the herring fishing on the coast at Kinsale?—I do not know. The boats that used to come over fishing were the Belfast boats, and they had a fishing of their own at Ardglass. That fishing has failed and they have not been able to keep it on. It does not pay them to go to the fishing at Kinsale for five or six weeks and be all the rest of the year idle.

179. Of whom are you speaking, the local men at Kinsale?—They never did fish.

180. Mr. ROCHE.—Don't they go to Howth, those Kinsale men?—Mr. O'Neill says they went. Perhaps there were some.

181. Mr. HOWARTH.—Is there any solution you can offer to smooth down any little friction between the two nationalities?—I do not know that I can offer anything. It only occurred to me the other day that if these men said " we won't go and fish for herrings until you choose to let us go, that is the 1st June; will you give up fishing mackerel on 1st June?"—It would be all right enough for these people to go to fish on 1st June, if they had the sea clear to themselves and if they could guarantee that the herrings would be there. My impression is that the herrings will not be there on 1st June.

182. Mr. GIBBS.—The Kinsale men say they have not the slightest objection to the Scotchmen going on 1st June?—I quite understand the meaning of that, if they delay till the 1st June that they won't come at all.

183. Mr. ROCHE.—Because they can get fishing elsewhere?—Yes.

184. Colonel Cadell.—What arrangement have the Scotch fishermen among themselves. Is there a close season by arrangement among themselves?—There is no close season. There is an arrangement with the Stornoway people. They say they should not commence fishing before 15th May. Other people agree with them and they commence fishing on 15th May by consent.

185. Mr. ROCHE.—That custom is universal in Scotland?—No, only at Stornoway.

186. Is there any arrangement at other places?—No.

187. Mr. GIBBS.—Why have the Stornoway men fixed upon that date?—To my mind they fixed that date because the herrings are not good enough before that.

188. Mr. ROCHE.—That is the only place in Scotland where there is found a custom of that sort?—So far as I know it is.

189. Mr. GIBBS.—The very same allegation is made by the Kinsale men that has been made by the Stornoway men—that the herrings are not fit to be caught before a certain date. What they are asking for is the very identical thing the Stornoway people have got?—On the contrary. I say the Kinsale herrings are fit. The herrings are sold in Stornoway at four or five shillings a cran—what would be two or three shillings per mease. At that time they are worth at Kinsale 15s. and 20s., which would mean 90s. or 40s. a cran.

190. How many Kinsale herrings go to the cran?—Two mease—about that.

191. How many at Stornoway?—About the same.

192. When do the July herrings appear here?—I do not know anything about that.

193. Colonel Cadell.—You said, I think, that the Scotchmen generally went from Kinsale to fish in Scotland. Do they not go to Howth first and fish for a while before going on?—They do go to Howth, and sometimes to Ardglass. Some years they have a good fishing, and sometimes a poor fishing after leaving Kinsale.

194. Mr. ROCHE.—The Howth fishing has fallen off very much, I think?—Very much indeed. That arrangement at Stornoway was not asked by the fishermen at all. It was asked for by the merchants simply because the fish did not suit their purposes. While we are at that I may tell you about the arrangement come to at Kinsale, not to let the boats fish herrings at Kinsale in April. That, I think, was in 1884. We, the buyers, ourselves considered that herrings in April were not required. We asked the Kinsale people to meet us. The Kinsale boatowners and fishermen met us in our quarters. There were no Scotchmen present at all; and we arranged between the buyers and

σ 2

Kinsale boatowners and fishermen that the date for the Scotch fishermen to commence would be on the 11th May. We informed the Scotch fishermen of that fact, and they agreed with it and went to fish on the 11th May. That was all **the** arrangement that was made. We made it for them.

195. Mr. Howkary.—Have the Scotchmen kept **to their part of the** bargain?—Oh, certainly.

196. Mr. Green.—As much as to say the buyers did not care to go to Kinsale and be there when they did not want to buy herrings? —We were buying mackerel at the time. We consider that in April we do not want any herrings.

197. Because the stocks in the English markets **had not run out?** —They would not make the value they should do.

198. Mr. Rogus.—When did that arrangement end?—It has not ended at all. The only thing I knew of it is that the year before last these fishermen created a good deal of bother. They came to me and said we should not fish herrings before the 1st of June. We very calmly told them we could fish where and how we liked, but they made such a threatening attitude that I considered it better to give way a little. I asked the men to stop in a week. They did so. We did lose the best week of the season.

199. Mr. Green.—How many Scotch boats have you engaged last year?—We had not them engaged. We sold them by public auction alongside the pier. We had something like forty Scotch boats, and nine or ten Irish boats.

200. Have you not engaged any by the season?—No; only if they did come there we sold them. I said there was nothing to prevent them coming, and if they did come I would sell their herrings on and after the 11th May, because I considered we were in honour bound by that arrangement.

201. How long is it since you gave up engaging Scotch boats?—I think it was about 1886, and we have since engaged mackerel boats.

202. Mr. Howkary.—The Scotch fishermen were perfectly satisfied with the arrangement as to the 11th May?—Perfectly; it was made for them and they did not object to it.

203. Mr. Green.—How much do you know a Scotch boat ever having made out of the herring fishing at Kinsale **in a season?**—The year before last I had ten Cockburne boats, and they averaged £300 each. They made all that in five or six weeks, some of them more and some of them less.

204. Mr. Rogus.—The **Irish demands** now are only three weeks in excess of that?—Yes.

205. There is only three weeks difference?—Yes; these three weeks will prevent the whole fishing.

206. Colonel *Cadell*.—Well, you were all satisfied before until the Irish made this extra demand?—They were satisfied when we put it to them. They would rather begin to fish on the 1st May, but when we said the 11th they agreed.

207. Mr. Howkary.—Would the days after the 10th May be better for the Scotchmen than the days before it?—Would it be a greater loss to the Scotchmen between 10th May and 1st June, or between the 1st and 10th of May?—If I was a fisherman I would prefer to commence fishing on 1st May.

208. Mr. Rogus.—The prices would be **better?**—There would be more herring and a longer time to be at it. I expect the prices would be better than further on in the season.

200. Mr. GREEN.—Would it meet the difficulty to any extent if the Scotchmen were allowed to fish from Castletown and Berehaven instead of Kinsale?—We do not know what restrictions might be put on.

210. But if they went to Castletown and the buyers went with them would that satisfy them?—I do not know. It might satisfy them.

211. Would you go and buy their fish?—There are only representatives of the buyers there. Not only that, but when they are sold all the preparation is made at Kinsale.

212. Is there any at Baltimore?—Quite as many people to buy, but the preparations for packing them is not there.

213. Colonel Cadell.—Are there the same facilities for exporting them there?—It is further from the market than Kinsale.

214. Mr. ROCHE.—Is there not a train going to be put on?—That is all right for a few.

215. Colonel Cadell.—Would they catch as many herring there as at Kinsale?—Very likely they would. It is the same coast.

216. Mr. GREEN.—I remember seeing Scotch boats fishing for herring off Valencia. Did they come from Cockenzie?—They came from Anstruther, I think.

217. Mr. HORNSBY.—At Castletown would they have the same facilities for getting their supplies to the market as they have at Kinsale? —That is the question.

218. Mr. GREEN.—They like Castletown as a harbour because they frequent it?—Yes.

219. Colonel Cadell.—Would it interfere with the hake fishing there?—The same as anywhere else. If they go to fish herrings at Castletown and Berehaven they might as well stop at home. They would not get the market.

220. Mr. GREEN.—It is all right for the fish but otherwise it is not worth while going?—Yes.

Mr. ROCHE.—It is a terribly out of the way place.

Colonel Cadell.—We might call any number of witnesses to repeat and confirm what John Brown has said, but I presume repetition is not what you require. But Mr. Green wanted to know something about the Howth fishing, so I will call Mr. William Dickson.

WILLIAM DICKSON, Cockenzie, sworn; examined by Colonel CADELL.

221. How often have you gone with your boat to Howth? You are the skipper of a boat?—For many years I went to the Howth fishing in the year 1873—twenty years ago.

222. Do you agree with everything that John Brown has said already?—You agree with him in all the statements made by him about the Kinsale fishing?—Yes; but I think John Brown omitted something I have experienced myself. The first year over I went to Kinsale two boats tried the herrings after all the other boats went away.

223. Mr. HORNSBY.—What year was that in?—In the year 1880; and the last time we shot we never saw one herring.

224. Colonel Cadell.—When was that?—It was about the 10th June.

225. The fish had disappeared altogether?—Yes.

226. And had dog-fish come on the ground or anything?—Some years they come very plentiful in the month of June.

227. And ruin your fishing nets?—Yes. I have had the experience

of that when they went all the way along to Dunmore—Dog-fish and
sharks too.

228. Mr. GREEN.—After the fishing stops at Kinsale, have you
ever tried it at Dungarvan?—Yes, I have tried Dungarvan.

229. Have you made any shots off Dungarvan or anywhere between Kinsale and Dungarvan?—Very seldom.

230. Where do you generally shoot your nets—what bearings on
the Old Head?—Sometimes westward off Kinsale Old Head and
sometimes eastward and very often right off Kinsale Harbour.

231. What is the reason you keep your boat there and not go to the
east? Because the buyers are at Kinsale and you wish to keep close
to them?—Yes.

232. With the greater part of what John Brown said you agree?—
Yes. But with reference to mackerel fry it swims so fast like a dart
that it goes through a herring net. It has no time to mesh.

233. Have you seen much mackerel drop out of your nets?—I have
seen one or two, but very seldom.

234. Have you seen any hake?—I have seen one or two, but I
never saw any quantity.

235. You never had five or six hundred?—No.

236. Do you ever remember having two hundred?—No; I never
had two score.

237. How many years have you been fishing at Kinsale altogether?
—I went in the year 1880, and I omitted some four or five years.
I dropped it and went to Lowestoft three years, and I went to Storno-
way three years, and to Shetland two years.

238. Have you fished to the westward of Kinsale, any part to the
westward?—I never was any further than Castletownsend.

239. When you went to the Howth fishing did you go from Kinsale to Howth?—I went direct to Howth twenty years ago, and the
fishing was good then.

240. When was the last time you went to Howth?—The Howth
fishing dwindled away, and I dropped going to it altogether, and
my experience is that all these early fishings have a rise and fall.
It is thirty-five years since I went first to the early fishing. I
went to Lowestoft, and my experience was that that was the case.
They dwindled down to less than 800. I went back to Lowestoft
again five years ago, and we got 140 mean.

241. Were you at Howth during the time when the fishing was
dwindling away?—Yes.

242. And were you fishing with the same industry as when the
fishing was good, and making as many trials?—Yes.

243. And you found the shots getting perceptibly less?—Yes.

244. What size of herrings were the Howth herrings compared
with the Kinsale herrings?—The first time I went to the Howth fishing they were a splendid herring, very few herrings could equal
them at that time. But when the fishing dwindled the size of the herring followed. There was a good deal of small fish amongst them.
Some boats would get good herrings for the whole shot, and others
would get altogether very small ones.

245. How many scores deep of nets do you fish with?—Fourteen score. The first time I went to the Howth fishing we had
fifty-four nets in the train, and sixty when we drifted.

246. How long was the head rope?—The net was sixty yards out
of the factory, mounted about forty-two yards—twenty or twenty-
one fathoms.

247. And the buoy lines were two fathoms?—Yes. At first when I

went the back rope was four fathoms, but the end was changed, it was changed to two fathoms or less back rope to pull the cork line uppermost.

248. Colonel *Cadell*—Do you think it would make much difference in the draw of the mackerel if you lengthened your buoy ropes? —As mackerel swim high there might be a little difference, but it would make very little difference in the end to the mackerel for all I get. I have got very few mackerel all the seasons over I was there.

249. What is the most you have got?—I do not think over I crowded anywhere over 600 or 700.

250. Mr. GREEN.—Do you use the back rope now, or do you haul by the foot line?—No, we haul by the back rope.

251. Have you sold any small mackerel in Kinsale?—I have sold all I have got, but I never got many.

252. Colonel *Cadell*—What would be the effect of having a close time up to the 1st of June. Would you go there after that?— I would have no use in going here at all. I would be making passages back and forward, and making no fishing at all.

253. It was stated by a former witness that some boats made £300 in a season at Kinsale. What do you think a fair average is? —There was two years that the average was near about £300, but unfortunately I was not there that year.

254. Mr. GREEN.—What is the cost of a train of nets?—Sixty nets cost £160.

255. How long do you consider they generally last. Of course you are always adding new nets, and taking away old?—If we do not lose the nets, and sometimes we are unfortunate, I have been very unfortunate, and lost nearly all the fleet and half of the fleet by bad weather and heavy takes of herring sometimes; but if you are fortunate, and do not go to the fall fishing at Yarmouth, a net will run four years, and perhaps five, and be a good fishing net, but you have to look after them well. Our nets are thirty-three or thirty-two meshes to the yard.

256. What is the cost of your fitting out expenses a year?—In the average of the boats I have been in the third part of the train has nearly been always new, sometimes nearly the half.

257. The sails and gear and all the rest of it—how much would you put that down at per annum?—A boat for herring fishing alone —£20 will fit her well out.

258. Colonel *Cadell*—What is the value of a boat?—Boats built now cost over £300.

259. Mr. GREEN.—How many men form a crew?—Seven.

260. What share goes to the boat?—The boat gets one share. The money is divided into seven and a half shares, and the boat gets one—equal to one man. The boy gets a half.

John Brown (the previous witness).—You asked Mr. Dickson there as regards the expenses of fitting out. Do you mean provisions and nets too?

Mr. HORNBY.—Simply the maintenance of the gear, rigging, and sails of the boat.

Mr. GREEN.—But there is the provisioning too.

261. Colonel *Cadell*—Do the provisions for the boat come out of the boat's share?—The boat gets a share after all expenses are paid including provisions. The boat gets a share of the clear money—not the realised money.

262. You were going to say what the average catch was of late

years. How many pounds did you make in a season, or about an average?—Taking away those two bad years I think £150 is counted something like a good fishing at Kinsale.

263. But when you speak of seven shares you are speaking only of that portion of the total take which is divided amongst the crew. Is there not a half of the take going to the boat to begin with?—When the owner of a boat has all the equipment belonging to himself and the gear likewise for going into the sea, he gets one half, and the crew the other half, and he goes along with them to divide the money —at that rate into fourteen shares. In some places they do that. But here the men are owners of the boat. Sometimes one man has the boat himself, sometimes four, sometimes three, sometimes two.

264. Mr. GREEN.—But the man that has not a share in the boat and does not own the boat, he only gets a fourteenth share?—Yes.

265. Colonel *Cadell*.—Would you be satisfied if the close time at Kinsale was fixed on the 11th May?—From my experience I would like better the 1st of May.

266. Mr. ROCHE.—If it was a compromise would you be satisfied with the 11th?—We would have to be satisfied, but the fishing would be better if it was from the 1st of May. To make peace we must come to that conclusion.

267. Mr. GREEN.—What effect would it have on your men going to Kinsale if it was fixed for the 20th May?—The 20th May would be too late. The time for fishing the herrings would be too short, sometimes ten days makes a mighty difference. We sometimes have bad weather one week and that cuts up the time.

268. Would it be worth your while to go at all if it was fixed at 20th May?—I do not consider it would be worth going to Kinsale.

269. But it would if fixed on the 11th?—We have had experience of that.

270. Mr. HORNSBY.—Is your experience that after the 1st of June it was useless to go to Kinsale for the herring fishing?—Yes, that is my experience.

271. Do you think the fish have left these waters on 1st June?—There is no use fishing after 1st June.

272. Mr. ROCHE.—Is that because the fish have gone away or because you have better fishing elsewhere?—Because the fish have gone away.

273. Mr. ROCHE.—Would you get better fishing elsewhere after the 1st of June?—There are no merchants to buy fish on the Scotch coast at that time.

274. Mr. GREEN.—There is after 1st July?—Yes.

275. It will take you all your time to leave and get to the Scotch coast and be ready for the Scotch fishing then?—Yes.

276. Colonel *Cadell*.—You are talking about the 11th May. Supposing a compromise came to be made—would it be better to say the second Monday in May, the commencement of a week. That would be better would it not?—Yes, we usually commence on Monday.

Mr. ROCHE.—It could only possibly make three days difference.

Mr. *Flynn*.—If you could fix anything it should be a date.

277. Mr. GREEN.—Are the nets used on the Kinsale coast the same nets as you use on the Scotch coast?—The same nets. When we go out to the fishing at Kinsale it is the whole train we use all the summer. We take the new nets away with us.

278. Do you ever think of taking mackerel nets to Kinsale and fishing for mackerel?—No, I never made up my mind to do that.

279. Would it not pay you to do that?—I have been told it would pay. The Scotch boats we had then were not so large as they are now, and when we went to Howth twenty years ago they prevailed upon us to go to Kinsale. But we thought the Kinsale coast rather too open, and we were content with what we had at that time.

280. Colonel Cadell.—Would you not like as early in May as possible?—Yes, as early in May as possible.

281. Mr. Green.—Supposing you were fitted out with mackerel nets and the 1st of June came would you think it worth your while to stop on for the June fishing at Kinsale—or would you rather get home for your July fishing as fast as you can?—I would drop it altogether even although I was fitted out with mackerel nets. I would never think of going to the herring fishing at Kinsale then.

282. Do you suppose it would pay the Scotch fishermen to take a train of mackerel nets to fish at Kinsale, and take a train of herring nets too with their chance, supposing the herring fishing opened on 10th May?—I think without the mackerel nets altogether, I think they have some little chance on the 10th May.

283. Mr. Boone.—They have better fishing here in Scotland. Is not that so?—They are fishing with the line for haddocks in Scotland all the time when we go to Kinsale. They drop the line fishing at home when the air gets warm. The haddock does not stand the heat in the summer and they do not realise anything. Fish is very scarce at home at that season.

284. Mr. Green.—Are the boats fishing haddocks now?—Yes, and they will be fishing up to the time when we are ready for the Kinsale fishing.

285. Mr. Boone.—You would not drop the Scotch late fishing? It is better than you can get in Ireland?—Yes.

286. Mr. Hornsby.—Supposing you did not go to Ireland what would you do? How would you fish in Scotland? What class of fishing would you carry on?—If I was not to go to Kinsale I would prefer to go to Stornoway or Lowestoft.

287. Mr. Green.—When does the fishing begin at Lowestoft?—It is a passing fish and except one year you may as well shoot your nets in this room as shoot before a certain day in June. It finishes up in the same way on July 12th or 13th or as early as 9th July—never any more than four good weeks in it.

288. Have you any idea where the herring go to?—I think they leave Kinsale on the 1st June. We thought always they went eastwards towards Dunmore.

289. What are they doing with themselves between 1st June and August and September?—Perhaps they go round the westward for all I know.

290. Have you fished at Dunmore?—Very seldom. Only once or twice I have shot nets.

291. Do you know when the herring fishing generally begins at Dunmore?—Perhaps there may be a lapse of time between it and the Lammas fishing at home.

292. Have you ever fished at Castletownsend?—Only one season. Not all the season, I went back and fore to Kinsale.

293. You have never fished from Baltimore?—I never was in Baltimore.

294. When you were fishing at Castletownsend were there any buyers there that salted and packed the herrings and sent them away?—A few merchants made a settlement with the house to give them so much a month.

295. They salted them?—The salt was taken from Kinsale to there, I suppose. I was not one of the boats that was settled with. I was not engaged. I went back and love from Castletownsend to Kinsale.

Joshua Porter, sworn; examined by Colonel Cadell.

296. You are the representative of the fish merchants Vallsall Brothers, Liverpool and Manchester?—Yes.

297. Have you been in charge of the Irish business?—Yes, sir, for fourteen years—since 1879 inclusive.

298. And you go to other places also?—Yes, sir, between Yarmouth and Kinsale, Peel in the Isle of Man, Grimby, and North Shields, that ends me till the commencement of the mackerel.

299. At those places does the mackerel and the herring fishing go on at the same time?—At Yarmouth and Lowestoft they keep separate boats and separate accounts, but the fishings go on simultaneously.

300. And the one fishing does not injure the other in your opinion?—I never heard any complaints about it between the traders or the fishermen.

301. Has there been a falling-off in the mackerel fishing at Kinsale, as far as you have observed?—Considering the proportion of boats fishing off Kinsale I do not think there has—not an appreciable one at any rate. There are many times now a fleet of 150 boats came in on the Saturday afternoons with a fair wind, because a number of them are going home to see their friends. They go out on Monday, and they do not see them again till the following Saturday. Perhaps twenty of them have gone to the westward stations where they had no ready market previously, and they had all to come to Kinsale every day.

302. And they land their fish at these westward stations?—Yes, sir, they get a ready sale for them at Baltimore and other places.

303. What represents the total amount of the catches of mackerel?—The delivery of mackerel at Kinsale is not nearly so great, but I think the total quantity of mackerel caught is not one whit less.

304. Mr. Horgan.—Is the total quantity caught off the south coast of Ireland as much as ever is was?—Yes, but it is more scattered. It does not all come into Kinsale, but also at Baltimore, Berehaven, Castletownsend and other places.

305. Do you think this fishing to the westward—the nets being always cast in that way—interrupts the mackerel from going eastward to Kinsale?—That is my theory.

306. And, therefore, reduces the number caught?—I believe it will. It will intercept a shoal of mackerel, and drive them seaward instead of going to Kinsale. This westward shooting drives them seaward. That is simply my opinion.

307. Colonel Cadell.—You consider there are as many mackerel on the coast now as there used to be?—Yes, there are as many cured and delivered to the English ports as ever, if not more.

308. Supposing you compared the last ten years with the previous ten years, what would be the difference?—The last ten years would show a considerable increase on the previous ten years—that is my opinion.

309. Would you not account for that by the railway communication being so much better?—The mackerel must be caught.

310. Mr. Roche.—There are more mackerel imported into England

now than ten years ago. Cannot that be accounted for by more railway communication?—I am quite prepared to say yes, it has opened many other places: Railway communication has done a great deal of it.

311. Mr. Horsley.—But still, surely, a heavy capture of mackerel conveyed to England by steamer is direct without touching the land?—Yes. I was leaving railway communication out altogether.

312. Mr. Grieve.—All yours go by steamers?—Yes.

313. Mr. Horsley.—What particular Irish railways do you suppose have been carrying large quantities of mackerel?—The Dingle Line, because it embraces a very large district; the Bandon Line, the Ballycastle Line, the Glaslein Line, which will carry them on to Tralee—forty miles.

314. What other railway?—The Fenit Railway.

315. That exhausts your list of railways, does it not?—Yes, that exhausts them until Baltimore was opened.

316. You can hardly place Baltimore on the railway stations?—It has a daily list of steamers.

317. Colonel Cadell.—Would you give your experience of the mackerel fishing in the years 1879 and 1880?—In 1879 we had an extraordinary fishing—considered one of the best fishings up to that time there had been. Older men than me, men who had been out fifteen or sixteen years, at that time admitted that it was the best they had known. But in 1880 when there had been not the slightest difference made—no curtailment of the fleet whatever, we had the worst season and the poorest delivery at Kinsale.

318. Was the number of Scotch boats similar in 1880 to what they are now?—In 1879 there were two Campbeltown boats, two or three from Auchrather, there could not be above a dozen altogether. There was such a small number that I did not take much notice of them. In 1880 we had, perhaps, a few more herring boats, but I could not be positive. We had a wretched disastrous fishing.

319. What sort of weather had you in 1880?—After the first two or three weeks the weather was very bad, accompanied with a lot of cold showers. That year, if I remember rightly, Good Friday was about the 26th or 29th of March, and I remember I loaded a steamboat the day before Good Friday that year. I have never seen anything approaching it any time since—just that one take was something like 150,000.

320. Do you consider the Scotch boats had anything to do with any falling off?—The Scotch boats were not there.

321. Do you think they had anything more to do with the falling off at Kinsale than they had to do with the falling off in 1880 as compared with 1879?—No, sir. I think it is an influence we cannot exactly determine—perhaps climate.

322. And that the Scotch herring boats do not interfere with the fishing for mackerel?—They assist us many a time to get lots of mackerel over to England.

323. Do they take them over for you?—No; the mackerel fishing would be so small it would not pay us. It would not be worth so much if we knew we had no means of sending them over.

324. Colonel Cadell.—To return to herrings. What is your opinion of the herring got at Kinsale in May?—I consider they are of good quality—the most marketable herring we get as a bloater.

325. Mr. Grieve.—Do you know of any of them being sent to Liverpool in such a condition that they were falling to pieces?—I never heard so. If so they were badly handled. Of course there are various ways of working them.

326. Mr. HOARNEY.—You being a fish merchant, having your head-quarters at Kinsale, would not this come to your knowledge if it occurred that these fish were rejected by the market authorities?—It might do so, if they happened to come to our own particular market. We land ourselves.

327. Would not common rumour bring it to you?—I have heard such remarks—that So-and-So's herrings could not be sold, but it never occurred to me it would be so.

328. It is possible that it occurred?—It is possible from the fish being handled, but not owing to the state of the fish.

329. Colonel *Cadell*.—And do you find a greater demand for the Kinsale herring in May than in June?—Yes, there is a better demand because the supply is there, and people are getting tired of the old salt herring; and are glad of something new sent fresh to the markets.

330. But are the herring sold fresh in the English market?—No; not to any degree. They are made into bloaters and kippers. Ours are all done for us. We get our sale from the fish curers.

331. Colonel *Cadell*.—And the demand gets less in June?—It does not get less, but there comes more supply. The Scotch fishing opens, and we have a large trade in Stornoway yet we can do with the Irish bloaters.

332. When do you leave Kinsale? When is the season over?—As a rule I am finished from the 20th to the 26th June, just as the Saturday may occur. I generally go to Peel. Of course we have large smoking places there.

333. Up to what date do you think the herring fishing may go on at Kinsale if the herring boats remained there?—I do not think the latest ever I saw herrings caught at Kinsale would be after 12th June.

334. So that if they remained after 12th June they would get nothing?—No.

335. Mr. GREEN.—Do you know of any Manx boats having tried it?—I have seen it mentioned recently there were several Manx boats tried it. Mr. Flynn mentioned some. Quite half a dozen gave it a fair trial. There was nothing for them to do at home, and they tried it for several days, but they got absolutely nothing. That might be up to 15th, 16th, or 17th June.

336. Is it the case that as soon as the herrings go into the English markets there is a perceptible drop in the price of mackerel?—The herrings instead of deteriorating the value of mackerel at Kinsale, I should say, in many instances tend to improve the price.

337. Colonel *Cadell*.—How, especially when you get small quantities?—They are getting carried over for nothing as it were, consequently I would rather say that having a good cargo of herring would not reduce the price.

338. Mr. GREEN.—I do not say that they depreciate the value of mackerel at all. The Kinsale fishermen say that when they come in from the mackerel fishing they found the herring boats had been in several hours before them and had loaded the steamer, and she had gone, and the mackerel were left on their hands because they had not enough to make another cargo?—No, sir, we could not decline to take the mackerel because, as a matter of fact, they are brought hours before we see them, and we are bound to take them.

339. You were fishing at Bantry. Did you draw, in the mackerel nets, some remarkably fair large herrings—two or three, or one or two in one net, in some four or five, or anything like that?—I have

found a hundred herrings got out of the mackerel nets—fill half a box.

340. How long did you run from Bantry?—We ran steamers from Bantry two years altogether—1889 and 1890.

341. You did not form any idea as to whether the herring fishing could be prosecuted there by boats going specially for it?—No, it is too far from the market for herrings. Herrings demand a quick despatch.

342. Did the steamer, after leaving Bantry, call anywhere else?—As a rule, no; because we were packing exclusively at Bantry. As a rule we could get a fair cargo for the steamer. It was more profitable to let her go on, to catch the market. We had a little steamer for the other stations. Often it was run to Fenit if it had not got sufficient at Bantry.

343. Would not the delivery of herrings under that system be just as rapid as sending from Kinsale is?—No, sir, the delivery of herrings would be one day later, and besides that, we have accommodation at Kinsale which it would cost us a very great deal to get at Bantry, and there are salt merchants, and we have nothing to do but order a cart to send us ten tons down to the pier head there, and a good pier to pack on.

344. If a pier was built at Bantry it would make matters better?—You would require to induce forty or fifty merchants to go there and bid over the prices to one another, before you would get the Scotchmen to go.

345. There is one question I would ask you. You say the great bulk of these herrings are sent over to England for curing purposes?—Yes, for bloatering.

346. Are there large quantities sent to Manchester, Birmingham, Sheffield, Leeds, Hull, Bradford and all the large towns in England, almost as fresh fish, as they are packed off from Kinsale?—There are a number of boxes sold so, but not above 10 per cent.

347. Because I always understood it was a theory that the Irish herring was not suitable for curing at that time of the year?—For bloatering it is an excellent bloater at that time of the year.

348. Colonel *Cadell*.—From a mercantile point of view, what date would you fix for the commencement of the herring fishing at Kinsale.—As the matter is already, so far as the traders are concerned, been agreed upon, the 11th May, I think, without any friction, may be fixed upon and would answer. It has worked very well with the exception of one particular year.

349. Mr. GREEN.—That arrangement for the 11th May is now in existence?—Yes.

Colonel *Cadell*.—Our men have been fishing before and after.

Mr. GREEN.—They have adhered to that rule of not fishing before the 11th, you say, and for us to make a rule saying the 11th May was the date at which the fishing was to commence, would practically be not to make any change at all.

350. Mr. ROCHE.—Recently, the Irishmen have objected to that, and they want the Scotch to commence on 1st June?—The 11th May is quite late enough.

351. Colonel *Cadell*.—Setting aside all national feelings, supposing it was at any other place, what date would you fix for the sake of peace?—I would say the 1st Monday in May.

Mr. GREEN.—I do not think there is any national feeling in it whatever. I think it is purely a question of the mackerel fishing. The Campbeltown fishermen go there.

Mr. Roche.—At Kinsale there was a very good feeling towards the Scotch. They simply think interfering with their fishing is an interference with their interests. They have no feeling against the Scotchmen. I can say that for myself.

Mr. *Porter.*—They want to protect themselves. The traders are extremely glad to see the Scotchmen.

Mr. Roche.—It is a pure trade question.

Colonel *Cadell.*—It is was only a pure trade question, witness says he would rather have it from 1st of May.

Mr. Roche.—The first Monday in May was what he said.

352. Mr. Green.—Do you think it would be a great loss to the nation at large if the herring fishing at Kinsale were abolished?—It would be a very great pity, in my idea, to see the prospect of letting the good food be lost, and prospect of good earnings. It is a benefit to the town of Kinsale, and do the buyers' benefit.

353. Do you think that if the herrings were not caught at Kinsale they would be caught at Dunmore, or some other place?—I have known such peculiarities among herring that I cannot say what would be the case.

354. Mr. Hornsby.—You expect there would be a loss of food to the community at large?—Yes, sir. So long as boats enough come to get good herrings from Kinsale, it would be a pity to cut them off from doing so.

355. If you take a certain number of eatable fish out of the sea, and send them into the market, it would be rather an Utopian idea to wait for these taking it into their heads to go to another part of the coast?—Just so.

356. Mr. Roche.—The case for the Kinsale fishermen is that it interferes with the mackerel fishing. They say that it injures the fishing?—I do not think so.

Mr. Hornsby.—They have got the idea into their minds, be it right or wrong. I do not think for a moment they would say so unless they thought so.

357. Mr. Roche.—Do you think, as a compromise, a date between the 1st and the 11th of May would be a good thing?

Mr. Green.—That would not be a compromise. It is what there is at present.

358. Colonel *Cadell.*—Were the Scotchmen parties to that compromise?—The Scotchmen admitted it by quiet consent. Of course there is nothing binding as to the date.

Mr. Hornsby.—It is an honourable engagement, and they kept faith.

John Brown, the previous witness.—It has been an understood date and the Scotchmen have been alluring to it of late. But we would rather have our choice to go when the fish is there. We know the fish are more plentiful on the coast at the 1st of May, but for the sake of peace, we as fishermen, are quite agreeable to go out on the 11th of May.

359. Mr. Hornsby.—How long have you been going out on the 11th May?—For the last six or seven years.

360. They generally come from the 1st to the 10th of May?—The boats arrive from the 1st to the 10th.

361. Have any of them fished before the 11th May at Kinsale?—We were eight days fully idle at Kinsale last year before we put a net in the water.

362. Mr. Roche.—When did you arrive?—On the 1st of May.

ARCHIBALD BUCHANAN, Cookmnie, sworn; examined by
Colonel CADELL.

363. Have you commanded a boat for many years?—I have commanded a fishing boat for 17 years.

364. Where have you been in the habit of fishing?—Kinsale, Howth, and Lowestoft for the past six years in the early fishing.

365. Do mackerel and herring fishing go on simultaneously at these places all the time?—For the last six years I have been at Lowestoft, we both were going on at one time, the boats shooting their nets alongside of each other.

366. And without any detriment to either?—Without any ill-feeling whatever, and no more quarrels between herring and mackerel boats than between herring boats among themselves—no more. I have seen where you could get herring, they would let you know. I have been told time after time by the mackerel men.

367. And have you done the same good turn for the mackerel men?—We do not get many mackerel to let them know.

368. Have you found the catches of mackerel and the catches of herring influence each other, one way or the other?—If there is a big catch of herring does that reduce the price of mackerel, and vice versa?—I do not think herring hurts mackerel much, but the mackerel hurts the herring a great deal.

369. Mr. GREEN.—You say at Lowestoft the herring boats and the mackerel boats shoot side by side. One of the witnesses here stated that the mackerel boats drift so much faster than the herring boats?—Oh yes; but you have to allow for that.

370. You would not shoot to get foul if you knew of it?—No.

371. Mr. HORNBY.—Have you ever fished off Kinsale?—Oh, yes; many a time.

372. What is your idea about this question of commencing the fishing?—The 1st of May is late enough for the herring fishing at Kinsale. There are more herring in the first week of May, than for the next month to come.

373. Do you agree with what the other witnesses said about Kinsale and the fishing there, and with what they said about the catching of small mackerel?—Well, I never got very many all the seasons ever I was there.

374. Have you ever had 10,000 small mackerel?—I do not remember any more than two or three hundred.

375. You never remember any boat having that?—No, it has never occurred in my knowledge.

376. When you sold mackerel to the buyers how many of these small mackerel might there be in a box?—I did not pay any attention to what number went into a box.

377. Were you not alongside the hulk?—Yes.

378. Did you not help to put them in?—It is a few years since I was there and I don't remember.

379. When does the Lowestoft mackerel fishing commence?—The 10th June. I do not think there is any fishing before that.

380. What size were these mackerel at Lowestoft in June?—They are not so large as at Kinsale. The small mackerel caught at Kinsale are nearly as good as the large mackerel at Lowestoft.

381. And they use smaller mesh nets, I suppose?—Yes.

382. In the herring nets when you do get mackerel do you get them at the top or the bottom of the net?—I got them at the top of the net. At Lowestoft we got them at the top and at the bottom.

383. Colonel *Cadell.*—Would lowering the net a fathom make much difference?—It would make very little difference for the few that I have caught.

384. Do you fish the herring nets deeper when fishing off Kinsale than Lowestoft?—Deeper at Kinsale. One fathom at Lowestoft and two at Kinsale.

385. Have you seen many hake in your nets at Kinsale?—No.

386. Have you ever seen mackerel or hake fry?—Never on one single occasion.

387. Do dead mackerel float or do they swim?—I never saw a dead mackerel float to my knowledge.

388. Mr. GREEN.—Have you seen many large mackerel drop out of your nets when hauling at Kinsale?—No, I never did.

389. Have you anything to say that you have not heard said already by the other witnesses?—Nothing any different to what they have said.

ANDREW BAILLIE, Cockenzie, sworn; examined by Colonel CADELL.

390. You have commanded a boat for many years?—For twenty years.

391. And have large experience of the Kinsale fishing?—Yes, sir.

392. Do you find your catches at the beginning of the season have realised as much or more than towards the end of May?—There was one year I had thirty-eight mease, early in May, and we got 17s. 6d. the mease for them. That was before that arrangement about the 11th.

393. Is that the best shot you ever had?—Oh no, sir; that was the second shot at an early period.

394. Mr. HORNBY.—How much had you in one shot?—Thirty-eight mease in the second shot early in May.

395. Do you find they get less towards the end of May?—There is a falling off in the herring passing by, and if you are not there to get them you do not get them.

396. Mr. GREEN.—The fishermen up the Shannon say that fishing down there off Kinsale in May breaks up the schools and spoils the fishing in the Irish channel. Do you think that likely to be the case?—I do not; but all Scotch fishermen know when they go to the west that the fish are coming east; we always got them coming east.

397. Colonel *Cadell.*—If they are going from Kinsale to Howth that shows that they have not broken up?—Yes.

398. Mr. GREEN.—Have you fished in the good years at Howth?—Yes; we tried it there last year. The year before last we got a few herrings there. It was in the month of June. We had £70 for two weeks at Howth.

399. How many shots do £70 represent?—Perhaps nine or ten shots.

400. Mr. HORNBY.—Is not the whole herring fishing on the east coast of Ireland falling off of late years?—I believe it has fallen off to some extent. About four years ago there was good fishing.

401. During the last three years it has fallen off to some extent?—Yes, but there is a great quantity of steam trawling. That is generally the cause of it. The Howth fishermen say so themselves.

402. Mr. GREEN.—Are you much interfered with by trawlers?—Yes; they do not trawl at night but go over the nets sometimes.

403. Do you think trawlers have anything to do with the falling off of the Howth fishing—are there trawlers in Dublin?—We believe it is the trawlers that are the cause. There is a great fleet of them.

'When I went there first I never saw any of them, but now they trawl right on the ground where we work the nets and we never got inside whether the fish are there or not.

404. Last year or the year before last you made a good week at Howth?—Last year we got nothing or next to nothing. After that week we made £70. We left because the herring fell off.

405. What was the lowest price you got for the herrings at Kinsale in May—you gave 17s. 0d. as a high price?—Yes, but we have got as high as 30s., and 25s., and 22s., and 20s., according to the quality and quantity.

406. How low has it fallen?—I think we have sometimes been as low as 8s. or 9s. There is one point about throwing fish overboard I should like to speak about. When we are coming ashore sometimes we get a thousand small dogs in redding up the nets. We put them overboard because they are useless. As for the 1st of June, I think the warm weather sets in on the 1st of June and the sharks begin and we have to leave. They do not come earlier than that.

407. Colonel Cadell.—Do you ever throw over gurnard and haddocks?—Not haddocks, but gurnard and any broken fish; just as at other places.

408. Do you ever throw mackerel overboard?—If it is broken, but not unless.

409. And no more than at other places?—No, when pulling in the net you may bruise a few with your foot and throw them overboard, but not otherwise.

Robert Walker, Fisherrow, sworn; examined by Colonel Cadell.

410. Have you been in command of a boat for many years?—For the past four years.

411. Have you been in the habit of going to Kinsale?—For four seasons.

412. How have you got on there?—I have not done very much myself.

413. When did you commence your fishing?—We have come to commence the fishing on 1st of May. We commenced on the 5th and 6th of May formerly. Last year it was the 11th of May, but I was not there at the time. They got very good catches last year when they began the fishing, and a good demand for them.

414. Did you get as good catches and demand towards the end of the month?—No, not so good catches at the end of the month.

415. Were the fish in as good condition at the beginning as at the end?—Splendid condition; fully better at the beginning than towards the end.

416. Did you catch many mackerel and hake in your nets?—Very few. I never saw any hako. Last year we got a little one about two feet long, that was all.

417. Mr. Green.—Did you catch a lot of those small hake?—No; I did not catch any small hake more than say two at a time.

418. What is the most you have caught?—I could not tell you that.

419. A hundred?—I do not think I got a hundred altogether.

420. How much herring did you ever get?—Thirty-five mease is the best I ever got.

421. What did you get for them?—I got 12s. the mease.

422. What did you get for the mackerel you caught?—For the mackerel we caught we sometimes got as high as 25s. The year before that we got as high as over 30s. a mease for the mackerel we caught. There were not many of that lot.

423. Did you ever throw mackerel overboard?—Unless it was a damaged fish you could not make any use of.

D

424. These are the only ones you have seen thrown overboard?—We have seen some drop out of the nets, but that is all. It would be very foolish for us to throw fish away that we get a living out of.

425. Have you ever got such small mackerel that you would get no sale for them?—No, I have not. I have been at Howth, and have many a time seen more small mackerel in one day in the winter time than I have seen landed at Kinsale.

426. What time was that?—That was in the end of September and October.

427. Would it be worth your while to go to Kinsale if it commenced on 1st June?—Oh, no. Mr. Murray came to me and I told him that from the very start. Even the year before last, when they stopped us from the fishing, we lost the best week of the fishing.

428. What week was that?—The week before the 11th May; I think it was the second or third week, I could not be sure. We had bad weather the following week and that was two weeks fishing gone. We lost the best week, and we might have done some good that week.

429. Mr. Hornsby.—You appear to have departed from the arrangement arrived at by the other Scotch fishermen not to fish before the 11th May, and appear to have fished on 1st May?—I have never been there at that time myself; I have fished from the 1st to the 3rd or 4th.

430. You could not exactly say when you commenced fishing?—I could not say. Mr. Flynn's books would tell you.

431. Did you fish before the 11th May, or did you not?—Yes, I believe I fished before the 11th May, but not before the 1st. From the 1st to the 4th or 5th May.

432. What is the first day you made a shot, you cannot remember whether you shot before the 11th May?—I could not say that.

Colonel Cadell.—I have nothing more to bring forward except the same evidence over and over again which could be repeated a hundred times.

Mr. Hornsby.—Well, there is no use for that. All I can say is, that we will consider very carefully the evidence we have received here to-day, together with the evidence we got in other parts of Scotland, and that we will devote our best intellects and deepest attention to endeavour to arrive at a solution of this very much vexed question, in order to try and prevent these unfortunate disturbances and disputes. I think it right personally, as presiding here to-day, to say how very much pleased I have been to see such an orderly and respectable class of fishermen here, and on my own part I think it due to them to thank them for their very orderly and fine behaviour.

Colonel Cadell.—All our thanks are due to you for the kindness and impartiality with which you have heard us, and endeavoured to get our men to give as much information as you possibly could.

Mr. Roche.—I think the fishermen are greatly indebted to Colonel Cadell for the very able way in which he has got up their case, just as well as any barrister would have done.

The proceedings then terminated.

ANSTRUTHER INQUIRY.

Tuesday, 31st January, 1893.

Her Majesty's Inspectors of Irish Fisheries held an Inquiry this day in the Town Hall, Anstruther, at one o'clock afternoon. Present—ALAN HORNSBY, Esq.; W. S. GREEN, Esq.; and CECIL ROCHE, Esq.; B.L.

Mr. *John Murray*, one of the officers of the Scottish Fishery Board, also attended.

JOHN WILLIAM SMITH sworn and examined.

433. Mr. ALAN HORNSBY.—Do you live here?—I live in Pittenweem, about a mile from here. My trade is carried on in this place.

434. You are a fish merchant?—Yes, sir.

435. Will you tell us your own story?—You know the subject matter?—My views are very simple. I mean to say that herrings caught in May in Ireland are equally as good as the herrings captured in June, if not better. My idea about it is, in respect to small mackerel, that there is a demand for them. I think they capture more in the short than in the larger mesh net.

436. Mr. HORNSBY.—In your opinion is there any large number of small mackerel destroyed?—There are a good number at times, unless they bring them in proper time, before three o'clock in the afternoon. If they are not brought in Ireland they are not marketable. They are for Ireland and there are lots of buyers.

437. Mr. GREEN.—You know the English buyers?—Certainly. I have been there for the last twenty-two years.

438. Mr. HORNSBY.—Kinsale is your headquarters?—Yes.

439. Do you think if the mackerel fishermen got a market for themselves there would be any complaint?—When they come in together there is a little bit of a clash. When they see the small mackerel they think it is prejudicing them in getting a proper price for their mackerel.

440. Mr. ROCHE.—The reason the mackerel people object is on account of the price?—Their objection is that they kill the small fry there—that is their objection.

441. You said something just now as to the price?—They meet a ready market at a small price—that is, the small mackerel.

442. Mr. HORNSBY.—Have you formed any opinion as to this early herring fishing in the channel?—I consider if they do not fish in the early months there is no use for them going there at all. We cannot get it to pay our expenditure on the mackerel fishing at that time. Three or four years ago the herring fishing began on the 11th May, if my memory serves me right. That was the best for that season. But at the end of the season the mackerel fishers said they would not allow them to fish till the 1st June. If they stop them till that time there is no use going there. The herring fishermen cannot keep up the outlay to pay for the few herring that is got. I consider the herring got in May equally as good as those got in June. I have seen better herring got in May.

443. You would not agree with evidence given to the effect that herrings got in May are in such a state that they would not stand the salt?—Certainly not. Last May we had some very good herrings. We salted them, and they gave satisfaction to all the merchants. We sent them to England, principally London.

D 2

444. About what size are the mackerel?—About half the proper size of the mackerel. It would take a hundred more to fill a large box than it would the proper sized mackerel.

445. Not more than that?—There are two sizes—the half box and the large box. Sixty mackerel would fill a half box, and it would take a hundred and a half of the others to fill it.

446. Mr. GREEN.—These mackerel put into the half box are they culled from the herring and the small mackerel rejected?—Oh, no, sir, the small are put amongst them and they take them as they come, the same as fishermen do anywhere.

447. How many boxes are there supposed to be in proportion to the herrings?—Sometimes as many mackerel as herrings; sometimes a few mackerel to twenty or thirty mease of herring, according to the fishing or according to the weather. I have seen herring boats come in without any mackerel at all; and I have seen them at other times come in with a few mackerel.

448. Mr. HORNBY.—What was the greatest take of mackerel?—About thirty-five or thirty-six hundred in one boat.

449. Have you heard about the quantities of small hake?—I have seen small hake, but very few shall immature hake. The mackerel boats take them as well as the herring boats.

450. Mr. GREEN.—The mackerel boats are not so much likely to take them as the herring boats?—I have seen them in the mackerel boats, but I have not seen many small hake.

451. You have not seen more killed in the herring nets than in the mackerel nets? Oh, yes, I have seen more, but not to notice.

452. Mr. HORNBY.—Under-sized hake?—I consider that the proper place to fish for hake is the Old Head and the Seven Heads of Kinsale, and that is a place that herring boats could not possibly put their nets.

453. Mr. HORNBY.—They go out in small boats? –Yes, they go out in small boats, and two boats go together. We have never seen any hake in any of the herring and mackerel boats, of course all the hake goes to the Old Head, and they dry them for their own consumption.

454. Mr. ROCHE.—Have you got any reason for the objections of the mackerel fishermen?—I think it has an effect on the market sometimes at Kinsale. If they made heavy catches of herrings the buyers might have an inclination to buy herrings instead of mackerel, and local buyers board these herring boats and buy the small mackerel from them instead of buying large ones. But I do not, personally speaking, think they do much harm to the mackerel fishers at Kinsale, because we generally put the herring boats on a hulk away from the mackerel boats altogether and let them put their herrings on the steamers.

455. Mr. GREEN.— What the Kinsale men say is, that when the herring boats come in early, having been fishing only a short distance from the land, and sold their herrings and small mackerel to the buyers, then the steamers go away, and very often when mackerel boats come in later in the day the steamer has got its cargo and has left, and they lose the sale of their mackerel in consequence of the herring taking away the markets?—Yes; that may be the case perhaps once in the month if the mackerel boats are calmed and cannot possibly get in their part of the cargo. They have to go a long distance, 120 or 130 miles to New Milford to put their cargo ashore, and it takes two or three hours before they can marshall the trains.

456. Have you an establishment in other ports besides Kinsale?—Yes.

457. Have you an establishment in Castletown?—I had.

458. And if the herring boats fished from Castletown, do you think they would have a sufficient chance of selling their herrings there, and would that obviate the difficulty?—It would obviate the difficulty in so far as they would not be clashing with the mackerel boats. Last year something like forty mackerel boats were fishing from Castletown, and there were no herring boats.

459. Do you suggest that it would be a good plan for the Scotch boats to take some other harbour, so as not to clash with the mackerel boats?—I consider there is no better harbour for the boats than Kinsale—large enough for both, if they could work in unison together.

460. Mr. Hocum.—Did you think the 11th May a very fair arrangement?—It pleased both parties at the time in the town of Kinsale.

461. Have you known the Scotchmen fishing before the 11th May?—Oh, yes; years ago.

462. Not since that arrangement?—No; Mr. Flynn told them distinctly not to come to fish for herrings till that time, and then after the 11th he would sell them, which I think was very fair. It was according to their own arrangement and they stuck to it.

463. Mr. Green.—You said a while ago that one reason why the herring boats leave Kinsale is because the buyers leave on the 1st of June. Do not the buyers remain longer than that if they can get the mackerel?—Yes, because the mackerel finish very early in June and they want herrings too. You must pay off the men when you pay the steamers off.

464. Have you been to Howth?—Yes, sir.

465. At Dunmore?—I have not been at Dunmore.

466. How long is it since you were at Howth?—Three years ago. There were not many last year.

467. Did you buy there?—I was there for seventeen or eighteen years every year.

468. Have you noticed that the number of herring that can be captured at Howth has decreased?—Something like fifteen or sixteen years ago plenty of herrings were got at Howth, but now they have gone away altogether. I do not consider that has anything to do with the Irish fishing we are speaking of now. I do not think they are the same class of herrings at all. That is my idea.

469. Have you any reason for thinking they are not the same class of herrings—the quality?—The herrings at Howth are full thick herrings, and always of the same quality. There is very seldom small stuff at Howth. But at Kinsale some days they are very good, and other days they are not so good.

470. Small?—Yes.

471. From your experience a boat cannot now make the same shots of herrings at Howth as you used to do?—No; Howth is virtually finished to my mind. I have not been at Howth for the last three years.

472. You said you were not at Dunmore?—No.

473. Do you think it would be possible for the herring boats to fish profitably further west than Castletown?—No, I do not think so, because the consequence of steamers going to fetch the herring further west than Castletown would prejudice us for the markets. We would not get them in in proper time. Kinsale is far enough. I would rather see them go over the way of Youghal.

474. Do you know whether they catch herrings off Youghal at that time of the year?—I do no know.

475. Of course there is no mackerel fishing going on there?—No; they must be engaged to go there

476. At Queenstown?—I have never had any experience of Queenstown. We had a boat engaged at Youghal some years ago, but it did not do much.

WILLIAM LINDSAY sworn; examined by Mr. HORNBY.

Witness (to reporters).—I do not wish my name to appear.

Mr. HORNBY.—What is your reason for that?

Witness.—My life has been many a time threatened in Ireland.

Mr. HORNBY.—Your name will appear; you may be prepared for that. Most likely it will go before Parliament.

Mr. *Murray.*—I do not think you need be ashamed of your name.

Mr. ROCHE.—I know Ireland as well as you, and you are in no more danger than I am in Scotland.

Witness.—I have seen people lose their lives there before now.

Mr. *Murray.*—It comes to this—if you are not to give your name the Chairman will not take your evidence.

Mr. HORNBY.—You must allow your name to appear.

Witness.—They may take my name if they desire. I may not be back in Ireland, and it will not matter.

477. Do you live here?—I live at Pittenweem.

478. You are a fisherman?—Yes.

479. Do you wish to tell your own story or be examined?—I will give you a rigmarole of my own.

480. Do not go through a rigmarole. Give us some succinct facts?—Yes.

481. Have you fished on the south-west coast of Ireland?—Yes.

482. How long have you been fishing there?—Twelve or thirteen years. I could not state exactly. I have been a dozen years at least.

483. You frequent Kinsale?—Yes, some years during that time.

484. Have you disposed of the herrings that you caught there at the market either to the English or the local buyers?—Yes.

485. What is the earliest you commenced to fish at Kinsale?—I have been there on the 1st May.

486. Did you fish on the 1st May?—Yes.

487. How long ago is that?—Perhaps ten years ago.

488. Well, then, what is your experience of the fishing for herrings at that time of the year?—Sometimes good, and sometimes not quite so good. They always commanded a fair sale.

489. Were they spawned or shot?—They all showed a shot appearance. I never saw any spawned fish there. I never did get that class of fish.

490. Were they in good condition for packing for the English markets?—So good that we could produce from 2s. to 5s. the hundred more than we can get at Anstruther at the present day.

491. When you say the present day, do you mean the present time?—Yes, the present time.

492. Did you ever have any small sold to local manufacturers?—Yes, for fish manure, if any dispute had arisen owing to the fish being too late in being landed. It is often done with large mackerel as well if the fish be too late. For instance, I once was landing fish to Mr. Flynn at 26s. per mease. The time came for the steamboat to go away, and I had three times as many to throw away as I got discharged, because the steamboats were gone, and there was no way of disposing of them. Night was on and they were useless.

493. Mr. GREEN.—Did you have many small mackerel?—Sometimes; other times scarcely any.

494. How many mease of small mackerel have you ever seen in one day?—I do not think I ever saw passing five or six mease in one day. That was the time we were stopped fishing.

495. Were they good and saleable?—All saleable. We got 4s. the hundred. Often as high as 10s. per hundred.

496. At the same time what was the price of the big mackerel?—There was scarcely any to be got at the time. It was that that made the good demand for what we were landing.

497. Four shillings the hundred for mackerel is a very low price?—Well, it may be low, sir, but I have seen them landing large ones at 2s. 0d.

498. How many of these small ones would go to a half box?—It depends on what you call a half box. There are so many kinds of boxes put in their appearance there.

499. There are only two?—I have seen all kinds.

500. Have you got many hake?—Very few, sir. Some days a few.

501. How many mease of small hake?—I never had a mease in my life nor yet half a mease nor a third of a mease. I never saw it passing twenty or thirty in a day. They were splendid, and there was a good demand for them.

502. How many miles have you fished from the land?—Twenty or twenty-five is about the furthest ever I was out—generally five, six, ten, and twelve miles.

503. Have the mackerel boats been near you?—Only when they could not get further out. They wish to go forty if they can manage it.

504. Can you tell us anything about how you find the schools of mackerel?—No.

505. Mr. HORNBY.—Have you anything else to say?—The first thing I would take notice of here is the prejudice that arises from ignorance.

Mr. HORNBY.—That arises everywhere. You have got prejudice in Scotland.

Witness.—You say we have got prejudice everywhere. Well, there is a harbour here where we meet from all villages. I do not belong to this village, but we meet all the way up and down the Forth and out and in there, and although we come in collision with each other's boats, there is scarcely a word exchanged, but if we get beside each other in Ireland there is a grievance.

Mr. HORNBY.—You are a more taciturn people here.

Witness.—This is a free country, and every man has a right to his own opinions. Is not Ireland as free to us as Scotland is to them?

Mr. HORNBY.—Yes.

Witness.—They come here and to Aberdeen and to other places they fish, and go up and down and get the greatest civility. Why do not we get the same in Ireland?

Mr. GARIN.—And so they do. The Scotch boats that go to the mackerel fishing on the south of Ireland meet with no objection.

Witness.—I remember one morning when the boats were not lying very comfortably, I asked an Irishman if he would be kind enough to make his rope bear better. He replied, "Do you know to whom you are speaking? Do you know that you are in your life's boat?"

Mr. HORNBY.—Well, I suppose he admired your boat so much that he said it was equal to a lifeboat.

Witness.—He meant it was my life.

Mr. ROOME.—We admit you have all the cardinal virtues.

Witness.—We wish fair play. I reckon without the Scotch fishermen that the Kinsale fishing would be a poor enough affair. My way for settling this would be to go back to 1801. That week that there were so many small mackerel about there was a very full landing—

some boats two, three, five, perhaps, more mess. I never saw such a
shoal of small mackerel. I told you what the prices were and how
they were appreciated both in the Irish and English markets. Bear
in mind what were those local buyers to do if the fish were not landed.
There was no fish landed by the large mackerel boats. There was no
large mackerel on the coast whatever. The Scotchmen were getting
a good few herring. I would say they were running from £40 to
£60 and £70 a boat for the week. That was the result of the Scotch
fishing for that year. Keeping the local buyers from going to Cork,
Dublin, Limerick, and other ports. And then the steamboats were
running for the English buyers. That was keeping the trade going
on. We were stopped on the first of the next week. We were not
allowed to go to sea. We were told our lives would be taken, that
our boats would be scuttled and so forth, and we gave way and lay in
the harbour. What was the result? Not a steamboat was sent across
to England with any one thing. The buyers could not get a thing to
buy, and the whole thing was at stagnation. The natives could not
get bread. I remember of a boat-owner saying "Do you know what
we ought to do?"

Mr. HORNSBY.—This is rather a waste of time. We are sitting here
as a Court of Inquiry. We cannot listen to what he said and what
he did not say to you. Give us anything you have in the way of facts.

Witness.—I was in company with the captain of a steamboat at
Cork this year, and he told me that when he was coming in from New
York——

506. Mr. HORNSBY.—That is not evidence.

Witness.—Yes, there is some evidence in this. He said "I was
coming from New York and I came through forty miles of mackerel.
When I came to Cape Clear I fell in with some boats and I told them
to go west. Those boats went west and fell in with the fish." He
wired to an agent at Milford Haven to send the boats west. They
went west and they got the fish on two different occasions. The next
time they went to fish they got no more of them, and the fish they fell
in with were on the south-west of Kinsale, and they sold at 26s. the
hundred. At last they would not go at all. A few boats happened
to be on the south-east on the following night, forty miles off, and
they also got a few, and they were no more found in this fishing. I
reckon they are a passing fish.

507. Mr. HORNSBY.— That is your opinion?—Yes.

508. Mr. GREEN.—Do you think it would be for the benefit of the
mackerel and herring fishing if you fished from another port instead of
Kinsale?—That has been suggested by Mr. Smith; what do you think
of it?—I have fished at other ports, but if you are not where the
buyers are how can you get them disposed of? I have been at Dunmore. There was only one buyer and if he was not open to take
them, there was nothing that could be done with them.

509. Mr. GREEN.—In order to shift to another port an encouragement system would have to be adopted?—I am much afraid that would
not do. We have to be wary of the buyers and there is plenty of
room for all.

510. Did you ever engage for the herring fishing?—I have never
engaged but it has been done.

511. Mr. BOOTH.—What do you think about fishing on the 11th
May? Would that satisfy you?—It is late enough. That is all I will
say about that.

512. Mr. GREEN.—Have you ever fished in June?—We always
seek away from there about the 7th, 8th, and 10th June—That is
the time we clear out of there.

513. Mr. BOURE.—Have you shot till 8th June?—Yes, sir.

514. Have you caught herrings?—They got rather scarce. They began to disappear at that time.

515. Mr. GREEN.—Have you any other difficulty in carrying on fishing in June except the buyers being gone and the fish having gone with them? Have you any other difficulties in shooting your nets in June?—The sharks and dogs come in. That is another thing. It clears out the mackerel.

516. Do you find every year the dog fish come in at the end of the herring fishing?—Not exactly every year, but generally.

517. Are they large dogs or small?—Very large dogs. It was not dogs last year, but we are always afraid of the sharks; they do so much havoc.

518. Mr. HORNEST.—What is your experience about hake fishing? Have you taken many small hake?—I have seen them. Some years I have not seen a score in all. It is generally large hake, and we get a good demand for them.

519. How many?—Sometimes seven or eight or ten at the most, and we get sixpence each for them.

520. Mr. GREEN.—Do you think having a longer buoy rope —three fathoms instead of two fathoms—would get over the difficulty of catching small mackerel?—I do not think it, sir. They go both high and low. Of course they are a surface fish if the weather is warm, but if the weather is cold they rather hang down.

521. Do you catch as much mackerel in the lower parts of the nets as on the top?—Generally through all. Once they get about the net they won't come into the net. I have been some years there and never killed any small ones.

522. When you are hauling the herring nets do you see large mackerel drop out of them?—No, sir; the nets are so hauled that the fish always circle back to the end up. You may see a chance one, perhaps two, for a shot, but there is that in herring also, just as it may happen.

523. Mr. HORNEST.—How many rows of meshes to the yard are there in your nets?—Thirty-one rows I have been using for five or six years. I used to have them longer, but I have adopted that; I think it is better for the mackerel.

524. What depth?—Eight inch four. Some work them shorter. They think it is better to let vessels and boats go over.

525. How many?—Some have one thing and some another. I have generally about 60; I have found them at 84.

526. What length of piece?—Sixty yards length we purchase. Forty yards when working.

527. When you have been out herring fishing do you come in contact much with the mackerel fishermen? Do you go to the same ground?—That may happen when it cannot be avoided in light winds and night setting in. But then we take every care to give no offence and give no trouble to them. We would rather suffer ourselves. I should like to say something here. Take the scientific view of mackerel. We got to learn that they have no natural enemies when they get about three months old; they are so swift they cannot be overtaken by any other class of fish.

528. Mr. GREEN.—Are they never found inside the belly of another fish?—I never did see them. Such a thing may happen. Fish get stunned or sick.

529. Mr. GREEN.—Such things will occur?—Dr. Day's statement is

that from four hundred and thirty thousand to five hundred and forty-six thousand eggs are produced by one mackerel. All the small mackerel killed in 1891, and there were more killed that year than all the years combined, would not make a difference in the number.

DAVID WOOD (BARRELL), sworn; examined by Mr. HORNBY.

530. Are you the master of a fishing boat?—Yes.

531. Have you been fishing at Kinsale?—I was one year at Kinsale about nine years ago.

532. When did you begin fishing?—We went about the middle of April, but we were not allowed to fish before the 11th of May. The Irish people made a close time. We left them and went to Castletown. We were allowed to fish there and we got good shots of herring at Castletown about eight miles off—good herrings and good quality. We came back to Kinsale after the time was up—the 11th May. I saw no small mackerel in my experience nor yet small hake.

533. Mr. GREEN.—Do you think it would be a good thing to have a close season for herrings anywhere?—Well, I would say it would be very good, provided it would make peace if the Irish people want a close time. The close time I would say would be the 1st of May to commence. It would be reasonable.

534. Would the 1st of June be any use to you?—The 1st of June would not do. It would be too late.

535. Mr. HORNBY.—What was the condition of the herrings you got in the early part of May?—The herrings were good; in good condition for spring herrings, no milt or roes in them; herrings that could stand going to market.

536. You did not see any large takes of undersized mackerel yourself?—No, I did not. Of course I was only one year, and my experience is very poor, but that is my experience. I saw no small mackerel or hake, and there is money to be made by going to Ireland provided you get the chance.

537. Mr. GREEN.—How many herrings did you get at Castletown?—As high as eight and ten to thirteen mease.

538. How much per mease?—3s. 6d. to 4s. the mease. There were no buyers, and I had to go to villages six or eight miles and retail the herrings myself. There is no use going there to fish when there are no buyers. Kinsale is the place for the buyers. If they are going to allow Scotchmen to go to Kinsale to fish they should just allow them to go on the 1st of May or bar them out altogether.

539. Mr. GREEN.—We do not want to bar you altogether. Would you not go to Baltimore?—I know nothing about Baltimore. Kinsale is where I have been.

ALEXANDER GARDNER, sworn; examined by Mr. HORNBY.

540. Are you master of a fishing boat?—Yes, sir, I have been both at the mackerel and the herring fishing. I have been round at Smerwick and the mouth of the Shannon fishing.

541. What time did you begin the fishing?—We used to go to the mackerel fishing about the middle of April generally. Perhaps the buyers came better about the 1st May. We considered that was a very fair time to start fishing for herring on the coast of Ireland as regards quality and numbers.

542. How many Scotch boats were there?—Three from the east

coast, a few from the Cantyre coast and Campbeltown, and very few from the northern counties of Ireland—County Down and so on.

543. Mr. Green.—Were you engaged?—Not the first year. We were engaged for two years after that for 25s. a mease by Lawson and Smith and by the same gentlemen at Smerwick.

544. Mr. Hornaby.—In your experience have you seen large quantities of small sized mackerel?—I have not seen many. I have used surface nets, and I have scarcely ever seen two score of undersized mackerel the whole six or seven years I used these surface nets.

545. What is your experience about the capture of undersized hake?—I never saw over a score of undersized hake, if it is undersized hake you call it. I maintain it is not hake at all. I have seen good sized hake.

546. Mr. Roche.—What do you call them?—I say it is something more like what we call in Scotland whiting.

547. Mr. Hornaby.—Why did you give up the mackerel fishing?—It did not pay. The Englishmen were too keen upon the herring and did not look enough after them.

548. What time do you think a fair time to commence herring fishing?—I think not later than the first week of May.

549. The beginning or the end?—I would say if possible the beginning. I have seen there for the month of May £400, and in June there has never been a herring there.

550. Mr. Roche.—You did not leave till the first week of June?—I have fished more what we call sun fish. They come in with the good weather and more heat, and the dogs, and sun fish, and squills as we call them—outside fish we think that they put the herring away.

551. Mr. Green.—You do not think the herring stop there? There would be no fishing after the 1st June?—I think they do not stop there whatever. They are a passing fish there.

552. Mr. Roche.—You continued fishing the first week of June?—Yes, we were in duty bound to fish our engagement out.

553. Mr. Hornaby.—You were not there the last two years?—No, 1879 was the first year I was there, and I continued going till the last two years.

554. When you fished did you catch generally mackerel the more westward you went?—The more out to sea is the best place, but we fished one and two to four or five miles off the Old Head of Kinsale.

555. Mr. Hornaby.—Have you any suggestion to make to throw oil on the troubled waters and live in harmony with the Irishmen?—I could not say. You are met to decide that question.

556. Would it satisfy you to begin herring fishing on the 11th May?—Better that than the 1st June. To put it at the 1st June would close it altogether.

557. Half a loaf is better than no bread?—I think it is a very fair thing the 1st of May. If you are going to the herring fishing, you could not take a man there to fish for less than four weeks.

Mr. Roche—It would give you more than that.

558. Mr. Murray.—Have you fished mackerel at Yarmouth?—No, sir.

559. Have you fished herring at the same time as the mackerel fishing?—Yes.

560. And they go on agreeably?—Yes.

561. Are the mackerel caught at Yarmouth much the same size as the small Irish mackerel?—Not so big as the Irish mackerel, a degree between the big Irish mackerel and the small Irish mackerel.

562. Mr. Hornaby.—What would be the difference of price between

the Yarmouth and the Irish of the small class the hundred?—I never saw so much Irish mackerel to know the difference.

DAVID WATSON, Cellardyke, sworn; examined by Mr. HORNBY.

563. Are you the master of a fishing boat?—Yes.

564. Are you the owner of one?—Yes.

565. What is your experience of the Irish fishing as regards the commencement of the season, the condition of herrings, and the quantity of small hake and mackerel?—As regards the beginning of the fishing, if we do not get begun on 1st of May it is useless to go. If you begin on the 1st May it leaves you four weeks. We consider that a very short fishing. Seven weeks we consider a fishing season.

566. Would it not satisfy you to commence on the 11th of May?—Well, the 11th May, that leaves you with less than four weeks for fishing.

567. When do you leave the south of Ireland as a rule?—The first week of June we fished the two years I was there, 1884 and 1885.

568. That is to say you fished on the end of the first week of June?—I could not exactly say. It is about the first week of June.

569. Have you at any time taken large quantities of undersized mackerel?—No, I have seen a hundred or two, but nothing worth speaking about.

570. Did you get a ready market for them?—I do not remember the price we got for them.

571. Did you sell them at a fair price or a low price?—Generally when we sold mackerel we sold them to local buyers, cadgers, and what not.

572. What condition were the herrings in in the first week of May?—They were just as good the first week as they were after.

573. Quite sound?—Yes, the first week we were there we got as good a price. That week we were stopped we all went home. That year we had nothing. The year before we had a good fishing.

574. Did you ever engage for the mackerel fishing on the south coast?—No.

575. Did you fish off the same ground as the Kinsale mackerel fishermen?—We very seldom were beside the mackerel boats, very seldom. They always went outside. Where we got most of our fishing was just about three miles from the Old Head.

576. What kind of net did you fish with?—Just the same nets, 32 and 31 meshes to the yard.

577. Mr. GARRS.—How many years were you at Kinsale?—Two years, 1884 and 1885.

578. You have not been there since 1885?—No.

579. How far west did you fish out of Kinsale?—We went into Youghal and Dungarvan, but there were no buyers, and we had to sell to the best advantage. Kinsale is the only place where the buyers are, and where there are no buyers we need not be there at all.

580. If the buyers at Kinsale went with you would you be quite satisfied to go to any of these places?—If there are plenty buyers, but the buyers cannot be at Kinsale and Youghal too.

581. Mr. Smith said there could be buyers at Youghal?—They cannot be at two places.

582. Have you any suggestion to make as to how this dispute should be settled at all?—No; no further than that we would like the 1st May for any man going to fish there, or it is useless going.

583. Are you thinking of going this year?—I will not be there this year. We cannot say when we may go there. I consider the 1st May late enough.

584. Have you been at Stornoway?—No, I have not been there.

585. What do you do when you do not go to Ireland at that particular season?—Ling lining.

586. Do you think there ought to be a close season for herring anywhere?—Well, it would be better if they had it at the right time.

587. Mr. Hornaby.—What time do you suggest?—For the Irish for the 1st of May, of course we hold out that. That leaves us only four weeks to fish. We consider that a very short fishing. Seven weeks is our fishing season.

588. Mr. Green.—When you went first did you go much earlier than the 1st May?—We left on the 13th April the first year I went there.

589. Did you ever make a shot before the 1st May?—We fished at once as soon as we got there, and got fish at once.

590. In the middle of April?—About the end of April.

John Louis, Buckhaven, sworn; examined by Mr. Hornaby.

591. Are you master of a fishing boat?—I am master of a boat.

592. Have you been at the herring fishing on the south coast of Ireland?—I have fished off Kinsale for five years.

593. What are those five years?—I believe it commenced about 1884, and each year following as far as my recollection goes.

594. What date did you commence the fishing for herrings?—The first season I left Buckhaven on 13th April, arrived on the 17th, and went to sea on the 19th.

595. Mr. Green.—Did you get any herrings at that time?—Three shots the first week and got £20.

596. Mr. Hornaby.—Were the fish taken then in good condition?—The fish were of a fair size and good to eat.

597. Were they also good to pack and send to market?—There was a good demand for them.

598. Mr. Green.—Do you remember what you got per mease?—I think they realised 18s. per mease.

599. Mr. Hornaby.—In your experience have you seen large numbers of undersized mackerel?—I could not say off the Kinsale coast. I have seen a small quantity, three or four hundred. I have seen them off Dungarvan after we left Kinsale.

600. What date?—The first year I went there we left Kinsale on the 5th June, and in the year following I fished from Dungarvan after the 5th June. It was there I saw them.

601. What about small hake—have you seen any large numbers of small hake taken up?—It was seldom over I saw small hake, so few, that I could not tell whether they were small hake or whiting.

602. Would it be the correct thing to say that the water was covered with small hake and undersized mackerel thrown out by the Scotch boats?—No.

603. What would you think about a Scotch boat having 30,000 small sized mackerel?—I could not say. The most I ever saw was one box, and that box brought 7s. 6d.

604. How many would be in the box?—I could not say.

605. What is the half box?—The box they sent the herring into. That was at Dungarvan.

606. What is the size of your nets?—Thirty-one to thirty-two meshes to the yard. I generally buy my nets that size.

607. How much did you make in the Irish herring season?—The first year I was there we commenced fishing and closed on 5th June—that year we realised £300.

608. What date did you stop?—We left Kinsale on 6th June.

609. What is your idea about stopping the herring fishing before the 11th May—do you think it would satisfy the Scotch fishers in Irish waters?—If you take the Kinsale fishing from me on the 1st of May it deprives me of the fishing.

610. What I ask you is this—Do you think that closing the herring fishing before the 11th May would satisfy the Scotch fishers?—I can only speak for myself. Any time I went to the fishing at Kinsale I had most part of my money before the 11th May. That is my experience. You can get more herring in the month of April than in May any time I have been there.

611. Mr. GREEN.—If you think you got more herrings in April why do you not go there in April?—I was engaged here at the fishing, and before I got ready to go I would have to leave this fishing; and another thing, the nights are too long for us to make so long a passage.

612. Have you gone to Stornoway?—I was only two years there when first I began fishing and then I stopped it.

613. Is there anything you would like to tell us?—The only thing is this—can you guarantee that we will catch any herrings after the 1st June at Kinsale as you have said?

614. Mr. HORNBY.—The state of things is this—it was represented to us by the Irish fishermen that the mackerel fishing is injured by the Scotch herring fishing in the early part of May, and we are holding these inquiries for the purpose of hearing what you have to tell us. After hearing what you have to say, I hope we will arrive at a conclusion which will promote harmony and good feeling between the two nationalities. But to say we have arranged the 1st June you are in a mistake there.

Witness.—Is it not a possible fact that the mackerel comes in there after 1st June?

Mr. HORNBY.—I think it is quite possible.

Mr. ROGER.—We have had no expression of opinion about that.

Mr. HORNBY.—The objection of the Irishmen has been to the one fishing on the same date as the other before the 1st June. Some years ago they said the 15th May; now they appear to rather change their ideas about that. But that does not for a moment bind us to fix the season on the 1st June.

615. Mr. GREEN.—Did you fish at Howth?—I fished there after I left Kinsale.

616. Do you think fishing at Kinsale does any injury to the fishing on the Shannon?—I have no experience of that.

617. Mr. MURRAY.—It is quite evident from the Irish evidence that the Scotch fishermen have been in the habit of throwing fish overboard. In your opinion what fish have the others and yourself been throwing overboard?—I never throw any fish overboard.

618. Do you catch gurnard?—I never throw any fish away except gurnard.

619. Small sea-dogs, sharks, and whiting—you throw these overboard?—We do.

620. These fish might have been mistaken for mackerel by others looking from a distance?—We throw all these overboard at Kinsale. We do not throw them overboard in the Tyne where we can sell them.

ALEXANDER KEAY, sworn; examined by Mr. HORNBY.

621. Are you the master of a boat?—I was, but now I am a curer.

622. Have you fished for herrings at Kinsale?—I went first to Castletown to fish.

623. At what time?—It was about the latter end of April.

624. What condition were the herring in?—They were very good at that time. We had as high as fifty-five meases of them at Castletown.

625. What price did you get for them?—Five and six shillings. There were very few buyers there.

626. If there had been more buyers would you have got higher prices?—We cannot tell; it is very hard to say.

627. The lowness in the price was not the result of the bad quality of the fish?—Oh, no. At Castletown that year we had twenty-five meases of herring on 22nd April. They were splendid herring.

628. Did you fish off Kinsale yourself?—Yes, sir.

629. What was your experience about finding undersized mackerel?—I have seen very few there until the first or second week of June. We went to Youghal and we got a good quantity of mackerel there. We had only one shot there.

630. What price did you get for them?—Youghal is a good sized place—they would sell there locally?—I could not say the price.

631. When you were fishing off Kinsale did you take large quantities of undersized hake?—No undersized hake or mackerel either. Off Baltimore there were very few undersized mackerel.

632. Mr. GREEN.—Did you ever fish at Baltimore?—No, all the one fishing.

633. What is your idea of the date when it ought to commence?—Give fair play to man and man, and the 1st of May is just late enough for anybody to go.

634. Have you been at Stornoway?—I have been at Stornoway two years past and seen the close time there. I believe it has done some good to that fishing.

635. When is the close time?—The fishing begins on 15th May.

636. Mr. ROCHE.—No fishing till 15th May does good?—It has done good I believe.

637. Mr. GREEN.—In Stornoway how was the fishing benefited by making a close season till 15th May?—My opinion is that the herring has come up the Minch more. They get leave to come nearer the shore, and everybody can get readier to them. The dog-fish are a great havoc to this fishing at the back end of the fishing in Ireland, and Stornoway too.

638. And Shetland?—And Shetland too. I hold it is no use whatever the Irish fishing after the beginning of May.

639. Mr. ROCHE.—Would the 11th of May do?—It is late enough I think it is not proper business for anybody to go after the 1st of May. A week or two sometimes makes a great difference.

640. Mr. HORNSBY.—Have you been at Yarmouth?—I have been at Yarmouth when the mackerel fishing and the herring fishing was going on.

641. Mr. GREEN.—You think the fish take the ground south of the Minch before they go on to Stornoway?—It is generally thought that. They believe that the fishing has done good to wait till 16th May. I believe in a close time for everybody.

642. You think there ought to be a close time?—I think there ought to be a close time when the fish is not in season. I believe they are in season in Ireland, and I do not see why we should not catch them.

643. Is it your experience that you get small mackerel in your nets?—I never saw them except at Youghal.

WILLIAM MAIN, District Fishery Officer, examined by Mr. HORNSBY.

644. How many registered first class boats are there here?—We have about 180. We used to have about 220; but within the last six years they have come down to about 180.

645. What has caused the decrease?—The old boats wearing out, and these large boats cost so much money they are not able to afford them. The fishing has been going down on the east coast.

646. Mr. GREEN.—And the boats are increasing in size?—Yes.

647. Do they invest about the same amount of money?—Yes, fully as much. The boats are more valuable.

648. Mr. HORNSBY.—What you say would rather tend to prove the importance of this Irish herring fishing for these men if their own local fishing has gone down. It would be more importance to leave Ireland open for them?—Yes.

649. Mr. ROCHE.—If you say there is as much money invested as before it is not going down. They have larger boats?—They have fewer boats, but larger boats.

650. But there is as much money invested now as before?—Yes.

651. Well, then, it is not going down?—The last four steam vessels cost £10,000.

652. Mr. HORNSBY.—What is the cause of the falling off?—The fishermen have not made so much money this present herring fishing. In 1883 there were 14,000 crans for the district from 1st January to 31st March, and these averaged 43s. 6d. per cran. In 1884, that was the first year herrings began to be imported from Sweden and Norway, the average price came down to 20s, owing to the foreign imports, and since 1886 till now, the average for all these years has been 11s. 11d. per cran. So that is a great difference.

653. I take it that your capture is equally as good but the price fluctuates?—Last year we had between two and three thousand crans. This year we have 5,500 crans, and the third part of the season not gone. The average price so far has yielded better than last year, 12s. to 13s., but that is on account of Sweden and Norway being blocked up with ice.

654. Mr. GREEN.—What was the price per cran at the other stations?—It depends on the quality.

655. What was the average price.

Mr. Murray.—Say in 1884?

The average for the east coast?—I cannot give any average for the summer fishing in the same year. This year the average price at Peterhead would be something like 16s. or 17s. per cran. At Aberdeen it would only be about 7s. 6d. to 10s.

656. Mr. GREEN.—Very much lower than at Peterhead?—That was on account of the difference in the quality. The Aberdeen boats fished further south; the Peterhead men fished rather north. From Aberdeen all the south there was a lower quality; Fraserburgh and Peterhead a superior quality.

657. Mr. Murray.—What is the difference between the herrings taken by surface and drift nets?—I am not aware. They get a greater quantity of small herrings those surface nets, but they catch a quantity of splendid herrings as well.

Mr. Murray.—The difference is so great that the boats were engaged at 18s. per cran for drift nets, and by the new method they were reduced 1s. to 4s. per cran, a fourth of value.

The proceedings then terminated.

MONTROSE INQUIRY.

Town Hall, Montrose,
Friday, 3rd February, 1893.

Her Majesty's Inspectors of Irish Fisheries held an inquiry this day in the Town Hall, Montrose, at five o'clock afternoon. Present—ALAN HORNSBY, Esq., W. S. GREEN, Esq., and CECIL ROCHE, Esq., B.L. Mr. John Murray was also present. There was a good attendance of fishermen.

Mr. HORNSBY said—We are sitting here rather late to-day in order to enable the fishermen, whom we have been informed were at sea, to give us some evidence. I presume you have all read this notice about the subject matter of the inquiry. We opened this inquiry in Ireland at Kinsale. We have also held meetings at Cockenzie and Anstruther; and now we are sitting here to-day to hear the views of such of you Scotch fishermen as fish in Irish waters, as to how some arrangement can be come to whereby the mackerel and herring fishing can be prosecuted at the same time without the one being injurious to the other, or to the vocation of the people of the different classes of fishing.

John West sworn; examined by Mr. HORNSBY.

658. Where do you live?—At Ferryden.

659. Are you the master or owner of a fishing boat?—The master.

660. Have you been in the habit of going to Kinsale for the herring fishing?—I was one year.

661. What year was that?—1885.

662. What time did you commence fishing that year?—I think we were there about the 18th of April.

663. What class of herrings did you get then?—They were a mixed class.

664. Some were in good condition and others were not?—Yes.

665. What proportion did the good herrings bear to the inferior ones —did you get more good ones?—Yes.

666. How did you dispose of your herrings?—The first shot went alongside the hulk, and we got orders to go alongside the quay with them for manure. They would not sell them.

667. Why would they not sell them?—The buyers would not allow us to sell them.

668. That was in 1885?—Yes.

669. You are quite clear upon the fact that the herrings themselves were fit for the market, the great proportion of them?—Yes.

670. What price did you get for them being sold as manure?—We got 5s. the mease.

671. Were there any other Scotch boats in the same position as you were?—I do not mind. There were not many out.

672. There was no doubt that these fish were in good condition for packing and being sold to the English markets?—Yes, they were good, most of them.

673. What quantity did you take?—We had five mease.

674. In your experience did you take any undersized mackerel in your herring nets?—None.

675. Or hake?—No, we got no hake.

3

676. I suppose your nets as regards the mesh and the depth are very much the same as those of the Anstruther men, are they?—All the same.

677. How far off the shore did you fish that time?—We were about seven miles from Kinsale Harbour.

678. You mean seven miles off the Old Head of Kinsale, or seven miles off the Harbour?—Seven miles off the Harbour.

679. Did you come across any boats fishing for mackerel?—No, sir.

680. Did you see them?—No.

681. Have any large mackerel fallen out of your nets?—No, we did not get a large one.

682. Any undersized hake?—No, sir.

683. How long did you stop at Kinsale?—We were there up to the end of June. (A voice, "May.")

684. Mr. ROCHE.—Better let the witness speak for himself.

685. Mr. GRAHAM.—Was it near the end of June you left?—Yes, we were among the last boats that left.

686. Mr. HORNSBY.—Did this occur more than once with the buyers?—It only occurred once. He gave us orders to go. We were idle for a week.

687. Who was that salesman?—It was Ketchpole.

688. After that, then, what price did you get the next time you went to him?—Eleven shillings the mease, I think. I do not remember what price we got for the next.

689. That would be in the early part of May?—We lay about in May and did not go to sea at all.

690. You told us you stopped in harbour for a week?—That was after we left.

691. When did you make your first shot?—I could not tell you the date. It would be well into May.

692. Mr. GRAHAM.—What have you been doing all the years since that year, at that time of the year?—I have been fishing out here. I have been at Shetland and different parts.

693. You gave up going to the South of Ireland?—Yes, because I could not get fish.

694. You could not get fish there. You did not get enough to pay for your trip?—No, they would not let us go and get them, and the salesmen gave us orders not to come.

695. After you began to fish did you not make a good season out of it?—No, after we stopped there we went to Howth.

696. All the time you were fishing there did you not see the mackerel boats fishing?—They were outside of us.

697. You saw them in the harbour?—Yes, but we never fished outside with them.

698. You never saw any small mackerel in your nets?—I have seen a few at the latter part of the time.

699. You did not sell any?—We sold some.

700. To the same buyer that was buying your herring?—No, we did not sell them to the same buyer.

701. Was there any reason for telling you not to go and fish when you went there first—was it because there was no sale?—No, they seemed to have met among themselves, and did not care about the Scotch boats going out.

702. Have you any notion about going back there again?—If it was to be made better I would like to go yet.

703. What would you call making it better—how could we make it better?—By getting begun earlier.

704. Then, you said your first shot of herrings were partly good and partly bad?—Most of them were good fine fish.

705. Were the bad ones small or soft?—Oh, they were soft.

706. Have you gone to Stornoway?—No.

707. Is there any other herring fishing you would be at at that season of the year?—No.

708. Did you ever fish mackerel?—No.

709. Mr. HORNSBY.—What would your idea be of a fair time to commence the herring fishing?—To my idea we should be allowed to commence after 20th April.

710. Would you be satisfied to commence on the 11th May—would it suit you to go there?—No, it would not; it is far too short.

711. Mr. GREEN.—And that is the reason you have not gone there again—because the season is too short?—Yes.

712. But that year you remained fishing till the end of June. What did you do till the latter end of June—did you get much fish?—No, we did not get much fish. We always remained on to see if it would be better.

713. What is your theory as to the fish going away from that coast?—I could not say. I did not know much before that year of the coast.

Alexander Cargill sworn; examined by Mr. HORNSBY.

714. Where do you live?—At Ferryden.

715. Are you master or owner of a fishing boat?—Master.

716. Have you fished off the south-west coast of Ireland?—Once.

717. Was that in 1885—the same year as the last witness?—Yes.

718. What quantity of herrings did you get—what date did you begin to fish to begin with?—We arrived on the 18th April. I think we were about three weeks there before we went out to fish—before they would allow us to go out and fish.

719. Mr. ROCHE.—Was that the salesmen?—I do not know whose blame it was.

720. Who stopped you?—The buyers told us there was no use of going. They would not buy them.

721. Mr. HORNSBY.—You did go out on the expiration of the time—what did you do?—We had 25 mease of herrings the first shot we were out.

722. What condition were these herring in?—Fair condition. We got 16s. a mease for them.

723. Did you sell these herring to the same buyers that refused you in the first instance?—I could not say. There are a lot of buyers there.

724. Did you take any undersized mackerel in you herring nets?—We got as many as we could eat, but never got any to sell.

725. What about undersized hake?—I never saw a hake all the time I was there.

726. How far off the shore did you fish?—About three miles off the Old Head of Kinsale was about as far as we went out.

727. Did you see the mackerel boats out fishing there?—Never one.

728. I suppose that was the best take you had—of 25 mease?—Yes, that was the largest take we had.

729. What is your idea about having a certain, so to speak, close time for herring off that coast—when would you be content to commence fishing?—Not later than the 25th of April at any rate.

730. Supposing the date was fixed later than that, would you give

B 2

up going—would you go to Ireland supposing it was fixed later?—No, I would not go later than that.

731. Where do you go when you do not go to Ireland in April and May?—We get fishing at home—cod fishing. There were over two hundred boats went away to Barra from Kinsale. They would not stop, and went to Barra and Castlebay.

732. What date did they leave?—I could not say the date. They stopped about a week—all the B.F. boats. There was no use men stopping there when they could not get fish.

733. They were not allowed to catch them?—That is so.

734. Mr. Green.—Did you make any shots at all on your way to Kinsale?—No, we never shot before getting to Kinsale.

735. Did you see any?—No.

736. You say you never saw small hake in the nets?—No, I never saw hake in the nets.

737. Did you have any small dogs?—Yes, plenty of small dogs—too many of them.

738. No other small fish?—No, I never saw whiting.

739. How long did you fish on to?—I think it was about the 10th June that we left, and we went to Howth to fish. There were boats stopped after us. I believe there was a good lot of herring came on the ground after we left, as far as I heard.

740. Was it good fishing at Howth?—No, we did not do very much at Howth.

741. Did you fish anywhere on the south coast, except from Kinsale—did you go to Castletownsend?—No, we only shot off Dungarvan once on the way down to Howth.

742. And did you get any there?—No, we got very few; seven or eight hundred.

743. What time did you begin fishing at Howth—was it in July?—No, it was in June. We were not long in going to Howth, three or four days.

744. Did you get herrings at Howth?—Yes, there was some good herring.

745. The same class of herring?—No, they were large herring there.

746. Larger than Kinsale herring?—Yes.

747. Had they spawn in them at Howth?—Yes.

748. Had they spawn in them at Kinsale?—A little. They were a different sort of herrings at Howth.

749. Would you say the herring caught at Kinsale are the same herring only younger?—Yes, I believe the same herring only not grown so big.

750. Did you ever go to Stornoway?—No.

751. Do you think it a good thing to have a close time for herring anywhere?—I could not say I am sure.

752. Would you like to have a close season for herring on your own coast?—I believe it would be good here.

753. And it would not be good in Ireland?—I don't know much about Ireland. I was not much there at all, but I have been fishing a lot here.

754. Would you go to Ireland if you had a longer season?—I might go to Ireland. I could not say. I would not go a date later than that.

755. Mr. Roche.—How many boats went from here?—I think there were ten boats.

756. Have none of these boats from here been there since?—Not one.

Walter Duff, Fishery Officer; examined by Mr. **HORNBY.**

757. How many boats are there registered here?—For our district, which extends from Dundee to Gourdon, there is about 600 of them, third class, and there is about 200 of the first class—202 I think.

George Coull sworn; examined by Mr. **HORNBY.**

758. Where do you live?—At Ferryden.

759. Are you master of a fishing boat?—No, sir.

760. You are a hand?—Yes.

761. Have you fished off the Irish coast?—Yes, sir; the same year as the others—1885.

762. Can you tell us what date you commenced fishing?—Well, I do not know if we had a shot at all before the time they were taking the herring. I do not think it.

763. Cannot you fix a date in your own mind about when you commenced—that is to say, you need not be exact as to a day or two. About when was it, in May or April, or when?—It was in May.

764. What class of herrings did you get?—They were just about half and half.

765. What price did you get for them per mense, do you know?—I do not exactly mind if it was 14s. or 15s.

766. How long did you remain there fishing?—It was the end of May before we left for Howth.

767. Mr. GREEN.—Are you sure it was not the end of June—did you leave in May?—I could not say if it was June or not.

768. Mr. HORNBY.—Did you get any small mackerel in your herring nets?—We got some for our own use—as many as we could use ourselves.

769. You did not sell any?—They would not buy them.

770. Would not the local buyers buy them?—No.

771. What did you do with the ones you did not use?—We used them all for ourselves.

772. Mr. ROCHE.—You used them all?—But we did not get many.

773. Mr. HORNBY.—Did you get any small hake in your nets?—Not that year.

774. You were only one year there?—I was three years there.

775. I thought you said at the commencement that you were only one year there?—I was two years before that. I thought it was that year you were asking about.

776. We want the experience of the men during every year they have been there. What is your experience of the three years?—The first year was a prosperous year.

777. What year was that?—Two years before that.

778. That would be 1883?—Yes.

779. What time did you commence to fish in 1883?—It was the 1st of May when we went there.

780. What time did you go out there to fish?—The 6th May was the first day we were out.

781. What herring did you catch then?—I do not exactly mind.

782. Had you a large quantity?—About four or five mense.

783. What condition were they in?—Of good condition at that time.

784. Were these mixed herrings you spoke about in 1885, got about the same date as in 1883?—They were better like herring at that time.

785. Mr. GREEN.—In that prosperous year you got a better class of herring?—Yes, there was plenty herring.

786. And a good class—large herring?—They were not large herring, but very fair herring.

787. Did you fish at Howth?—Yes.

788. This is the same year?—Yes.

789. Were the herrings at Howth much larger?—They were terrible big herring—large herring.

790. You said a while ago you did not get small mackerel in 1885, but you did in the other years. Did you not say that?—We got some —not many.

791. Or small hake?—Very few.

792. Plenty of small dogs?—Yes; we do not want to make a close season for dogs.

793. Did you get gurnet—you never saw any nouds or whiting in your nets?—No.

794. Nothing but herrings and a few mackerel?—Nothing but herrings—some of them small mackerel.

795. Did you ever sell the small mackerel—could you get anybody to buy them?—We never got many to sell. We could always make use of them.

796. Mr. HORNSBY.—Supposing we fixed the season to commence herring fishing as 11th May, would you consider it worth your while to go there to fish?—It is rather late in the season.

797. What date would you propose?—I think the 25th April is as late as we could take it.

798. Mr. GREEN.—Did you ever see any signs of herring about sea on your way to Kinsale?—No; I never saw any herring in the water.

David Anderson sworn; examined by Mr. HORNSBY.

799. Where do you live?—At Ferryden.

800. Are you a master or owner?—Master, sir.

801. How many years have you fished on the Irish coast?—I was only one year, sir—in 1885.

802. What date did you commence to fish in 1885?—It would be about 20th April. When we got there and when we got cleared up and went ashore, the buyers said they would not take any herring from us before the 10th May. We went to the market on 10th May, and they told us they would need another eight days before they would take them. They said they would not take them before the 18th

803. Mr. GREEN.—And who were the buyers that told you that?— There were different buyers. I do not remember.

804. You do not know their names?—No; we would have got herrings if they had allowed us to take them. The reason they would not take them was that it would interfere with the selling of the mackerel. They wanted the mackerel season done before they began the herring.

805. What condition were the herring in on the first day you were allowed to go to sea?—They were pretty good. We had sixty mease the first shot we were out.

806. When you say pretty good, that is a vague term?—There were about two parts good.

807. How many these?—Sixty mease.

808. What price per mease did you get?—We got 16s. 6d., but there were herrings sold at 16s. and 17s. that day.

809. When you say two parts were good, do you mean two-thirds were good, three-thirds representing the whole?—Yes.

810. Did you take any small mackerel in your nets?—I saw few small mackerel.

811. What do you call few?—We sold 200 one day. We never sold any more after that.

812. What price did you get for them?—I cannot remember what we got. We got very little.

813. Five shillings?—We did not get that. I think we got three shillings.

814. What were these mackerel sold for—were they sold as food or manure?—They were sold for food.

815. Did you sell them to the small local buyers?—Yes, it was a small buyer that got them. The buyers would not have anything to do with them. He was a small buyer, and it was eight days before we got the price of them. He had to go there and hold on till we got it.

816. What size were these mackerel, roughly speaking?—They were about the size of a good sized herring.

817. How far off the shore were you fishing when you got these mackerel?—We were ten miles off.

818. Were there any mackerel boats near you?—No, sir; I never saw one shoot their nets all the year we were there.

819. Had you any undersized hake in your nets?—We got a very few.

820. What do you call a very few?—We got about two dozen one day, I think.

821. Were they fit for sale?—They were not fit for anything. We had to throw them overboard. They were no use to anybody.

822. What is your idea of a close time for herrings off that part of the coast of Ireland?—That was the first year we were there, and I have never been there since. If I had known they were going to treat us as they did I would not have been there that year. They kept us too long hanging there. When I went there the quality was as good as when we started.

823. It was not the Irish fishermen that objected?—Oh, no the Irish fishermen never said anything to us. I never, indeed, saw a more civil class of men in my life. It was the buyers who objected to us going to sea. There was herring—more than when we started to fish. I believe it was the 20th when we got a start made, because it came on bad weather.

824. Supposing the 11th May were fixed as the date for the fishing to commence in that part, would you go every year?—I think if they started the fishing about the 1st May, that would be as little as would do the fishing any good.

825. You do not think it would pay to fit out and go there commencing on the 11th of May?—It would depend upon the season. It was a bad season that year, and it seemed there were more herring in the fore part than the latter part of the year. We heard that there were some herring on the coast after we went down to Howth, but I do not know if it was true.

826. Unfortunately, we have no control over the elements?—Oh, no.

827. Where have you been fishing, now, at the time of the year

you would be in Ireland—say in April and May?—We have been fishing at home, cod-fishing, and fishing on the coast of England.

828. How many years did you fish off Howth?—I was one year there.

829. What did you do there?—Very little that year. About £60 altogether.

830. Mr. GREEN.—What do you think was the cause of the buyers refusing to buy your herrings?—They thought it was spoiling the sale of the mackerel.

831. Did you think it did spoil it?—They did not give us a chance to spoil it. They did not take the herring.

832. Did it ever happen when you came in with the herrings that you gave a good cargo to the steamer, so that she went away and was not there when the mackerel boats came in?—No, I do not think so, all the time we were there. There never was so much herring as to let the boat go away without mackerel.

833. Did you clear your nets of the herrings at sea as you were coming in?—Yes, every day.

834. And heave the rubbish overboard?—We threw the small hake overboard, what we had. They were for no use and no money.

835. How many had you?—About two dozen is as many as we had.

836. Some of the mackerel men said they have been following the herring boats in towards the harbour, and that they have seen great numbers of small fish in your wake?—If they had been following our wake they would never see very many small fish.

837. Did you throw anything else overboard?—That was the only thing. I do not see how they could do it. The distance they were off the land, and the herring fishermen were off the land, would enable the herring fishermen to be in a long time before the mackerel fishermen.

838. What depth were your nets?—They are in the fishing two fathoms strap—that is as far as underneath the water is concerned. Our nets are eight fathoms below that.

839. If you were fishing three fathoms strap would it prevent your catching mackerel?—I do not know. I do not think it would make any difference.

840. Mr. HORNSBY.—What would you say about a witness who told us that ten thousand small mackerel were got by one Scotch boat?—I never saw it.

841. Would you be very much surprised to hear it?—Yes, I do not think that it is true.

842. Mr. ROCHE.—How many Scotch boats fish from Montrose and other Scotch ports?—I do not know, I am sure. I believe 350, or close up to 400.

843. Off the coast of Kinsale?—Yes; only ten from this port.

844. Mr. HORNSBY.—Would it be true to say that it is not the fact that you have thrown out large quantities of fish from your nets before coming into port?—Not that year. I can only speak to one year. I never saw it all the time I was there.

845. Is there anything else you wish to say. You seem to be an intelligent man?—There is nothing I can say, only that if we got the chance to fish when we got to Kinsale, we would have got more money. I think all our boats were in debt that year. Of the ten two cleared their way.

846. Most of the other boats came away in debt?—Yes, we did. We

did not get a chance to clear our voyage. We lay about a month, all the boats lashed to one another on the beach, and we did not get a chance to do anything.

847. Mr. CARSY.—Is it not the fact that a great many herrings were got after you left?—There was a lot of boats left at the same time as we left. There were very few boats that stayed, and we heard that these boats got some herrings after we went away. We only heard that after we went down to Howth.

Charles Anderson sworn; examined by Mr. HORNSBY.

848. Where do you live?—At Ferryden.

849. Are you master of a fishing boat?—Yes, sir.

850. How many years have you fished off the Irish coast?—Two years, sir.

851. What years?—In 1883 and 1885.

852. When did you begin to fish in 1883?—22nd April, sir.

853. What did you do then?—The first shot we had forty mease, sir. We were engaged at 12s. the mease from 22nd to 30th April.

854. What condition were the herring in?—Very fair.

855. That is an unknown quality. Cannot you state distinctly what proportion were good herrings, and what you would call of inferior quality?—There was not what you would call of inferior quality. Three parts of them were good, and one-fourth inferior.

856. When did you stop fishing in the year we have been talking about—1883? When did you leave Kinsale?—I would think it would be the 1st June. We were engaged from the 1st till the 5th May at 15s. the mease. After 5th May we had 30s. the mease.

857. Who were you engaged by?—Sayers and Holloway.

858. That year were you interfered with by the buyers?—No, sir.

859. Were you taking any quantities of undersized mackerel during that year?—No, sir; we had very few.

860. What is very few?—Just much about the same as what you have heard. The first year I could not say we had any. Certainly in 1885 we had a few.

861. How about hake in 1883 and 1885?—I never saw any small hake in 1883.

862. In 1883 and 1885 did you fish about the same distance off the land?—Yes, sir.

863. You were well clear of the mackerel boats each time and did not see them?—No, sir.

864. What is your idea of a close time for herrings off the Irish coast?—It was on the 22nd April we started and that was the quantity of herring we got. That was what we were engaged for 12s. from 22nd April to 30th April, 15s. from 1st May to 5th May, and after 5th May, 30s. to the end of the season.

865. What would you call the end of the season? When did you stop fishing?—In time for going off to the fishing at home.

866. What is your idea about the 11th May as the date to commence upon? Would you be in favour of that?—I would not be in favour of the 11th May to make a start.

867. What date would you be in favour of?—I would say, the 22nd April. We started then and got plenty of herring, and the buyers did not complain of the quality.

868. Are we to understand from you that supposing the 11th May was fixed as the date you would not find it worth your while to go

there?—It would not be worth our while to go there on 11th May, because we have about nine or ten days sailing before us.

869. Mr. GREEN.—You said you were engaged for part of April at 12s. and part of May for 30s.?—Yes, sir.

870. Why was there such a great difference in the engaged price in April and in May?—I do not know, sir, but I can give you that as a fact.

871. If you got as good herrings in April as in May would not they be worth a great deal more in April on account of their being scarce in the English markets?—It would have been a great deal more value to us if we had not been engaged. Two boats got thirty mease at 40s. the mease; I reckon we would have got 30s. that day if we had not been engaged.

872. Is it not the case that the small price in the early part of the season and the bigger price at the latter part of the season is because the herrings are rather inferior at first to what they are afterwards?—There was one bad day before we went out that time. We went on board a D. F. boat and asked what he had got and what quality. He said they were very good. He had been there a year or two before that. He said they were a short thick fish, and he said if you take notice you can almost know the difference after this date. That is what he told us.

873. They would be growing?—Yes. Of course he had been there for a year or two before that, and we were never there before.

874. But the reason why they give the 30s. in May, is because they are sure then of getting a better class of fish?—For that I could not say. The market must be better at the commencement than at the end.

875. Why did you think they objected to take herrings till the 11th of May—they did object in 1885?—Yes, they objected as soon as we went there. They never gave us a chance to go.

876. Had they anything to say about the condition of the herrings, or whether it accounted for the cutting down of the price of the mackerel?—That is all the idea we had of it. If the herring had come into the market, it would have sent down the price of the mackerel. We might have been right or wrong; I could not say. That was our idea that it kept down the price of the mackerel if the herring boats kept going to sea.

877. Is it because of the period for commencing being the 11th May that you have not gone back to the Irish coast?—Yes, sir.

878. That was your reason?—Yes, sir.

Mr. *Murray.*—That exhausts the witnesses who have been at Kinsale.

William Mearns said he had not been at Kinsale, but would like to be heard.

Sworn and examined by Mr. HORNABY.

879. Where do you live?—At Ferryden.

880. Are you master or owner of a fishing boat?—Master and owner too.

881. Will you tell us exactly what you want to tell us, as briefly and succinctly as possible?—I have heard the evidence a good deal, and though I have never been at Ireland, I am greatly interested in fishing matters. Of course the fishing industry concerns me very much, and seeing the question in the papers some time ago, it was a matter of interest to me, I do not know how soon I may be in Ireland, and of course fishermen are always growing up. I heard some men giving evidence as to a close time. My opinion is this, I would require a close time upon every fishing—a close time that would suit everybody —a proper reasonable time.

882. How would you fix a time that would suit everybody?—I mean this. As soon as fish are good and marketable, it is a pity to restrain men from taking them. The Scotch fishermen have thought that by curtailing it, they are deprived of from four to eight weeks fishing. Being stopped till the beginning of June, just means that the great bulk cannot go. It is taking rights from Scotch fishermen that they should have. I question, whether according to international law, French men could land and fish in Ireland at Galway, Waterford, Dublin, Belfast, and some other places at any season of the year. I think it is a pity to cripple a great industry like the fishing, if you gentlemen could so arrive at a conclusion to suit all parties as near as possible, and not to cripple up the Scotch fishermen from going to any part of the Irish fishing. We all belong to one island.

883. Mr. Roche.—You do not belong to Ireland?—As fishermen, I think we have quite a right to go and fish in Ireland. Cutting off May, practically cuts off the Scotch fishermen from having any interest in the Irish fishing.

Mr. Hornsby.—It is not our object at all to drive away the Scotch fishermen, but to try and arrive at some amicable arrangement between the men fishing for herrings and the men fishing for mackerel—the two classes of fishing. There is nothing else in the question. It is simply this friction that has occurred on some occasions.

Mr. Roche.—We wish to encourage the Scotch fishermen to come to Ireland.

884. Mr. Green.—Have you fished at Stornoway?—I have never been so far as Stornoway. I have been at Shetland and south in Norfolk and on the Yorkshire coast.

885. Do you think it would be a good thing for you to take mackerel nets to Ireland in the spring of the year and fish for mackerel?—Our men have not generally thought of trying mackerel in Ireland. We have never gone in for mackerel nets. Only two fishermen in Cellardyke tried it, but they have never been gone into by the fishermen generally.

886. Mr. Hornsby.—It would not be worth while trying experiments by some Scotch fishermen?—It might.

887. What would you think of the 11th May to commence?—According to the evidence, taking men who have been there from year to year, they seem to think from the 25th of April till the 1st day of May a reasonable time to want the fishing. Later than that they seem to think curtails the fishing so much.

888. Would not half a loaf be better than no bread? And if you could manage to meet the mackerel men half way and give ten days I think it is only reasonable that the fishermen should do that as near as possible. Of course we would not like to be unreasonable or take any undue advantage?—If fish are good and marketable it is a pity they cannot be taken.

889. Mr. Roche.—According to evidence it does injury to the mackerel fishing?—It is really a question of the mackerel fishing against the herring fishing.

890. Mr. Green.—Have you been ever fishing off Lowestoft?—Yes.

891. Have the mackerel boats fished near you there?—Yes, I have seen them fishing alongside the herring boats—at Yarmouth, generally speaking. When we went there the mackerel boats were giving it up. I have known them being together some weeks after the herring boats started, and they never seem to have come in contact. There are not many small mackerel got there but what is the proper size for use.

Mr. HORNBY.—We are only too much obliged if any witness will come forward and supplement what you have said by his own statement.

Mr. *Mearns.*—I am very glad you gave me a chance to say a word. Our industry would not need to be crippled by any means. This means keeping perhaps three or four hundred Scotch boats at home which might be making a livelihood in different parts of the island.

Mr. HORNBY.—We are very much obliged to you for what you have said. We will adjourn this inquiry now to our next place of meeting—Buckie on Tuesday, the 7th.

Mr. *Charles Anderson.*—I beg to move a hearty vote of thanks to the Commissioners for altering the hour of the meeting, so as to make it convenient for the fishermen to attend.

Mr. HORNBY.—It is a source of gratification and pleasure to us to see such a very respectable class of men as we do see at all our inquiries in Scotland—intelligent, respectable, orderly, in every way very much to be admired.

The proceedings then terminated.

BUCKIE INQUIRY.

Fishermen's Hall, Buckie, Banffshire,
Tuesday, 7th February, 1893.

Her Majesty's Inspectors of Irish Fisheries—ALEX HORNSBY, Esq. (in the chair), Rev. WM. SPOTSWOOD GREEN, and CECIL R. ROCHE, Esq., Barrister-at-Law, held an inquiry this day in the Fishermen's Hall, Buckie, with reference to the custom of fishing by nets for herrings off the South Coast of Ireland before the 1st of June in each year.

Mr. *John Murray*, Leith, one of the officers of the Scottish Fishery Board, attended the meeting to render any information or assistance which the Inspectors might require during the inquiry. Dr. *Duguid*, Chief Magistrate of Buckie, and President of the Moray Firth Fishermen's Protection Association, appeared on behalf of the fishermen at the inquiry.

Mr. HORNSBY in opening the proceedings said:—We commenced these inquiries in Ireland in December last, and our first inquiry in Scotland was at Cockenzie on the 23th of January. We also sat at Anstruther on 31st January, and at Montrose on 3rd February, and now we sit here to-day to hear the evidence of any of you Scotch fishermen who go to fish for herrings off the South-West Coast of Ireland. The object of our inquiry is to endeavour to arrive at some arrangement under which the Scotchmen who fish herrings and the Irishmen who fish mackerel will agree and be satisfied, and some arrangement which will be to the benefit of the fisheries as a whole—not to injure either branch of the industry. Your Chief Magistrate here has kindly undertaken to examine such of you witnesses as wish to come forward. (To Dr. Duguid.) You had better call your witnesses.

Dr. *Duguid*.—First of all I must express our thanks to the gentlemen who have come here to-day from Ireland, for the purpose of making these inquiries and investigations. You are all aware that there has been some difference of opinion between our Scotch and Irish fishermen at Kinsale, and that, perhaps, has, I think, been the cause of some of our fishermen ceasing to go and prosecute the herring fishing there. The Irish Fishery Board are anxious that a stop should be put to these differences, and if possible, that a mode of amicably carrying on the fishing should be arranged, and they have come here to get whatever evidence we may be able to lay before them on that point, and we **are** certainly very much indebted to them, for their courtesy in coming here. I hope that the result of this investigation may be to, perhaps, make a better opening to our fishermen on the South-West Coast of Ireland without, at the same time, doing any injury to the native fishermen there.

Alexander Reid sworn; examined by Dr. Duguid.

892. Are you the master of a fishing boat?—I was master **of a** fishing boat.

893. And you have been a fisherman all your life?—Yes, sir.

894. You have been in the way of going to the Kinsale fishings sometimes?—Yes, sir.

895. How often have you been at Kinsale fishing?—Once.

896. Only once, when?—In 1886.

897. What time did the herring fishing commence there that season? —It commenced about the middle of April.

898. When did you arrive there?—On the 15th.

899. Of April?—Yes.

900. And did you commence fishing immediately? Did you go to sea next day or when?—Yes, the following week. We went in the end of the week.

901. So that you commenced fishing about the 18th or 20th April?—Yes.

902. And did you get herrings at that time?—Yes, we got some herrings.

903. But perhaps not heavy shots?—No.

904. When did you begin to have heavy shots?—Later on there were plenty of fish.

905. When did they become plentiful?—From the beginning to the middle of May.

906. And what quality of fish did you get?—They were good for the season of the year.

907. What quality of fish would you have had at the beginning—when you commenced about the 20th of April? Were they of good quality then?—Yes, they were of good quality. As good as we could get along the coast. The quality was pretty fair for the season of the year.

908. Would you have had full fish at the beginning of the season?—I would not say that we would have had full fish then.

909. But they were good marketable fish?—Yes.

910. And what price would you have got for them at that season?—They were very little.

911. What would you have got, do you remember?—I hardly remember the price; but it did not pay at that time.

912. Did the price improve afterwards as the season went on?—Yes, the prices improved as the season went on.

913. Did the quality of the fish improve as the season went on?—Yes, sir.

914. About what time was it that you got good full fish?—They were in good condition from the middle to the end of May.

915. Were they good eatable fish before that time?—Yes.

916. But they were superior fish by the end of May, were they?—They were of better quality before the end of May.

917. And the price was rather low at the beginning of the season, but it improved afterwards?—Yes.

918. Were there many boats there that year?—Yes, there were a good few boats there.

919. How many, could you say?—I could hardly tell.

920. Were there hundreds?—Yes, there were hundreds.

921. From all parts?—Yes.

922. Were they mostly Scotch, English, or Irish?—A good few were Scotch.

923. A great many were Scotch boats?—Yes.

924. Was the majority Scotch?—Yes.

925. Were there many English boats?—There were some English boats.

926. Any Irish boats fishing for herrings?—I could not say that there were any Irish boats fishing for herrings.

927. There was a fleet of Irish boats fishing at the same time for mackerel?—Yes.

928. At the same time?—Yes.

929. Did the herring fleet and the mackerel fleet ever come into collision? Were they fishing on the same grounds?—No, I never saw them in collision.

930. Did they fish over the same grounds?—There was always a good distance between the two fleets.

931. They were separated from each other?—Yes.

932. Did you catch mackerel in your nets then?—We caught a few small mackerel, but only a few.

933. Did you catch any hake?—No, I don't think we caught any hake at that time.

934. But you had small mackerel?—Yes.

935. Many?—No, not many, a few.

936. And what did you do with them?—We gave them to the first one that we came across to sell.

937. Sold them to the first buyer?—Yes.

938. Had you as many of them as were worth selling?—No, no. We never expected to make anything of the mackerel.

939. Might you have had about a dozen or two?—A hundred would be about the most that we got.

940. Were they full or undersized mackerel?—Oh, undersized. They were caught in the net. Our nets would not take large sized mackerel.

941. Were they good to eat?—No, I do not think they were good to eat.

942. When you are fishing at home here you sometimes catch mackerel in your nets?—Yes, we get mackerel here as well as there.

943. How many would you get?—Very few in number.

944. Would the mackerel here, on our coast, and the mackerel at Kinsale, be pretty much the same size of fish?—Much about the same.

945. And yet, though there were a good many mackerel about where your nets happened to shoot, you only got a few stray mackerel?—Just a few.

946. Your nets would not catch them?—No.

947. That is the reason. There will be plenty of mackerel here on the coast though you do not catch them?—We cannot catch them. They fall out of the net when they die.

948. They do not get into the net?—No, they are not meshed in the net.

949. They come striking against the mesh then?—Yes.

950. And cannot get in but just go back?—Yes.

951. Have you any idea whether there should be a close time at Kinsale for the herring fishing?—Not if the herring were saleable; if there was a market for them.

952. You have an idea that there should be a close time when fish are not in season, or not good marketable fish—that it is better not to be fishing for them?—Yes, it would be better to prevent the sale of immature fish.

953. You believe that immature fish should not be caught?—Yes.

954. When do you think it would be prudent to commence fishing at Kinsale?—I think the 25th of April would be early enough to begin the fishing at Kinsale.

955. And at that time, by the 25th of April, would you get good fish?—You would get good marketable fish.

956. You have not gone back to Kinsale?—No.

957. Why?—Well, we did not get much satisfaction the year we were there. There was not much competition and sometimes we were knocked about rather more than we should have been.

958. Explain what you mean by being knocked about?—Well, when we sold our fish sometimes we were the whole day before we could get them discharged.

959. How did that happen?—Being in the hulks we did not get our turn sometimes. The Irishmen used to be served before us.

960. Did the mackerel boats there do anything to inconvenience you in your fishing?—No.

961. But in the delivery of the fish?—Yes, we never met them until we came ashore.

962. When you got there did the native fishermen interfere with you in any way?—That was just the way they did.

963. Well, how did they interfere with you?—I never saw much interference except when selling fish at the hulks. You had to wait your turn until the Irishmen were cleared, and sometimes the detention may have caused the loss of a shot at sea.

964. They did not do anything else?—Nothing that I saw.

965. You are in the way of going to Lowestoft fishing, are you?—Yes.

966. And there is a mackerel fishing there?—Yes.

967. Is it carried on at the same time as the herring fishing?—Yes.

968. By different sets of fishermen?—Yes.

969. And did the two fleets work harmoniously there?—Yes.

970. You never had any trouble there?—No.

971. Did you catch mackerel then in your nets at Lowestoft?—We caught mackerel in the nets just as at Kinsale, but we did not make a market of them.

972. You did not catch sufficient to make a market?—That is it.

973. Were you fishing nearly on the same ground as the mackerel fleet?—Yes.

974. And they will be getting good shots while you will be getting virtually none?—Nothing to speak of.

975. Mr. HORNBY.—What was the first day that you fished at Kinsale?—About the 18th or 20th of April.

976. In the fish you took what was the proportion of good marketable herrings and inferior ones? You had some inferior ones, had you not?—Well, we had mixed herrings.

977. Well, what proportion did the really good marketable herrings bear to the inferior herrings?—There was over a half, I believe, of good marketable herrings.

978. Were these herrings that you took good firm herrings that would stand salting, packing, and transporting to England? Were they in that condition or were they soft?—I may tell you that we did salt them ourselves at that time. The curers salted them, I mean, when we discharged them, so that I suppose if they salted them it looked as if they were marketable.

979. What price did you get per mease for them?—I can hardly remember.

980. Was the price low, or what?—The prices were very good the first week or so, but I suppose that was because there were no herrings caught before that.

981. Yes, but can you tell us about what the price was?—I think the first we sold were about 6s. a mease.

982. Did you ever hear when you were there that the buyers objected to your going out before a certain date?—No.

983. We have it in evidence elsewhere that the Scotchmen complain that the buyers would not take the fish before a certain date. Do you know anything about that?—No, I know nothing of that, sir.

984. There are two questions I should like to get some explanation of. Where did these English boats that you met at Kinsale come from?—I hardly remember where they came from.

985. Can't you say where they came from?—I think they were Penzance boats.

986. Oh, the Cornish boats. Any Lowestoft boats there?—Yes, there were some of them there too.

987. You complain that you were delayed very much at the hulks in bringing in your fish and getting discharged. Is it not a fact that the mackerel and the herrings are discharged at different hulks, and that they are treated by different people altogether?—No, I have discharged herrings and I have seen mackerel discharged at the same hulk.

988. Oh, because we have it in evidence elsewhere from different fish buyers that there are two distinct hulks?—I cannot help that. I have discharged herrings at the same hulk as the mackerel boats.

989. You speak exactly of what happened to yourself; that is what I want to know?—Yes; well, that is what happened to me.

990. That is very important now. When did you leave Kinsale that year—how long did you fish there?—Until about the end of May.

991. Well, were the herrings plentiful then, or had they gone off the coast?—They were not very plentiful, but were better in quality.

992. What price were you getting then?—The herrings went as high as 16s. a mense.

993. Don't you think the fact of your only getting 6s. a mense rather tended to prove that the herrings were of inferior quality?—No, I don't think so.

994. But herrings coming into the market at that early period ought to command good prices if they were good—ought they not?—Yes; but it is the competition that makes the prices.

995. How many Scotch boats were there fishing there the year that you were there?—I can hardly tell you distinctly.

996. About how many—I don't tie you down strictly?—I should say about a dozen. I think that is about the number, but I am not exactly sure.

997. But I thought that in your direct evidence to the Chief Magistrate you stated that there were very large numbers?—I meant by that the whole of the boats for Scotland, taking in Cellardyke, Burghead, and Hopeman.

998. Well, taking all these localities, how many Scotch boats were there at Kinsale when you were there?—I should say 150.

999. And out of that about a dozen from here?—Yes, sir.

1001. How many Lowestoft boats were there?—I could hardly tell you.

1002. Well, roughly—I am not tying you down to a particular number?—Well, I believe there were about a score that I can remember seeing. I do not know if there were more than that or not.

1003. Well, now, what would you think, supposing you were prohibited from fishing for herrings off that coast before the 11th of May each year—what is your idea on that point? I know that you have stated that you want to commence in April, but I want to get some reasons from you for that?—Well, I would think that the Irishmen were taking too much liberty.

1004. Yes; but please devote your attention to this. You are a skilled fisherman and an intelligent man, and the question is this:—Do you consider that in that early fishing when the herrings, as you have told us yourself, fetch a very low price, is it a wise thing for a large fleet to carry on fishing there at so early a date?—Not if the herrings do not pay, but if the herrings pay the fishermen and the buyers, then I think it is quite right.   F

1005. But will 6s. a mease pay either the fishermen or the buyer?—Well, I am not sure whether it would pay or not; but if they got plenty of them it might.

1006. What was your largest take at Kinsale?—Well, I can hardly remember.

1007. What about then—give us an idea?—I think about eight or ten crans was our highest take.

1008. Where did you shoot your nets—were you near the mackerel fishing? Were you on the same ground as the mackerel fishermen when you shot your nets?—Not just on the same ground.

1010. How far off them were you?...Well, they might have been two or three miles off, or one and a half miles off some nights, if they were not following each other when they were fishing.

1011. How far off the land did you shoot your nets?—From fourteen to twenty-five miles.

1012. You have answered this question already when put to you by the Chief Magistrate; but have you had any undersized mackerel in any great quantity?—No.

1013. Have you seen any hake?—No.

1014. Are your nets of the same class as those used by the men who have appeared before us at Anstruther and Montrose?—Yes.

1015. The same number of rows and knots to the yard?—Yes.

1016. And you have got the same length of rope?—Yes.

1017. How many meshes deep are your nets?—Eighteen score deep.

1018. And what depth do they sling generally?—About 9 fathoms.

1019. How many pieces of net are there in a train?—55 or 60.

1020. What is the length of each piece?—60 yards and some 55 yards.

1021. Mr. *Murray.*—Not mounted—what is the length of a net mounted.

The *Witness.*—Oh, it is the length of a net mounted you want?

1022. Mr. HORNBY.—Yes.

The *Witness.*—20 fathoms.

1023. Mr. GREEN.—When the herrings were of different qualities at the beginning of the season, and when you brought them to the hulk, did the buyers make any difference between them—did they select them, or did they give the same price whether they were large or small?—They were sold just in the lump.

1024. Just as they were?—Yes, they were sold by the mease. They were put up for sale and purchased by the mease.

1025. Did the buyers make any difference by selecting them before being sold off?—No, I never saw any selection made.

1026. You said awhile ago that you were in danger of fouling the mackerel nets your were so close to them?—No, I beg your pardon, I never said that. I said that sometimes the mackerel fleet were about 1½ miles and 2 miles off from the herring fishing boats, and that they never fished through each other just for fear of that.

Mr. ROCHE.—Yes, that is what I understood you to say.

1027. Mr. GREEN.—What price did you get for small mackerel?—We sold them to the first man who came round. We never tried to make money out of them. It was the herrings that we were looking after more than the mackerel.

1028. Mr. ROCHE.—Do you know if there is a close time for the herring fishing at Lowestoft?—For herring fishing?

1029. Yes?—Well, not that I know of.

1030. There is in Stornoway, I believe?—Yes.

1031. But not at Lowestoft?—No, the fishing is open the same as on the east coast.

1032. Mr. HORNBY.—Is there anything you wish to add to the questions we have asked you, and to the answers which you have given?

The *Witness.*—I should like to keep the time open for the fishermen from the 25th of April, or from the 1st of May—either of the two dates—so that the Scotch fishermen could go there and fish for herrings the same as they do at Lowestoft and Yarmouth. Another thing I would like is if you would petition the Government to give us a better sea police to prevent trawlers coming within enclosed waters.

Mr. HORNBY.—I quite agree with you there and we certainly will adopt your suggestions, and we are glad to be fortified with your opinion.

Mr. ROCHE.—We are quite of the same way of thinking as yourself in that matter.

1033. Dr. *Duguid* (to Witness).—You are in the way of going to Stornoway fishing?—Yes.

1034. Do you find the quality of the fish at Kinsale and at Stornoway pretty much the same?—About April they are pretty much the same fish.

1035. Would Kinsale fishing be earlier than Stornoway?—The fish are better quality at Kinsale in the early part of the season.

1036. Mr. ROCHE.—In the early part of the season would you have better fish at Kinsale than at Stornoway?—Yes.

1037. When is the close time at Stornoway?—The 10th of May.

1038. Dr. *Duguid.*—The 15th of May is it not?—Yes.

1039. So that you think there could be a profitable fishing at Kinsale for two or three weeks before the Stornoway fishing commences?—Yes.

1040. Mr. ROCHE.—Could you fish for a couple of weeks at Kinsale before the fishing commences at Stornoway?—Yes.

1041. You say the 15th of May is the close time at Stornoway?—Yes.

1042. Supposing you were to begin fishing at Stornoway at the same time as you propose doing it at Kinsale, would you get a good class of fishing?—You would get better fish at Kinsale than at Stornoway; but I believe you would get as marketable fish as there is to be got during the whole season about the middle of May or the 1st of June at Stornoway.

1043. Dr. *Duguid.*—So that you could have a profitable fishing and a good fishing at Kinsale before you could have it at Stornoway?—Yes, good enough fish for the market; at least, they are very good fish for food.

1044. Mr. HORNBY.—Are we to understand from your evidence on that particular part of the inquiry that it would not pay you Scotchmen to go to Ireland to fish supposing you could not commence before the 11th of May? Do you think it would pay you to go and commence on the 11th of May?—No, it could not do that if we were to leave here on the 11th of May or be there on the 11th of May.

1045. I said commencing to fish on the 11th May, and not leaving for the fishing grounds on that date?—No, it would not pay, and the reason I would give is that the time would be too short.

1046. What time do the great bulk of the men stop fishing for herrings on the Irish coast?—From the 25th to the end of June. Some of them remain as long as to the end of June I have heard.

1047. Mr. ROCHE.—Fishing for herrings?—Yes.

1048. Mr. HORNSBY.—From the 11th of May to the end of June you would have forty-one days?—That is not a very long time.

1049. It is not a very long time, but you see it is much better to come to some amicable arrangement. Although I have said that some of the men remain till the end of June, the most of the boats leave long before that time—about the middle of June—to come back to the late fishing here.

1050. What is your experience, and the general impression of the fishermen here with reference to the date at which it would be time for you to stop fishing for herrings off that coast—I mean the time when it would not pay you to remain?—I think it would be time for everybody to stop about the middle of June.

1051. Dr. *Duguid*.—Is it a fact that at Stornoway the fish go round the Butt in a sort of stream, and that if you begin fishing there too early you break up the shoal of fish and spoil your chances afterwards?—Yes.

1052. Sometimes the fish come up the Minch, and if you begin fishing too early you break up the shoal?—Yes.

1053. There is not the same chance of doing that at Kinsale?—No, it is open sea at Kinsale.

1054. So that even if you caught the fish there you don't break up the shoals and spoil the future fishing?—No, because the coast is in a straight line direction.

1055. Mr. GREEN.—Do you fish at Barra?—Yes.

1056. Do you fish there earlier than at Stornoway?—There are engagements made for Barra; I think they generally stick to their agreements when they go there.

1057. Dr. *Duguid*.—But you commence earlier at Barra?—I am not sure.

1058. But you might do it?—Possibly.

1059. Mr. ROCHE.—What length of sea is under close season at Stornoway?—The Minch itself is about from the Shiant Isles to Cape Wrath. That is about 120 miles.

1060. And that is under close season?—Yes, it prevails over all that water.

1061. 120 miles you say?—I understand the close time extends from the Orkneys to the Mull of Kintyre.

Dr. *Duguid*.—From the Shiant Isles to Cape Wrath is sixty or seventy miles. The close time that prevails at Stornoway is not a legal close time, but simply one made by the fishermen themselves in their own interests.

Mr. ROCHE.—We know that, and therefore it is the more important as showing what has been done without legislation.

1062. Mr. HORNSBY.—Would you approve of this mutual arrangement being extended from Cape Wrath to the Mull of Kintyre?—Yes, I would. I mean from Orkney to the Mull of Kintyre.

1064. What season do you approve of for that district?—From the Orkneys to the Mull of Kintyre.

1065. Yes. When would you commence the herring fishing there? —I would commence from the 10th to the 15th of May, which is soon enough at Stornoway, and the same at Scrabster and for the Barra fishings.

1066. Why not the same for Kinsale?—Because I think Kinsale is an earlier place. I may be wrong.

1067. But certainly, according to your evidence you do not appear to get much profit for your herrings in the early part of the season?—

I told you. I thought that was accounted for by the want of competition, and curers don't go there until they get good fish to buy.

1068. Buyers you mean?—Yes.

1069. But surely the buyers there for mackerel would buy the herrings too, in order that they might make up a cargo for the steamer, if the mackerel were short?—That depends if the mackerel were scarce, but there were plenty of mackerel there the year that we were there. About that season of the year there were plenty.

1070. But you had no difficulty in obtaining buyers?—We could not get much remuneration for our fish.

1071. There were plenty of people to buy them though?—I do not know that there were plenty of them. I heard several Scotch fishermen complaining that there were not many curers there.

James Thain sworn; examined by Dr. DUGUID.

1072. Are you the master of a fishing boat?—Yes.

1073. Are you the owner as well?—Yes.

1074. And you have been going to the sea as a fisherman all your life?—Yes.

1075. And you have had a pretty large experience as a fisherman both here and in other countries?—Yes.

1076. You have fished, I think, in Scotland, England, Ireland, and in America as well?—Yes, I have fished all these parts.

1077. In America, too, I think?—Yes.

1078. Have you ever been fishing in Kinsale in Ireland?—Yes.

1079. How many seasons were you there?—I went over there about the month of April. I was there about six weeks.

1080. You were only there one season?—Yes.

1081. When was that?—That was eight years ago come April.

1082. That would be in 1885, was it?—I believe it would.

1083. Then what period of the year did you go there?—I left Buckie on the 1st of April.

1084. On the 1st of April?—Yes.

1085. When did you arrive at Kinsale?—I arrived there about the 9th of April.

1086. When did you commence fishing?—I commenced fishing about eight days after that.

1087. About the 17th or 18th?—Yes, as near as I can remember.

1088. Did you get good fish when you began?—Well, the fish were good for common food.

1089. But not for curing?—I could not say that they were good for curing at first.

1090. But good for food?—Yes.

1091. That was at the very beginning—about the 18th or 20th of April?—Yes.

1092. Did the quality improve pretty fast?—Yes, at the time that I left they were very good.

1093. When did you leave?—I left about the 4th or 5th of May, I think.

1094. And the fish were of good quality then?—Yes.

1095. Were they good for curing purposes then?—Yes.

1096. Were they good for any time before that?—They were not so good at first, but they improved every week.

1097. At the beginning of May they were good fish?—Yes.

1098. What price would you have got for your fish?—The most that I realised was 6s. 6d a mease.

1099. How does a mease stand with a cran?—I do not remember very well.

1100. The mease would be about half a cran?—That is our calculation.

1101. So that there would be about two meases to the cran?—Yes.

1102. So that the price you were getting would actually be about 12s. to 13s. a cran?—Yes.

1103. And wouldn't 12s. or 13s. be a good price for early herrings?—Very good.

1104. So that you did not think 6s. or 6s. 6d. a very poor price for your early herrings?—No, we thought it fair enough for the first start.

1105. At Kinsale there is a large mackerel and hake fishing going on at the same time?—Yes, but we get no hake there.

1106. No, but there is a mackerel fishing going on there?—Yes.

1107. Did you get any mackerel in your nets when you were fishing for herrings?—Nothing to speak about.

1108. Just a few?—Yes, just a few.

1109. Just pretty much as at home?—Just such like.

1110. Were any of the mackerel that you caught undersized?—Yes.

1112. But quite few?—Very few.

1113. Nothing to interfere with the mackerel fishing?—Our nets were all underneath the mackerel there.

1114. Did you fish upon the same ground as the mackerel boats?—They went further out than us.

1115. So that the two fleets were not mixed together?—No.

1116. Did you fish with your nets at the same level as the mackerel fishermen did?—No, our nets were three fathoms underneath the water.

1117. So that the mackerel swim above the herrings?—They are what you call a surface net.

1118. And the herring fishing is deeper down?—We use three fathoms.

1119. Do the mackerel and herring swim pretty much in different depths?—The mackerel are always above the herring.

1120. The mackerel swim nearer the surface than the herring?—Yes.

1121. So that practically your nets do not interfere much with the mackerel?—No, not in a sense.

1122. There are plenty of mackerel on our coast at the time of the herring fishing?—Oh, yes; you get mackerel in the nets as easily on our coast as at Kinsale.

1123. And you have just as many here as at Kinsale?—Yes, at times.

1124. At the mackerel season?—Yes.

1125. But practically then the mesh of your net is too small to interfere with the mackerel?—It does not hurt the mackerel at all.

1126. If the mackerel came the way of your nets, it would not go into them? They knock against the nets and go back again. You may get a few caught by the fin.

1127. Do you think that there should be a close time at Kinsale for the herring fishing?—I would adopt a close time.

1128. What is your idea of the proper time to commence at Kinsale?—I would say from the 25th of April to the 1st of May or thereabouts.

1129. That is to say the fishing might be commenced say from the 25th of April to the 1st of May?—Yes.

1130. Not before the 25th of April nor later than the 1st of May?—No.

1131. You are in the way of going to the Stornoway fishing?—Yes.

1132. Do you think that the Kinsale fishing might be commenced earlier than the Stornoway fishing? Are the fish at maturity sooner at Kinsale than at Stornoway?—Yes.

1133. So that you think there might be fishing at Kinsale for a few weeks before the Stornoway fishing?—Yes.

1134. And that our fishermen might go to Kinsale at the end of April and fish for a few weeks, and then go to Stornoway?—Yes.

1135. And that the fish at Kinsale would be quite as good quality then as they would be at Stornoway a few weeks afterwards?—I would think so.

1136. You have not gone back to Kinsale in recent years?—No.

1137. Why?—We did not get much encouragement at the time we were there.

1138. In what way?—There was not much competition for buying herring. They would scarcely buy the herrings from us, and then we required some protection at sea sometimes. We were there to stick up for our own rights.

1139. What were you afraid of?—Just the people there.

1140. The Irish fishermen?—Yes.

1141. Did they threaten you in any way?—I never had any words, but the Irish fishermen would have done it very fast if they could. I have come across some men before who complained.

1142. One reason why you did not go back then was that you felt you were in danger?—Yes; and there were not enough of buyers.

1143. So that there were two reasons—want of competition and the opposition of the native fishermen?—Yes.

1144. Supposing you were going back there, are you sufficiently acquainted with the present state of matters as to say that the competition now is better than when you were there?—I do not know.

1145. I mean of recent years?—I do not know.

1146. Mr. HORNSBY.—You advocate commencing to fish herrings off the Irish coast, say, on the 25th April. The herrings you caught there at first fetched a very low price; didn't they?—Yes.

1147. These herrings that you caught, were they in a proper condition for being packed, salted, and sent to the English markets?—Yes; for common food.

1148. That is not an answer to my question. I asked were the fish in a proper condition to be packed and salted and sent to the English markets, and fetch a price in the large towns, such as Birmingham, Sheffield, Liverpool, and Manchester?—I am no judge of that. It is the buyer who is the judge of that.

1149. But you are a fisherman, and you ought to know when the fish are in good condition?—I know when they are good for common food.

1150. But you know perfectly well whether herrings are in proper condition or not?—I have some idea, but not so much judgment as buyers.

1151. Well, according to that idea, tell me in what condition were these fish for transportation to the English market?—They were good enough for present use.

1152. When you say present use, you mean for sale to the local buyers?—No; I mean to be sent away on a journey occupying a day or two to the English markets.

1153. Don't you think the price is a very fair criterion to go by as to the condition of the fish, unless there has been an enormous glut in the market?—Yes.

1154. How many Scotch boats were there fishing there?—I should say over 100 round the coast.

1155. Would you be content to go to Ireland and commence fishing on the 11th of May?—That would be rather late. That is the time we go to Stornoway.

1156. Putting Stornoway out of the question, don't you think the fish would be in better condition in May than in April on the Irish coast?—The fish would be far better in May at Kinsale than at Stornoway.

1157. That is not the question I am asking you. Do you think the fish would be in better condition on the 11th of May than on the 25th of April?—Yes, I think they would.

1158. Your sole objection therefore to the date of the 11th of May is that you would rather be at Stornoway at that time?—No, that is not my whole objection. The herrings would be better on the 1st of May there than at Stornoway.

1159. I see. You get better herrings in May in Ireland than in Stornoway?—Yes.

1160. Is there any mackerel fishing carried on off the Scotch coast?—No; there is not a great mackerel fishing carried on off the Scotch coast, but there is a good mackerel fishing on the English coast.

1161. You have mackerel fishing off the Yarmouth and Lowestoft coast, I think?—Yes.

1162. Do the mackerel men and the fishermen fish over the same ground there?—No, I have never been in contact with a mackerel boat there either.

1163. You keep away from them?—Yes, or else they keep away from us.

1164. When you were fishing off the Irish coast, provided you did not get right on the ground of the mackerel men, did they interfere with you, or did they complain at all?—No, we never happened to be in contact one way or the other, except in fair weather without wind.

1165. Did you receive any incivility from the Irish fishermen?—Very little. One man was very uncivil one day.

1166. Oh, yes; there is a black sheep to every flock. But, on the whole, were they not very civil to you?—Oh, yes; I could not complain at all.

1167. Were you ever threatened?—Oh, no; I could not say that.

1168. Did you ever hear of any Scotch crew being threatened by the Irish fishermen?—Yes, I have heard of it.

1169. You did complain in your evidence to the Chief Magistrate, I think, about there being a want of buyers, didn't you?—Yes.

1170. Do you attribute the low price to want of competition amongst the buyers, or what?—I think so.

1171. That, coupled with the inferior quality of the fish?—I beg your pardon, I did not catch that.

1172. Is that coupled with the fact that the fish were of inferior quality when you first started?—Yes, they were not so good as when I left.

1173. Why did you leave so early?—Because of the want of competition.

1174. But, surely, there were more buyers who came afterwards?—I could not say, I do not know that.

1175. Were the mackerel buyers there at that time?—Yes.

1176. Would they take your herrings?—Not so long as there were mackerel.

1177. Supposing they wanted to make up a cargo, would they not take your herrings?—Yes, but they always took delivery of the mackerel before the herrings.

1178. Did you deliver your herrings at the same hulk as the mackerel?—Yes, once.

1179. Where did you deliver the other times?—At the slips at the beach.

1180. Is it not a fact that there are two hulks there, one for mackerel and one for herrings?—No, there were just other two boats that I heard of went alongside the hulk I went to on the day in question, but there were eight or ten mackerel boats, and the buyers took delivery of all the mackerel before the herrings.

1181. Because we have got it in evidence—I mentioned it to the last witness—from a very large English fish buyer, that there are two hulks at Kinsale, and two different staffs of men employed, one for packing the herrings, and the other for mackerel, for the steamers to Milford?—That may possibly be the case since I was there.

1182. Mr. Roche.—It is eight years since you were there?—Yes.

1183. Mr. Green.—Do you go to Stornoway?—Yes.

1184. Do you fish at an engaged price there?—No.

1185. Did you ever fish at an engaged price there?—Yes.

1186. What is it generally? Was it lower at the beginning of the season than towards the end?—We have had early prices at the earlier part of the fishing.

1187. Was the early price a lower price?—Oh, yes.

1188. Do you go to Stornoway now?—Yes.

1189. And about what date did you begin to fish there?—From the 15th, for the last few years.

1190. That was on account of the close season?—Yes, and I think they are trying to get it a week earlier this year, if possible.

1191. Do you think the fish are in good condition earlier?—The buyers think so.

1192. Mr. Roche.—What other boats were fishing the year you were at Kinsale?—They were from Fifeshire.

1193. Were there any besides Scotch boats fishing there?—Oh, yes, there were some mackerel boats from Lowestoft.

1194. How many would there be there?—There were two small steam boats that year.

1195. Any others?—Yes, I think there were some luggers. There were a few whatever.

1196. Mr. Hornby.—When were you fishing off the American coast?—Oh, it is five years come the month of April.

1197. Did you see the purse seine net used there for mackerel?—No.

1198. You do not know anything about its use?—No.

1199. You know it is prohibited by the American Government, don't you?—I beg your pardon.

1200. You know it is illegal now by the law of America to use that net at certain seasons?—Yes.

1201. Dr. *Duguid.*—It was in Canada you were fishing?—Yes.

1202. Mr. Hornby.—Oh, in Canada, was it?—Yes.

1203. Dr. *Duguid.*—About New Brunswick?—Yes.

1204. You were not in the State waters?—No, I was away down the Bay of Fundy.

1205. When you were at Kinsale was there a demand locally for the herrings or simply the mackerel?—Particularly mackerel.

1206. There was really no local demand for the herrings?—Very, very little.

1207. The Irish about Kinsale don't care to eat the herrings if they can get the mackerel?—No.

1208. If they did not get the mackerel they would take the herrings? —Yes.

1209. So that the herrings at first were really almost entirely for the English markets?—Yes.

1210. It did not interfere with the consumption of mackerel in the native markets?—None in the least.

1211. What about the price of early fish at Stornoway?—I think it used to be about 15s. a cran for May fish. I have seen men engage for prices from £1 per cran.

1212. When you used to be engaged it was about 14s. or 16s. for May fish and £1 afterwards?—Yes.

1213. That would be equal to 7s. or 7s. 6d. per mease?—Yes.

1214. And sometimes a little less?—Yes.

1215. If you had 6s. or 6s. 6d. for a mease at Kinsale that was only about 1s. less per cran than what you would be getting at Stornoway for May fish?—If the fish were scarce at Stornoway you would get £1 per cran for early fish.

1216. That is when scarce?—Yes.

1217. Were you engaged at £1 per cran?—Yes, our share.

1218. In the month of May?—Yes.

1219. But then you had bounties in these days?—Yes.

1220. And when you had more per cran you had less bounty?—I have had £1 per cran and £20 bounty.

1221. What price would you get for early herrings for the last few years at Stornoway?—Very often the early fish if not plentiful sold best.

1222. But when the whole fleet is fishing they are cheap enough?— They come down a little.

1223. Mr. HORNSBY.—Have you as many buyers at Stornoway at that time as you would have at Kinsale, or more?—Just now.

1224. No, in May, when you go up?—Oh, yes, any amount of buyers.

Dr. *Duguid* asked if there were any other fishermen present in the hall who had been at Kinsale.

No one answered, and

Mr. HORNSBY said—If there is no one else who wishes to give evidence on the subject we must now adjourn this inquiry to our next place.

Mr. ROGER—Is there not some sick fisherman to be examined?

Dr. *Duguid*—Yes, there is a sick fisherman confined to bed, who was at Kinsale.

Mr. HORNSBY.—Is it fair to a sick man who is in bed that we should worry him any more?

Mr. ROGER—And would he wish to be examined himself?

Mr. *Murray*.—I think it is hardly desirable.

Dr. *Duguid*.—I am his medical attendant, and I can vouch for his condition, but if you wish to go——

Mr. HORNSBY.—I hardly think it is worth while. The fact is present to our minds that the great mass of their body are out at sea earning their livelihood and cannot be present; we will always recognise that fact, of course. We take these men here to-day more or less as spokesmen for themselves and for all their comrades who are not here.

Dr. *Duguid*—There are only a limited number of our fishermen from Buckie who have been at Kinsale. I have spoken to the greater part of them, and I think their evidence would only be a repetition of what you have heard.

Mr. HORNABY.—It seems there are about 12 boats go from Buckie to Kinsale.

Dr. *Duguid.*—Yes, but lately there have been none going from this particular town.

Mr. *Murray.*—One or two go from Portessie.

Dr. *Duguid.*—Yes, there is one. I called at the skipper's house and found that he was at sea, and his wife was very doubtful if he would be at home in time for the inquiry. We have spoken to him before, but he was very doubtful if he could get to the inquiry. If he had not gone to sea with the rest of the crew it would have meant the boat lying ashore for the week.

Mr. HORNABY.—This inquiry is now adjourned to Burghead on Wednesday, 8th February.

Dr. *Duguid.*—Allow me to thank you, the Commissioners, for the kind way in which you have conducted the inquiry, and I hope, and we all hope, that some result may come of your visit here—that our fishermen may find an opening with you, and that that opening may be of benefit and use to your people as well as to ourselves.

Mr. HORNABY.—We are very glad to come here, and all I can say, and I am sure I am speaking the views of my colleagues at the same time, is that here in Buckie as elsewhere I can only repeat what I have said before, that we are delighted to see such a set of respectable men.

BURGHEAD INQUIRY. ·

Free Church Hall, Burghead, Morayshire.
Wednesday, 8th February, 1893.

Her Majesty's Inspectors of Irish Fisheries:—ALAN HORNSBY, Esq., (in the chair), Rev. WILLIAM SPOTSWOOD GREEN, and CECIL R. ROCHE, Esq., Barrister-at-Law—held a similar inquiry to that of Buckie, this day, in the Free Church Hall, Burghead, Morayshire.

Mr. *John Murray*, Leith, Officer of the Scotch Fishery Board, was present to assist the Commissioners. The Rev. Robert Niven, Minister of the Free Church, Burghead, was also present, and handed in a statement prepared by himself and representing the views of the fishermen on the subject matter of the inquiry.

Mr. HORNSBY.—We are sitting here to-day to take the evidence of any of the Burghead fishermen who may wish to come forward and give us their experience of the herring fishing off the south-west coast of Ireland. We have already sat at several places, as you are aware by the notice, in Scotland, and one place in Ireland. We are now anxious to hear the evidence of any of you men who have gone to Kinsale in any particular year—what your experience is and what your ideas are as to this proposal to fix a time before which herrings should not be captured off that part of the Irish coast. Is there any one here to represent the fishermen, or do they represent themselves?

Mr. *Niven*.—The men have requested me to prepare a statement of their experiences, and their views in connection with this question. It is adhered to also by the fishermen of Nairn, Lossiemouth, and Hopeman. Including Burghead, these are the four places within the Findhorn Fishery District, and we propose to hand it in to you.

Mr. HORNSBY.—Would you like to read it?

Mr. *Niven*.—If it would serve the same purpose.

Mr. HORNSBY.—I think you had better read it, because these gentlemen of the Press would very likely wish to get a portion of it.

Mr. *Niven*.—The information in this paper was gathered on the 7th day of January, before any of your meetings were held in this country.

The following is the document prepared and handed in by Mr. Niven:—

"The following statement prepared from information gathered from the fishermen of Burghead, N.B., who have been in the habit of fishing at Kinsale and other parts on the Irish coast, was submitted to and approved by them at a meeting held on Saturday, 21st January, 1893, and by their authority and on their behalf, as also of any others who may adhere to them in it, signed by their chairman for presentation to Mr. Alan Hornsby, Rev. W. Green and Mr. Cecil Roche, Inspectors of Irish Fisheries, on their visit to Burghead, 8th February, 1893, to make inquiry respecting the question of the Irish Mackerel and Hake and Herring Fishery dispute.

"Crews of herring fishers have been accustomed to go to Ireland to prosecute their calling for upwards of twenty years. At first Howth was the port from which we fished, beginning our operations about the fourth week of May in each year. While engaged at this fishing, we were told by mackerel fishers from Kinsale that herrings were plentiful on their coast during the months of April and May. We were induced by this information to give it a trial. About the year 1880 four boats proceeded from our village to Kinsale, and started fishing about the end of April or first of May. These crews met with good success. Herrings being plentiful and of good quality, were eagerly bought and good prices obtained. Encouraged by these results, more of our number went to Kinsale the following year, and we have continued, in varying numbers, to go there year after year up to the present time. Our endeavour has been to reach it by the end of April, as we have felt it would not be worth our labour to be there at a later period, the main body of the herring shoals having passed Kinsale eastwards by the end of the third week of May. Some of our number considered the propriety of proceeding at an earlier date, by the end of March in fact, to this port, that they might fish during the month of April as well as the first three weeks of May. It came to nothing, owing to the length of voyage at a season of the year when the weather is not quite settled and promise of a safe and speedy passage could not be entertained. Also the sea being open to the South of Ireland, if the weather were the least boisterous nothing could be done with herring nets, and the men must lie idle in harbour. We were never too early to find fish or buyers for them.

"In prosecuting our calling as herring fishers we carefully avoided proceeding to sea among the mackerel fleet. We do not require to do it. The herring shoals have always in our experience been found within the mackerel schools. To the best of our judgment we get herrings at a distance varying from four to twenty miles off shore. The mackerel fleet goes from thirty to forty miles and the most of their fishing is done beyond twenty miles. Our capture of herrings is made as a rule about eight miles off. We have gone among the mackerel fleet on some few occasions after the men told us of getting herrings in their nets, but we failed to get any. In our judgment the few herrings they got were stragglers from the main body of the herring schools, as the few mackerel we have caught in our nets may be considered as stragglers from the mackerel shoals. In the matter of these two fishings as far as we can see and speak truthfully neither do our respective fishing grounds or interests in any way clash.

"We are aware that for some time our work as herring fishers has been viewed with disfavour by the mackerel fishers owing to the fact that unavoidably we have taken mackerel in our nets. We do not go to Kinsale to fish for hake or mackerel, and we do not welcome either for the destruction they cause to our gear. Our business is to take herrings; for their capture our nets are prepared and put into the sea. That we take some of both kinds of fish as also blackfish we admit, but of hake we seldom see one that is full grown in our nets, and not more than a dozen that are immature, if even so many at one haul. Mackerel are more plentiful in them and are about twelve to fourteen inches long. We do not get them always, and we think that of an average during the season we are in Kinsale, a hundred and fifty of this fish in our nets each night they have fished would be a fair statement. We have seen the figures given recently at Kinsale by our Irish brethren, but we cannot check them as we have kept no records of our work and consider them extravagant.

"What mackerel we take is sold to buyers for Irish consumption, principally hawkers who sell them in the neighbourhood of Kinsale, or carry or send them inland to places where demand exists for them, and where they can be purchased at a price within the reach of the inhabitants. Part also of our takes of herrings is disposed of in the same way. So far as we know neither directly nor indirectly do we come into competition with the mackerel fishers whose fish are almost invariably sent to the English market at that season, and if for their protection a close time for herring fishing be adopted ending with the fifteenth or thirty-first day of May, a portion of the people in the South of Ireland will be deprived of an article of diet, wholesome, nutritious, good, and cheap.

"We are inclined to believe the fishing of mackerel during the greater part of the year is injurious to this industry, if injury can be done by drift net fishing to a species of fish so prolific as mackerel is known to be, and not the few thousands of fish taken by the Scotch boats in the herring season. These latter are immaterial to affect the numbers or reproductiveness of the shoals. Decline had been known in all fishings followed again after a time by revival. The supply of food for the mackerel will doubtless greatly affect its movements and numbers around the coast. We are also of the opinion that the hake fishing has not suffered through our operations as herring fishers, and if hurt can be attributed to any mode of fishing it must be to beam trawling, which is known to take the mature and immature and does not spare the female fish when gravid and about to spawn. In this latter matter the trawlers do injury that cannot be calculated. In this fishing also decline may be expected at recurring periods (its history shows that) followed by revival. The haddock fishery in Dublin Bay may be cited in support of our opinion. For years it was impossible to get haddocks there, now they are found in paying quantities, and men who formerly went to sea with herring or other nets devote their whole time to their capture.

" We consider that a close time for herring fishing at Kinsale, ending either with the fifteenth or thirty-first day of May, will not help either the hake or mackerel fisheries on that coast, while it will destroy that of herrings. The fishing practically closes itself by the third week of May, the fish having gone eastwards into the channel. We follow them by the fourth week of May to Howth. We would not go to Kinsale for herrings in June, our experience being that they are not to be had there in that month, and if they were, the numbers of blue sharks in that sea at that season would altogether destroy our nets.

"Finally, we desire to say our relations with our Irish brother fishers have ever been most pleasant. We do not regard them as being the originators of the agitation in this question of hake and mackerel versus herrings, and that if they had been left to their own judgment we believe they would not have stirred it. We also utterly and unconditionally repudiate any statement made by any man speaking in the name of any of our Scotch fishermen as to race hatred, religious creed, or politics as having any bearing upon the question. Our hearty desire is that we should live on good terms with our Irish co-workers in the fishing industry, and each of us prosecute his own calling, there being in our judgment sufficient room for us both, and that we both are doing our fellow-citizens in Great Britain and Ireland a real service in capturing for their consumption such excellent food fishes as herring and mackerel.

" ALEXANDER MAIN, Chairman."

" Signed also at the same time on behalf of Hopeman fishermen, represented by a deputation of their number who were requested to attend the meeting at Burghead and represent them at it.

"ALEXANDER MURRAY, Chairman of Deputation."

Mr. *Nivn.*—The Nairn men have signed the following document for attachment to this paper :—

" We, fishermen in Nairn, having an interest in the Irish herring fishing at Kinsale, at a meeting held in Nairn on Saturday, January 28th, and having read and considered the statement prepared by the Burghead men, adhere to them in it, and authorize the Chairman of our meeting to sign this paper in our name and on our behalf for attachment to the copy to be presented to the Inspectors of Irish Fisheries at their meeting in Burghead on 8th February, 1893.

" JAMES MAIN, Chairman."

A similar document was signed in Lossiemouth, the terms of which are as follows :—

"The fishermen in Lossiemouth having an interest in the Irish herring fishing at Kinsale, at a meeting held in Lossiemouth on 7th February, 1893, having read and considered the statement prepared by the Burghead men, adhere to them in it, and authorize the Chairman of the meeting to sign this paper in our name and on our behalf for attachment to the copy to be presented to the Inspectors of Irish Fisheries, at their meeting in Burghead on 8th February, 1893.

"A. COWIE, Chairman."

I may say that there are two fishermen from each of the villages, Burghead, and Hopeman, and from Nairn, present to give evidence. The Lossiemouth men are all at sea, and they said when they sent their adherence to our statement that the Burghead men would represent them. In the name of the fishermen I have to thank you for coming here to make inquiry into this matter, which affects the fishermen of both nations.

Mr. HORNBY.—Will you examine the witnesses?

Mr. Niven.—I would prefer not.

Mr. HORNBY.—Will you give us the names of the witnesses?

Mr. Niven.—Certainly. Daniel Main and John Ralph, Burghead. I may state for the Commissioners' information that at an informal meeting it was arranged that perhaps one man from each of the villages should be taken.

Mr. HORNBY.—Yes.

Mr. Niven.—One from Burghead, one from Nairn, and one from Hopeman.

Mr. HORNBY.—Of course we really only want to get the evidence of some representative witnesses who command the confidence and respect of their comrades, and who will act as spokesmen for them. We don't want to go over and over the same thing again and again.

Mr. Niven.—These are representative men who have been chosen at meetings of the fishermen called for that special purpose.

Mr. HORNBY.—That is just the very class of men that we want.

Daniel Main sworn; examined by Mr. HORNBY.

1225. Do you live here?—Yes, sir.

1226. Are you the master of a fishing boat?—Yes.

1227. The owner or part owner?—I am owner and master, and have been for forty years, of a fishing boat.

1228. When did you fish off the Irish coast for herrings? How many years were you there?—About twenty years ago.

1229. That was your first time?—Yes.

1230. What was your last time?—Last year.

1231. And how many years did you go between? How many following years?—The four years before last year I was absent; that is all the time I have been absent for twenty years.

1232. Well, now, at what date, about, did you actually commence fishing there?—We always tried to commence if possible at the 1st of May, and I have fished about a fortnight in April one year.

1233. And were you fishing for herrings in that year in the middle of April?—Yes.

1234. Well, when you commenced in April in what condition were the herrings then that you caught?—We found them very good herrings.

1235. What price did you get per mease for them?—We got about the average of 15s. a mease.

1236. At what date was that?—In April.

1237. Were these fish bought by Irish buyers, or by English buyers for the English markets?—By English buyers for the English markets, the most part of them.

1238. As you went on in the season into May did you find the herrings improve in condition, or what?—We always reckoned the 1st of May to be the best quality of herrings.

1239. You think that they were in the best condition then?—Yes, about the first part of May.

1240. What do you call the first part of May, do you mean the 1st day of May up to the 7th or 8th of May?—Yes, they improved then, and we reckoned they were up to their best condition by the 14th of May.

1241. Their prime condition?—Yes, about the 14th of May.

1242. Well, what is your experience—have you taken any undersized mackerel in your nets?—Well, we take very few.

1243. About how many, roughly speaking?—I think 300 or 400 would be a high enough average for what we took at a time, except last year. I never saw so many in any year as last year.

1244. What numbers did you take last year?—About the average I have already stated.

1245. How did you dispose of these mackerel?—We disposed of them both to the English merchants and to the Irish buyers.

1246. What price did you get from the English buyers?—We have sold them as low as 2s. 6d., and as high as 15s. per hundred.

1247. What is the cause of that great variation in price—was it because there was a greater demand at one time than another, or was it that the mackerel were very inferior?—No, according to the demand.

1248. The market price?—Yes, as we find in all fish.

1249. How many of these mackerel would go to a box?—Well, for the most part it is 100 I have seen put into a box. That is the common number.

1250. I am speaking now of the smaller class of mackerel you know? —Yes.

1251. What has been your experience with reference to undersized hake—have you come across them? We never saw any hake that was worth taking any notice of. We have seen them entering one at a time, but they were so few in numbers that we seldom took any notice of them.

1252. When fishing, did you fish off about the same ground as the Irish fishermen fished for mackerel?—No; except it was very dull weather, we scarcely ever saw the mackerel fishermen.

1253. I suppose your idea is conveyed in the reverend gentleman's statement as to the date for commencing to fish? What date do you think you ought to commence to fish?—Well, I think the 1st of May would be the proper time to commence the herring fishing in Kinsale.

1254. Do you suppose that it would pay you and other Scotch fishermen to go to Ireland to commence on the 11th of May? I would not go at all if it was later.

1255. Suppose you were to commence on the 11th?—We were confined last year to the 11th, but it made the time very short.

1256. When did you give up last year?—We left about the 1st of June. I could not say the particular day.

1257. Early in June?—Yes, all the times I have ever been there, the fish always failed about the same time.

1258. About the first week in June, is it?—Yes.

1259. Do you remember any particular year before there were any arrangements come to, when buyers declined to buy fish from you at a certain date? We got that in evidence at the inquiry we held the other day at—

Mr. *Murray.*—Cockenzie.

Mr. HORNBY.—No, I think it was Montrose, was it not, where it was stated that the buyers declined to buy the fish?

Mr. GREEN.—Yes, it was at Montrose.

1260. Mr. HORNBY (to witness).—Did you ever find the buyers declining to take fish from you at a certain date?—No, sir. The first herrings that I caught there, the buyers were as ready to buy them as anything.

1261. How many boats are in the habit of going from Burghead and its immediate vicinity to Kinsale do you know?—I think we would average about eight boats for a year.

1262. Eight?—Yes, sometimes more and sometimes less, but I think that would be a fair average.

1263. Mr. Murray.—But is that from the vicinity, or from Burghead alone?—From Burghead alone.

1264. Mr. Hornsby.—Oh, well then, if you take in these fishing places in the immediate vicinity. Take the Findhorn Fishery District?

Mr. Murray.—We will ask the fishermen from the different districts.

1265. Mr. Hornsby.—Very well, then. You will speak for eight boats from Burghead.

The Witness.—Yes.

Mr. Niven.—It is stated that there are about thirty boats go from the whole district to Ireland.

Mr. Hornsby.—Can we get at what that stretch of district is?

Mr. Niven.—From Lossiemouth to Nairn.

Mr. Wm. Main, fisherman, Nairn.—There would be over fifty boats from Lossiemouth to Nairn.

Mr. Murray.—I estimate them at forty-five.

Mr. Niven.—Better to take that number then.

1266. Mr. Green.—For sixteen years you have been going to Kinsale.

The Witness.—I have been about thirteen years at Kinsale, and the rest of my time at Howth.

1267. When you went there first the buyers were quite ready to take your fish, and give good prices for the first fish?—Yes, sir.

1268. Did you find a difference in the prices you got later?—The prices varied according to the market.

1269. But in some places we got evidence that 6s. per mease was the opening price paid by the buyers, and some got better prices in the early fishing?—Yes.

1270. Can you explain that?—Well, one man might get the one price, and another man another price, according to the time he was there. It is not supposed that the same price is got all the day over.

1271. No. Did you fish from any other part on the South coast of Ireland except Kinsale?—Kinsale, Howth, and Ardglass. These are all the places I have been in, and I have sold the fish from 6s. a mease to £3.16s. a mease in my time.

1272. About what shot of herrings would you make at Kinsale—what was the largest shot of herrings you have got at Kinsale?—Fifty mease.

1273. In a night?—Yes, I had as high as fifty mease.

1274. When you went there first were there any other **boats fishing** herrings besides the Scotch boats?—There were a few **Campbeltown** boats, and there were a few Irish boats.

1275. Well, last year, did the buyers object to take the herrings?—No, sir; there was one buyer insisted on us going down to Queenstown, and he would come down there with stuff for us and sell the fish.

1276. Was that suggestion before the fishing began at Kinsale?—When the Irishmen objected to us coming before the 11th, there was one buyer there who said he would go down and take stock along with him if we would go. We would not go for the sake of keeping peace along with the Irish fishermen.

1277. You would not go?—No, we would not go to keep peace with the Irish fishermen.

1278. But if you were fishing from Queenstown don't you think you would get over part of the difficulty?—It would depend if the buyers would go there. We could fish out of the one place as well as the other if the buyers went there.

1279. If you were fishing from Queenstown, do you think there would be the same objection on the part of the Kinsale men?—I could not say as to that.

1280. One of their objections is that the herring boats come in, and very often give the cargo to a steamer, and the steamer goes away early in the day, and that then there is no steamer for the mackerel?—I don't think that.

1281. Have you ever found that the case?—No, I don't think that.

1282. And you think there would be no use in attempting to shift the herring fishing from Kinsale to another part, in order to get over the difficulty?—No, I don't think it would be any use, and I think it would be a great loss to Kinsale to do it.

1283. Mr. HORNABY.—As a matter of fact, have you read the evidence that was taken at the inquiry at Kinsale?—Yes, sir.

1284. You have seen it?—Yes.

1285. You think the statement therein about the very large takes of immature mackerel are not correct?—Not so far as I have seen, but it may be.

1286. But is it possible that a good, intelligent fisherman like you would not have heard if mackerel were taken in large quantities; it would be a matter of common conversation amongst the Scotch fishermen, would it not?—There were some taken, but I could not say what quantity.

1287. Would you say that 10,000 would be a fair limit in one boat in one night's fishing—do you think that is correct?—It might happen on a day, but it is not a common thing.

1288. Is it possible that it could happen?—It is possible that it could happen.

1289. But it is not probable?—No.

1290. Mr. ROGER.—Have you ever fished at Stornoway?—Yes, sir.

1291. Is there not a close season established there for the herring fishing?—It is by the consent of the fishermen themselves.

1292. They have established a close season?—Yes.

1293. It is to their own interests to do it?—Yes.

1294. And it is not proposed to extend that?—No, I don't think it is.

1295. Beyond Stornoway?—Not as far as I know. We were trying to extend it over the East Coast for our own benefit.

1296. Are you in negotiations with any other fishermen to make a close time all along the East Coast for your own benefit?—Yes, we were trying to get it done for our own benefit, because last year we had too great a quantity of fish.

1297. It would be beneficial for your fishing if you were to have a close season round that coast?—The fishermen seem to think so.

1298. That is owing to the over-quantity got last season?—We had to throw a good quantity into the sea, and gave plenty away for manure.

1299. Don't you think it would be equally beneficial for the Irish fishers to have a close time as you have found it here?—No, it would do away with it altogether to do the same to Ireland. After the month of May there are no fish to be got in Ireland as far as we are acquainted with the shores.

Mr. *Niven.*—Would you kindly allow me to put a question?

Mr. HORNABY.—Surely.

1300. Mr. Niven.—It is not proposed to establish a close time for herring fishing in the interests of any other fishing?—No.

1301. It is not so proposed by you?—No.

1302. And the close time at Stornoway is because of the immaturity of the fish that have been caught there?—Yes, and I believe the buyers are more for it for the sake of the fish than even the fishermen are.

1303. And likewise the idea of a close time too for the East Coast is because of the immaturity of the fish taken before the 15th of July?—Yes, and the over-quantity that we have seen.

1304. Mr. Roche.—How long has the close time been in existence at Stornoway—how many years?—I could not say. It is only a few years.

1305. A few years since?—Yes.

1306. Mr. Green.—Do you think that the close time in Stornoway is owing to the herring schools being broken up by fishing for them too soon? Is that one of the reasons for the close season—that if they are fished for too soon it would break up the schools before they got into the Minch?—Yes, it would break up the schools, but it is not so much for this as because the fish are not up to the proper quality at that time at Stornoway. Every different fishing station varies in its quality of fish at the same season of the year.

1307. Do you think fishing at the mouth of the Minch would break up the schools and prevent them congregating near Stornoway?—Well, it might. I could not say.

1308. Mr. Roche.—What is **the date at Stornoway—the 15th of May?**—Yes.

1309. And what is the proposed date for the East Coast—have you heard of it?—The 10th of July, I think.

1310. For the East Coast?—Yes. Every station, of course, alters its date.

1311. Mr. Green.—The fishing at Stornoway is a spring fishing, is it not?—They fish all round Scotland every day of the year. My boat is there fishing at Stornoway now.

1312. Yes, in spite of the close season being agreed to?—There is no close season now.

1313. There is no close season now at Stornoway?—No, it only includes from a certain day in April to a certain day in May, I think.

1314. But here, on the East Coast?—It is the same.

1315. The close season, then, it is proposed would be from a certain date in the spring sometime?—A certain day in May to a certain day in July for the East Coast.

1316. Mr. Murray.—From a certain day in June you mean?—Oh, yes; I beg your pardon.

1317. Mr. Niven.—What is the quality of the herrings that you get at Kinsale as compared with, perhaps, the best fish that are got at the West Coast—the Barra fish in the month of May?—I would reckon the Kinsale herring fully as good as the Barra fish in the month of May.

1318. Would they be equal to the Barra fish in the month of June, the best season of the year for the Barra fish?—Well, I think they would. They are of very good quality. The Irish fish are about as good quality as I have seen.

1319. In your reply to Mr. Hornsby as to **the quality of the fish at** Kinsale you insisted that from the 1st to the **14th of May was the** season at which they were best?—Yes.

1320. During that fortnight?—Yes.

1321. Do you know if it was the case that there was a close time at

g 2

Stornoway or on the West Coast, enforced statutorily at one time?—I do not think so.

1322. Enforced by law, I mean?—Oh, yes; I remember about 30 years ago there was a close time, but it had to be given up.

1323. What was the date?—The 20th of May.

1324. From the 1st of January?—Yes.

1325. What was the reason for it having to be given up can you tell? —I do not know the particular reason. I suppose it may have been because there were so many different opinions about it. That is the most I can say.

Mr. HORNBY.—Was that close season a mutual arrangement also?

Mr. *Niven*.— No, enforced by Act of Parliament, I understand.

Mr. HORNBY.—I suppose the fact is that the Scotch Board had not the machinery for enforcing the Act of Parliament. I suppose that was it.

Mr. *Murray*.—Oh, yes; we enforced it.

Mr. HORNBY.—Well, was it repealed?

Mr. *Murray*.—Yes, in consequence of the opposition to it from different quarters.

Mr. HORNBY.—How long was that law enforced?

Mr. *Murray*.—About two or three years, I think.

Mr. *Niven*.—Was it the same Act as applied to Lough Fyne?

The *Witness*.—Yes.

William Main, Nairn, sworn; examined by Mr. HORNBY.

1326. You live here—you are a native of this place, are you?—No, Nairn, sir.

1327. You are representing the Nairn men now?—Yes.

1328. Are you the master and owner of a fishing boat?—Yes, sir.

1329. You have fished off Kinsale, I suppose, for herring?—Yes, sir.

1330. When did you first go to Kinsale?—In 1880.

1331. And you have been there every year since?—No, only for six years.

1332. Did you go six years from 1880?—Yes.

1333. You stopped in 1886 then?—Yes.

1334. Well, now, when was the first date, about, that you commenced fishing at Kinsale?—The first year I went there, in 1880, I commenced in the last week of April.

1335. As regards that particular year, what condition did you find the herring in at the end of April there?—Good herring and plenty of them, and owing to that, we went back the next year in the month of March.

1336. For one moment, confine yourself to 1880. What price did you get for those herrings, do you remember—what was the average price?—I think we averaged about £1 a mease.

1337. What would be about the lowest price you got per mease?—15s. I think was the lowest that we got that season.

1338. And your opinion as a practical fisherman is that these herring at that time of year were in prime condition for exportation to the English markets?—They were, sir, especially that season.

1339. They were firm, and would stand salting and all that?—Yes.

1340. Still talking of 1880, did you come across many undersized mackerel?—Very few, and very pleased we were when we saw a few, because they realised good prices then.

1341. What prices, as a matter of fact, did you get for them per hundred?—From 15s. to £1 per hundred.

1842. What was about the greatest quantity that you got at any one fishing?—I have seen one day something about 600 or 700, I think. That was the most I have seen.

1843. With one boat?—Yes.

1844. Now, what would be about the average size of these **mackerel**?—From 10 to 13 inches, off and on, thereabouts.

1845. Did you come across any immature hake?—No.

1846. None?—No.

1847. What distance off the land, as a rule, did you fish herrings?—Well, I have shot from two to twenty miles.

1848. Did you come across the mackerel men there?—No.

1849. You have been talking up to this time about 1880. What was your experience in the remaining five years as regards quality, and what dates did you commence; as a rule, in fact, in 1881, 1882, 1883, 1884, and 1885?—Well, in 1881 we went in the month of March, and we got a very boisterous passage. It would be well on in April before we landed there, and the first time we got to sea we got a good catch of herring. I think we got either 10 or 12 mease.

1850. That would be in April?—Yes.

1851. About what time in April—the middle or the beginning of it?—It was well on to the end of April. There was a long time to wait.

1852. What was your opinion of the condition of the herring in that year when you first started?—They were very good—very fair.

1853. What price, about, did you get in 1881 per mease?—The price was not so good that season at the commencement, but in the last week of April I remember we got the best price we got the whole season. The last week of April and the first week of May were the weeks for the best prices.

1854. What about was the price do you remember?—If I remember right, we got as high as 80s. a mease.

1855. What was the lowest price?—15s.

1856. Have you noticed that the herring improve as the month of May goes on up to a certain date?—Yes.

1857. I want you to give me your own views about this. When do you think the Kinsale herring at its perfection, and would fetch the highest price?—Oh, well, they are about their best in the first and second week of May.

1858. Then about the other years—what was your experience of these other years, to come down to your last?—All round, much about the same.

1859. Your best year was 1880, was it?—The best year was 1881.

1860. Was that because you got a better price or heavier take?—There was a better price—better money.

1861. After 1881, did you find the fishing falling off, or what?—No, it stood up pretty well.

1862. Were the prices lower?—Yes.

1863. But they stood up afterwards?—Yes.

1864. How many boats go from Nairn to Ireland?—The first year I was up, there were only three Nairn boats, and then they increased up to something about twenty the last year I was there.

1865. Have you any idea how many went last season, for instance, from Nairn to Ireland?—Just one boat.

1866. There is one question I want to ask you, more for my own information than for anything else. When you were at Kinsale, did you land your herrings at the same hulk as the mackerel men landed their fish, or had you different hulks?—The same hulk, pretty often.

1367. But was it invariably, or only occasionally. What was the usual practice?—If it were English buyers, the fish were always landed at the same bank, but it it was local buyers, they were landed on shore.

1368. But you had English buyers buying mackerel and herrings at the same date. The statement has been made to us that the Scotch fishermen were delayed at the banks by reason of the mackerel men being there, and consequently they lost a voyage. It was said that the buyers would not take the fish till it was too late, and that then the fish were sold at a sacrifice?—I have seen that, and suffered it myself too. It is my own experience.

1369. On the other hand we have had buyers before us who have given us evidence that there are two distinct staffs of men, one for the mackerel business and the other for the herring, and two different banks. That is what I want to get at. Mr. Green reminds me that that may have occurred since you were there?—Possibly.

1370. What is your idea of a close time—a date before which you should not fish?—I believe in a close time in all fishings.

1371. What would your idea be of a fair time to commence herring fishing off the south-west coast of Ireland?—As late as you could make it, I think, would be the 1st of May. That is my experience the six years I was there.

1372. When do you generally find it imperative to leave there for home?—Generally the first week in June.

1373. Would you consider the 11th of May too late to commence?—It is too short a season for such a long voyage to make from Scotland.

1374. Mr. Ross.—Which route do you take in going to Ireland? Do you go up the Canal?—Yes, up the Caledonian Canal and round the Mull of Kantyre.

1375. Mr. Holdout.—These boats which go to Ireland, assuming that they remained at home, where would they fish at that season of the year—in May say?—They would go to Stornoway to pursue the fishing at home—the fishermen who were fishing now the line and net.

1376. I suppose your nets are about the same size and construction as the nets of the other men from Anstruther and Montrose?—Oh, yes.

1377. Mr. Green.—Have you ever fished at Howth?—Yes.

1378. Were you fishing at Howth the same year as you were at Kinsale?—Yes.

1379. How did the Howth herrings compare with the Kinsale herrings? Were they considered better?—I always thought them better.

1380. Do you mean by better, larger or in better condition?—Better in quality.

1381. Did you ever know of the Kinsale herrings being so soft at the commencement of the season as that they would not bear being packed in salt?—No.

1382. Did you ever hear of them going bad before they reached the English market?—The last season I was there—that was how I left there before the season was done—they said that the quality was not good, and there were no prices for them, and we left Kinsale and went to the Howth fishing.

1383. Was that at the end of the season?—That was about the first weeks in May.

1384. They said the herrings were not good then?—There was no good quality on the ground at the time.

1385. Do you think from your own experience that the herrings fished were of inferior quality?—Yes, they were not so good in quality.

1386. Two fishermen in the body of the hall interposed at this stage, and said they had fished that season, and the herrings were the same all along.

1387. Mr. Niven.—Last season, round the east coast, was the quality of the herrings inferior—that is in the late fishing?—They were pretty fair, I think.

1388. What was the quality of the fish at Aberdeen?—They were of very poor quality them.

1389. Was that the case all the year round?—All the year.

1390. Then sometimes there will be good quality and sometimes an inferior quality of fish?—Oh, yes. On the same grounds at the same season of the year there are different shoals of fish not of the same quality. It is not the date that makes the quality of the fish at all.

1391. Mr. Green.—You got as good herrings then as at the beginning of the season?—Yes.

1392. Mr. Niven.—You spoke of fishing at Stornoway. Have you fished also at Barra?—Yes.

1393. The two ports are from 80 to 100 miles separate?—Yes; it is Barra I mean when I said Stornoway.

1394. That is the last fishing, though?—Yes, I should say so.

1395. And Barra fish are better quality on the whole than Stornoway fish?—Yes.

1396. Then the statement made by the former witness as to Kinsale fish being about equal in quality to Barra fish would mean that they were superior to Stornoway?—They are.

1397. And at an earlier season of the year than you are accustomed to get fish at Stornoway?—Yes.

Alexander Main sworn; examined by Mr. Hornsby.

1399. Where do you come from?—Hopeman, sir.

1400. Are you the owner and master of a fishing vessel?—Yes.

1401. How often have you been at Kinsale fishing?—Four times.

1402. What years were they?—That was in 1882, 1883, 1884, and last year.

1403. Well, now, what time, as a rule, during these years have you commenced to fish?—As a rule about the 1st of May, or possibly within the first week of May during the first years.

1404. That was up to 1884?—Yes.

1405. What condition did you consider the herring that you took in the early part of May?—I considered them very good.

1406. What price did you get per mease?—Varying from 17s. to 26s. Possibly sometimes 30s.

1407. I suppose I may say varying from 17s. to 30s.?—Yes. I may state that there was one year that we sold them for 1s. That was in 1884, the year that the buyers stood out against us and we had to leave.

1408. That was the year—we have got it in evidence—that they refused to buy from you? Yes, and we had to sell them for manure that year. That is the explanation of the price.

1409. Well, now, what time do you think the herring off that coast are in the best condition for the market? Well, I should say, to the best of my judgment, about the first half of May. They are in very good condition then.

1410. What is about the best take that you have had in any of those years?—The best take I have had was 60 mease.

1411. Were they all good fish?—All good fish. That was last year.

1412. By-the-by, what time did you commence to fish last year?—On the 11th.

1413. Of May?—Yes.

1414. This last year was your best year?—No, I had a good year in 1888.

1415. What was about your capture then?—The whole catch.

1416. No, your best take?—I think it was about 45 mease.

1417. And did the price over you got last year compare with the price that you got in other years?—It was lower last year as a rule.

1418. Did you find large quantities of immature mackerel getting into your nets last year?—Occasionally.

1419. Did you notice an increase last year over the previous years?—No, not as a rule. There were occasionally one day or which the catch was larger.

1420. What was about the greatest quantity of small mackerel that you got?—I would say about 1,000.

1421. You got 1,000?—Yes.

1421a. In one haul?—Yes.

1422. What would be the average size of these mackerel?—They would range from 10 to 13 and occasionally 14 inches.

1423. What price did you get for these per hundred from the buyers?—The day that we caught the most mackerel they were very cheap. We sold them to Mr. Flynn for 6s.

1424. Have you any idea of what Mr. Flynn did with them? Did he send them off to the English markets?—Yes, he did.

1425. Have you any reason to suppose that any other of the Scotch boats got about the same quantity?—I could not say, I did not observe the others. It was a late night that night, and everybody was so busy with themselves that I did not observe.

1426. Have you come across much immature hake?—Very few, scarcely worth noticing—last year especially.

1427. When you fish herrings off the Kinsale coast, do you come across the Irishmen fishing mackerel?—No, I never came into collision with them but once, and that was in calm weather. I think that was in 1882.

1428. How far off the land, as a rule, do you fish?—As a rule from eight to twenty-four miles. We generally went off twenty-three or twenty-four miles last year, as we found the best fishing grounds at that distance. There was good fishing got inshore from about eight to twelve miles, but we rather preferred going twenty-four.

1429. Well, what is your idea as to a good date to fix to commence herring-fishing off the south-west coast of Ireland?—I think 1st May would be a very suitable season both for quality of fish and demand for them.

1430. What is your opinion about the 11th of May?—If we could not get the 1st we would have to be satisfied with the 11th.

1431. Supposing that the 11th was the time fixed, do you think that many Scotch boats would continue to go to Kinsale?—I believe a good few would be inclined to go.

1432. Have you ever fished off the English Coast at Lowestoft?—Yes.

1433. How have you got on there? You get mackerel fishing there too?—Yes, occasionally.

1434. Are the two fishings carried on simultaneously there in a harmonious manner?—Yes, as a rule, to the best of my judgment. The mackerel fishers keep inside there, generally to the south side of the herring fishers, but I have seen them together occasionally.

1435. How many years have you fished off Lowestoft and on that coast?—About seven years.

1436. Have you met many of the Lowestoft boats at Kinsale?—No, very few. I have seen one or two, I think, mackerel boats especially.

1437. Mr. Green.—Have you been fishing from any other part of the Irish coast besides Kinsale?—I have fished at Howth and Ardglass occasionally.

1438. Were you fishing last year at Howth?—Yes.

1439. What takes did you make there?—Very little, I think. I tried it twice. We had fourteen mease one day, that was the most we got there.

1440. Were there good prices?—No, 14s. I think, were realised for them.

1441. Was there good competition among the buyers?—No there was no competition, that was the reason why the prices were so low.

1442. The herrings were very good?—Well I have seen them better at Howth. They were very inferior last year.

1443. But comparing the herrings that you got 30s. for at Kinsale, were the herrings you got at Howth as good, and did they fetch as good a price?—No.

1444. They were not as good?—No.

1445. Have you fished for a great number **of years at Howth?**—Three years.

1446. When was the first time you were there?—It was in 1882.

1447. Were the fish good then?—Yes.

1448. Have you seen any change in the fish there—in the amount of fish caught?—Yes, a great change last year.

1449. A falling off?—Yes, a falling **off. In 1882, I think, I saw as** high as 96 mease landed at Howth.

1450. By one boat?—Yes, I remember **of one boat that had over** 100 mease, and sold them at 5½s.

1451. The Kinsale herring fishing **was going on that year, was it** not?—Yes.

1452. Do you think there is any truth in the idea that the fishing at Kinsale breaks up schools before they get to the Irish Channel?—I could not say. The fish have a habit of going to the eastward at Kinsale. We generally saw that, and we followed them to the eastward.

1453. When you got the first shots at Kinsale did you find the herrings more to the westward?—Yes, as a rule. Last year especially the herrings were very permanent. They stayed a long time on the one spot, but they inclined to the eastward, we considered.

1454. Did you make any shots eastward on your way home?—Not except Howth.

1455. What time did you consider it to be the close season at Stornoway?—The 15th is the close season at Stornoway at the present time.

1456. From what date?—From the 15th of May.

1457. When do they begin fishing?—They are fishing there now.

Mr. Niven.—The 15th of April is the date at which the close time begins.

Mr. Green.—It begins then?

Mr. Niven.—Yes, and lasts one month.

1458. Mr. Green.—Are you anxious for a close season on your own coast?

The Witness.—I would, for our own benefit.

1459. What length of close season do you think would be sufficient?—Well, we think it might be from a certain day in April to the end of May.

1460. Mr. *Niven.*—To the end of May or 1st of June. Is it not the case that the fish you get round the coast here—take the Moray Firth for one spot—in the first of June are scarcely worth taking?—Yes.

1461. Poor in quality and in price?—Very immature.

1462. Then, do you happen to know anything about what the quality of the fish round the Aberdeenshire coast may be?—They are equally the same.

1463. So that a close time as proposed by you is really in the interests of the food supply of the nation?—Yes.

1464. Then there would be a fair quality of fish had, and a remunerative price obtained?—Yes.

1465. In fishing at Lowestoft, do you get mackerel in your nets?—Occasionally. I have got as high as 600, 700, and 800.

1466. And in taking them into the harbour there and exposing them for sale you were welcomed with them as much as if you had been a regular mackerel fisher?—Just the same.

1467. Any trouble arising through that?—No trouble whatever. We never found any trouble with mackerel in Lowestoft. There were always ready disposals.

1468. Mr. GREEN.—How long did you remain at Howth when fishing there?—Last year we stayed about eight days.

1469. And you don't think it would pay you to remain there?—No; it was for that we left.

1470. Was it because you were anxious to get home to your own fishing?—Not exactly, but it was because it did not pay us that we left.

1471. Were there many of the local men fishing?—A good few, but not so many as I have seen.

John Ralph, Burghead, sworn; examined by Mr. HORNBY.

1472. Are you the owner and master of a fishing vessel?—Yes.

1473. How many years have you been going to Kinsale?—Ten years.

1474. One after the other?—Yes.

1475. What is the last year you have been there?—Three years ago.

1476. That would be 1890?—Yes.

1477. What is your usual practice? Upon what day did you commence to fish actually?—The 1st of June.

1478. Mr. *Murray.*—May, you mean?—Yes, the 1st of May.

1479. Mr. HORNBY.—What condition was the first shot of herrings in that you got on the 1st of May?—They were in good condition.

1480. Would you, as a skilled fisherman, consider them in first-class condition for the English market?—Yes.

1481. Were there any proportion of them not so good? In what condition was the great bulk?—The herrings were very good for the market.

1482. Every year did you commence about the same date?—Generally, always about the same date.

1483. About the 1st of May?—Yes, when we reached there.

1484. And your experience is that for ten years at the 1st May the herring you got were in prime condition for the market?—Yes.

1485. What price did you get, now, for these early takes in May, as an average?—15s. to £1.

1486. It varies?—Yes.

1487. When do you get your heaviest takes, when you begin, or when the month advances a little?—It is commonly about the first that we get the heaviest takes—for the first week or fortnight.

1488. But did you find them increasing as the month of May went on; that is to say did you find that you got heavier fishing on the 15th of May than on the 1st of May?—Just at times.

1489. Did you come across in any one of these ten years much miniature mackerel in your nets?—I daresay sometimes we got a few, and sometimes not.

1490. What is the greatest number you have taken in one year? During the whole of your fishing in any one season there, what would be the bulk of the mackerel that you took?—About 1,000 was the highest shot I ever saw of mackerel.

1491. Supposing you remained at Kinsale for three weeks or a month, what do you suppose would the take of mackerel amount to in that time?—Not very much. Perhaps you may get them one day in the season, and sometimes not at all.

1492. Could you not give me a rough idea as to what quantity of that fish you would take?—About fifty mackerel a shot.

1493. Mr. Gibson.—Is that the average?—Yes.

Mr. Nixon.—Taking twenty shots that would **amount to 1,000** mackerel according to his judgment.

1494. Mr. Horsac.—What price did you get for these mackerel per 100?—Commonly about 10s.

1495. Were they sold to English buyers or to local buyers?—When we got any quantity of them the Englishmen bought them, and when we only got a few we sold them to the local buyers. I think there were two buyers from Cork who used to come there, but I forget their names.

1496. What about immature hake? Have you come across them in any quantities?—No, I did not see any of them.

1497. How far off the land did you fish as a rule?—From ten to twenty miles, sometimes five miles. That is when you get a south-east coast.

1498. Did you come across the men fishing mackerel when you were shooting your nets?—No.

1499. Are they away from you or near you?—Yes; **they are away** south.

1500. What is your idea about the proper time to commence herring fishing off the Irish coast?—I think about the 1st of May.

1501. Supposing it was fixed at the 11th of May would you go there?—I might try it for a year as an experiment and see how it would suit.

1502. Mr. Nixon.—Have you ever fished in April at Kinsale?—One year.

1503. What was **your experience then**?—**There were plenty of her-**ring to be got then.

1504. About what time did you begin?—About the latter end.

1505. Say about the 20th?—Yes, about the 20th.

1506. And if you had been there earlier do you think you would have got fish?—Yes, I think we would get fish there now.

1507. Do you remember the proposal in our village here to make some alteration in connection with the observance of the Sacrament of the Lord's Supper, to enable the men to go away earlier, say about the end of March. Do you remember ever hearing that talked about?—Yes, I have been away before the Sacrament.

1508. Yes, but did ever you hear it mooted that there should be a change made in connection with the observance of the ordinance, so that the men might get away about the end of March, or the beginning of April?—Yes, I remember that quite well.

1509. That was entirely on account of the men finding it profitable to them to fish in April in Ireland?—Yes.

1510. And they would have gone as early as it was possible for them to go?—Yes, that is quite correct.

1511. Is there a kind of fish, the black fish, you get in your nets?—I have seen them, but I do not suppose they are hake.

1512. Are these an edible fish?—No, we never ate any of them.

1513. Do you know of any fishing at all, that a close time was instituted in connection with it, in order to protect another fishing?—No.

1514. Have you ever heard of anything of the kind, that a close time was instituted for one kind of fishing in order to protect another fishing being carried on at the same time, and in the same year?—No, I never heard of it.

1515. Mr. Carson.—All these ten years that you went to Ireland, some years were good and some were bad?—Yes, sir.

1516. Could you tell us, now, what years were good years for the herring fishing, and what years were bad? Was 1880 a good year?—The first year was far and away the best.

1517. Was 1881 good or bad?—Good.

1518. Was 1882 good?—Yes.

1519. Was 1883 good?—Yes.

1519a. And 1884?—Yes.

1520. 1885 was as good?—Yes.

1521. And 1886?—Yes.

1522. And 1887?—No, I think 1887 was bad.

1523. And 1888?—Bad, too. The last three years that I have been there were bad.

1524. Well, was it because those years were bad that you gave up going?—Yes.

1524a. How were they bad? Was it that you did not catch so much, or was it that the price was low?—I think the fish were not on the ground.

1525. You did not make the same takes?—Not the same takes.

1526. From what you heard fishermen saying who have been there last year, would you be inclined to go this coming season?—No.

1527. Was that last year you were there a good season?—Yes. The last year I was there, I was up as far as Baltimore.

1528. Did you fish from Baltimore?—I had two shots.

1529. And sold the fish at Baltimore?—Yes.

1530. Did you fish from Castletownsend?—We were in Castletown, Youghal, and Dunmore. We began at the Tuscar, and fished up to Dunmore.

1531. That was in 1890?—Yes, we got a good deal of fish at the Tuscar, and came into Baltimore, and could not sell them.

1532. Was that to the westward of the Tuscar?—It was west of the Tuscar.

1533. Did many of the boats fish down in the west that year?—No, I was about a fortnight or three weeks after the others. The blue sharks began, and we had to go off the ground.

1534. About what time did the blue sharks begin?—About the middle of June.

1535. Mr. Niven.—About the middle of June, would you not be on your way home?—Yes, we were forced to go home.

1536. And was that from Howth or Kinsale?—No, that was from Dunmore.

1537. During the first part of May, you find the best time for fishing herrings, do you not?—Yes.

1538. What about the last fortnight of May? Are the herrings anything plentiful during that time, or do they fall off?—They fall off.

1539. Coming, say, to the fourth week of May, what kind of takes have you made in any of these ten years that you spoke of having been in Ireland?—Some years you would get them, and some years not; If a man hits them, he gets them, and if not he misses them.

1540. Have you come across sharks or dog fish in the end of May?—Yes.

1541. You have got them, then?—Yes.

1542. Were they plentiful?—Yes.

1542a. As plentiful, say, as in the Lowes fishing?—Not the same kind of dogs. They are larger. What they call blue sharks.

1543. And they are equally destructive, or more destructive than the dog fish?—More destructive than the dog fish to the nets.

1544. In the month of June, what have you ever done? Have you tried the fishing at Kinsale in the month of June?—Yes.

1545. And what did you make of it then?—Nothing.

1546. Would that answer apply practically to the four weeks of May?—I think it would.

James Macpherson, Hopeman, sworn; examined by Mr. Hennesy.

1547. Are you the owner and master of a fishing boat?—I have been part owner for over twenty years.

1548. How many years have you been going to Ireland?—I was four years at Kinsale.

1549. What four years were these?—I commenced in 1880, and omitted 1881.

1550. You did not go in 1881?—No, sir.

1551. In 1882, 1883, and 1884 you were there?—Yes.

1552. What time did you commence actually to fish herrings?—We arrived on the 5th of May and commenced operations upon the 8th of May.

1553. Was that about the same date that you always commenced, or was it only for one of these years?—No, last season we commenced about the 25th of April.

1554. In 1880 when did you commence?—The 5th of May we arrived.

1555. You arrived on the 5th of May?—Yes, and commenced on the 8th of May.

1556. In 1882 then?—We commenced on 1st May that year. There were four boats from Hopeman.

1557. Well, then, 1883?—We commenced about the same time.

1558. And in 1884?—We commenced fishing on the 25th of April, in 1884.

1559. That was your last year?—Yes, sir.

1560. What condition did you find the herring in when you commenced fishing?—Fair.

1561. When you say fair, do you mean that they were middling or do you mean that they were prime marketable fish?—There was room for them to improve.

1562. Does that apply to each year in May. The early part in May was best; did it apply to only one year?—As a rule the 1st of May. There was room for them to improve up to the middle of May. They got to their prime about the middle of May.

1563. But these herrings that you took then on 1st of May were they in sufficiently good condition for exporting to the English markets? Were they firm enough for packing and so on?—Oh, yes, sir.

1564. Did you come across many immature mackerel in any of these years?—Very few.

1565. What about hake?—We saw none, hardly. **I saw six large** hakes one day, but that was all I saw for the season.

1566. Which of these years from 1880 to 1884 was your best year at Kinsale?—1882 was the best year.

1567. Was that as regards both capture and price?—The prices were about the same.

1568. What about the average price per mease in 1882?—The price ranged from 15s. up to 20s.

1569. Were you engaged then fishing on your own behalf?—No, sir.

1570. What would you think of a close time fixing the fishing to commence on the 11th of May at Kinsale?—I should think it would make the fishing there too limited to commence it on the 11th of May.

1571. That is to say you think your season would be too short a one?—Too short altogether.

1572. What date would you propose?—Well, I would suppose about the first of May. Longer than that I would not think of going myself at all.

1573. You would not go?—No.

1574. How many boats as a rule go from Hopeman?—There were about 25 one year, but as a rule, taking them on an average about 12 or 15 boats.

1575. Going every year?—Yes, about 12 boats is an average.

1576. How far off the shore did you fish?—From seven miles to twenty miles, but I have shot as near as two miles. The former, however, was the general distance.

1577. At any of these distances did you get amongst **the mackerel** men?—No, sir.

1578. Have you fished at Lowestoft?—Yes, sir.

1579. What is your experience of fishing herrings there?—Well, I have got mackerel. The first year I went up was in 1880 and I have got as high as 1,000 mackerel in the nets, and they sold about 25s. a hundred.

1580. What comparison would these mackerel that you got there bear to the Kinsale mackerel?—Oh, they were larger in size at Lowestoft.

1581. The Lowestoft mackerel were better?—Yes, by far.

1582. Was there any idea there amongst the local fishermen that your fishing for herring was injuring their branch of fishing?—Oh, none whatever. For instance, I was there last year and there was a mackerel boat shooting inside of the herring fishing boats. He was fishing for mackerel but when he went to haul he got nothing but clean herring—large herring—with mackerel nets. He could not haul his nets out amongst them.

1583. Have you ever fished anywhere else off the Irish coast besides Kinsale?—I have tried the fishing at Dunmore.

1584. What did you do at Dunmore?—I shot off Dungarvan and landed forty mease at Dunmore.

1585. What date would that be?—That would be about the 12th of June. We were doing nothing at Kinsale and we left—two boats—and shot on the route.

1586. What price did you get?—15s. per mease.

1587. How many Scotch boats were there fishing?—There were four or five boats when we were there, but the fish they landed were very immature, not the same quality at all. They shot away to the south-east.

1588. Not the same quality?—No, not the same quality as we had away to the westwards. They shot their nets going to Hirwih off the Tuscar and got small fish, very immature. The fish that we got off Dungarvan were very large. There was only one buyer there and that was the reason why the price was so low.

1589. And there was no competition?—No.

1590. Mr. Green.—What is your experience in fishing right through the season? Do you get sometimes a shot of herrings that are in worse condition and then another shot may be of much larger and better condition?—Some days better and some days worse, but as a rule when we fish the size of the fish is according to the size of the mesh.

1591. Have you different sizes of meshes in your ling?—Some men are sometimes abler to get new nets than others, according to the age of the nets; and the meshes are always larger.

1592. The old nets are more shrunk?—Yes.

1593. Did you see many large mackerel dropping out of your nets when hauling them in?—Very few.

1594. Do you remember any of the herrings you got at Kinsale being so soft that they would not bear salting?—No, sir, I never knew that in my experience.

1595. Nor never heard **of the** herrings you got being rejected **in** Liverpool?—No, sir.

1596. Do you think all that you got if properly handled, were sure to reach the English market in good condition?—I am sure that they were properly handled by us. But what way they were handled after they were landed I could not say.

1597. Mr. Niven.—In fishing off Kinsale have you sometimes come across large shoals of fish and sometimes smaller?—Sometimes.

1598. About what size?—Well, the size would be about eleven inches or thereabouts. From ten to eleven inches. As I said already it depended upon the size of the mesh that we had. If it was a narrow mesh we would get smaller fish.

1599. Do you not also in connection with the fishing there, as in the fishing round our own coast here, sometimes get a better quality of fish which would take the trade marks in the salting season here—those which would take the mattie brand and those which would take the crown brand?—I have seen them here that they would take the crown brand amongst immature fish, but very few. I have often seen that the thicker they are sometimes they are the smaller fish.

1600. You mean that the more numerous the shoal the fish are the smaller?—Yes.

1601. Then you get sometimes fish of better quality off the Irish coast, and sometimes not so good?—I have seen that in my experience.

1602. Have you ever got any mackerel in Scotland?—Very few. Two or three at a time was the most that I have ever seen.

1603. Comparing them with that you took at Kinsale, would they be anything like the Kinsale mackerel?—They were larger.

1604. As large as at Lowestoft or inferior?—Just about the same size as at Lowestoft.

1605. Mr. Green.—Supposing these herrings you catch at Kinsale were cured, what brand do you think they would take?—I would say about the medium size.

1606. What would that be—matties?—Full crown matties.

1607. That would be about the size of the fish that you catch?—Yes.

1608. Mr. Niven.—Your nets will shrink after two or three years backing from thirty-two to thirty-four meshes?—After they have been three years working there are only thirty-four rows per yard.

1009. They are so sharp then, at that time, that if a herring gets its nose into them there is no chance of its getting off?—None.

1010. They will take big as well as little fish?—Yes, they are so sharp. The wide nets that they have will take little fish.

1011. But on the whole, the quality that you get there is superior to the cuttle brand on the coast here?—Oh, yes, in my experience I think they are of better quality and stronger fish.

1012. Would you compare them with the Stornoway fish? Last year at Stornoway, I think they were better in quality?—I had not been in the habit of fishing at Stornoway until last year, but they told me it was an exceptional year for good quality.

1013. Have you fished at Barra?—Yes, for a long time.

1014. Compare the Barra quality in the month of May with what you get at Kinsale in the same month?—I would say much about the same for years.

1015. The Barra herring is a longer kind of fish, but it is of the same quality as the Kinsale fish? It is of a fairly good quality?—Yes, it is a fair quality.

Alexander Main, Nairn, sworn; examined by Mr. HORNSBY.

1016. Are you the owner and master of a fishing vessel?—Part owner, sir.

1617. How many years have you fished off the Irish coast?—Seven years.

1618. What seven years were those?—From 1880 to 1887.

1619. At what date did you commence to fish as a rule?—Well, sir, we took no particular notice of any date to commence there. We always left home on the 1st of April, and if we got a very good passage we commenced as soon as we landed there in April.

1620. What is the earliest date at which you have ever fished at Kinsale?—I believe I fished it on the 12th April.

1621. You could not say what year that was?—The year, I think, was 1882.

1622. What did you do that year?—We did very well, sir.

1623. What condition did you find the fish in that you took on 12th April?—The fish were very good.

1624. What price did you get?—We got good prices, from 15s. to 30s.

1625. Do you consider that as the time goes on, getting into May, the fish improved in condition?—I could not say so much about that. Of course they improve up to the 1st of May, but I could not say much about their improvement after that date.

1626. Have you come across many of these immature mackerel?—Yes, a good few, sir, and very glad to get them at times, because we always realized money for them when we got them. I do not see why a Scotchman should not catch them as well as an Englishman and a Manx man. We go there to make money.

1627. There is a good deal of common sense in that. What is the greatest quantity of mackerel that you have got?—Sometimes 600, and sometimes none at all.

1628. What price as a rule did you get per 100?—About 15s. a 100.

1629. Did you get any that were unsaleable?—No, sir, never.

1630. You never got any that were purchased for manure?—No, sir, never.

1631. And how about immature hake? Have you come across

much of them?—No, we got altogether one or two at a time. They were small hake.

1632. About what distance from land have you been in the habit of fishing at Kinsale?—Well, it varied from four to twenty miles, and sometimes twenty-five miles, just according to how we found the fish.

1633. You never came across these mackerel boats, did you?—No, sir, we always tried to keep clear of them, and gave them a good wide berth.

1634. What is your idea as to fixing a date to commence fishing off the Irish coast—that part of it which you visit? –My idea, sir, is if we are to get the fish there at all we ought to be allowed to fish on the 1st of May, because later than that it would be excluding Scotch fishermen altogether. The herring begin to decay after the middle of May. The best takes we have always obtained were got in the first of the season.

1635. Speaking for yourself now, would you give up going to Ireland —as a matter of fact, rather, you have given it up—but would you go to Ireland again for the purpose of the herring fishing off the south-west coast if you could not commence before the 1st of May?—Not me. I would not be inclined to go at all.

1636. Have you fished off Lowestoft?—Yes, sir.

1637. Have you taken mackerel there when fishing for herrings?—Yes, we have.

1638. In large quantities?—Well, we got as high as 600 and 700 sometimes.

1639. About the same as you got in Ireland?—The very same.

1640. What was the quality of the mackerel?—Very good, sir—small and big—just mixed.

1641. What price did you get for them at Lowestoft?—Sometimes £1 and 2s. per hundred according to the demand.

1642. Mr. GREEN.—What month is it that you fish in at Lowestoft?—In November and December.

1643. Mr. *Murray.*—October, surely?—Oh, yes, October. and November.

1644. Mr. GREEN.—Are you able by going to different places to keep on fishing for herring nearly all the year through?—Yes, sir.

1645. At this time of year you can catch herrings on your own coast?—Yes.

1646. And then you prefer to go to the south of Ireland?—Yes, sir.

1647. And when that is over where would you go?—Down to the east coast.

1648. The east coast of what?—Of Scotland.

1649. And fish there until when?—Until sometime about September.

1650. And then you go to Lowestoft?—Yes, sir.

1651. And that finishes the year?—Yes, sir.

1652. Out of all the fishings which do you look upon as the most remunerative?—Our east coast fishing we always depend upon most.

1653. Is that the summer fishing?—Yes, sir.

1654. Have you been fishing for mackerel anywhere else except off the Irish coast?—I have never fished for mackerel.

1655. I beg your pardon, I mean fished for herrings?—Yes, I have fished in Scotland, England, and Ireland. I have been round to Sheephaven.

1656. Have you fished off the Donegal coast?—Yes.

1657. What year was that?—There are no fish to be found there but wild beasts and seadogs.

1658. What year was that, I am asking?—I think that was in the year 1879.

H

1659. Did you go further west than Sheephaven?—We went up to Ardglass.

1660. From Ardglass you went to Sheephaven?—No, we went from Sheephaven to Ardglass.

1661. Where did you shoot when you were at Sheephaven? Did you shoot off Tory Island?—Just beside Tory Island.

1662. Did you get many herrings?—No.

1663. Were you line fishing at the same time?—No, we were not at the lines.

1664. Did you remain long there?—We stopped a fortnight I think; a week too long.

Mr. *Murray.*—That exhausts the evidence here, sir.

Mr. HORNSBY.—We will consider the evidence taken at all the different places in Scotland along with the evidence that we have taken in Ireland. It may be necessary for us to take some further evidence in other places, but of course we will consider the evidence as a whole, and our earnest desire is to arrive at some conclusion which without driving the Scotchmen away from Irish waters will still afford a certain amount of protection to the fishers in these waters. It is very hard to please everybody, but we must try and do our best in the matter. We are very anxious that it should not for a moment be supposed that it is at all our intention to legislate for one class of fishing as against another; but our object in this inquiry is to arrive at some conclusion which will be for the benefit of the fishers as a whole and not as a purely local question as between two different classes of fishermen. Upon these lines we will endeavour to arrive at some solution of the question. We are very much obliged to the reverend gentleman here for the assistance he has given us, and to the fishermen for their orderly conduct here to-day as has been the case elsewhere.

Mr. *Nixon.*—Allow me in the name of the fishermen in the Findhorn District to thank you, Mr. Hornsby, and your colleagues in this inquiry for coming here and making inquiry respecting this matter. We feel that we have indeed received a great kindness in the Inspectors of the Irish Fisheries coming to Scotland to make this inquiry, and that we have been received, as it were, into a confidence that we had no reason to expect. Our men here, and the others with whom I have spoken, have expressed themselves as highly pleased indeed that you should have considered them, and have asked their experience in connection with the matter of their profession round your coasts, to enable you to come to some judgment. Of course we can only hope as you yourself have indicated that some solution of this problem will be arrived at which will bring peace and good will to all the fishermen around these coasts.

CAMPBELTOWN INQUIRY.

Town Hall, Campbeltown,

Tuesday, February 14th, 1893.

Her Majesty's Inspectors of Irish Fisheries—William S. Green (in the Chair), and Cecil Roche, Esq., B.L.—held an Inquiry this day in the Town Hall, Campbeltown, at three o'clock, afternoon, pursuant to public notice. There was a large attendance.

Mr. Green said—We have come here to-day in accordance with a wish that was expressed by several gentlemen in Scotland with regard to this Inquiry we have been holding about the herring fishing and the mackerel fishing on the South Coast of Ireland. I will read the notice, "Whereas it has been represented that the custom of fishing for herrings off the South Coast of Ireland before the 1st June in each year is detrimental to the mackerel fisheries off said coast, and as fishermen from Scotland are interested in the question, the Inspectors of Irish Fisheries hereby give notice that they will hold inquiries into the matter at the following places in Scotland." We have come here to-day knowing that some of you come to Kinsale in the spring, and we will be very glad if you will give us any information you can, and whatever evidence you consider pertinent to the subject, to enable us to arrive at a decision, and if possible to settle this very long vexed question. If any persons here wish to be examined as witnesses they may come forward and we will be glad to hear them. Whether will we take the evidence ourselves, or will any magistrate or anybody undertake the case for them?

Bailie Paul.—On behalf of the fishermen here, and in the absence of the Provost who could not be here, we give the Commission a very hearty welcome—knowing that they will do what will tend to bring back the prosperous days of the Kinsale fishing. Our fishermen here are all practical men. We have amongst us also Councillors who are real practical fishermen—Councillor Rae, Ex-Councillor Campbell, and Councillor Ronald Robertson—these are all men whose opinions are worth something. I have no doubt if you call upon them and ask them to make any statement, they will be able to throw some light on the subject. We are very much obliged to the Commission for coming here.

Robert Rae sworn—examined by Mr. Green.

1665. Do you wish to make a statement from your own experience?—I may make a short statement or you can question me as you wish. I have been in the habit of going to Kinsale since the year 1879. That was my first herring fishing. In that season we started on the 7th May to fish, and we got fish the very first day—that is, herrings. In the following year we thought we would start a little earlier, and

H 2

we arrived there in the end of April, to start fishing on the 1st day of
May. In the very first shot—I recollect it—it was a very thick night
—we got no less than forty meas of very fine herrings. Mr. Michael
Paul was the gentleman who gave us £2 per mease. He was the man
who bought the herrings during the season, and he afterwards told me
he had done very well, and made a very good profit. And in my experience I think the 1st of May would be a reasonable time to start the
herring fishing at Kinsale. On the second or third year after going
there, I forget which, there was a slight difference got up between us
and the Kinsale fishermen about the price of mackerel. Sir Thomas
Brady and others came down and had a meeting in a meeting-house
in Kinsale with both the Irish fishermen and the Scotch fishermen.
There was a difference of opinion between the two parties as to what
the date should be, and we, the Scotch fishermen, were in the minority.
We were taken into an ante-room by the Commission and we were
asked if we would accede to the 10th May. In consequence of the
little slight difference between us we did accede, and then, of course,
the Kinsale fishermen when they were told what we had acceded to
they agreed to that. It was a mutual agreement between the fishermen
and the Irish Board at that particular time. The 1st May or from the
1st to the 10th May is the time that should be arrived at. In my experience I have fished on to the 10th or 17th June from Kinsale as far
up as Dungarvon, and in the last fishing I had half a hundred small
herrings and half a hundred mackerel.

1666. How many years have you gone to Kinsale?—I went from 1873
up to 1883, and then afterwards to Bantry, Smerwick, and round that
coast up to 1887. I have been going to Ireland for thirty years—to
Howth, Kinsale, and round as far as Shannon.

1667. Did you commence as a herring fisher?—Yes.

1668. Did you keep herring fishing all the time?—We started
mackerel fishing in 1879 and kept up that.

1669. Did you stop fishing for herrings and begin fishing for
mackerel?—Not for some time. We began with our herring nets. We
were not successful one year and gave it up altogether; and then we
fished till the first day of June, or about that date, for mackerel and
then came to Howth and fished herrings there until the Howth fishing
failed, and then we went to Aberdeen and Orkney and Shetland for the
late herring fishing.

1670. Did the value of the herring fishing decrease in the last years?
—Yes.

1671. You did not give up the herring fishing on account of having
got out of herring nets?—No, not at all.

1672. Why did you give up the herring fishing?—Because we found
it did not pay after the mackerel fishing finished.

1673. Why did you change to the mackerel train from the herring
train?—Because we considered it better mackerel fishing from the 1st
March till the end of May. That was three months fishing mackerel.

1674. During the time the Scotch boats are fishing for herrings you
think the mackerel fishing is more valuable?—I thought so at that
time.

1675. Your actions showed it?—Yes.

1676. When you were fishing for herrings did you get many small
mackerel?—A few; not many.

1677. Did you catch anything to sell?—Yes, the most ever I saw was
two dozen. I have seen half a dozen, and I have seen none at all.

1078. Mr. ROCHE.—Did you get them yourself?—No, but in one of our boats.

1079. Mr. GARRR.—What did you get for the half box of small mackerel?—I could not tell you. They gave so much. There were two of our boats fishing. They sold at the same price as I got for any mackerel out of my mackerel nets.

1680. Do you ever remember getting any small hake?—No, I do not; I have seen a few—sometimes a dozen, sometimes half a dozen.

1081. Have you seen many large mackerel fall out of the nets?—A few, but they were not well caught in the nets.

1682. Those mackerel would have to be killed?—Undoubtedly.

1683. And they would sink?—Yes.

1084. From your experience as a mackerel fisher do you think the herring fishing injurious to the mackerel fishing?—I do not, sir.

1085. And, as a mackerel fisher, you would like to see the herring fishing going on?—I would; but not sooner than the 1st of May.

1086. Mr. ROCHE.—Why do you say that?—I will tell you my reason. I think it would practically have a little influence in reducing the price of the mackerel earlier in the season. But on the other hand, I would consider it to be a great drawback to prevent fishing for good wholesome herrings fit for human food, and allow them to go waste from 1st May till say the 10th June.

1687. Mr. GARRR.—What was your experience of the condition of the herrings got about the 1st May?—Splendid fish.

1688. Did you sometimes get inferior fish?—Oh, yes.

1689. Did you sometimes get a shot of very inferior fish—fish that would not bear salting?—Oh, no, I never got that.

1090. You never heard of any fish of yours being rejected?—Never.

1691. Then when you were discussing the matter before with the Howth men did they object to the herring fishing at Kinsale?—No, I never heard any objections by the Howth men. We never had any consultation.

1692. Mr. ROCHE.—What is the difference between you and the Kinsale men?—They wanted to prevent us from fishing herrings, so that the one fishing would not clash with the other.

1693. Mr. GARRR.—As a mackerel fisher did you find the price get down as soon as the herrings came in?—No; I tell you, sir, that towards the middle of May, before there was a herring fishing boat went there in my experience, the mackerel fell in price considerably. It is a natural consequence.

1604. When you were fishing herrings, were you fishing with the mackerel boats, or were you fishing inside them?—Very much so—always inside them. On many occasions we would not see the mackerel boats at all. The one fleet did not see the other.

1695. Did you ever find a case when the herring boats came in they filled the steamer, and sent it away?—I never saw that in my experience.

1696. When you did catch small mackerel, were they always saleable?—I never saw them yet but they could be sold, although sometimes not at a very remunerative price.

1697. The Kinsale men state that a tremendous number of small mackerel were of no use and could not be sold, and were thrown into the sea?—I saw that from a report in the *Cork Examiner*. I never saw it in my experience.

1698. Have you been fishing on the Kinsale coast from 1873 to 1887?—Up to 1883 I was at Kinsale, and between Kinsale and Baltimore. The years afterwards I was along about Bantry and the mouth of the Shannon.

1699. When fishing at the mouth of the Shannon, you would only be fishing for mackerel?—Yes.

1700. Did you get any herrings?—The most ever I got was 200. Very fine herrings they were.

1701. Do you think the 10th of May you agreed to at that time, or the 11th of May is a reasonable time?—If I were to have any say in the defining of the date, I would put it at the 1st. However, I see by several gentlemen's evidence here for the sake of coming to a mutual peaceful arrangement, I think the second Monday of May.

1702. Mr. Roche.—The second Monday of May?—As far as I am concerned I would accede to that.

1703. Mr. Green.—You think the second Monday of May better than nothing?—It is generally the case that it begins on Monday. But if I had the defining of the date I would prefer the first of May.

1704. Are the men who leave here more interested in the mackerel fishing than the herring fishing?—At one time they were more interested in the mackerel fishing, but not so much now-a-days.

1705. Are the boats taking to the herring fishing more?—Yes. There are not so many boats in the town as there were some years ago.

1706. If we had come here some years ago is it possible we might have heard a different story?—I do not think it. I do not think the men are so far left to themselves as to turn about that way.

1707. Mr. Roche.—Suppose the 10th May was fixed do you think Scotch boats would generally go?—I think they would, a good number of them.

1708. How many boats go from here?—I do not know. I think there were about sixteen or seventeen mackerel boats; but there was a number of herring boats at one time.

1709. Mr. Green.—Have you ever fished at Sheephaven or anywhere else on the north coast of Ireland?—Never; there are some in the ball I believe who have tried it.

1710. What sort of weather had you in the early part of the mackerel fishing?—I have seen us not later than the year 1885 three weeks lying in harbour for stormy weather. Of course that spoiled the fishing considerably for that season. That was the end of March and beginning of April.

1711. Have you any suggestion to make other than what you have told us?—No, I have nothing further to remark.

Archibald Campbell sworn, examined by Mr. Green.

1712. Do you belong to Campbeltown?—Yes.

1713. Are you a fisherman?—Not practical, but I am a boat owner.

1714. Have you been a fisherman?—In my early days I was a little at it, but only a little.

1715. How many boats do you own?—As a matter of fact just now I daresay three boats belong to me.

1716. Are they mackerel or herring boats?—Mackerel and herring boats.

1717. Have they gone to Kinsale recently?—No, they have not been at Kinsale mackerel fishing since 1889. They stopped the mackerel fishing.

1718. Have they gone to Kinsale since?—No.

1719. When they did go to Kinsale did they take herring nets or mackerel nets?—Generally mackerel nets first and other nets; and they used what would be most remunerative for the time.

1720. Did they fish out both seasons?—Some years they were engaged for a certain time—from some day in March on to the 1st of June at a fixed price to a buyer, but the years we had no engagement we took herring nets and stopped the mackerel fishing at the time the fishing fell off.

1721. If you were not engaged and free what time would you put the mackerel nets ashore and take herring nets aboard?—Just as a matter of convenience.

1722. About what time?—Perhaps about the end of April.

1723. And would you give up the mackerel fishing for the herring fishing at the end of April?—Yes.

1724. Have you gone to Kinsale yourself to look after the boats?—Yes.

1725. And you have seen them coming in?—Yes.

1726. You know what they took?—Yes.

1727. Did they kill many mackerel in the herring nets?—It depends entirely on the size of the nets fished with. The herring nets are generally thirty-two meshes to the yard.

1728. In that net did they kill many mackerel?—Always one or two, just as on our own coast.

1729. Did they kill many?—No; the herring nets hang so much deeper than the mackerel.

1730. How long is the buoy line to the herring nets?—Three fathoms and a half or perhaps four fathoms.

1731. And did they fish that length?—Yes.

1732. Some boats told us they generally fished two fathoms of a buoy line?—Perhaps so; a great many do not fish a buoy line at all, but on the surface.

1733. Is it the custom for the boats here that the spring back is at the bottom of the nets or at the top?—A few boats adopt the surface nets, but not generally on this coast.

1734. They generally have the net pulling a spring back?—Yes.

1735. Is that the plan in use at present?—The back from the top is the usual method.

1736. Have you seen any hake killed in the herring nets?—Not many.

1737. There has not been several boxes full of small hake thrown over-board?—I have never heard of it. The crew was always able to use the hake they got.

1738. Do you think five or six hundred hake were ever killed in your herring nets?—I never heard of it.

1739. Did you ever hear of small collops or any fish being killed?—Oh, yes.

1740. In large quantities?—No, not in large quantities. One or two now and again.

1741. What time do you consider the herring fishing fairly to commence at?—I have seen good herrings in April in the mackerel nets. I would not believe the numbers would be remunerative to fish before the 1st of May.

1742. Do you think the bulk of the herrings are not in good order so early as that?—My opinion is that they are in quite as good order in April and May as later, and after that every particular part of the coast has its own season for a good season—mackerel fishing in May till the beginning of June; then the Howth fishing a little later—perhaps about the beginning of June; and later the Ardglass fishing commences. All these come in their season, just as by rotation; and on our own coast here we have several seasons. Our herring season does not begin till June in Shetland, and in some other places it is very much later.

1743. How do your boats occupy themselves throughout the year? They go to Kinsale in March?—Yes.

1744. And leave Kinsale in June. Where do they go?—Generally to Howth.

1745. And when they leave Howth?—Well, of late years we did not follow the Howth fishing so much since we started the Shetland fishing. From 1880 or 1884, we left off the Howth fishing and went to Shetland, and fished there, perhaps, two or three months, and laid up our boats as soon as they came home.

1746. From your experience do you think a close time for herrings is good on any part of the coast?—I believe it is, but so long as our Norwegian friends are allowed to send herrings into the country at all seasons of the year, I have very little faith in a close season for any kind of fish. So long as that is done it will always spoil our markets no matter what the fish is. That is my opinion.

1747. Then you are against a close time on any part of the Scotch coast?—Well, provided you stop the Norwegians.

1748. You mean a close time for him from the 1st January to 31st December?—From the 1st January to the 1st January of the following year. I believe that has more to do with the great grievances than all the other things put together.

1749. When the mackerel fishing stops, the herring fishing stops—I want to know how it stops?—It stops by the shots getting smaller and smaller, or the herrings getting fewer and fewer, so that you leave it to go somewhere else. The numbers in both years of herrings got beautifully small, because the season for them coming on the coast has passed away.

1750. Have you been out in the boats yourself when they were making shots for herrings or for mackerel?—Oh, well, occasionally.

1751. Did you find when you were looking after the sales of the fish —I suppose you did sometimes?—Mostly the skippers of the boats attended to that.

1752. Did you find when the herrings came in in large quantities that it cut down the price of the mackerel?—If we were engaged it would be no difference what the price was.

1753. If you were free?—Naturally, the price would fall for mackerel; if we got a good price for the herrings we were quite as well pleased.

1754. Do you think the 11th May is a good time, or the second Monday in May is a good time for the herring fishing to begin?—I think the 1st of May is late enough for beginning.

1755. You have given up going there since 1880?—Since 1880.

1756. Why did you give up?—Just because I lost £100 almost every year for three year.

1757. Why did you lose in these years and not in previous years?—Just because there was a better fishing. The last year about the close of 1889, we had nights ashore in consequence of storm.

1758. But then of course storms always did not prevent you?—One year may be stormy weather.

1759. Did you find a diminution of the mackerel fishing?—If we did not get them.

1760. I mean shot for shot, I suppose you would always have an average?—Sometimes we had good shots and sometimes very low.

1761. What years do you remember to have been good mackerel years?—I could not say at this moment.

1762. Do you think that the recent years were worse than the years, say, ten years ago?—Oh, yes, very much worse.

1763. And big shots that used to be made cannot be made now?—No, nor the price either.

1764. Mr. Rocha.—The price you attribute to the Norwegians?—I believe it has a great deal to do with it. They come in here with herrings to the London market. What we used to get £1 a cran for from Mr. Murray, fishcurer, Fraserburgh and Aberdeen, are considerably reduced now, because these herrings come into the market at 3s. or 4s. a barrel, and are all sold in the London market. I want to remark this, that the herrings got in Norway are stored in the steamers that come into London. They take these fish and put them into the barrels literally in a starved condition, and unfit for food, in my opinion. They are kept in that store, and undoubtedly they are starved, because they have no liberty to look for food and are unfit, consequently our price is spoiled in this country.

1765. When do the Norwegian herrings begin to come in?—Four or five years ago.

1766. What date do they begin to come in?—Usually in the middle of the summer on to the end of the year, unless circumstances prevent them coming in. Of course stormy weather will always have something to do with it.

1767. Have you nothing now that you would like to say further?—No.

1768. Mr. Rocha.—There is one thing I want to ask. You say the 1st of May. Suppose now it was the 11th or 10th, don't you think it would be better to have a fixed date than the second Monday of May, which would vary so much. The second Monday of May might fall on the 14th. It would be a very uncertain and irregular day?—I think the 1st of May.

1769. But some intermediate date would be better, if it was thought right to fix it?—A fixed date, in my opinion, would be the best. I am afraid it will make very little difference to us. I am not sure that either mackerel boats or herring boats will leave this year for Kinsale?

1770. Had you any last year?—There were one or two.

1771. Mr. Green.—This is a very interesting matter, because we want to find out very distinctly why it was it paid you so well ten years ago, and why it does not pay you now?—It was no uncommon thing, perhaps, to get £2 a hundred for mackerel that now you get as many pence for.

1772. Mr. Hendry (District Fishery Officer).—Do you think Irish interference has anything to do with it?—There has sometimes been disturbances.

1773. Mr. Green.—That has never interfered with the price?—No.

1774. You think you cannot catch as many mackerel in the shot now as ten years ago?—I do not think they are so easily caught now as then. Of late seasons we did not get so many, because we were round to Bantry and Smerwick the last three or four years.

1775. You were engaged then?—Yes.

1776. Do you think giving up the engaged system is detrimental to the fishermen or not. It has been given up to a great extent?—I could not say as to that. If they got fish they were always sure of the price. If they got them and were not engaged they were at the mercy of those who bought them.

1777. If you want this year to fish would you be more likely to make a big shot off Bantry or Kinsale?—The fish are earlier at Kinsale, going further north of course they will feel the cold.

1778. Do you say the price is worse now than it used to be?—Of late we have not got so much for them.

1779. Was there not a good price last spring?—We were not fishing last spring.

Dugald Robertson sworn; examined by Mr. Oakum.

1780. Do you belong to Campbeltown?—Yes.

1781. Are you a fisherman?—Yes, sir.

1782. Are you owner and skipper?—Yes.

1783. Have you gone to Kinsale?—Yes.

1784. When were you last there?—Fifteen or sixteen years ago. I was there about the days Mr. Rae spoke of—1873—four, five, or six years in succession.

1785. Were you herring fishing then?—Yes.

1786. Were you a mackerel fisher?—No, I never fished mackerel—herrings all the time.

1787. At that time was there any dispute between the herring and the mackerel fishermen?—Yes; I remember disputes at that time.

1788. What was it about?—They found fault with us for fishing for herring before the end of the mackerel season.

1789. Was it about cutting down the price?—They said so.

1790. Did they find fault with you for killing small mackerel?—No, I never saw small mackerel.

1791. How far from the shore did you begin to shoot?—As a rule five miles.

1792. Were the mackerel boats near there?—No, as a rule, they were out of sight.

1793. Did you fish at any other port?—I fished at Howth and Ardglass.

1794. Did you fish at any other ports?—No, I was never further west than that.

1795. Did you sell the small mackerel that came into the herring nets?—Yes.

1796. Did you catch as many as would fill several boxes?—No. I never saw more than a cran at one time—as a rule about a basket.

1797. And were they all saleable?—Oh, yes.

1798. When did you begin to fish in those years?—The first year I went there was on the 14th April, I left here for there. I do not remember when we arrived.

1799. What was the date of your first shot?—I could not say.

1800. Do you remember when you began to fish?—I remember we proceeded straight on and fished the first night. I could not say how long we took on the passage—perhaps a week.

1801. It was in April?—Oh, yes, in April.

1802. Did you make a good shot?—A fair shot.

1803. Did you have any difficulty in selling them?—Yes, there was some difficulty in selling. Buyers did not care for them, they were not in good condition.

1804. They were too soft?—They were out of season. The proof of it is that Scotch fishermen won't eat them in April, and then the buyers did not like to sell them either.

1805. Did they think they would be unsaleable?—I never saw a price for them in April.

1806. When does the price improve?—Well, the end of May.

1807. The end of May?—Yes.

1808. When is the best price?—The 1st of June is the best price. I remember that year in the end of May we got about 10s. a measure and in June 10s. the hundred.

1809. Is that just because of the better quality?—Yes, just because of the better quality.

1810. What do you think a fair time to commence that fishing?—I would say any time about the 10th would be a fair time.

1811. And you think when the herrings first come on the coast that they are poor?—They are poor.

1812. And do they improve?—They improve in May daily.

1813. And you are a herring fisherman altogether?—Yes, I never fished mackerel.

1814. Do you think a close time is a good thing for herring?—Yes, I do, because they are not fit for food.

1815. Well, do you think if the date we have spoken of—the 10th or 11th of May—were fixed, do you think there would be a sufficiently long season left to make it worth while for herring boats to go and fish for herrings on that coast?—Oh, yes.

1816. When would you say the season ended for herrings?—During the years I have been there we had always to leave about the end of June on account of sharks which come in great shoals and destroy the nets. We had always to leave for that.

1817. Mr. ROCHE.—But you fished on till then?—Yes.

1818. Mr. GAMBLE.—Then you go to Howth?—Yes.

1819. Have you been to Howth in recent years?—No, we have not been there since I was at Kinsale.

1820. At that season where do you fish now?—Campbeltown.

1821. Do you ever go to Stornoway to fish?—I was once at Stornoway.

1822. You have not got mackerel nets at all?—No.

1823. Did you ever find small mackerel in your nets?—Yes, I remember one time counting 114.

1824. The size of herrings?—No, we would not get them as small as that. They were about two foot long. They were so good that they were split and cured.

1825. Did you ever kill a thousand in a shot?—That was the most I ever saw. About a score was the average. That was the first year. They were more plentiful last year.

1826. Do you fish with four fathom ropes?—Yes.

1827. When you did get them, where did you find them in the net?—Generally at the bottom. The strength of the fish caused the foot of the net to roll over, and they were in a bag so to speak.

1828. Did you ever see many large mackerel drop out while hauling in the net?—No.

1829. What was the last year you went there?—1878, I think.

William M'Millan, was the next witness called. He rose in his place, and said—I corroborate all that Mr. Rae says. I think what he has said is quite sufficient. I agree with everything he has said.

1830. Mr. GREEN.—Are you a skipper?—No, I am a boat owner.

Archibald Cook sworn; examined by Mr. GREEN.

1832. Are you a boat owner or fisherman?—Both.

1833. And you are the master of your own boat?—Yes, for the last thirty years.

1834. Have you gone to Kinsale?—Yes.

1835. When was the last time?—The year before last I was round to Bantry—in 1891.

1836. Have you been going to the south of Ireland continuously up to that date?—Yes.

1837. For thirty years?—Not altogether; for twenty years.

1838. You must have been round there at the very commencement of the mackerel fishing?—Not at the commencement. In 1873, I went round there to the herring fishing.

1839. Were you herring fishing all the time?—When we went there first, I shot three boats at the herring fishing.

1840. For several years you kept to the herring fishing. When did you begin the mackerel?—Next year.

1841. Did you take separate fishing boats?—Yes.

1842. You took the small boats to the herrings?—Yes.

1843. What was the biggest shot of mackerel you remember when you went round there first, when you began mackerel fishing at Kinsale?—I have seen eight or ten thousand, and four and five thousand.

1844. What would be the biggest shot you might count upon now?—We sometimes get that up to the present, but they are not so plentiful those big shots as they used to be for a number of years past.

1845. You have seen a falling off in the mackerel?—Oh, yes.

1846. There is no doubt of that?—The quantity of boats on the ground is bound to shift the fishing. Heavy mackerel fleets shift the fishing as well as anything else.

1847. Were you fishing to the west of Kinsale?—Yes.

1848. How far round?—Bantry and Dingle.

1849. You were engaged at Bantry?—Yes.

1850. All round there the boats were not so thick as at Kinsale?—No.

1851. Did you find bigger shots there?—When we went round there first we had bigger shots than at Kinsale.

1852. I suppose the reason you have not gone on to Bantry these last years, is because of the engagement system having been dropped?—These last few years the fishing fell off there also. Whatever the cause is, it was not for the heavy fleet. The fleet covered Howth, Bantry, Dingle, and the Skellies there.

1853. You found the fishing fell off there to?—Yes, it fell off considerably in the last three or four years.

1854. The last couple of years you were at Kinsale. Where were you fishing? At Kinsale itself?—From Kinsale down to Cape Clear.

1855. Did you find you got mackerel as early as you used to get them round that coast?—Oh, yes. These last few years they have been later according to the weather and the winds. If it is a strong prevailing easterly wind, it keeps them longer from coming. In a season like this they are earlier as far as my experience goes.

1856. Were you fishing both herrings and mackerel at Kinsale, and along that coast?—Oh, yes.

1857. Did you fish herrings off Bantry?—No; but there have been some Scotch boats there.

1858. Did you continue the herring fishing on that coast all the years you were there, except the years you were at Bantry?—We continued for four or five years—the smaller boats—from 1st May till 10th or 15th June, when the fishing commenced to slack, and then the Howth fishing began. The buyers cleared out when the season was up, and you have to follow the buyers.

1859. Why did you not go there in 1862?—The last year I was there it did not pay; and other people that were staying at home were making more money, and we thought we would take it easy for a year or two.

1860. As a fisherman, would you prefer the engagement system or fishing free at Kinsale?—I would sooner be engaged. We had then more peace, and the material was more in safety.

1861. Can you remember the days you began herring fishing?—I think it would be about the 8th or 10th May. Mr. Rae and I went there at the same time. We were the first Scotch boats that went from the west coast.

1862. But the west coast boats began the herring fishing before the east coast boats?—Yes.

1863. Were your first years good years?—Oh, yes.

1864. Did you notice when you got your first shots of herring, that the quality of the fish was worse than afterwards?—The first shot I had myself was seventeen or eighteen mease of as fine herring as I could wish, and I got some 25s. for it.

1865. Mr. ROCHE.—Do you agree with the last witness who said they were not fit to eat?—I do not know. They would not have the same flavour as the May herrings.

1866. Do the Scotch fishermen refuse to eat them themselves?—They do not care for them, unless they can get nothing better. They would sooner have a bit of mackerel.

1867. Mr. GREEN.—Do you think from the 10th May on is long enough?—I think it a very fair time. The herrings both on this coast and round there are the same quality of fish. They are in prime condition at the same time of the year.

1868. You would be fishing at Campbeltown if you did not go to Kinsale?—They are earlier round there.

1869. Did you ever fish round the north of Ireland?—There were a few Campbeltown boats round at Sheephaven; they got some good shots too, but they did not stay very long.

1870. You have had such long experience, if you say anything to throw light on this vexed question we would be very glad to hear it. I have asked all the questions I can think of to bring out your knowledge?—For my own part, if there is going to be herring fishing at all it should not be later than 10th May.

1871. Mr. ROCHE.—Do you think a close time a good thing to have?—Oh, yes, but not later than the 10th May. If you make it later the season is gone. Men coming from the east coast are prevented from going to sea for a week or two.

1872. You would be satisfied, the fishermen here would be satisfied to begin on the 10th?—Oh, yes.

1873. As far as I see the time you are there you have very good fishing?—In June the fishing slacked a little at Kinsale, and, as Mr. Robertson said, the sharks come in.

1874. Mr. GREEN.—What was the best price you got for herrings at Kinsale?—We have got as high as £2.

1875. Did you ever throw them overboard?—No, we are too glad to see them.

1876. Had you ever to sell them for manure?—No.

John M'Kinlay sworn; examined by Mr. Gamm.

1877. Are you a fisherman?—Yes, sir.

1878. Are you a boat owner?—Yes, sir.

1879. You have been a master?—Yes, fourteen or fifteen years a master.

1880. Have you gone to Kinsale?—Yes, sir; I was in Kinsale in 1875; that was my first going.

1882. When were you last?—I was there four years altogether—two years at herring and two years at mackerel; the first years were the herring fishing.

1883. And then you took to the mackerel fishing in the third and fourth?—Yes.

1884. Did you take herring nets with you?—No, sir.

1885. When you were fishing for herrings, when did you commence the fishing?—I believe it would be about the 10th; it took us eight days in passing down.

1886. When you went down you made the first shot about the 10th May?—Yes.

1887. What condition were the herrings in?—I thought the herrings were in very good condition as far as I could understand, and I know in Barra I never saw better herring.

1888. You go to Stornoway too?—Yes, I was in Stornoway and Barra.

1889. Does the fishing at Kinsale commence sooner?—I suppose it is sooner; we never commenced sooner.

1890. What are you employed at before going down to Kinsale?—At codling fishing.

1891. Do you find that fishing remunerative up to the time you go to Kinsale?—Yes, to the middle of April, very good.

1892. Then you fit out for Kinsale?—Yes.

1893. Since you gave up going to Kinsale, where do you go?—Just in the channel about here.

1894. Did you get a good price?—I think we sold them at 35s. a mease.

1895. At the commencement of the herring fishing?—Yes.

1896. Do you think the herring fishing at Kinsale is injurious in any way to the mackerel fishing?—I do not think it in the least to my knowledge of the fishing, because the mackerel boats were far outside—forty, fifty, and sixty miles outside—and the herring boats only a few miles off the shore. I did not see anything injurious about it.

1897. Did you get any small mackerel?—I never saw small mackerel but as good as got in mackerel nets.

1898. But they were small?—I don't think it.

1899. Would not 150 go into a half box?—I don't think it. I don't think there was 150 altogether.

1900. You have fished up in the Stornoway fishing. Is there not a close season?—It is since I was there; I think among themselves, as far as I understand.

1901. Then you have no experience of the fishing there?—No.

1902. Did you fish from any part to the west of Kinsale?—I never was further west than the Cape.

1903. Did you fish from Castletownsend or any of these places?—No, never anywhere but at Kinsale.

1904. You were fishing two years for herring and two years for mackerel?—Yes.

1905. Did you remember what number of mackerel you killed of a night?—About a couple of thousand, or three or four thousand. I sold four thousand about 20th May.

1906. How many nets did you fish?—We had forty-four.

1907. Did you ever see a lot of small hake in your herring nets?—No, sir, I saw very good hake, and I got a good price for them too. I sold as high as two score in a shot.

1908. Were they two feet long or so?—Yes, and three feet.

1909. Were they at the foot of the net?—So far down you could hardly get them out.

1910. Do you remember what you got for the first shots of herrings?—I do not remember. I know we got 35s.

1911. Why did you give up going down there?—Since I got a boat of my own the fishing on the coast here is better than going down to the south seas.

1912. Mr. Rocm.—Are you in favour of a close season for herring?—No, sir, I would not be for a close season to fishermen leaving here to go down to Ireland. I think you should give them from the 1st May. That would give them over a month to fish. When it comes to June the fishing is gone and the buyers go with it.

1913. You do not agree with the other witness who say the 10th?—I believe the fish is as good on the 1st as the 10th. I think the 1st of May would be a fair time. It would give them about four weeks to fish. As for hurting the market I never saw it.

John Martin sworn; examined by Mr. GREEN.

1914. Are you a master?—Yes, sir.

1915. And have you been long fishing?—Thirty or thirty-five years.

1916. Have you gone to Kinsale?—I have.

1917. When did you commence to go there?—I think it would be fifteen or sixteen or perhaps eighteen years since I went first.

1918. When did you give up going?—Oh, well, it is about thirteen or fourteen years—about that time.

1919. You went four consecutive years?—Yes.

1920. Why did you give it over—you went down to try it?—Yes.

1921. Why did you give it over?—We did not find it was a very beneficial fishing for us. It was a very short fishing.

1922. Are you speaking of herring fishing or mackerel fishing?—Herring fishing—I never was at mackerel fishing.

1923. Was it a bad year the last year that you were there; what caused you to give it up?—I believe it was the worst I had been at there. It was not altogether but what it paid pretty well, because we had the Howth fishing before us. I think that was the reason we were going to fish there at all.

1924. You took the two fishings?—We had a month, and another month before us at Howth and Ardglass.

1925. Why did you give up going to Howth and Ardglass?—I could not answer that very well. I think it is the buyers and not the fishermen.

1926. Do you think fish could be got there if the buyers went there?—Yes; if the buyers were there, they could be got there.

1927. Can you give any reason for the buyers having left if the fishing is good; where do they go instead?—They are going to other places that never used to fish in those years. Stations have been opened up on the whole of the east of Scotland and England that had not been in existence then nearer the market.

1928. Have you been fishing here off your own coast?—Yes.

1029. Do you notice any falling off in the fishing on your own coast?
—I do.

1030. Has there been a steady falling off?—Very steady for the last twelve or fifteen years.

1031. And you cannot make the same shots now of a night's fishing?
—No, we cannot.

1032. Are you sure it is not one year bad, and another year good—just an occasional bad year on your coast?—No; I have taken notice of a very steady falling off.

1033. Do you think fishing for herrings down at Kinsale can be injurious to the mackerel fishing—do you think that breaks up the schools, and injures the Howth fishing?—I cannot answer that question. It is not for me to judge of that.

1033a. Have you ever fished at Stornoway?—No, but I have fished at Barra Head, and all along there.

1034. Have you been there since they made the close season?—No.

1035. When you were fishing at Kinsale did you get small mackerel?
—Very few I ever saw.

1036. You never got several boxes?—No, no, I never got a half or quarter box of small mackerel.

1037. Mr. ROGER.—Is it the herring fishing you say is falling off so much?—It has fallen off at Howth and here.

Mr. ROGER.—According to this return (handed by Bailie Paul) for 1885, it does not seem to have fallen off much.

Mr. GREEN.—In 1877 it was very good. You say it has fallen off since then.

Mr. ROGER.—In 1885 you were a great deal better than you were in the seventies.

1038. Mr. GREEN.—Have you changed your nets in recent years?—Yes.

1038a. Do you fish longer and deeper nets than before?—Yes, the seine net makes a great difference now.

1039. Is the mesh of the seine net much smaller than the mesh of the drift net?—Very little; some of them as large as the drift net mesh.

1040. If you had a smaller mesh, do you think it would have an injurious effect?—You would catch smaller fish.

1041. Would it not be a bad thing to catch undersized herrings?—I believe it would. If we could leave them alone they would be better in the sea.

1042. Do they lift them with the boat-rope between two boats?—Yes.

1043. They have not got a running rope round the foot of them—a rope through rings?—No.

1044. What date do you think would be a good time to fix for Kinsale fishing, so as to satisfy the mackerel men and satisfy the herring men?—Well, I think, taking notice of the fish that I fished there very early in May—perhaps about the 8th or 10th—I found them better fish than any fish I ever got in any other place at that time on that coast, and very much better than our own, namely, Lough Fyne, in the month of May—larger and finer.

1045. Those herring you got down at Kinsale, of course they are not full herrings?—No, they are not full.

1046. They are not full at any time they fish down there?—No.

1047. Are they firm down there?—They are better than any fish ever I have fished in the month of May on any coast I have been on.

1048. Do you think if they were salted would they make as good a sale as the west coast matties?—They would make better. If the matties were killed in May they would make better matties.

1949. Do you think it would do to have a close season?—I would think it would be good to have a close season throughout the whole country if you say that we would not be annoyed with foreigners sending fish into the country at that time.

1950. Do you think it would be good to have a close season at, say, Kinsale?—I think it would be good for any place to have a close season, but in the circumstances I would not advocate a close season.

1951. Why would you not advocate a close season?—Because other countries send fish in and take money from us that would otherwise go into our pockets. We can fish in May, and if we were debarred from doing so it would give a premium to other countries and we would be to blame.

Archibald Campbell re-examined by Mr. GREEN.

1952. How many boats have ever gone from here to the Kinsale fishing at one time?—I should say about twenty boats to the Kinsale fishing between herring and mackerel. I mean those who went to Howth and Ardglass did not go.

1953. How many boats went to Kinsale, Bantry, or any other southern ports?—(*Robert Rea*)—About forty boats. Seventeen went to the mackerel fishing for a period of years, and I have seen as many as twenty to twenty-five going to the herring fishing.

1954. Mr. ROCHE.—To Kinsale?—Yes.

1955. Mr. GREEN.—The South of Ireland—Kinsale and along to the Cape?—Yes.

1956. Mr. *Hendry*.—These mackerel boats went to the herring fishing as well?—(*Robert Rea*)—Yes, when we thought that mackerel were not paying us as well as herring we put ashore the mackerel nets and took aboard the herring nets till we thought it would pay better to go to Howth.

1957. How many men are there to a boat?—Seven men and a boy to the mackerel boats, and six men and a boy to the herring boats.

Mr. *John Murray*, Officer of Scottish Fishery Board, examined by Mr. GREEN.

1958. If you will kindly tell us what you know about a close season. Mr. Murray has gone all round the coast with us, and has been of the greatest possible help to us, and has in the most efficient way possible arranged these Inquiries, and told us the best places to go to, and in every way has helped us. And now before we part we want to get from his great experience some ideas regarding the close times that have existed on the Scottish coast and that do exist, whether they may be arranged by legislation or by mutual consent of the fishermen.

Mr. *Murray*.—Well, gentlemen, with reference to the question of close time I speak under some reserve, as it is a question that is very much discussed at the present time from both sides. I may shortly state the history of legislative close time and say that in 1860, in deference to public opinion at that time, which chiefly originated in Glasgow, a Close Time Act was passed which came into operation on the 1st of January, 1861, and the capture of herrings was prohibited from the 1st January to the 31st of May, from Ardnamurchan to the Mull of Galloway. A further close time period from Ardnamurchan to Cape Wrath came into operation from the 1st January to the 20th May. After a few years it was found that in the northern section considerable opposition arose, and in consequence an Act was passed in 1865 which repealed the close time north of Ardnamurchan, but continued the

I

close time south of Ardnamurchan with a slight modification, namely, that close time began on 1st February and continued till 31st May between Ardnamurchan and the Mull of Galloway. That close time continued in strict operation about six years. I was engaged in enforcing the provisions of the Sea Fisheries Close Time Act of 1860 and 1865, for about twelve years. In consequence of the restrictions of jurisdiction introduced by the British and French Sea Fisheries Convention of 1868, the previous Close Time Act became imperative, and since that time there has been practically no close time enforced. Under the last clause of that Act it was provided that fish taken in contravention of the Close Time Act were not permitted to be landed, and the nets were liable to forfeiture. So that up to the present time, I believe, the Close Time Act continues in the statute book, but so far as I know it is quite in abeyance everywhere. I think public opinion is generally in favour of a close time, southwards of Ardnamurchan, because it is considered that the fish are not sufficiently ripe to be taken before the end of May. With regard to close time for sea fish I may say I have had a good deal of experience in enforcing close time, but I am not in favour of a close time for herrings. It was not beneficial in any respect.

Mr. ROCHE.—Is that on account of the difficulty of enforcing it?— No, it never tended to the increase of herrings, and it prevented fishermen from industriously following their occupation. A short regulation period immediately preceding the season for the capture of ripe herrings might be beneficial and of some utility; but in no case should the capture of herrings be prevented to be used as bait. I have known great hardship and privation caused by preventing the capture of herrings for bait. At the present time all the close time I would be in favour of would simply be, a short commercial regulation period preceding the time when the herrings would be sufficiently ripe for the market and curing. I am not aware I can add very much more.

Mr. ROCHE.—I quite agree with my colleague, Mr. Green, as to the great service given to us during the time we have been in Scotland by Mr. Murray. Mr. Murray has been of the most valuable assistance on every occasion. I think it is also right to say, we are greatly indebted to Mr. Eastmont, the Chairman of the Scottish Fisheries Board. On the occasion when we consulted him, he assisted us in every possible way. We are greatly indebted to him, and to Mr. Murray also, for the assistance they have given us. Mr. Hornaby is unfortunately unwell.

Mr. Murray.—I thank you very much, gentlemen. It has been a great pleasure to me to be of any service in this Inquiry. I thank you very sincerely.

Bailie Paul.—I propose a vote of thanks to the Commissioners. I hope the interview will be productive of good.

Mr. GREEN.— We are very much obliged to you for the kind way we have been received, and the information that has been given (Applause). I wish to express our appreciation of the manner in which Mr. Hendry, the District Fishery Officer, has carried out the arrangements for our meeting here.

Archibald Campbell said—I would just like to amend one part of my statement, with regard to the size of the mackerel nets I was in the habit of using—generally about twenty-three to twenty-four rows to the yard. The ordinary herring net was thirty-two.

The Inquiry then concluded.

PEEL INQUIRY.

Court-house, Peel, Isle of Man,
Saturday, 11th March, 1893.

Her Majesty's Inspectors of Irish Fisheries —ALAN HORNSBY, Esq., (in the chair), Rev. WILLIAM S. GREEN, and CECIL R. ROCHE, Esq., B.L., held an inquiry this day, at the Court-house, Peel, Isle of Man, pursuant to the following notice :—

"FISHERIES—IRELAND.

"32 and 33 Vict., c. 92, and the Acts incorporated therewith.

"Herring Fishery—South Coast of Ireland.

"NOTICE.

"Whereas it has been represented that the custom of fishing for herrings off the South Coast of Ireland, before the 1st of June in each year, is detrimental to the Mackerel fisheries off said coast ; and, as fishermen from the Isle of Man are interested in the question, the Inspectors of Irish Fisheries hereby give Notice that they will hold inquiries into the matter at

"THE SEAMEN'S SHELTER, PEEL, ISLE OF MAN,
"On Saturday, the 11th day of March, 1893,
"At the hour of Twelve o'clock, noon.

"Of which all persons interested are requested to take notice.

"By order,
"M. P. DOWLING,
Secretary.

"Dated at the Office of Irish Fisheries,
"Dublin Castle, this 3rd day of March, 1893."

Mr. HORNSBY opened the proceedings :—I presume the subject matter of this Inquiry has been fairly ventilated here in Peel amongst the fishermen, and there is just then, first, to make a few explanatory remarks. At the request of His Excellency the Lord Lieutenant of Ireland, as representing Her Majesty the Queen, we have been asked to hold an exhaustive inquiry into this question, as to when the herring fishing should commence on the south and south-west coast of Ireland, complaints having been made by the Irish fishermen that the early herring fishing is injurious to their branch of fishing. This matter has cropped up from time to time in Ireland, but we have never until now, held an exhaustive inquiry into it. We have held a series of inquiries in Scotland, and we thought it would be only just and fair to the Manx fishermen to come over here and hear their side of the question, so as to endeavour to arrive at some satisfactory conclusion for the benefit of the fishermen at large. We cannot hope to satisfy everyone, but

I 2

must try to do our best for the fishing industry, and the question of a good supply to the English markets. We take this opportunity of expressing our thanks to His Excellency the Lieutenant-Governor of this Island, and to the High Bailiff of Peel, both which gentlemen have given us valuable assistance, and made several suggestions which we have adopted. We are also obliged to the gentlemen who have attended here to-day to assist in laying before us the facts of the case. Now, Mr. Graves, will you call the witnesses?

Mr. *H. T. Graves* called *William Mylrea*, and said:—Will he come forward or stand in the box? You do not require to administer an oath.

Mr. Hornby.—Yes, we administer an oath.

Mr. *Graves* (to witness).—Then stand in the box. (To the *Inspectors*)—This is the Admiral of the Manx fishing fleet.

William Mylrea sworn; examined by Mr. Hornby.

1059. You fish for mackerel off the south-west coast of Ireland?—Yes, sir.

1960. For how many years?—About 31 years, I think, sir.

1961. In carrying on your mackerel fishing, do you come in contact much with the men who are herring fishing?—Yes, sir, we cannot get clear of them always.

1062. How far off the shore do you fish?—Sometimes three or four miles off, to sixty or seventy, according to the way we strike fish.

1963. Do you come much in contact with these herring fishing men?—We do not. We generally fish high off, but the other boats that fish lower in, must come in contact with them. I do not believe in shooting with the Scotch herring boats, because they are like a wall on each side of you.

1064. Have you any personal knowledge of great quantities of undersized mackerel being taken in herring nets?—I have not seen them; because I have not happened to be there when they were coming in, but I have been told by people in Kinsale, and by buyers, that there were.

1065. What do you know of mackerel striking against the nets?—They will die and fall to the bottom.

1066. But you have not seen this yourself?—We can prove that in our own herring nets.

1967. What proportion of them would you get?—We might get one out of five or six, or perhaps more than that. They roll away out of the nets, and if we want a good-sized mackerel, we try to roll the net on him.

1968. Have you formed any opinion whether this early herring fishing is injurious to the hake fishing?—I think it is, because they catch a power of small hake.

1969. Have you seen that yourself?—Yes, sir, I have seen that.

1070. What suggestions would you make to us, as fixing a time before which herring fishing should not commence?—It should not commence before June at all, or sometime in June.

1971. About what time in June?—For my opinion, I would say the 10th or 20th.

1072. Have you any idea as to what time the herring leave the Irish coast?—I do not know, because we leave them there.

1973. What time do you leave Ireland, generally?—We leave generally about the 20th or 25th.

1074. And are the herrings still on the coast then?—Some say that there are plenty of herrings there then, and some say that there are not.

1975. That is a matter of dispute?—Yes, sir.

1976. Supposing the Scotch fishermen swore there were no herrings, would you not contradict them?—Yes, I would.

1977. Would you swear there were herrings there?—Yes, I would.

1978. In sufficient quantity to make it pay to fish for them?—I do not know about that, sir.

1979. In your idea they should not begin to fish before the 20th?—I would not object to them beginning to fish on the 1st of June, but it would be better on the 20th.

1980. Suppose the Scotchmen say, "If you do not let us fish before the 1st of May, it will not pay us to go there"?—We cannot help that. As some of them said to me, they allowed they were doing an injury to the mackerel fishing, and were killing the small fish, but could not avoid it.

1981. Where did those men come from?—I could not say where they came from, I was just talking to them on the quay.

1982. Mr. Grady.—Scotchmen, they were?—Yes, sir, Scotchmen.

1983. How did they happen to speak about it?—They were talking about the mackerel fishing and small fish. They could not avoid killing small fish, they said.

1984. There was a proposition made some years ago to start at the 10th of May. It was a suggestion made at Kinsale to extend the period later on, to the 20th. Do you think that would meet the case?—I think it would be a bad time, because the month of May used to be our best mackerel time, and it is nearly done up altogether since the herring fishing commenced.

1985. How many boats go from this port to Kinsale?—I do not know how many go to Kinsale. They are scattered over the coast.

1986. But how many go to the Irish fishery altogether?—I suppose about 150 or 160.

1987. Mr. J. G. Corrin.—That is from Peel?

Witness.—I think it would be somewhere about that.

1988. Mr. Grady.—About how many go from Port St. Mary?—I could not say how many.

Mr. Graves.—About 100, I should think.

Mr. J. G. Corrin.—There will be about 250 from the two places.

1989. Your boats from this island go entirely for the mackerel fishery? They do not fish for herrings?—No, sir. Not until we come home again.

1990. Was there a time when Manx boats used to take a herring train?—Yes, sir.

1991. How long ago is that?—A good many years ago.

1992. About how long?—I could not say.

1993. How many?—I suppose an odd boat had herring trains with them twenty years ago.

1994. How many boats?—Just an odd boat.

1995. Mr. Grady.—What has been your experience with regard to the commencing of the mackerel fishing? Is it as early as it used to be, or later?—The way I have experienced, I think it lies a good deal on the water. Some years you will get them later, and others earlier, but I think it has been a deal later these seasons gone by.

1996. Might that not have been on account of the weather?—It might have been on account of the weather, as far as I can judge.

1997. Have you noticed any decline in the mackerel fishing off the Irish coast?—Yes, sir.

1998. In what way? Do you think the same amount of mackerel is caught, or is it only that a smaller shot can be made by each boat? Do

you think as large shots can be made now as used to be?—You can
make the same shots, but you do not get the same quantity of fish.

1999. Since when have you noticed that the mackerel are decreasing?
—I think it is decreasing since the herring fishing commenced, with the
Scotch boats.

2000. Mr. Rocna.—How long is that?—Fifteen or sixteen years.

2001. Mr. Green.—What would you call a good shot of mackerel
off the coast of Kinsale?—Perhaps five or six thousand, but I have seen
a great deal higher.

2002. Is that at present?—It is seldom you happen on that now,
there is oftener a few hundreds or tens of hundreds.

2003. What would have been a good shot fifteen years ago?—A few
years ago I remember 10,000 or 12,000, and over 30,000. They do
not get that now, sir.

2004. Is it because there are more nets in the water?—In my opinion
it is more on account of the herring fishing nets, because they sink a
deal lower in the water, and nearer the top of the water as well.

2005. Mr. Rocna.—Has the fishing been steadily decreasing for the
last fourteen years?—Yes, some years I have been of the opinion that
some years when the Scotch boats have been up they have done very
little at the herring fishing, and the next year there would be few boats
up, and that year the mackerel fishing would be better.

2006. That is, that when there are few Scotch boats the mackerel
fishing would be better?—Yes, sir, that is it.

2007. Mr. Green.—You have been fishing at Baltimore and Castletownshend?—Yes, sir, and at the west. In recent years I have been
fishing mostly from Kinsale, sir.

2008. From your experience of the western fishing do you find that
the mackerel have decreased there—that is, west of Baltimore—as much
as Kinsale?—I cannot say that, because I have not been fishing there
these years.

2009. I suppose some other fishermen will give us that, because the
Scotchmen do not fish, except out of Kinsale, you said there were
plenty of herrings on the Irish coast in the middle of June?—Yes, sir,
I should think there would be.

2010. Do you go to the herring fishing at Dunmore?—No, sir.

2011. Do any of the Peel boats go?—Not many these years, but
there has been an odd one.

2012. The Scotchmen said the herrings left the coast at Kinsale in
June, and you think they remain there in June?—I suppose so, if they
would fish, but it comes to their own time, and they are inclined to go
to the east. They do not stop to fish then.

Mr. Hornsby.—Now, Mr. Graves, would you like to ask the witness
anything.

Mr. Graves.—No, I was only trying to get out that the mackerel
fishing had declined since the introduction of the Scotch herring fishing.

2013. Mr. Hornsby.—I suppose, in giving this evidence, a great
many of the masters of your fleet agree with you?—Witness.—Yes, sir.

2014. Is there a unanimity of opinion among you?—A lot of our
boats go to the east coast, and I think, perhaps, they will be debarred
from giving evidence, because there may be a feeling against them when
they get there.

Mr. Hornsby.—That is one of our reasons for coming to hear evidence here to-day, but after all, I do not think there would be anything
of that sort.

2015. Mr. *Graves* (to *Witness*).—Mr. Hornsby asked you, whether the fishermen were all agreed as to the advantage this would be?—They are all, I think, sir.

2016. Mr. ROCHE.—Had you any meeting among you to arrange evidence, or anything of that sort?—No, sir, we had not.

Mr. ROCHE.—There is no reason why you should not have had.

2017. Mr. GREEN.—Have you seen any of the small hake?—Yes, I have seen them thrown overboard, and some of them in their nets.

2018. What size were they?—Some of them would be the size of herrings, and some smaller, because they get doubled in the mesh of the small net, and get caught that way.

2019. From your observation, how many of these small hake would be caught by a boat in a night?—I should think a thousand, and perhaps more.

2020. You have observed the fish sufficiently closely to be able to say a thousand would be caught in a night?—I have not been there when they were taking the nets in, and when they knew there was an ill-feeling against that kind of fishing, they would pitch them overboard.

2021. You have seen them drop them over?—Yes, sir.

2022. Mr. ROCHE.—Were you at the mackerel fishing last year?—Yes, sir.

2023. You have been fishing in Ireland regularly?—Yes, every year.

2024. Mr. HORNSBY.—Have you ever fished off the coast of Scotland for herrings?—Yes, sir.

2025. At Stornoway?—Yes, sir.

2026. Do you agree with the evidence given to us—that the herrings in May on the south coast of Ireland are in better condition than at Stornoway at the same time?—The buyers at Kinsale complain of them not being of good quality.

2027. As a skilled fisherman, what is your opinion of the condition of the herrings at Kinsale in the month of May?—My opinion is, that I have seen them of very poor quality. Towards the end of May they would be mending a bit.

2028. What would be their condition in June?—In June they would be a little better quality again.

2029. Would it be correct to say that they would be good enough for market, but that the fishermen would not eat them themselves?—That is a matter of taste. There have been fish I would not eat.

2030. Mr. ROCHE.—We had evidence in Campbeltown that the fishermen would not eat these herrings themselves. Is that your opinion?—They might eat one an odd time—them as was not very fanciful.

2031. Mr. *Graves.*—Mr. Green asked you if there were more now in the water now than formerly, and whether you thought the falling off of the fishing was attributable to that?—I do not know whether he meant herring nets or mackerel nets.

Mr. GREEN.—I meant mackerel nets.

2032. Mr. *Graves.*—Are there more boats fishing than formerly?—Not of our boats, but I do not think the whole fleet is larger than years ago.

Mr. ROCHE.—That is the Scotch fleet.

Mr. *Graves.*—The whole mackerel fishing fleet—Irish, Scotch, and Manx.

John Quirk sworn, examined by Mr. HORNBY.

2033. Do you live in Peel?—Yes, sir.

2034. Are you the master of a fishing vessel?—Yes, sir.

2035. Have you been in the habit of going to Ireland for the mackerel fishing?—Yes, sir.

2036. For how long?—For twenty-nine years.

2037. Continually?—Yes; year after year. I never missed a year.

2038. Have you come much in contact with the boats fishing herrings there in May?—Yes, sir; I have come across them occasionally.

2039. Have you any knowledge of large quantities of immature mackerel being taken by them?—I have seen them throw small mackerel over the side.

2040. You have seen them?—Yes, sir.

2041. In any large quantity?—I have seen them heaving quantities over the side, and more than that, I have seen them floating on the water and washed in on the beach.

2042. They could not be any other fish but mackerel, could they?—No, sir.

2043. You saw them sufficiently well to know?—Yes.

2044. Have you seen anything of small hake?—I have seen them putting hake over the side as well as mackerel.

2045. What is your idea of fixing a date for the fishing of herrings off that coast? What limit of time should be fixed?—I should say it should not be commenced before June, anyway.

2046. What date would you say?—I am not exactly prepared to say that, but I would say the 10th or 20th at the earliest.

2047. From your knowledge of the subject do you think it would pay the Scotch fishermen to come there so late in the season?—Well, I could not say as to that.

2048. When do you suppose the herrings leave the coast there?—I do not think the herrings leave the Irish coast at all, I think it is the boats that leave the fish.

2049. But the Scotchmen have come forward, man after man, and say that the fishing after June is not good, and they have to leave?—I have seen them taking large quantities, and leaving there, and going home to their own fishing.

2050. Then you say they leave simply because it does not suit their own ends to stop there?—Yes, that is it.

2051. Do you think that a lot of these large mackerel strike against the herring nets and drop out, and are not taken?—I think that when a large mackerel strikes against the net it is killed, and then it sinks.

2052. Mr. GREEN.—Have you been fishing from Castletown-Berehaven?—I have been fishing from Baltimore and Castletownshend.

2053. The Scotch fishermen do not fish down so far west as that?—Yes, they fish at Baltimore and Castletownshend.

2054. But not many? Are there many Scotch boats fishing out of Baltimore?—I do not know how many, but I know there is a portion of their fleet at Kinsale, and a portion at Baltimore. The greater portion would be at Kinsale.

2055. Have you noticed any falling off in the mackerel fishing since the herring boats began fishing?—Yes, sir.

2056. Could you give us any idea of the proportion of that falling off?—In my opinion it is through the herring boats there taking the small mackerel.

2057. I mean, would you compare the hauls of mackerel before the herring fishing commenced with the hauls common nowadays since the herring fishing commenced? I want you to say what you consider an average take of mackerel per night now, and say, 12 or 15 years ago?—Do you mean the large quantities.

2058. I want to know what quantity you would consider a good take fifteen years ago, and the amount you would consider a good take now, in one night?—I would consider a good take of mackerel fifteen years ago, six to ten thousand, but it is seldom we get that now.

2059. Do you ever get that quantity now?—We do not, except forty or fifty miles off; we do not get the large catches we did in former years in-shore, since the herring boats have been fishing there.

2060. Then has the effect of the herring fishing been to force you further from the land than formerly?—I have been with the herring boats shooting myself, and it was very difficult to get from them.

2061. Do not the Scotch boats fish off the land as well as close to?—I have seen them forty or fifty miles off, but not many of them, but if we knew there were quantities of mackerel three or four miles along the coast, we cannot put our nets in the water there, because we cannot drift with them.

2062. Why not?—We would lose our nets by driving against their floats; for that reason we do not know whether there is mackerel in-shore or not; we cannot put our mackerel nets in the water when the herring boats are there.

2063. You cannot drift along with the herring boats?—No, we would drift faster.

2064. And you would therefore be in danger of fouling their floats?—Yes, sir. I have known a Port St. Mary boat lose his train on the Scotchmen's floats.

2065. The last witness said there were 150 or 100 boats going from Peel to the mackerel fishery?—Yes, sir.

2066. What time do you usually go there—you are just starting now, I suppose?—Yes, but in former years we would be going about the first of March; we would consider this late.

2067. Then you start about the middle of March, and how long do you continue there—to the end of June?—Yes, sir, or sometimes we finish June there.

2068. So you are nearly four months off the Irish coast?—Yes, sir.

2069. During which time you are entirely engaged in the mackerel fishing?—Yes.

2070. How long do the Scotchmen remain there? We have it from other sources, but I do not think they remain nearly so long as that?—I have seen them there in April, and there are quantities of them there in June.

2071. About the middle of June they go away, do they not?—I think they are gone before that.

2072. Then you are on the Irish coast about twice as long as the Scotchmen?—I should think about that.

2073. Mr. *Graves.*—You have seen large takes of mackerel at Kinsale, 20,000 or more. I mean in former years?—Yes, sir.

2074. Have you seen fishings of that sort lately—for the last few years?—I have not seen them to my knowledge, for the last fourteen or fifteen years.

2075. Was it considered an unusual thing to see takes of fifteen or twenty thousand then?—No, sir.

2076. Is it usual now?—It was not unusual then, but it does not happen now, to my knowledge.

2077. Mr. J. *Loughby*, M.R.—Which month in the year used to be the best fishing month for mackerel?—the month of March.

2078. Was that a better month than May?—May would be the best general fishing, but we had not the quantities of fish in March. Since the herring fishing boats have gone there the fishing is not so early.

2079. What is the cause of it?—I do not know.

2080. May used to be a good month for fishing, and it is not now?—Yes, that is it.

2081. What, in your opinion, is the cause of that?—In my opinion it is the herring boats—we cannot fish with them. The herring boats fish for herrings on the ground where we used to fish for mackerel, and now we are driven off, because we cannot fish with them on any ground. In May and June the mackerel boats used to be spread over the coast, low in and high out, but it is not so now. We cannot prove the ground in-shore, because of the herring boats, whether there is any mackerel or not.

2082. Why not?—We would destroy our nets if we put them in the water with them.

2083. Mr. Green.—You said awhile ago that when you commenced fishing there March was a good month?—Yes, sir.

2084. And now March is not so good?—No, the fish is not so early as in former years.

2085. That cannot say anything against the herring fishing, because they do not come in March?—I think it is because they take the small mackerel, and the fish is not so early. We used to get a good quality of mackerel in March, and we don't get that now since the herring boats have come, and year after year it gets worse.

2086. Mr. Roome.—Do you observe that if there are few Scotch boats the fishing is better the following year?—Yes, I agree with that. That would account for it.

2087. Mr. Green.—Have you any idea of the amount of mackerel taken by these Scotch boats on a special occasion?—No more than some of the Scotch fishermen have told me they would be getting as high as ten meases a shot; we do not count them in meases, but in hundreds and thousands, but that is the way they count their herrings.

Mr. J. G. Corrin.—Ten mease would represent six thousand immature mackerel.

Witness.—A Scotchman from the Moray Firth told me that last year or the year before.

2088. Mr. Green.—Have you ever seen them throwing the small mackerel overboard?—Yes, I have seen them often.

2089. And have you passed close enough to the small fish to see what they were?—Yes, sir. The herring boats are lower in than we are, and when we come in we go round their stern, and often we are close up to their stern, and see them throwing small mackerel over and hake too, and we have passed close enough to these small fish to see what they were.

2090. Is it not a fact that mackerel will sink?—Yes, they will.

2091. But you say you have seen them?—They will sink, but still we have gone close enough to see they were mackerel.

2092. Are you sure these fish were not injured fish?—No, sir, they were not, because I have seen them afterwards. I have seen them when they would not have time to heave them overboard outside, when they would be picking their nets when they would be inside, and they would be heaving the small fish into the lough, and I have seen the small mackerel in upon the beach.

2093. Mr. Green.—How large were they?—Some of them would not be as large as a herring.

John Moughlin sworn, examined by Mr. Hornsby.

2094. Do you live in Peel?—Yes, sir.

2095. And you are the master of a fishing boat?—Yes.

2096. How many years have you been going to Ireland?—Twenty-six years.

2097. Every year?—Yes, sir.

2098. Have you come in contact at all with these Scotch **herring** fishermen?—I have seen them often.

2099. What is your experience of the capture of undersized mackerel by them?—My experience is that they catch any amount of them, because I have seen them.

2100. How many have you seen in one boat?—To the best of my knowledge I have seen over 5,000 in one boat alone. We were putting mackerel on board of the hulk on the 17th of June, I think, the year before last, and some of the chaps drew my attention to this boat putting herring in the same hulk, and I went to look for myself, and saw there the bulk of the fish—4,000 or 5,000 mackerel, if there was one.

2101. That was in the one boat?—In the one boat. I believe they were put overboard this same evening afterwards when they went to sea, because there was no demand for them.

2102. Then, why would they bring them in?—I suppose they brought them in because they thought they might get sale for them. They do get sale for lots of them if the other mackerel is scarce, because I have seen them boxed on the quay at Kinsale many a time. There would be about a hundred and a half in a box.

2103. How large were they?—About six inches long.

2104. What price would they get for them?—They were getting 5s. or 6s. a hundred, sometimes.

2105. Who bought them?—Local buyers. They were sold to all sorts of buyers, local and others too. Ones that are there buying mackerel all the time, English buyers I suppose they are.

2106. Did you ever hear about undersized mackerel being sold for manufacturing into manure in Kinsale?—I have heard of it, that they have been carted away, but I have not seen it. We are not very often ashore, because we are at the hulk, and are not often at the quays, and they nearly always discharge at the pier head.

2107. Have you seen many small hake taken?—I have seen them taking the nets, and shaking overside what I **think** would be hake, anyway.

2108. Could you judge the quantity?—You could not tell what quantity, as you might be sailing with them an hour, and them heaving over regularly.

2109. How many could they throw overboard in the time?—They might have time to heave a thousand over.

2110. What is your idea of a good date to commence the herring fishing there?—My idea is that they do a lot of destruction to the mackerel fishing anyway.

2111. Mr. Graves.—But what date would you say the herring fishing should commence?—Not before the middle of June at all, I would say.

2112. What date in June?—Not before the 14th or 15th.

2113. Are the herring on the coast at that time?—It is my opinion that they are. In June last year we have shot with the mackerel nets, and we have been getting a hundred or two hundred of herrings in the mackerel nets. If we caught a hundred or two hundred in the large mesh nets, we might get sixty meshes with herring nets. It is only the large ones we catch in the mackerel nets.

2114. About what date was that? About the 10th or 12th of June.

2115. What is your opinion of the condition of the herrings off the coast in the month of May?—They are not in good condition until the latter end of May, or the 1st of June. I have seen them, and heard people saying they were not worth buying, and in fact, they were only getting about 1s. a hundred in May for the first herring they were catching.

2116. From your knowledge as a fisherman, would you say that the herrings in May were soft, and would not stand salt?—My opinion is they are not worth, except for selling a few fresh as a commodity, as a servant to the people who ate them. Of course, herring is a fish that sells well all round the south-west coast of Ireland in small quantities, and in county Kerry too.

2117. Have you noticed, in your boat, a great falling off in the take of mackerel in the last few years?—Yes, sir, in the last fifteen years.

2118. Do you connect the falling off with the advent of the Scotch fishermen?—Yes, that is about the advent of the Scotchman, and that is the falling off of the fishing, so far as the Irish sea fishing is concerned. There are no fish in Arklow now, and none in Howth, and you can trace it back to that time.

2119. But that may be supposition?—Well, it may be. The most the fish they get at Dunmore, and I do not know what way that fish travels, whether it goes on the Welsh coast, or the Irish coast, or down channel.

2120. You mean herrings?—Yes, sir.

Mr. Grouse.—That is not what Mr. Hornsby asked you.

2121. Mr. Hornsby.—No, but he has enlarged upon it, that is all—(to Witness.)—What Irish ports have you fished from besides Kinsale?—From the Shannon to Kinsale.

2122. In places where you do not come across these troublesome Scotchmen, is the fishing as bad?—I do not know what you say.

2123. I want to know if, when you are fishing at a part not frequented by Scotchmen, you notice that the fishing has become lighter there?—Some years there might be more mackerel than others, and you might be fishing at one place one year and another the next.

2124. What I want to draw your attention to is, whether it is thought mackerel are becoming lighter on the coast by some reason in natural history which we are not at present prepared to explain, or whether it is entirely due to the Scotch fishermen fishing for herrings in May?—The mackerel fishing is lighter on the coast than it was fifteen years ago.

2125. But where the Scotchmen are not, you do not notice much decrease?—No, I have not noticed much decrease on the westward.

2126. Have you been much at the westward?—I have been seven or eight years at county Kerry, and have been fishing at Kinsale before that, and then I went back to it. There have been Scotchmen round the coast of Kerry, but they could not prosecute the fishing there because of the dogs—the dog-fish.

2127. Mr. Room.—Is there any place where you do not meet the Scotchmen?—That is the only place. There were a few up there, but they did not stop any time. That is from Dingle to the Shannon. Generally speaking there are no Scotchmen there—there may be a few, but not many. There were a few fishing out of Valencia a few years ago.

2128. Then that is the place where you see the least of the Scotchmen?—Yes, that is the place where you meet less Scotchmen than anywhere else.

2129. Have you found the fishing there getting worse, as in Kinsale?—I cannot say that it did. Of course the last year I was fishing there there was as much mackerel as the first year I went to it.

2130. Then there was no falling off?—I could not say there was much falling off. There was not the same falling off as in Kinsale.

2131. Mr. Hornsby.—You say you were fishing at Kinsale, and then went for a few years to Kerry, and for the last few years you had come back to Kinsale?—Yes, sir.

2132. Can you give us any reason for your returning?—The reason is not in regard to the fishing at all, but because we were engaged to fish around there, and the prices were not suiting. That is what stopped us from going round. And there were too many boats going round too; that is another point.

2133. Then have your been engaged for the last two years?—No, sir.

2134. Were you engaged all the years you were fishing on the Kerry coast?—Yes, all the years we were on the Kerry coast we were engaged.

2135. What were the years?—From 1882 I think.

2136. Mr. Gunn.—What is the first time in the season, generally, you notice herrings in the mackerel nets?—Well, you will in May, but some years you would not come across them in the mackerel nets at all, or hardly in the herring nets, because you might not be fishing where there were schools of herring.

2137. Do you get herrings in March in the mackerel nets?—I never saw any in March, that I know of, at all. I have seen lots of herrings at the westward in the month of April in the mackerel nets, and from that up to June, and the latter end of May.

2138. What other kind of fish did you notice in the mackerel nets besides herring? Do you get any white trout?—An odd one, sometimes.

2139. Mr. Graves.—Are the ports adjacent to Kinsale as Baltimore and other places, affected in the same way as Kinsale by the herring fishing?—The mackerel is a fish that travels, it does not stand to the one place all over the coast, I suppose they go from one place to the other.

2140. You do not understand me. Are the takes as good at Baltimore and Castletownshend as in former years?—They are not as good on any of the south-west of Ireland, or in none of the ports adjacent to Kinsale. I would earn as much money in May fifteen years ago as I would earn for the whole season now.

2141. Mr. Hornsby.—Are there many Scotchmen fishing in those ports?—A few in Castlehaven. One of our local buyers has had boats in Castlehaven fishing for them one year.

2142. Mr. Graves.—Do you think the destruction of immature fish at Kinsale would affect those ports?—I think it would affect any place, because I think they are own and the same mackerel; and, besides, they do not get the third of them. I have had a thousand in the herring nets myself off Hartlepool, and where we were getting one, ten were getting away, and we were trying to roll the net up, and get them in because we were getting a good price—3s. or 4s. a score.

2143. Mr. Gunn.—Have you been fishing for herrings off Lowestoft?—Never further up than Flamborough Head.

2144. Mr. Reeves.—Lowestoft is south of that?—Never further south. I mean and never further north than Aberdeen and Peterhead.

2145. Mr. Gunn.—It is said that the price of mackerel suddenly

falls when the herring fishing commences at Kinsale?—Yes, I have
noticed that. When the herring comes in in quantity the mackerel
goes down in price.

2146. Is that an important reason for stopping the herring fishery?
—I would not stop it for that. Every man has a right to go to fish, if
it was not for herring the mackerel fishing. That is what I say,
because you can stop no man from fishing, I suppose, if it is lawful.

2147. Mr. Roche.—Have you ever gone to the Irish coast for the
autumn fishing?—No, some of the Peel boats have gone.

2148. Mr. Graves.—How many years ago do you consider that the
autumn fishing commenced?—Four or five years ago, I should think.

2149. Have you noticed any falling off in the spring fishing since
the autumn fishing commenced?—I have noticed a falling off for nine
or ten years before they went to the autumn fishing at all.

2150. Have you noticed that it has made any perceptible difference
in the spring fishing?—I cannot say whether it has made any perceptible difference, but I say the falling off in the mackerel fishing has
been now for the last fourteen or fifteen years.

2151. Mr. Graves.—The mackerel fishing is not profitable now?—
Not at all.

2152. The men scarcely earn enough to support themselves?—No,
and it is not supporting the boats, and when it is not good for the boats
it is not good for the men. It used to be that they could make a living
and the owners keep boats and now they cannot do it at all. These last
fourteen or fifteen years some have been doing well and others have
not. It is not a general running fishery as twenty years ago to fourteen
years ago. Then, nearly every year in Kinsale would nearly all do
good season, from five or six hundred pounds to three or four hundred.

2153. It is an exception now that a boat does fairly well?—Yes, it is
the exception now for a boat to get £300.

2154. Mr. Graves.—Does the fishing season last now as long as it
did then?—Yes, it lasts now as long as ever it did.

2155. Mr. Graves.—When did you start for the fishing at that
time?—I have never moved to the mackerel fishing until the 17th of
March very often.

2156. Mr. Graves.—And when did it end?—I have been in Peel on
the 10th and sometimes the 1st of June with £400, and not going out
of here before the 17th of March.

2157. Is the price as good now as then?—The price was as good the
year before last as then, if not better. I have earned over £300 in
May, at 10s. a hundred—over £300 in four weeks. That was seventeen or eighteen years ago, and different other boats would do it besides. If you got thirty or forty miles off, you would get 4,000 to
5,000 every night you would go.

William Moore, examined by Mr. Horsley.

2158. Are you master of a fishing vessel?—Yes

2159. Have you been going to the Irish mackerel fishing?—Yes, I
have been going to Ireland for thirty-one years.

2160. What is your experience now, of the action of the herring
fishing on the mackerel fishing?—My experience is the same as those
who have given evidence before you. I can hardly add anything to it.

2161. You agree with everything the former witnesses have said?
—I do sir.

2162. Have you of your own personal knowledge seen large quantities of undersized mackerel taken?—Yes, I have, by the Scotchmen.

2163. About what quantity have you seen?—From two to three, and four or five thousand, and so on.

2164. Is that for the whole season?—No, for the one catch.

2165. How often did you see that occurring?—It is not very often I would be coming across them, but a chance time I would happen to see them, perhaps four or five times in the season.

2166. Mr. Redom.—Would the quantity you state be caught by one boat?—Yes, one boat would catch that.

2167. Mr. Horshaw.—On each of these times how many would you say you saw? On each occasion?—Perhaps from three to four thousand.

2168. Have you ever seen large quantities of undersized hake?—I could not exactly tell, because they throw them out of the nets, and it is a fish that will float. To see them, they float on the surface, and therefore, when you have not seen them in a hulk in the boat you cannot tell the quantity, but I know there have been large quantities of them going catching.

2169. Have you seen large quantities of them floating?—We have seen them floating on the surface both inside and out.

2170. Do you agree with the former evidence as to the condition of the herrings in May?—They are not good then. They are very soft and not good tasting. They are not good eating.

2171. Do they improve in quality later on?—In the month of June they improve very much.

2172. When do you think the great shoal of herrings go off that coast?—I don't think they hardly go off the coast at all. I have been one of the best hands mackerel fishing, and I have seen us on the 27th and 28th of June with large herrings in the mackerel nets, and I have seen signs of herrings there, because we very often say where there is a large body of herrings there is a sign with it, as the hog, or something like that, and I believe that there are large schools of herrings there from the month of June out.

2173. Do you suppose the Scotchmen go away because the buyers are gone?—They do not go away because the buyers are gone, but because their own fishing is on.

2174. What is your idea as to the date on which herring fishing should commence off the Irish coast?—I would say not before the 1st of June at any rate. I would be strongly in favour of not before the 10th or 15th of June, but not before the 1st at any rate.

2175. Do you agree with the former evidence as to the falling off for the last fifteen years or so in the take of mackerel off that coast?—I do. If you kill the young by fishing you cannot catch very much old—they are not left to get old, or grow big. If you kill all the children you cannot expect to get men or women.

2176. That is the converse of that—Will you kill all the men and women, you won't get any children. (Laughter.) You would say that the 1st of June is a fair date on which to commence the herring fishing?—Yes, not before that.

2177. You would not say the 15th May?—No, sir, I would not.

2178. Why not?—Because my opinion is that the small mackerel that the Scotchmen kill in May, by the month of June have grown larger, and they are not likely to kill so many of them in the herring nets. The mackerel is a fish in which there is a small fin about half an inch from the mouth, and when it is in the herring mesh it is held, and there drops back to the bottom if it is any size, but the small fish mesh

2179. Have you fished from any Irish ports besides Kinsale?—I have fished from Kinsale to Castletown Berehaven, but no further west.

2180. At Castletown Berehaven, did you find a falling off there?—Well, no. It is not very much I have fished out of Castletown Berehaven, but chiefly from Kinsale to Baltimore.

2181. Have you found a falling-off at Baltimore?—Yes, I have found a falling off at Baltimore these last fourteen or fifteen years—a big falling off. I do not think we kill half the mackerel we did from fourteen to thirty years back.

2182. Then you agree with the former evidence that the mackerel fishing off the Irish coast is not a very paying concern?—Not in these days.

2183. Mr. Graves.—Neither for the native boats nor for the Manxmen?—Not for anyone.

2184. Mr. Gibbs.—Have you seen many small mackerel thrown in the sea?—No, for the mackerel is a fish that does not very often float, but I have seen them in bulk. We have seen them in the bulk, and I have seen them when, perhaps they would not throw them overboard in the lough, because the fishermen would see them; but you would see them in a heap.

2185. But if the Scotchmen say they only throw away broken fish; and that all the mackerel they catch are saleable; would you consider that correct?—I would not consider that correct. The smaller you get the mackerel the softer it is, and the rarer bruised. The larger it is the more squeezing it will stand.

2186. Mr. Roche.—You have been fishing over there a long time?—Yes.

2187. During the last nine or ten years—to go back for ten years—have the Scotch fishermen been decreasing in number then? Have there been less there during that time than before?—Some years we get double the quantity there is for years. There are not the same number there every year.

2188. Are they getting less in number?—I daresay they will be.

2189. We have the returns here from the Harbour master at Kinsale, but I want to know what you think?—I have seen 200 there some years, and not 50 other years.

2190. Mr. Roche.—According to the evidence of the Harbour master at Kinsale, that we have here, he says that in 1884 there were 165 Scotch boats; in 1886 there were 106; in 1887, 33; in 1888, 40; in 1889, 45; in 1890, 10; in 1891, 49; and in 1892, 30; so that you see the Scotchmen were decreasing in number every year, and as they were getting less the herrings were getting less too—the mackerel, I mean?—No, if there were such a small fleet of them out the mackerel would be more plentiful.

2191. Don't you say that for the last ten years the mackerel fishing has been getting steadily worse? If we can prove that there were less Scotchmen there than before, how do you account for that? The mackerel should be getting better according to your argument?—I cannot account for that.

Mr. Roche.—No, more can I according to the figures here and what you say; you should have a good deal more mackerel than what you have.

2192. Mr. Holdship.—At any rate your opinion is that the mackerel fishing has decreased?—It has gone down more and more.

2193. Mr. Gibbs.—Have you ever been herring fishing there?—No, never.

2194. Have you ever been herring fishing in Howth?—Yes, I have.

2195. Have you noticed any decrease in the herring fishing in this Channel?—Yes.

2196. Since when?—I may say that has been for twelve to fourteen or fifteen years; twelve, at any rate.

2197. What was the last good year?—Not these last ten or twelve years, but I could not say exactly.

2198. Have you any reason to give for that decrease in the herring fishing about Howth?—No, I cannot give you any reason for that.

2199. Mr. Hornsby.—How long did you go to Howth?—It is very seldom I ever went to it in the summer time; we used to be going in the fall of the year, beginning in the month of October and November.

2200. What was your first year for going there herring fishing?—It would be about thirty-three years ago.

2201. Did not the herrings desert the Howth coast altogether for some years and go back afterwards?—Yes, they did. I may say they have all but deserted it at the present.

2202. Mr. Greer.—When you had done with the mackerel fishing at Kinsale, what fishing did you next go to?—From here across to the Irish shore; fishing from Peel for herrings.

2203. How long does that last?—That fishing will last for the months of July, August, and September.

2204. And then, after September, what fishing did you go to?—We used to be going to the fall-fishing in October and November, and then our season is done.

2205. And do you fish from Ardglass, or any of these other places?—Yes, from Ardglass, or any place convenient on the Irish shore.

2206. Have you ever been at the Dunmore fishing?—No, sir.

2207. When the herring fishing ends here, I want to know how does it end; is it when the takes of herring get fewer and fewer, when they get smaller, why do you give it up?—I believe that is the way they get smaller, once going out in September the herrings are going on the ground for spawning, not close by here where we can fish them but on such as a coral bank. They are lumped into a heavy shool and go away to spawn. That is what makes them fall off here in the latter part of the season.

2208. And you do not pursue them here when they go away to spawn?—Well, yes, at times, at Douglas, but it is all spawn fish we get there at that time of the year.

2209. Mr. Graves.—Mr. Roche puzzled you a little time ago when he asked you how it was the mackerel fishing did not keep equal with the number of Scotch boats. For instance, there were 180 boats at one time and it dwindled to ten or twenty, and you did not understand, you said, how the mackerel fishing did not keep in train, must the injury have been done when the 180 boats were there?—It is possible, I think I brought that out pretty clear.

2210. Mr. Roche.—Don't you think they would recover in seven years, when there were not forty or fifty boats fishing?—I do not know that it is possible.

2211. Mr. Hornsby.—At one time you would have 200 less than another time there, and the inference is that you would suffer most severely then?—Yes, but when there was a great injury done it would take a long time to pull it up again.

2212. Mr. Graves.—Do you know the reason the Scotch boats fell off in number?—Because the fishing was not paying.

Mr. Roche.—That is, of course, the herring fishing was not paying

K

2213. Mr. *Graves*.—If it had paid them they would have increased in number?—Yes.

2214. Mr. *Jonghin*.—Might not a great injury be done to the mackerel fishing when 180 boats or so were there, by scaring the fish away to some other coast, and the fish never coming back to Ireland again?—Yes, I think I explained that.

2215. Mr. ROCHE.—Are we never to get them back at all, is that your inference?—The year 1864 is nine years ago, and because then there were about 200 Scotch boats there, you say they had annihilated the mackerel on the Irish coast?—That is my opinion.

Very well, but that is rather strong, you know.

2216. Mr. *Graves*.—I do not think you mean that, but that the quantity is diminished in consequence?—Yes, diminished in consequence.

2217. Mr. ROCHE.—I would think they might recover in ten years?—The last two or three years there have been better catches of mackerel than there were nine or ten years ago.

2218. Oh, there have been?—There were larger catches.

2219. And better fish?—Yes, this eight or nine or ten years since, because there have not been so many Scotch boats.

2220. Then the mackerel fishing has not got worse those last few years?—From the last fourteen years down.

2221. Mr. HORNBY.—Can you tax your memory sufficiently to go back ten years, and tell us the good years and the bad years? Taking a period of ten years, can you give us your best and worst years? It is not a very easy thing to do, I know?—No, it is rather hard to state that clear.

Yes, it is rather difficult.

2222. Mr. GREEN.—But which is the worst year you have had in the last five years?—I think four years ago was the worst year I have had, but it might not have been the worst for all the rest. That was the worst year I had, but at the same time there might have been some of the boats good that year—it might have been the best year they have had for the last ten years.

Mr. HORNBY.—Are there any statistics we could get to show the receipts for a series of years? We might judge them.

Mr. *Graves*.—So far as my own boats are concerned, I think I could give the figures, but not at once; it might take some time.

Mr. ROCHE.—Of course you see the importance of it. If the takes vary in proportion to the number of Scotchmen of course your case is conclusively proved.

Mr. *Graves*.—I could give the earnings of the boats year by year for the last twenty years—say, a score of boats.

Mr. ROCHE.—For, say, fourteen years, would be all we would want.

Mr. *Graves*.—And I could get similar statistics from the other owners.

Mr. *Jonghin*.—I could give the last fifteen years.

Mr. HORNBY.—We would be very much obliged, if it was not too much trouble.

2223. Mr. *Graves* (to *Witness*).—Does the mackerel fishing pay you more now?—No, it does not. If there was any other occupation you would not get the men to follow the mackerel fishing now.

Finn Quirk examined by Mr. HORNBY.

2224. Are you a master of a fishing boat, living at Peel?—I am, sir.

2225. How long have you been going to the Irish Coast?—For thirty-one years.

2226. Well, perhaps, you can tell your own story of what you consider the effect of those Scotch herring boats upon the mackerel, in taking undersized mackerel and hake?—I saw them one day, the Scotchmen alone, putting them over-side, and another man told me he killed 50,000 every week, and only sold about a thousand. I have seen them kicking them overside.

2227. Have you seen them doing so often?—I saw them several times last year.

2228. How many times?—Perhaps six or seven times.

2229. For what length of time were you near enough to observe them? How long were you observing them each time?—One day we were about five minutes looking at them, and they were heaving them overside as we passed them. We were, perhaps, three or four minutes going past them.

2230. And in that time they heaved over a considerable quantity?—Yes, as far as I could see.

2231. Where did that happen?—Coming inside of the Bullman.

2232. I suppose you are not able to speak of undersized hake?—Yes, I have seen hundreds of them floating in the lough—thousands of them.

2233. Have you seen that often?—I have seen them several times.

2234. What do you define as several times?—Maybe a dozen times, or seven or eight.

2235. Mr. *Jonghin.*—In a year?—Yes.

2236. Mr. HORNSBY.—How long have you seen this going on?—Since the Scotchmen came.

2237. Well, now, what is your idea about the date on which the herring fishing should commence?—Since it commenced they have injured the mackerel fishing.

2238. But you would say to stop all herring fishing until what date?—The first of July, I think.

2239. Would not that practically stop the herring fishing there altogether?—As soon as the middle of June comes, the Scotch boats are gone, for they are only engaged to stop there for a certain time, and as soon as the Stornoway fishing commences, they are leaving.

2240. What time do you observe them leaving there?—From the 15th to the 22nd of June, more or less.

2241. Do you suppose there will be any quantity of herring at Kinsale in the month of July?—I have not done much for the month of July, but I have seen plenty in June, when we would be coming home.

2242. Are the herrings in better condition in June than the month of May?—Yes, I think so.

2243. What has been your experience in your thirty-one years mackerel fishing off the Irish coast? Has your capture decreased year by year, or what?—It has fallen the last ton or twelve years.

2244. Ten or twelve years?—Yes. Before the Scotch boats came, once May came in, got three or four miles off, and you were sure of three or four thousand, and that was the time we made our season.

2245. Do you agree with the last witness that the fishing has improved for the last two or three years?—Well, I do not know.

2246. What has been your actual capture for the last two or three years? Has it been better or worse?—Worse.

2247. Mr. ROCHE.—For the last two or three years?—Yes.

2248. Then you don't agree with the last witness?—No.

Mr. *Groves.*—I am afraid he was speaking from his own personal experience.

Mr. ROCHE.—That is quite right.

2249. Mr. HORNBY.—Could you tell us the worst year you have had in Ireland?—These last two or three years.

2250. What did you do last season?—Was it a bad season?—Yes, over all.

2251. Was the season before bad too?—Yes, it was not much better.

2252. And as to the season three years ago?—An odd boat might have done a little, but it was an odd boat.

2253. Then your idea would be to stop all herring fishing off the south coast of Ireland?—To a certain limit.

2254. Stopping it to the first of July practically stops it altogether?—Yes.

Mr. GRAVES.—Do you think he understood that question?

2255. Mr. HORNBY.—Would the fish be on the ground then?—No, they are going away when the fish are on the ground.

2256. Mr. GRAVES.—Would you fix the first of July as the beginning of the herring fishing there?—Yes; I think it should be stopped.

Mr. GRAVES.—The other witnesses said the first of June.

Witness.—The Scotch destroy nets as well as fish.

2257. Mr. ROCHE.—I think you would like to put the Scotchmen off the coast altogether?—No, I do not want to put any man off a living.

2258. Would that not practically stop them fishing there altogether?—No, I think not.

2259. Then you think the herring fishing could commence on the first of July with profit to them?—Yes; at Dunmore, some of them, I suppose, fish to the end of July.

Mr. GRAVES.—His idea is that the two fishings should not go on at the same time.

Mr. ROCHE.—Quite so.

2260. Mr. JONGHIN.—Is it possible for the herring and mackerel boats to drive together?—No, it is not.

2261. Mr. ROCHE.—They are inconsistent, the two fishings?—Yes.

2262. Mr. JONGHIN.—Then the herring boats off Kinsale fish on the ground in May, where you used to get very large takes, and May was the best month in the year for you?—Witness.—Yes.

2263. Mr. JONGHIN.—How far off the land do they fish?—From five to thirty miles off.

Mr. ROCHE.—I understand the contention of these men is—and of course it is perfectly right that they should so contend—that the two fishings are inconsistent.

Mr. GRAVES.—That is clearly the opinion of this witness.

Mr. HORNBY.—Surely it would be better to have a give and take policy. The extreme demand of the Irishmen is that the fishing should be stopped until the first of June.

Mr. GRAVES.—The other men are more modest than this man is. They may think as this man, but they do not like to say so.

Mr. HORNBY.—But when a man is on his oath he must speak as he thinks. Modesty is all very well, but when a man's pocket is concerned we do not often see it. (Laughter.)

Mr. GRAVES.—I think all the men would like to see the fishing stopped.

Mr. ROCHE.—Then let them say so. It is for us to draw a conclusion, but let them say what they think.

Mr. JONGHIN.—If the herring boats fished more east, towards Dunmore, they would not interfere with the mackerel fishing so much, but, in May, they fish on the very ground where our men used to make good mackerel fishing, and monopolize that ground.

Mr. Hornsby.—The Scotchmen contradict all the evidence we have got from these men here to-day, because they say they rarely see these mackerel boats at sea. We have pages of evidence to that effect.

Mr. Joughin.—The mackerel boats are bound to keep away. May used to be the month for mackerel fishing, fourteen or fifteen years ago, but now it is one of the worst. In May the fish used to come up to the surface, and you could get four to six thousand within a few miles off the land, but since the herring boats have come and fished on the ground there, they have driven the mackerel boats forty or fifty miles off.

Mr. Hornsby.—But do not the herring boats **fish on** different grounds at different times?—They were at first.

Mr. Joughin.—If they go out there they drive the **mackerel boats** further out.

Mr. Hornsby.—How do you reconcile the fact that the two fishings can be carried on at the same time at Lowestoft?

Mr. Joughin.—I think, perhaps, the Lowestoft nets are mounted differently to our nets here. They are deep nets, and mounted accordingly like the herring nets, but here they are foot-rope nets, and shallow on surface, but the herring nets are deep nets. The mackerel boats drive quicker than the herring boats, and they foul each other.

2264. Mr. Gaker.—You have been along side of a Lowestoft boat at Kinsale?—Yes.

2265. Are their mackerel nets different to yours?—They use fly nets, with no sole ropes, but the top is on the surface the same as ours.

2266. The Lowestoft nets you see on the South Coast of Ireland are the same as the Manx nets?—Yes.

2267. Do you think that altering the herring nets, and making them fish with shorter straps, or anything of that sort, would meet the case?— I don't think it.

2268. Do you think limiting the depth of the herring nets, and making them fish on the surface would do?—Altering the depth of the herring nets?

2269. Yes?—I do not think it. They have always deeper nets.

2270. It was suggested to us in Scotland that an alteration might be made in the herring nets?—Then, I do not think they would get much herring.

2271. Have you fished from Baltimore or Castletown Berehaven?—Yes.

2272. Would you not be clear of the Scotchmen altogether there?— There would be a few there. They are fishing from the west south-west to the south south east off the Old Head, and up along the shore off the Seven Heads, and from that to forty or thirty miles off.

2273. Do they, from your experience, go in the direction of Bally-cotton?—Yes, sir, some.

2274. Do you think they would get as much **herring east, towards** Ballycotton?—I will not say that.

2275. Would it be any benefit to you if they were kept east?—They would not come across us then.

2276. Do you think you would be able to shoot your mackerel nets in the same water as occupied now by the herring nets, if they were kept out?—Yes.

2277. And would that be an advantage to you?—Yes.

2278. Mr. Rogke.—About what distance do you fish from the land usually?—About thirty to fifty miles, more or less. It is according to how the fish work.

2279. That is for the mackerel?—Yes, that is in the first of the season.

2280. And where do the other men fish?—You will get some of them out with us.

2281. They go out with you?—Yes.

2282. Mr. GROVES.—What was a fair average earning for a man fifteen or twenty years ago at the mackerel fishing?—From £15 to £25, or £20 a man. The average might be £20 a man.

2283. And what is the average now?—Maybe £2 or £3 (laughter), maybe none at all.

2284. It may be interesting to ask this man what his earning was last year?—I am not rightly sure—about £160.

2285. About how much a man?—About £6.

2286. You think £5 would be a good average?—Yes.

2287. It has come down to one-fourth of what it was?—Now it has.

2288. To what do you attribute that?—I do not know.

2289. Do you attribute it to any extent to the Scotchmen?—The most of it, because the month of May used to be the time we depended to do a fishing.

Mr. GROVES.—The mackerel fishing has come to a very grievous state; perhaps more than you have any knowledge of.

Mr. ROCHE.—We know that.

James Gorme sworn, examined by Mr. HORNSBY.

2290. Are you a master of a fishing vessel?—Yes.

2291. How long have you been fishing off the coast of Ireland?—Thirty-one years.

2292. You have heard the form of evidence we have been taking, can you tell us if it agrees with your experience as regards the herring fishing, and undersized fish being taken, and so on?—Well, my opinion is like the previous speakers: that the mackerel fishing has gone so bad it is not worth following it, and I think it is through the herring fishing.

2293. Have you seen, yourself, large quantities of undersized mackerel in the herring nets?—Yes, hundreds and thousands.

2294. Hundreds of thousands?—Yes, among the fleet.

2295. How many hundreds of thousands, to begin with?—I do not know, because for the last two or three years the Scotch fleet is very large.

2296. How many hundreds of thousands, now?—I have heard that many of the buyers say that some of the boats had 30,000 to 40,000.

2297. But yourself?—Well, I cannot say, but I have seen thousands thrown over the side.

2298. You saw them yourself?—I have seen a great many myself, but we were not going much among the boats.

2299. But you had an opportunity of seeing, roughly, how many dozen, say, on each occasion?—I cannot say, but I have seen them shaking the nets coming in, and throwing mackerel and small hake over the side.

2300. What quantity would they be throwing over?—I have seen considerable quantities.

2301. What is your opinion as to the date on which the herring fishing should commence?—About the first of June, I think; I do not think it would do much harm then.

2302. You would not approve of the 15th of May?—Well, May was the principal month we had to do a bit of a season, and now we are getting nothing then, we may say.

2303. To what do you attribute this great decline in the mackerel fishing?—I think it is the killing of the small mackerel. They destroy more small mackerel than would do a season for us. There has not been a right mackerel fishing since the herring fishing commenced here, and not what I call a right fishing.

2304. One of the other witnesses said that the last two seasons were slightly better than the previous years. Do you agree with that?—Well, fifteen or sixteen years ago, the last week in April and the first week in May, I was booking myself down for £100 each week, but the last couple of seasons we had about a couple of shillings each week.

2305. Mr. ROCHE.—Was it better before that?—Well, three or four years ago was a bit better, but the Scotchmen stayed at home for a year or two. The last two or three seasons were the worst of all.

2306. Have you fished anywhere as well as at Kinsale?—I have fished as far as Berehaven, but I was not much there. I was principally at Kinsale.

2307. Have you ever fished at Lowestoft?—No, sir.

2308. Mr. GREEN.—Have you followed the herring fishing at Howth?—Yes, all my days, as long as it was worth following, but there has been nothing there for the last fifteen years, I may say.

2309. Have you formed any opinion as to the cause of the falling off them?—Well, we may form opinions enough, but to say it, we can't.

Mr. GREEN.—Do you want any more evidence?

Mr. HORNSBY.—Well, if the great mass of the men agree with the evidence that has been given, it is no use going over the ground again.

Mr. GREEN.—Well, you might have one or two on the other hand.

Mr. ROCHE.—Ask the men generally, then.

Mr. GREEN.—Are there any men in the room who followed the autumn mackerel fishing in Ireland.

A VOICE.—Yes, sir.

Mr. GREEN.—Will you come forward then.

Mr. ROCHE.—As to the cross-examining of these witnesses, I am the principal person who has done it, but they must not imagine that because I cross-examine them about a point, that I take any special view—it is to get the knowledge from them. I simply want to test them.

James Moore sworn, examined by Mr. HORNSBY.

2310. Are you a master of a fishing vessel?—Yes.

2311. For how long?—For upwards of twenty years.

2312. What is your experience of the effect of the herring fishing on the mackerel fishing off Kinsale?—Well, I think the herring nets being shot there so early in the season has a great deal to do with the falling off, because they catch a deal of the small mackerel.

2313. Have you seen them?—Yes, I have seen them throwing them over-side. The Scotchmen, as a rule, clear their nets as they haul. They save the herrings, and the small mackerel they generally throw away. Of course the boats that fish mackerel have got their nets to them earlier in the morning, as a rule, and we go past these boats, hauling their nets, and I have seen them myself throwing the mackerel overboard, as long as we would be in their sight. When we would be gone too far we would not be seeing them, of course.

2314. But would they be throwing the fish out continually?—Yes, they would be throwing them out continually, and throwing out small hake as well, and we would see them floating in the water.

2315. The hake would float?—Yes; the mackerel generally sink, but the hake float.

2316. How many years have you been going to Ireland?—About twenty-seven or twenty-eight years. I am a master of a boat for twenty.

2317. Have you fished at other places on the coast as well as at Kinsale?—I have fished from Kinsale, Castletownshend, and Baltimore.

2318. Do you find as a great a decrease at Castletownshend as at Kinsale?—The herring fishing has been going on off Castletownshend nearly as much as Kinsale.

2319. What has your capture been at Castletownshend as compared to Kinsale; do you get better fishing off Castletownshend or Kinsale?—I consider them both about the same fishing ground, they are very close by each other.

2320. Do many Scotch boats fish out of Castletownshend?—I have seen about fifty Scotch boats in Castletownshend myself.

2321. Were those men lying there, or did they come out of Kinsale?—They fish out of both places, there was one year I think there was one buyer there, Mr. Bridson, but then they engaged there; I have seen fifty of them fishing out of Castletownshend.

2322. What date would you propose to allow them to commence herring fishing?—Not before the 10th of June, I do not think the herring is eatable before that, they are very soft.

2323. Mr. Round.—Not before the 10th of June?—No, sir.

2324. And the herring is not eatable before than?—Well, they are not so good.

2325. Are they bought by the buyers before then?—Oh, yes.

2326. They are good enough for the English market?—Well, they buy them. What they do with them afterwards I do not know.

2327. Mr. Hornsby.—Have you been at the autumn mackerel fishing?—I have.

2328. What class of fish do you get then?—They are a smaller class of fish than we generally get in the spring and summer.

2329. Much smaller?—Not much.

2330. Are they of good quality?—They are better fish. They are much sweeter, but they are smaller.

2331. You do not suppose the autumn mackerel fishing, since it has been started some five or six years ago, would have any effect on the spring fishing?—I do not think so.

2332. What is your reason?—Because we got mackerel as early, since the autumn fishing commenced, as we did before. We got mackerel quite as early in the spring since as before.

2333. Mr. Green.—Do you not think, since the autumn mackerel fishing commenced, a great many more young mackerel are killed than were ever killed by the Scotch boats?—No, sir; I do not think the mackerel we catch in the autumn are younger than the mackerel we catch in the spring, but of course they are smaller in themselves. In fact, they are done spawning, and clean, and much sweeter to eat. I do not mean to say they are a younger fish.

2334. Mr. Jenkins.—Do you fish for them with the same sized mesh?—Yes.

2335. Mr. Green.—Have you seen any other small mackerel killed besides those caught in the drift nets during the autumn mackerel fishing? Have you seen them caught by any other means than the drift net and fishing in the autumn fishing? Have you been in any place where they were killing them by any other method?—No, sir. I never saw those same nets working. They have been taking large quantities with them, but I never saw them.

2336. And you think any amount of those autumn mackerel being killed would have no effect on the spring mackerel?—I don't think so.

2337. Have you heard of the amount of fish taken in the seines in the autumn fishing?—Yes, sir. I have heard of as high as 20,000 taken in the seine nets.

2338. In what bay?—In some of the bays to the north-west, but I never saw it.

2339. Mr. Rocha.—Do you know anything of those purse seine nets?—No, sir.

2340. You have never seen them?—No, sir.

2341. Mr. Green.—Where have you been engaged in the autumn fishing?—In Castletownshend.

2342. Mr. Green,—Do you agree with the other witnesses as to the damage done by the herring fishing to the mackerel fishing?—I do, sir.

2343. You have heard the evidence of the other witnesses?—Yes, sir.

2344. Mr. Rocha.—Do you think the two fishings can go on together?—No, sir, they cannot be carried on together.

2345. Why not?—Well, one injures the other—in fact, we destroy each other's nets; we cannot drift together.

2346. Mr. Green.—And if they were out of that would you expect to catch mackerel in the same waters as that in which they now shoot their herring nets?—Yes, sir, because, as a rule, we generally get the most mackerel where they shoot for herrings, and we are obliged to keep from them entirely, sooner than do any damage.

Mr. Green.—Is there any man in the room who has followed the herring fishing at Kinsale?—

Mr. Rocha.—Has anyone anything fresh to tell us, because there is no good going over the same ground.

Mr. Green.—If we could get any man who has actually fished for herrings there, we might get something fresh.

John Zachariah Quirc sworn, examined by Mr. Hornsby.

2347. Are you the master of a fishing vessel?—No, sir, not at present, but I have been.

2348. Have you been fishing for herrings on the Irish coast, at Kinsale?—Yes, sir.

2349. Did you come across many small mackerel when you were fishing for herrings?—Yes, sir.

2350. In what quantity?—I cannot tell the quantity, sir; but large quantities of small mackerel and hake.

2351. What do you do with them?—We generally put them overside.

2352. Would you not get a price for them if you sold them?—We might get 6d. a hundred for them, sometimes.

2353. What is your idea as to herring fishing and mackerel fishing going on simultaneously?—I think it is doing destruction to the young fish.

2354. Why did you stop herring fishing off that coast?—It was hard to get a crew to go from here to fish herrings, or I would have followed it every year; but our men here felt rather delicate about going up there.

2355. What is your opinion as to the condition of the herrings in the month of May, as against June?—Well, for the first of May they were long enough, plenty of length, but narrow; and if you cooked them they were quite green inside. As I heard a man say here, some might eat them for the novelty of the thing; but, for my own part, I would prefer a salt herring out of the barrel.

2356. What would be their condition in June? Would it improve?—At the end of May they would be very nice to eat, and they would be still better in the first of June, improving by the week or by the day, I may say.

2357. And when do they reach the zenith of their perfection?—I beg your pardon?

2358. Mr. Groves.—When are they at their best?—In June, I think, they are as good as a man may care.

2359. Mr. Roche.—How many years were you herring fishing?—For six or seven years.

2360. And whom—lately?—Four or five years ago.

2361. Mr. Hornsby.—Do you agree with the evidence that it is impossible for the two branches of fishing to be carried on at the same time and place?—They can be carried on, but they must keep apart.

2362. Suppose there was a fair give and take policy adopted, could not the two be carried on?—Yes, but they must keep apart, because the mackerel nets float, and the herring nets are sunk perhaps eight yards deep, or four or six. Large vessels and steamboats go over them.

2363. Have you ever fished at Lowestoft?—No, sir.

2364. What date would you fix upon which to commence the herring fishing off Kinsale?—Well, about the first of June. Herrings are very fair then.

2365. Mr. Green.—Have you fished the season out completely at the herrings on the Kinsale coast?—Yes, sir.

2366. What led you to stop fishing?—The sharks come on the ground there, and drive us away, we have to go, or we would have no nets at all.

2367. It is not because the fish get scarce?—No, sir; one shoal goes away, and another comes, and that is the way I believe it is.

2368. Mr. Roche.—At what date did you stop fishing?—We stop about the 20th of June.

2369. If you began to fish about the 1st of June, and then you say the sharks come about the 20th, that only gives them about three weeks fishing?—Yes.

2370. And that would not be worth a man's while coming from Scotland?—No, it would not.

2371. Then practically starting the fishing on the 1st of June would stop the fishing altogether?—Yes, because the Scotch boats have to go back.

2372. Mr. Green.—Then there would be no herring fishing there?—Well, I think it would be much better to fish generally on the coast to the east in the summer time.

2373. You think you would get them at the east?—We would get them to the east if we did not meddle with them, sir.

2374. Mr. Roche.—What number of men are engaged at Kinsale?—We have had it from other sources. In the herring fishing?—First of all we want the herring fishing. How many boats will there be?—Well, some years there will be more, and some less.

2375. I want to find out whether there are more herring or mackerel boats there?—The mackerel boats are longer there.

2376. How many boats are engaged in the mackerel fishing, and how many in the herring fishing?—Well, I have seen, I suppose, 500 mackerel boats fishing there, and some years there will be sixty or eighty, or a hundred, or 150 herring boats. There will be two or three times more mackerel boats than herring boats.

2377. And for a longer period?—Yes; there are a greater number of men, and they are there for a longer period.

2378. Mr. HORNSBY.—What time of year do you commence to fish herrings?—Generally about the middle of May.

2379. Do you find much difference in your price in May and June?—We get a very much better price in June.

2380. Do you shoot with the mackerel boats?—I have seen us shooting with the mackerel boats, one evening in particular, and we were not very far apart when we began to shoot; but the mackerel boats generally shoot on the wind, and the herring boats a little off the wind. When we were done shooting, we were a good way apart, so next morning we were both in Castletownshend, and I think he had 300 of mackerel, and we had about 2,000 mackerel in our nets. (Laughter.)

2381. Mr. JONGHIN.—Small ones?—Small, and large too, we got them sometimes rolled up in the nets. They could not mesh, and rolled themselves in it.

2382. Are the mackerel a good size?—They are very large, some of them, but most of them are small.

2383. What price would you get for them?—Well, perhaps we got sixpence a hundred.

2384. Mr. HORNSBY.—Who do you sell these mackerel to?—Local buyers. I think, anyway, they were not mackerel for the English market at all.

2385. Mr. GAGES.—What was got for the big mackerel that was caught the same day?—They would get a price for their mackerel, but they always thought the mackerel caught by a herring boat were smaller, and would not give much for them.

2386. Were you always able to sell the small mackerel?—Sometimes we could, and sometimes we couldn't; but we killed a power of hake. They generally meshed in the net.

2387. How large were they?—About eight inches long I expect.

2388. And about how many of them would you have in the net?—Hundreds of them. I pitied the hake more so than the mackerel. I was really feeling for the hake. I was saying, times, it was a shame killing the hake. They were no manner of use, and if they were left to swim and grow they would be of some use to some man some day. We have got baskets of them in a night.

2389. Could you tell us how many you would catch?—How many boxes?—Well, we have got baskets, but I could not say as to boxes.

2390. Would you catch the hake close to the surface?—They would be all through the net, up and down.

2391. Do you catch pollack or other small fish?—No, sir. There was a class of fish we caught—we could not get a name for it, nor the natives either—we thought at last it was young ling we were killing. They looked something like it.

2392. Do you know a fish called whiting-pollock?—Yes, sir; we caught a few of them.

Mr. HORNSBY.—Well, is there any use our going over the same ground?

Mr. GRAVES.—There are plenty of witnesses here, but I imagine they will be all the same.

Mr. HORNBY.—I suppose you all here, fishing in Irish waters, agree with the evidence given to-day?

Voices.—Yes, sir.

Mr. ROGHE.—If not, if there is anyone who does not agree, he had better come forward.

Mr. GRAVES.—There is no one who does not agree.

Mr. Morrison.—I do not think there is anyone that does not agree.

Mr. HORNBY.—Well, gentlemen, we are concluding the inquiry here as far as the Isle of Man is concerned, but we are going on to Lowestoft and Yarmouth, and when we have got the evidence in train and are able to digest it, we will endeavour to arrive at some solution of this very perplexing question, which will be of course submitted to the Government who will then decide upon the measures they will take in Ireland. The Lowestoft mackerel fishing is not of so much importance as the Irish mackerel fishing, but we are going there to take evidence now.

Mr. GRAVES.—We have a strong view on this matter, and we trust that the result of this inquiry will be that a close season will be arrived at and fixed.

Mr. HORNBY.—Of course at the present juncture it would be premature for us to express any opinion on the matter.

Mr. GRAVES.—It is our hope all the same.

Coastguard Station, Lowestoft,

March 15th, 1893.

Her Majesty's Inspectors of Irish Fisheries, ALAN HORNBY, Esq. (in the Chair), the Rev. WILLIAM S. GREEN, and CECIL R. ROCHE, Esq., R.L., held an Inquiry this day (Wednesday, 15th March, 1893), at the Coastguard Station, Lowestoft, pursuant to the following Notice:—

"FISHERIES (IRELAND).

"32 and 33 Vict., c. 92, and the Acts incorporated therewith.

"HERRING FISHERY—SOUTH COAST OF IRELAND.

"NOTICE.

"WHEREAS it has been represented that the custom of fishing for herrings off the south coast of Ireland before the 1st of June in each year is detrimental to the mackerel fisheries off the said coast; and as fishermen from Lowestoft are interested in the question, the Inspectors of Irish Fisheries hereby give notice that they will hold inquiries into the matter at the *Coastguard Station, Lowestoft,* on *Wednesday,* the 15th day of *March,* 1893, at the hour of one o'clock, P.M., of which all persons interested are requested to take notice.

"By Order,

"M. P. DOWLING, Secretary.

" Dated at the Office of Irish Fisheries,
Dublin Castle, this 3rd day of
March, 1893."

Mr. HORNBY briefly explained the object of the Inquiry, and said—The Inspectors have already sat at various places in Scotland, and also in the Isle of Man, at Peel. We intend to conclude our investigations at Yarmouth, and when the evidence accumulated has been considered, we shall arrive at some conclusion as to the best course to adopt in the matter, and report to His Excellency the Lord Lieutenant of Ireland. The point in dispute is that the early herring fishing injures the mackerel fishing off the south coast of Ireland. The Scotchmen are not prepared to admit that, and in fact some of them will not do so. The fishermen of the Isle of Man and the Irishmen are of opinion, the latter most emphatically, that the herring fishing does do injury. We want to know the opinion of the Lowestoft men themselves on the matter.

The first witness sworn was Mr. *John Breach*, a member of the Lowestoft Town Council. He was examined by Mr. HORNBY as follows:—

2393. You are a boat owner, I believe?—Yes, sir.

2394. And you reside in Lowestoft?—Yes.

2395. Well, now, what can you tell us about this matter—but perhaps you had better tell your story in your own way?—Well, sir, it is a good many years ago since I was fishing off the coast of Ireland—perhaps nearly ten years ago. But I went for six or seven years successively before that.

2396. How many years did you go to Ireland altogether?—About seven years.

2397. In what capacity did you go?—I went as master of a fishing boat.

2398. You went fishing for mackerel?—Yes, sir.

2399. You did not go for herrings?—No, sir.

2400. What is your experience—what time did you commence fishing?—Well, till the last year or two there was no herring fishing prosecuted. When I first went—but this man (pointing to another of the witnesses present, Mr. Benjamin Reynolds) will give you a better explanation later on. The last year I was there several boats came from out the Bristol Channel, up the Irish Sea, by the Isle of Man, Campbeltown, and all up there. Scotchmen also used to come down there. I used to fish off Queenstown, and the Scotchmen fished to the eastward of us.

2401. Did you fish out of Kinsale?—Yes, sir. Sometimes we fished out of Baltimore, but more often out of Kinsale.

2402. What do you think was the greatest number of Scotch boats that went there?—I should say about ninety- not more than that. That would be, of course, about eighteen years ago.

2403. I think they used to go there in great numbers about fifteen years ago?—Yes, probably.

2404. Did you come very much in contact with these Scotch boats?—No, not a great deal, because they fished to the east of us.

2405. Did you form an opinion as to their taking any quantities of undersized mackerel?—I can hardly say much to that. I don't think I took much notice of it.

2406. You know nothing about the injury done to the undersized mackerel or hake, do you?—No, sir, I can't say I do—only what I have heard from other people.

2407. Did your men fish with the same nets? Are the mackerel nets the same as those you fish with up your coast? Just describe them?—We had twenty-one rows to the yard for Ireland—for what we call the Irish fishing, and we have twenty-five rows to the yard for our own fishing.

2408. Now, what opinion have you formed upon this question?—I believe the herring boats destroyed a tremendous lot of mackerel. They must destroy a lot—any one would know that. I have heard fishermen say that the Scotch boats have come in with a lot of mackerel—small ones—in their nets—what we call cock mackerel. There have been a lot of large ones amongst them. As an experienced fisherman I should say that they destroy a lot.

2409. By the Rev. WILLIAM S. GREEN.—On your own coast do you find that the herring fishing interferes with the mackerel fishing?—Well, we don't like to see the Scotchmen come so soon, for we think they destroy a lot of mackerel.

2410. By Mr. HORNBY.—What time do the Scotchmen go there?—About the 20th September.

2411. Oh, you are speaking of the autumn fishing?—Yes, sir.

2412. Ah, that is a different matter. What date would you fix for herring fishing to be carried out to commence off this coast?—I think about the 10th or 12th May.

2413. That is fixed by agreement. I think it was a mutual arrangement?—That is so; but it has not always been adhered to by the Scotchmen.

2414. Do you agree with the Irishmen or the Scotchmen?—I, as a mackerel man, agree with the Irishmen. It is to our interest to do so. If you limit it to the 1st of June you will do good, and the Scotchmen will fall to it.

2415. Yes; but do you think it would suit the Scotchmen?—Yes, I should think so.

2416. How many weeks' fishing would they have then—not more than two weeks at the most?—I don't know. I can't say anything about that. Most of times now our boats leave Ireland and find mackerel right down in the north-west. After the season gets up they will go down to Berehaven.

2417. You think a fair date to commence herring fishing would be the 1st of June?—Not, if I was a herring man.

2418. But what do you think would be for the benefit of the mackerel fishing?—If they were not to go at all it would be best. These fine Scotch nets—eight or ten fathom deep—are so fine that they stop anything that comes against them—just like a wall up and down. Rare fishermen those Scotch fellows are! They have nets to catch fish!

2419. The question is this—a large portion of the community fish in these waters?—Yes, but the Scotchmen are our masters.

2420. Englishmen, Manxmen, and Irishmen fish in the waters?—Yes. They all go mackerel fishing—the same as our people.

2421. What is the general opinion of the Lowestoft men as to the date. I suppose they have formed an opinion?—They say that they thought the Irishmen had come to a very fair understanding. Our men's opinion is that it should be about the 10th or 12th of May. They thought it was fair between them. I think I am right in saying so. The Irishmen have taken it into their own hands, and they felt it was good.

2422. Would you say the 15th May was a fair date?—Say the 20th. As I repeat, we thought that the 10th of May was very fair. But if they got the 20th, all of us would consent to that—it would be better. We Englishmen come away into the western ocean forty or fifty miles to the south-west of Scilly. The Kinsale fishing has not been a paying game of late years—not by a very long way.

2423. Have the men here found that the mackerel fishing off Kinsale has fallen off?—A good bit since I first went.

2424. Have they ever attributed it to any particular cause?—I, as an experienced fisherman, cannot form an opinion. There is so much difference in the seasons. Some years you will have an abundance, others none at all. To put it in plain words, if you were killed when young you would not live to be an old man. They attribute the falling off to the Scotchmen destroying them.

2425. Do your men at all attribute the decline of the mackerel fishing to the Scotchmen fishing for herrings in large numbers?—I cannot give you an answer to that.

2426. Do you think the mackerel fishing commenced to decline when the Scotch fishermen came in large numbers to fish for herrings early in May, and perhaps in April?—Certainly I do. When I first went to

Ireland, we used to try for mackerel off the Old Head of Kinsale. I have known my brother to catch mackerel right in the line of the Old Head of Kinsale, but they don't think of catching mackerel there now. A man told me he was only sixteen miles from the Old Head of Kinsale, and saw great mackerel in the month of March. The season gets later now, somehow or other.

2427. By the Rev. WILLIAM S. GREEN.—That is since the Scotchmen came there ?—Yes, sir, I believe it is.

2428. How many boats do you have go from Lowestoft to Ireland ?—About twenty-five.

2429. They are gone away to the west coast, to Berehaven ?—Yes, sir.

2430. Why do they prefer fishing off Kinsale ?—Because they believe they get mackerel first.

2431. Do the Scotchmen drift as fast as the others ?—They drift with the tide.

2432. It has been said that the mackerel boats cannot fish with the herring boats, on account of the former drifting faster ?—Well, the herring nets are down five or six fathoms, but I don't think there is a great deal of difference.

2433. Do you find much difficulty ?—We often come into collision.

2434. When the nets do come into contact who fares the worse ?—We got off as best we can, and they do the same. The Lowestoft men generally suffer less than the Scotchmen, because their gear is so fine, and our boats are so heavy.

2435. If your nets come foul of the herring nets, do they get foul of the floats ?—Yes. If they are not very strong they come off, and lose the nets.

2436. Do you ever notice here that they kill small mackerel when fishing for herrings ?—Yes, sir; we kill hundreds and thousands ourselves. We cannot avoid it.

2437. Are the mackerel which the Scotchmen catch saleable ?—Yes, sometimes they get 2s. or 3s. a hundred. It all depends upon the quality and quantity. When there is an abundance they will not look on little mackerel, and when mackerel are scarce these little ones will perhaps sell for 5s. or 6s. a hundred.

2438. In order for mackerel to get caught in the herring nets, they must be about the size of herrings ?—Not necessarily, because a mackerel shoots quicker.

2439. How long do your boats fish mackerel on this coast (meaning Lowestoft) ?—About five or six weeks. Some of them don't give up till the latter part of November.

2440. Have you found from your own experience of your own boats in Kinsale waters—have you found that the price of mackerel falls when herrings get caught ?—I cannot give an opinion of what it is now, only what it was. Of course it all depends. When people are engaged in buying herring they don't buy mackerel, and the other way on.

2441. Are your boats engaged by any buyer ?—No, we are fishing free.

2442. How many boats go from Lowestoft to Kinsale ?—Twenty-one or twenty-two.

2443. This year about the same ?—Yes.

2444. Mr. HORNSBY.—Is there any other point you would like to mention, or anything else you would care to say ?—No. I think I have told you all I can with reference to the matter.

Mr. HORNSBY.—Thank you. The evidence you have given is most important.

Benjamin Reynolds sworn, was examined by Mr. HORNBY as under:—

3445. What is your name?—Benjamin Reynolds.

3446. And you live at Lowestoft?—Yes, sir.

3447. Are you the master of a fishing boat?—Not now, but I have been.

3448. You are an owner?—Yes.

3449. How many years did you fish in Ireland?—About seven, sir.

3450. What was your first year?—About fifteen years ago.

3451. What was the first year the Scotchmen went there in large numbers?—I cannot say. There was a great quantity when I went. But I can't say how many there were.

3452. Did you ever come across these Scotch boats fishing mackerel when you were after herrings?—We have never been foul of their gear.

3453. Have you been inside of each other?—Yes, we have been inside of each other.

3454. Have you ever seen any large takes of undersized mackerel?—I cannot say I have ever seen them take any. But I have heard other people say they have done so.

3455. Have you ever seen them take hake?—Yes, I have seen them have some very small hake. When I used to go we didn't shoot in amongst the Scotch boats. If we had wind enough we didn't shoot amongst them, because we considered it was of no use.

3456. Did you shoot on the same ground as the Irishmen?—Just the same. Yes, all amongst them.

3457. Have you formed any opinion as to what date would be the best for the herring fishing to commence?—No, I have not.

3458. As an experienced fisherman what would you consider the right time to commence?—I can't say at all. I don't know what time the voyage commences, and I do not know what time it finishes.

3459. You have heard about this mutual arrangement as to the 12th of May?—Yes.

3460. Would you think that a satisfactory date on which to commence, or would you think it too early?—I think that after about the 12th May it does not interfere with the Lowestoft boats, because they mostly leave there and go to the westward.

3461. Just direct your mind to Lowestoft for a moment. What would be of benefit to the mackerel fishing?—The later the herring boats began the better it would be for the mackerel fishing.

3462. Not to drive the Scotchmen away altogether, what would you think a fair date to commence?—Well, I should say about the 15th of May.

3463. I suppose from the 15th to the 20th?—Yes, sir.

3464. Is there anything you wish to say yourself about this matter?—Well, we always considered, when I went to Ireland—we always attributed the falling off of the mackerel at the Old Head of Kinsale to the herring fishing. Before the herring boats came there we used to get plenty of mackerel from the Old Head of Kinsale to the Galley Head, and the Scotch boats got an abundance. If the Scotch boats shot their nets there we seldom got any mackerel. The last voyage or two of us being there we did not sell any mackerel in Kinsale. We could not get them at all. We met the fish quite to the west, and had to fish to the Caps. Then we used to go to Baltimore, and bring mackerel to England, or where we could. We attribute the falling off to the Scotch fishing, but we could not say for certain.

3465. What was the last year you fished off Ireland?—About seven years ago.

3466. What do the Lowestoft fishermen say amongst themselves?—The

Lowestoft fishermen are against the herring boats being there so early. That is their opinion. They believe it does a lot of harm.

2467. What date do they commence to go from Lowestoft to Kinsale?—The most of them leave this week. We had some that went away on Monday. The remainder will go next Monday. They will all go away within this week.

2468. Are there some boats not yet gone?—Yes, several. Well, there are seven or eight, perhaps, that have not gone, certainly not more.

2469. Well, now, why have we not got the evidence of these men?—You might be able to do so if you went down to the fish market.

Mr. Breach (a former witness).—I will go and see if I can fetch any of them in, as they might be able to tell us a good deal.

By Mr. Hoosear.—Yes. It is most important that you should get them. This is a very important question to you people.

2470. To Mr. Breach.—Would the men come if you went and talked with them?

Mr. Breach thought they would, and thereupon departed in search of further witnesses.

In the meantime the examination of Mr. *Reynolds* was continued.

2471. Mr. Gream asked—Do you fish for mackerel off this coast too?—Yes.

2472. Do you find that the herring fishing going on at the same time as the mackerel is objectionable?—We have two mackerel voyages here. We have one voyage which commences about the 1st of May. This last ten or twelve years we have had another mackerel season which commences about the 20th September, that is when the herring boats destroy so many mackerel. We have had shoals of mackerel about that time. The Scotch boats come about the 20th September. At that time our Lowestoft boats are fishing for herrings in the North Sea—off Lincolnshire, off Grimsby. All about there the Scotch boats destroy a lot of mackerel in the herring nets. Likewise our own boats do the same, if there are any mackerel about when they come here. As a rule at that time of the year our boats fish for herrings further off than they fish for mackerel. They don't fish amongst them at all. The herring boats fish twenty-five to thirty miles from Lowestoft, while the mackerel boats on an average don't fish more than ten to twenty miles from Lowestoft. When the herring boats, especially the Scotch boats, do shoot in amongst the mackerel boats, they kill an enormous lot of mackerel. The Scotchmen destroy a lot of them, because their nets are so fine and deep. Our Lowestoft boats do not commence here very seldom under October.

2473. As a matter of convenience in shooting nets, quite apart from the killing of immature fish, is it difficult to fish when the mackerel boats are mixed up with the herring boats?—Yes, it is difficult. They keep as far apart as it is possible for them to do. They don't often shoot amongst each other—not more than they are obliged. If a boat is herring catching up here, he does not stop in amongst the mackerel boats, as a general rule.

2474. How many boats are you sending to Ireland this year?—I am sending only one to Ireland this year.

2475. Is there anything else you can add, or anything else you would like to say?—No, I think not, sir.

William Burroughs sworn and examined by Mr. Hoosear.

2476. You are a boat owner?—Yes, sir.

2477. And you live at Lowestoft?—Yes.

2478. Now, what do you know about this question?—Well, I can't say I know a great deal about it.

2479. Have you ever been to Ireland?—No.

2480. How many boats have you got?—I have two boats.

2481. The most convenient way perhaps would be for you to tell your own story—what you know about this?

The witness manifested a reluctance to answer, and Mr. HORNBY continued.

2482. Your boats go to Ireland?—Yes.

2483. How many years have they gone?—They have gone about fifteen years.

2484. Year by year?—Yes, every year.

2485. Are they there this year?—No.

2486. But they are going?—Yes—they haven't left yet.

2487. What have your returns been during the last few years—have they been falling off or increasing—have you noticed any variation?—Yes; they have been falling off.

2488. Since when?—I should say during the last five or six years.

2489. Have they fallen off to any great extent?—Yes, a good bit. We don't get money from that side (meaning Ireland).

2490. I mean that side—we are speaking entirely of that side now. To what do you attribute that falling off?—Well, to the scarcity of fish.

2491. Do you attribute this scarcity of fish to the Scotch fishing for herrings?—That has been the report of the men who go from Lowestoft.

2492. That, I suppose, combined with other causes?—Just so.

2493. Have you formed any opinion as to whether this herring fishing should be stopped before a certain date?—Well, gathering from what I have heard the crews report, I should certainly say that the 20th May would be a very favourable time—very favourable indeed.

2494. Have your men ever complained of the herring fishing?—Yes, sir.

2495. By the Rev. W. S. GREEN.—Have you heard them complain about the length of the season—have they said it has changed?—I have not heard them make any complaint that way.

2496. Is the season shorter than it used to be?—The complaint I have heard them make is of the scarcity of fish at Kinsale. That has driven our boats further into the channel, because there have been no mackerel along the Irish coast during the last five or six years.

2497. When do they expect to meet the fish?—About the 1st May, or the last week of April.

2498. Mackerel?—Yes.

2499. When do they begin to fish?—About the latter part of April or the beginning of May. I have sent there fifteen years and have never got anything till the latter part of April. They never went further round than Baltimore and Kinsale.

2500. Do they complain that they cannot make as large takes for a night's fishing as they used to do?—I have heard them complain of that. Whether this is owing to the Scotch boats going there I cannot say.

2501. How many nets do your boats carry?—About ten score. That is a fair average. Some carry a few more. Each net is about thirty yards on the lint. A set net would be about two or three and twenty yards on the net rope.

2502. Do they shoot the whole?—Yes; they shoot the whole.

2503. How many score deep?—From six to seven score. That was last year. They have added another score this. Six score used to be the usual depth.

2504. Would you use thirty yards—that is after being mounted?—No, twenty-two yards after they are set upon the rope.

2505. By Mr. Ceon. Roorn.—I believe you fish here for mackerel and herring?—Yes.

2506. Do you think those two fishings can be carried on without injury to one another?—Not without injury to the mackerel.

2507. That is your experience here in Lowestoft—in your own waters?—Yes; I have been most on this coast and can understand the fishing here, though I have never been to Kinsale.

2508. Your experience is that the fishing altogether here does injure the mackerel?—Yes; this last year or so the mackerel laid very close in, and the herrings have laid further off; so there has not been so much injury done by the Scotchmen on that account, as they went further away. So they have not killed so many mackerel.

2509. By Mr. Hornsby.—Which is the greater number of boats fishing from here—say, should?—I suppose the mackerel boats exceed the herring boats. I can't say though.

2510. By Mr. Roorn.—We had evidence given us in Scotland by Scotch fishermen that Lowestoft is a place where the herring and mackerel fishings were carried on with great satisfaction. Do you admit that?—Yes, for the first month. From the first week in September to October—that is the injurious part. After that they go for herrings further off.

John Butcher examined by Mr. Hornsby.

2511. Do you live in Lowestoft?—Yes, sir.

2512. Are you the master of a fishing boat?—Not now, sir.

2513. Were you a master in Ireland?—No; I was mate of a vessel that went round to Ireland.

2514. How many years were you fishing off Ireland?—About six or seven years.

2515. What was your last year?—I can hardly say. I should think about 1851.

2516. Are you going there this year?—My boat has gone. We sent it away yesterday.

2517. Are you the owner of a boat?—Yes; managing owner.

2518. Have you formed any idea as to when this herring-fishing should be allowed to commence off the South Coast of Ireland?—I have not formed any idea. I have heard the Irish people complain about it.

2519. Do you think there is any justice in their complaint?—Yes, I do [with great firmness].

2520. Any of the years you were there were you near the Scotchmen when you were fishing?—Yes.

2521. Did you see any quantity of undersized mackerel taken in their nets?—Yes.

2522. How often did you see that?—Two or three times.

2523. Roughly speaking, what quantity?—About two thousand.

2524. How about hake—did you see any undersized taken?—Yes.

2525. In any large quantity?—No.

2526. Did you find that you had to shift your ground in consequence of the Scotchman going there?—We had to go further west.

2527. How much?—To the Fastnet.

2528. The first year you went there were there any Scotchmen there?—No, sir.

2529. Then what year did you commence to go further west?—After I had been there—about 1885 to 1886.

2530. From 1885 downwards?—Yes.

2531. Well, now, what do you think would be just and fair to all sides? What date would you propose for the commencement of the herring-fishing off the coast of Ireland?—I can hardly say. I have not been there for some time.

2532. As an experienced fisherman, what are your own ideas?—I never was catching herrings there.

2533. But you saw herrings being caught there?—Yes.

2534. If the herring fishing injures the mackerel fishing, what date would you fix?—20th May.

2535. That would be a fair time?—Yes.

2536. By the Rev. W. S. Green.—Is your boat gone west this time?—Yes.

2537. Is she engaged?—No.

2538. Do you think the price will be as good in the West as in Kinsale?—No, I don't think so.

2539. Then why does your boat go there?—Because we think about catching mackerel first that way.

2540. Will she go eastwards afterwards?—It all depends on the fishing.

2541. Have you noticed that the fishing has been falling off at all?—Yes.

2542. Do you remember your boat making a good shoot long ago?—When I first went there I have hauled as much as thirteen or fourteen thousand at once.

2543. Do you think there is much chance of getting that now?—No.

2544. What is a good haul now?—About two thousand.

2545. Do you think they will get two thousand now as often as you got ten thousand when you first went there?—No.

2546. Have you noticed anything about the season getting earlier or later—did you get mackerel earlier in the times gone by?—No; I don't think there is any difference. The milder the weather the earlier the fish come.

2547. By Mr. Roche.—About the herring fishing here—do you find that it interferes with the mackerel fishing here?—That all depends where the herrings lay and where the mackerel lay.

2548. Then it does interfere?—Yes.

2549. Have you caught any mackerel when fishing for herring?—I have seen mackerel drop away from the net.

There were no other witnesses present, and as Mr. Breach did not return with more witnesses the inquiry closed after Mr. Hornsby had thanked those who had given evidence for their attendance.

GREAT YARMOUTH, 17TH MARCH, 1893.

Her Majesty's Inspectors of Irish Fisheries, ALAN HORNBY, Esq., the Rev. WILLIAM S. GREEN, and CECIL R. ROCHE, Esq., LL.L., attended at the Coast Guard Station, Yarmouth, at one o'clock, p.m., pursuant to the following Notice:—

" FISHERIES—IRELAND.

" 39 & 33 Vic., cap. 99, and the Acts incorporated therewith.

" HERRING FISHERY—SOUTH COAST OF IRELAND.

" NOTICE.

" Whereas it has been represented that the custom of fishing for herrings off the South Coast of Ireland, before the 1st of June in each year, is detrimental to the Mackerel fisheries off said Coast; and, as fishermen from Yarmouth are interested in the question, the Inspectors of Irish Fisheries hereby give Notice that they will hold inquiries into the matter at the Coast Guard Station, Yarmouth, on Friday, the 17th day of March, 1893, at the hour of one o'clock p.m., of which all persons interested are requested to take notice.

" By Order,

" M. P. DOWLING, Secretary.

" Dated at the Office of Irish Fisheries.
    " Dublin Castle, this 3rd day of March, 1893."

It appeared, however, that no one in Yarmouth was interested in the matter, inasmuch as no trader or boat owner attended to give evidence before the Inspectors. Accordingly the inquiry was not opened.

INDEX.

	Page
REPORT,	iii
APPENDIX, No. 1.—Boats attending the South Coast Mackerel Fishery in 1892,	2
APPENDIX, No. 2.—Evidence taken at Inquiries,	3

KINSALE INQUIRY.

Names of Witnesses.

	Page
James Coleman,	4
Timothy Hayes,	5
John M'Colgan,	6
William Alcock,	7
John Coghlan,	8
John Riordan,	11
James Coleman (recalled),	14
John Riordan (recalled),	16
Michael Newman,	16
R. A. Williams,	17
Adam M'Carthy,	18

COCKENZIE INQUIRY.

	Page
John Brown,	24
Hugh Flynn,	30
William Dickson,	37
Joshua Porter,	42
Archibald Buchanan,	47
Andrew Baillie,	48
Robert Walker,	49

ANSTRUTHER INQUIRY.

	Page
John William Smith,	51
William Lindsay,	54
David Wood (Birrell),	58
Alexander Gardner,	58
David Watson,	60
John Logie,	61
Alexander Keay,	62
Wm. Mair (District Fishery Officer),	64

MONTROSE INQUIRY.

	Page
John West,	65
Alexander Cargill,	67
Walter Duff (Fishery Officer),	69
George Coull,	69
David Anderson,	70
Charles Anderson,	73
William Mearns,	74

BUCKIE INQUIRY.

Names of Witnesses.Page.
Alexander Reid, ... 77
James Thain, ... 85

DURGHEAD INQUIRY.

Daniel Main, ... 95
William Main, ... 100
Alexander Main, ... 103
John Ralph, ... 106
James Macpherson, ... 109
Alexander Main, ... 112
Statement by Rev. Robert Niven, . . 114

CAMPBELTOWN INQUIRY.

Robert Rae, ... 115
Archibald Campbell, ... 118
Dugald Robertson, ... 122
William M'Millan, ... 123
Archibald Cook, ... 124
John M'Kinlay, ... 126
John Martin, ... 127
Archibald Campbell (re-examined), . . 129
Robert Rea (re-examined), . . . 129
John Murray (Officer of Scottish Fishery Board), . 129

PEEL INQUIRY.

William Mylrea, ... 133
John Quirk, ... 136
John Monghtin, ... 139
William Moore, ... 142
Evan Quirk, ... 146
James Gonna, ... 150
James Moore, ... 151
John Zachariah Quine, ... 153

LOWESTOFT INQUIRY.

John Breach, ... 158
Benjamin Reynolds, ... 161
William Burroughs, ... 162
John Butcher, ... 164

DUBLIN : Printed for Her Majesty's Stationery Office,
By ALEX. THOM & Co. (Limited), 87, 88, & 89, Abbey-street,
The Queen's Printing Office.